THE JAI

He felt a familiar ang   inside him. Eucliff
was a good example of how the Chinese were
being corrupted, their culture eroded, their
countryside altered by speculative land deals.
It was the same wherever the British went.
India, Africa, Malaya, China: whatever they
saw, they changed — as if that was the natural
way of things. They did not learn the local
languages except in order to teach the natives
English. They built their churches and
imported their own god and tried to subvert
the local deities. They eradicated customs
without having anything better with which to
replace them. They brought their own
business practices which they expected to be
adopted, their own laws to be obeyed, their
own merchandise to be purchased. They even
brought their own diseases of influenza and
gonorrhoea to add to the local scourges. When
they could not get their own way with the
natives they ruled by division, pitting tribe
against tribe, clan against clan, religion
against religion; when that failed, they
brought in their troops and their gunboats.

THE JADE PAVILION

Martin Booth

ARROW BOOKS

Arrow Books Limited
62 - 65 Chandos Place, London WC2N 4NW

An imprint of Century Hutchinson Limited

London Melbourne Sydney Auckland
Johannesburg and agencies throughout
the world

First published by Hutchinson 1987
Arrow edition 1988

Printed and bound in Great Britain by
Anchor Brendon Limited, Tiptree, Essex

ISBN 0 09 952650 6

for
Roy Lewis

Prologue

Above the gate the lettering in the stone plaque had been picked out in new black paint. During the war the sun and neglect had peeled the original but now the lettering was plain and stark: PROTESTANT CHURCH AND OLD CEMETERY (EAST INDIA COMPANY 1814).

The sun was stiflingly hot. The frangipani trees issued their heady scent as they had for a hundred years but every other shrub and flower in the graveyard seemed bored or resting. There was no breeze. One morosely coloured bird whistled plaintively in the deep shade by the lower wall where the foliage hung thickly over the stonework. Even their footsteps were muffled by the oppressive heat of the air.

'Why do we have to come down here?' asked the seven-year-old boy walking by the woman's side. He had refused to hold her hand as they had descended the moss-strewn steps: he was growing up now, was beyond all that. 'It's very hot and gloomy. All these graves . . .'

'We just have to,' she said.

'Why?'

She made no reply.

'What's the point? They can't hear you. They can't see you.'

The pair passed the gateway to the top terrace and reached the lawn of the lower. The grass was tough and stringy with rigid veins and sinews in the blades, perfect for making thumb-screechers. The boy plucked one carefully, pinching it with his nails to prevent the saw edges cutting

1

him and blew through his fingers. The squawl he made alarmed the bird which stopped whistling and flitted away through the shadows.

'Stop that!'

The boy was cowed and apologised.

'Look at this!' He was standing before an oblong slab of grey stone set against the terrace wall.

'It's in funny words,' he commented and read aloud, ' "*Ter Gedagtenisse Van Der Weledelen Heer Pieter Kintsius Eerste Super Carga Opperhoofd Der Neederlandsche Oost Indische Compagnie intRykvanChina Gebooren Te Amsterdam En Overleeden Te Macao Den 25 Iuny 1786 in Den Ouderdom Van 53 Iaaren.*" ' He mispronounced or misread most of the epitaph.

'It's a Dutchman.'

'It *was* a Dutchman,' the boy corrected her.

'Was.'

If, at that moment, she had seen a ghost, it would have been Philip Haversham's. He would have been talking discreetly to the two weeping amahs he was about to present with their final salary; he would have turned and seen her, smiled in his serious innocent way and blown her a kiss then scampered off, blushing . . .

To the boy, moving on, the tomb of the great artist, George Chinnery, was as big as a small house. It even had a miniature garden in front surrounded by a low iron railing with spikes on it.

To the left of the tomb was a tangle of creepers and blossom. The woman pushed them aside with her foot. The grave they hid was fashioned of a poor quality stone. Already the damp and the heat had eroded one corner and ants were busy carting cut fragments of leaf into a crevice they had discovered beneath it.

Most of the gravestones bore verses or memorials. There was none before her, merely one name: Mulrenan 1948.

'Is that it?' the boy asked as they left slowly, climbing the steps.

'Yes. We shan't come back,' she told him firmly.

Parked at the curb outside the gate was a shining new 1950 model Chevrolet. The coarse glare of the sun rebound-

2

ed off the black metal panels and a thin mirage danced over the bonnet. The driver held the door open for her.

'You get in, Alec. I won't be long.'

'Where are you going?'

'Nowhere special. Just wait here a second.'

The boy obeyed and entered the closet of heat inside the automobile.

She shut the car door firmly and stepped across the pavement, weaving her way through a group of coolies who were resting on their haunches, smoking and tossing coins in a game of heads or tails. One was chewing on a stick of sugar cane and spitting the pulp into the gutter.

The house on the junction of Rua do Patane and Rue dos Curtidores was occupied, though delapidated. The roof above the balcony on which she had so often sat was sagging and the railings had rusted. On the scarred and peeling window frames she could make out vestiges of blue paint. The shop on the ground floor was boarded.

She went through the gateway to the small courtyard at the rear. There was no one about: it was the hour of the day when those with sense hid themselves from the sun. The windows over her head were shuttered against the blistering heat.

From her handbag she took a short iron spike. Her gold chain bracelet rattled on the polished steel as she stooped. It took her less than ten seconds to insert the metal prong under the step and yank the stone askew. From the cavity beneath she lifted a chamois leather bag, holding it from below in case the leather had rotted. Had anyone seen her they would have noticed not so much her furtive actions as the complete absence of emotion in her face; and that would have puzzled them all the more.

When she returned, the coolies were all departing but for the one with the sugar cane. He gazed at her briefly as she passed him by, tentatively held out his hand for *kumshaw*, but she ignored him. He spat a mouthful of pulp in front of her feet, but she seemed not to notice.

'Are we ready now?' the boy enquired as she carefully placed her handbag on the leather seat.

'We are,' she said with an air of finality. 'Indeed, we are.'

A rickshaw halted by the car. Lashed into the seat was a garishly painted paper model of a building. Along its façade was glued a paper notice: it read 'Bank' in English and Portuguese.

'Today's the Festival of The Hungry Ghosts,' the boy observed.

The coolie hauled on the shafts of his rickshaw and headed off along Rua Tomas Vieira, the sun glancing off the varnished ribs of the seat.

'Yes,' his mother confirmed, 'it is,' and she instructed the chauffeur to drive to the Hong Kong ferry pier.

'But the ferry doesn't sail for three hours, mama.'

'Then we'll wait in our cabin,' she said.

As the Chevrolet pulled away from the curb, the dull brown bird glided up to perch beside the plaque over the cemetery entrance. It bobbed its head between the two green-glazed pilasters and started to chirp.

A Piano-Playing Man

1

A cabaret pianist does not have to concentrate upon the music he is playing. He is not controlled by it as a concert pianist is, governed by sympathies and musical innuendoes, by the exacting demands of art; a light pedal here and a hard there, a delicate touch for one section and a thumping hammer of the keys for another. Fortissimo and pianissimo are not words in his vocabulary. The nightclub pianist has only to allow his hands a will of their own much as a typist must: he does not see the ivory or the ebony, nor does he really hear the notes any more than the typist sees the words or hears the dent of the letters on paper.

As Mulrenan looked up from the piano, his eye alighted as it always did upon the two racing stucco charioteers. The one in front was riding hard, his long hair streaming in the wind, whilst the one trailing was cracking a whip, the thin line of cord meandering across the wall. The pillars on either side, with their Corinthian capitols, he assumed were the starting and finishing posts in a race that would survive as long as the plasterwork clung to the stone. He who was winning was, Mulrenan thought, the one with the luck, the Irish one.

Beyond the pillars, through the windows, was a scene as far removed from classical Greece as any surrealist could contrive. Outside, there was a harbour a mile wide before a mountainous island. On the island shore was a city from which one white skyscraper thrust up like an altar. Behind it, buildings appeared to be crawling up the lower slopes of the mountains. Plying across the sea was a ferry with a

7

stove-pipe funnel and several three-masted Chinese junks. Riding at anchor were ocean-going steamers, around each of which clustered a bobbing throng of sampans and lighters. Grey warships lay alongside a grey dock, the silhouettes broken by fluttering white ensigns and the sunlight glinting on the brass mouths of the deck guns.

Leaning against the art deco panelling of the wall behind him was the double bass in its black leather case. On a dais stood the drum kit, the cymbals reflecting dim gold in the tropical sunlight and, before it, five music stands arranged in a haphazard pattern, bearing sheets of music from the previous night. From each stand hung a cloth emblazoned with the insignia of the band, an incongruous mixture of East and West — a grinning mandarin in a bobbled hat holding a clarinet. The banners hung like lance pennants at a medieval jousting tournament.

It was an appropriate comparison, in Mulrenan's opinion. Every night, from nine-thirty until one, the upper crust of the European community of Hong Kong gathered here to join their own contemporary tournament. It was far more genteel and refined than its distant predecessor but no less cut-and-thrust, certainly no more merciful. The wounds were less readily recognised, the blood that flowed was metaphorical, but the close combat of primitive battle was present all the same. Ladies and lovers were vied for, pacts sealed or shattered, social treaties suggested with as much etiquette as was once given to the lungeing of a pikestaff, the swinging of a spiked ball on a chain.

Through the windows shone the brilliant light of an early afternoon unfiltered by blinds or curtains. Across the parquet flooring, glistening from daily polishing, the glare cut a narrow oblong close to the sills. Over his head the ill-disguised ventilator, set into the slightly domed ceiling and painted in what the hotel management claimed was the colour of the sky after a rainstorm, caused a delicate down-draught upon the few empty tables, rippling the petals of the roses in the vases and tickling the starched serviettes folded to represent white rosebuds.

They were tiny trademarks of *The Rose Room*, once the

8

banquetting hall, now an excellently appointed restaurant which could be thrown open in conjunction with the *Roof Garden* to form a massive ballroom capable of seating eight hundred.

His fingers reached the end of *Clair de Lune* and the music trailed off with a delicate flourish. A few hands applauded from the nearer tables.

The diners were a motley lot: businessmen discussing their affairs with hands pressed under their chins as if praying to the great gods of trade; Americans with their wives doing the world — there was a liner berthed in the Kowloon Docks; women taking tiffin together without their spouses, their heads close together in the conspiracies of gossip; at tables laid for two were earnest, quiet couples oblivious of the other customers and the cursory, knowing glances of the women. There was not a Chinese seated at any of the tables.

A waiter approached him, dressed in black loose-fitting trousers and a white high-collared jacket with polished silver buttons in place of the traditional knotted cloth ones. On his feet were soft, slipper-like black shoes. He was carrying a silver-plated tray upon which balanced a crystal glass tumbler.

'You wisk-ee, Mist' Muwennun.'

Mulrenan looked up from the keyboard.

'Thank you, Ah Loong. Just what I need.'

He took a long sip, the cube of ice nudging his lip. As usual, the scotch had too much water in it and the chlorine could be tasted through the spirits. He did not complain.

'Is lunch ready?' It was a rhetorical question, for he knew it would be. It was a part of the deal, the overall package of service and perks.

'You tiffin offa' dere,' the waiter replied, using a word for a meal to which Mulrenan was still not fully accustomed. Ah Loong indicated a table laid for one in a corner at the other end of the room, by the entrance from the bar.

Mulrenan's contract demanded he provide 'social music appropriate as an accompaniment to midday drinks' from half past eleven for an hour, take a half an hour break then

9

play what he privately called 'trough music' from one until two-fifteen. He would then be due his lunch. He was also obliged to play cocktail music in the evening from seven to nine-thirty and, when asked, perform at tea dances or sit in with the dance band if their pianist, an asthmatic Frenchman with a predilection towards cognac, was indisposed. If the manager requested it he was also bound to play in one or another of the company's hotels on Hong Kong island.

He walked to his table, put down his whisky and began to eat. He was in no hurry, for the afternoon was his own. He pierced the chilled prawns one at a time, dipped them in the lime mayonnaise and followed the hors d'oeuvres with a cold roast beef salad and another weakened scotch. By the time he had completed his meal the clientele had departed.

2

Two amahs were dusting the sills while two others skated across the dance floor, large rags bundled round their feet. The air was rich with the aroma of polish and chalk. Several waiters were stripping and relaying the tables.

Mulrenan collected his sheet music and shuffled the pages into a brown manila envelope with a crest upon it above the name — *The Peninsula Hotel*. He tucked in the flap so the crest was hidden, then made his way down to the ground floor. He did not take the lift, as that was reserved for guests.

The stairs were richly carpeted, the brass rods buffed up with Brasso in such a way there was no stain on the fabric. Once, he had seen the polishing being done in the very early hours of the morning: a bell boy rolled newspaper behind each rod and the man cleaning them had not only rubbed those sides that showed but had revolved each rod so it was cleaned the whole way round.

In the spacious lobby, he stood behind a German naval

officer who was leaving a leather briefcase for safe deposit. On its front was an embossed silver swastika. The receptionist handed the man a receipt before turning to serve Mulrenan. He did not look up as he filed the carbon copy of the German officer's chitty.

'What can I do for you, sir?

His English was good, lacking the local accent: as a Eurasian, he had been educated in one of the local schools which permitted the entry of those of mixed or Chinese extraction. When he saw whom he was addressing, his tone changed.

'Hello, Sean. How's things on the top floor? Busy wooing the ladies?'

'Tinkling along, Joseph. Still stroking the white and black ones. Not many ladies to woo.' He leaned forward on the counter. 'Plenty of women.'

The receptionist smiled briefly, looking around to ensure the comment had gone undetected.

'I suppose you want . . .?'

Mulrenan nodded.

The clerk spoke in Cantonese to one of the office boys sitting at a desk behind the heavy wooden counter, who got up and went through a door marked 'Office Staff Only'.

'I don't understand why you can't do your business below,' Joseph said, casting his gaze down at his feet in a meaningful manner.

On the ground floor of the hotel was a branch of The Hongkong and Shanghai Bank, its shining wooden counters as substantial as those of the hotel, its brass tellers' grills just as well Brasso-ed as the stair rods, its vaults more secure than the hotel safe.

'Because', Mulrenan replied. 'I like to make my deposits in the big place itself. There's something about crossing the harbour with my fortune in my pocket. You should know the feeling, being at least part Chinese: it's the fun of the gamble. Plenty of pickpockets between here and Central.'

The clerk did not flinch at what would have been a considered insult from any other European; he knew exactly what Mulrenan was and how he thought from a conversation they had had in the late summer of 1938 when the pianist had first arrived in the colony fresh off the Imperial Airways seaplane flight.

They had first met in the hotel lobby when the manager had asked the clerk to show Mr Mulrenan to his room: the hotel had given him free lodging for a month, to give him time to find himself a place to live. It was not practice for the musicians to live in.

A single room at the back of the hotel was alloted to Mulrenan. The clerk followed him up to unlock the door and ensure the bellboy with the bags was doing his job. In those days Joseph Collins was in charge of breaking in new non-menial staff. Pianists were considered non-menials.

Mulrenan dumped his heavy overcoat on the bed and plumped himself down beside it. He looked tired but still had an energy to him that caused his fingers to fidget and his eyes to dart.

'I doubt you'll wear that coat except for a few days in the winter. At the very most,' said Joseph: then he introduced himself.

'Is that a fact?' Mulrenan answered, accepting his hand and shaking it firmly, even roughly. 'For sure, it's as hot as hell itself today. If I saw little red imps with tridents dancing a hornpipe on the pavements I'd not bat an eyelid.'

'Have you had a good trip?' the clerk went on, helping Mulrenan to lift his largest suitcase on to the dressing-table stool. The bellboy had left, aware that fellow workers did not tip. 'It's so quick these days. Compared to the ship . . .'

'Not too bad. There was some rough weather after Colombo and we had to turn back to Trincomalee. Stayed an extra night there.' Mulrenan snapped the locks of the case. The brass catches thumped solidly against the dub-binned leather. 'It was raining hard in Singapore.'

'It always rains hard in Singapore,' Joseph remarked. 'Every day around noon. Pelts down, I'm told. It's so regular they say you can set your watch by it.'

'That was the one! We landed about midday. They took us ashore in a motor boat to the jetty. Streaming down, it was. Warm as a bath.'

12

He opened the lid of his case, resting it back on its straps, letting free the aroma of good-quality cowhide, and started to thrust a tuxedo on to a hanger.

'Have you been to Singapore yourself?'

Joseph's reply was cautious and apprehensive. Any second now the truth would be out.

'No. Actually, I've never left Hong Kong.'

'Really, is that a fact . . . ?' It was a statement this time. 'Then how come you're here? Didn't you come out, recruited from one of the . . .?'

'I was born here.'

It was then, inexplicably, that Joseph decided he had an affinity with the new pianist. It was nothing he could define or justify, merely a deep-seated reaction to the man: just as he could assess most customers before they had even signed in.

Recognising people for what they were was a part of the skill acquired in hotel work. A flourish of the fountain pen, a look at the bellboy, a glance over the baggage: in such insignificant motions he could tell the character of a complete stranger, immediately know he would be the type to complain to the maitre d', or tip generously, or surreptitiously request a woman, or be downright bloody-minded to the Chinese roomboys.

'I'm not British. At least, not in the sense you are. My father was English and — but — my mother Chinese. They are divorced now,' he added, as an excuse.

To his surprise, this information did not get the customary retort, the one in his youth he had found so painful, but which had numbed now to an ache, a mixture of apology and dismissal much like condolences offered at the funeral of a distant and unloved relative. Instead, the pianist leaned back on his bed and laughed.

'I shouldn't let that worry you. Because you're half-caste doesn't mean you're not as good as the rest. Probably means you're a damn sight better.'

Flabbergast, the clerk made no answer. He stared at the stranger sitting on the bed, an ivory-backed hairbrush in each hand.

13

'Think of it this way,' Mulrenan said. 'Look at greyhounds. You know what greyhounds are?'

Joseph shook his head. 'Grey dogs of some sort?' he ventured.

'Ah, well. Never mind.' Mulrenan was not prepared to break the flow of his parable with a lesson about dogs. 'Think of race horses. Think of those fine Arab stallions the gentry ride. The big businessmen from the big companies. The hongs. The men who think they own China. The wheelers and dealers. Think of them. Tall, erect horses, shining with health and breeding. Proud as peacocks, strutting round the ring at the races — I know you have races here, though I'll bet you don't go to them . . .'

Joseph shook his head again. The sudden volubility of a man who until now had spoken only in short, non-committal sentences shocked him.

'You seem to know a lot about Hong Kong,' he interrupted. Perhaps, he reasoned, by speaking himself and changing the subject he might silence him or reduce him to brevity once more.

'Of course I do. Research. You don't think I'm going to fly halfway round the bloody world to play piano in a bar I've not looked into, do you? Not at £112 per ticket. One way! And it's a long way —' Mulrenan's voice lowered and, for the one word, bore sadness — 'home. Anyhow. Horses,' he continued, not to be deterred, 'those Arabs. They win races, for sure. They run like mercury across a steel plate. But watch them in the gate or at the starting post. Prancing about. Finnicky. Flicking their tails. High-strung as their owners. Under starter's orders. The flag drops. Down the course they go. How they go! But try riding one over a field, put him in the shafts of a trap. Nothing. Bloody useless. What do you use for the good things, the important things in life? Easy. You use mongrels, with all the good points of their parents and the high-strung shennanikins bred out. That's you. I could tell as soon as I met you that you're the better off for the decanting of bloods.'

He was momentarily silent.

'That's how it strikes me, anyhow,' he went on. 'And, for

your information, I'm as British as you are. My father was Irish, but my mother English.'

He grew serious. 'Sometimes, though . . . Of course, it's not the same for everyone. Sometimes you can't help the hate.'

'Hate?'

'You know. Hating . . . What the hell!' The Irishman's mood suddenly changed. 'How long does the laundry take? Or do they call it *dhobi*? No,' he answered himself, 'that's in India. I've not a clean shirt to my name.'

3

He crossed the road to Statue Square, dodging between black saloon cars, cyclists, red and green rickshaws, coolies with loads suspended from poles and pedestrians. As he walked around the effigy of Queen Victoria under her cupola he reflected how even the statues of the British were shaded from the sun.

Across the other side of Statue Square stood the most impressive building in the crown colony, the head office of the bank, euphuistically named 'The Bank', The Hongkong and Shanghai Bank, the controller of local currency and trade its building twice as big as any other building in the city, an imposing monolith in grey-buff stone with a top like an elongated and stepped pyramid, its apex sliced off. The roof might have had a slit in its top for the insertion of coins, so much did it look like a money-box.

Pausing for a few moments, Mulrenan watched, wondering how long it would be before some passing coolie, a bamboo pole over his shoulders, stretched out his hand to touch one of the bronze lions. Already, in just the few short years since 1935 when the building had been completed, the animals had become symbols of good fortune, the rub of a paw or the touch of a tail promising riches.

He did not have long to wait. An amah walked by carrying a bamboo basket in which a hen scuffled and clucked. She changed hands with the basket and lightly stroked the lion's flank. The chicken, dislodged from one side of the basket to the other, squawked loudly.

Mulrenan, smiling to himself, made his way inside. The banking hall was vast and cool, as if dictating that good commercial sense was never warm. Upon the Swedish marble floor stood thick square columns of Ashburton marble supporting a vaulted roof enriched by a mosaic of vast proportions illustrating the spirit of the age. To those prepared to crick their necks the mosaic portrayed in classical terms the taking-over of the mystical Orient by the industrial West. To Mulrenan, it was a gross and tasteless proof of what the British did to the culture of nations who stood in the way of colonial progress.

'Good afternoon, sir. Can I be of some assistance?'

The young man who had addressed him was wearing a lightweight grey suit, a white shirt and deep blue tie; on his wrist was a watch with an expanding steel strap. His right hand jacket cuff was slightly shined. He looked unmistakeably a bank worker.

'I'd like access to my deposit box, please.'

'Certainly, sir. May I have your name?'

Mulrenan gave it, then waited while the official lifted a section of counter, passing into the private area of the banking hall. He checked a file lying on a glass-topped desk at which sat another, more senior official. When he returned, he was accompanied by his senior, whom Mulrenan vaguely recognised.

'Mr Mulrenan. Good afternoon, sir.' The man turned to his assistant. 'You were quite right to call me, but Mr Mulrenan is a regular and valued client.' He turned back. 'Will you follow me?'

Mulrenan was ushered into the vault anteroom, signed his name in a ledger and was shown to a private cubicle. His deposit box was brought by a Chinese in the uniform of the bank messenger staff. The man placed it carefully, almost sacramentally, on a table, the only furniture except for an upright chair, then politely withdrew.

From a slit pocket inside the waistband of his trousers Mulrenan produced a key with a complicated pattern cut in the tongue. He unlocked the box and, from each of the side pockets of his trousers, took a small pouch made of chamois leather. He did not open the two pouches but squeezed them gently to assure himself of their contents. With difficulty, for there was little space available, he put them in the box, locked the lid and pressed a button on the wall. Almost at once the messenger returned and the box was taken back to the vaults.

In the banking hall once more, Mulrenan joined a short queue for a teller. Reaching the head of the line, he deposited three thousand Hong Kong dollars in notes.

4

The funicular Peak Tram slid into the station, halting just short of buffers from which the grease was running in the heat. There had been only three or four passengers but more were queueing for the return journey up the mountain. Mulrenan was the only European adult, the others were either the servants or the children of the wealthy who lived on The Peak. It was nearly four o'clock, and the children were returning from the Central British School where afternoon lessons during the summer term ended just after three.

Predictably, the school-children sat in the first class, front end of the tram. They avoided the very front seat which was specially reserved, a traditional relic from the days when it was kept exclusively for the governor and his family. Mulrenan considered taking the seat himself but chose instead the third class section at the rear where normally only servants would sit. The advantage of the third class was that the seats had no protecting wall and one could slip into them without using a door; a running board provided a step up to the wooden slat benches. Without the coachwork, one was open to the elements which in rainy weather meant a dowsing but in hot weather provided a cooling breeze.

As soon as Mulrenan was settled, the servants out of deference sitting apart from him, the driver gave his signal, a bell rang tinnily and the tram set off, running past a row of hibiscus bushes and across a bridge of girders over a nullah before tilting for an ascent of over a thousand feet.

Above May Road the upbound tram passed the downbound, Mulrenan watching idly as it went by, his eyes nevertheless carefully scanning the passengers. Where the tracks turned in a cutting at eight hundred feet, below the Barker Road station, the tram stopped. The other had halted lower down the mountain: if one stopped so did the other, for they were on opposite ends of the same cable. The car in which Mulrenan sat rocked as the steel stretched and contracted.

Below Mulrenan's feet, thick jungle dropped steeply to the city. By the roots of a succulent plant, the branches of which almost brushed the side of the tram, he could see a cobra curled in a patch of shadow. As the tram started again, the snake raised its head and spread its hood but, before it could unwind and escape into the undergrowth, the tram had moved on.

At the terminus the children were collected by motor cars or sedan chairs. The servants, many of them laden with bundles, set off on foot. Mulrenan crossed the narrow road to a small cafe discreetly positioned behind a low stone wall and tall bushes. At weekends The Peak Cafe was a favourite spot for Europeans walking on the mountain or visiting it to admire the views. In midweek it catered for few clients.

Mulrenan walked through the entrance in the stone wall and into the warm semi-shade. At the rear was a patio of sorts arranged with folding chairs and metal tables covered with gingham cloths. Overhead draped flowering creepers, the main branches supported on a wooden trellis. The patio was deserted except for a waiter who stood up expectantly as Mulrenan looked round at the empty tables. The man evidently hoped his movement would encourage the customer to stay and order.

Mulrenan tapped the glass of his wrist watch to make certain it was working. Perhaps it was fast: he had had trouble with it ever since arriving in Hong Kong. The humidity seeped into the clockwork despite the fact the watch was guaranteed waterproof. He grudgingly accepted its faults, for it was British-made and that, to his mind, suggested inferior quality. It did not matter: soon he would be able to afford a Swiss watch.

Beside the Peak Tram terminus an observation platform under a small, Chinese-style roof of ceramic green tiles. He made his way across the road into the shade and leaned upon the railing. Before him was spread the vista of Hong Kong, the harbour and distance shimmering in the late heat of the day. Beneath was the city of Victoria, the white buildings stark against the greenery of the mountainside as if they had been bleached rather than whitewashed.

Another two Peak Tram arrivals produced more passengers but not one of them sought the shade of the cafe.

From the observation platform, Lugard Road wove around the side of the mountain, disappearing into the lush trees. To pass the time, Mulrenan set off along it, pacing himself so he would not grow too hot or walk too far. The mountain air was not as sticky as the city atmosphere, but it was still very hot.

Butterflies as large as house martins drifted in slow flight ahead of him, their wings bending and iridescent in the light shafting through the branches. Smaller butterflies darted at his feet, a cloud of them shimmering up from where they had been drinking at a trickle of water seeping from the rock. Their pale wings resembled breaking glass rising into the air as if a sharded window pane was trying to reconstruct itself. There was no birdsong: in lieu, cicadas and crickets scratched unseen in the undergrowth. Mulrenan met no one until he reached the end of the tunnel of trees and bamboos.

A coal coolie, his panniers empty, had come down from a

house built precariously into the hillside above the road. As he walked the panniers swung from the pole across his shoulders and yet, relieved of his load, the man still bowed, unable to straighten even when his burden was absent. He was dressed only in baggy pantaloons and his upper body was coated with coal dust. His tanned skin showed through where rivulets of sweat had run across his torso. Around his head he had wrapped a strip of rag above which his close-cropped hair stuck coarsely upward.

The coolie did not see Mulrenan until he was at his side and jumped with surprise, side-stepping quickly to let a European by. Mulrenan having already made a similar gesture, the two of them stood for a moment with the coolie nonplussed. He was not used to having anyone make way for him even when he was carrying heavy loads of coal. With a semi-scurry, the coolie turned and set off: he did not smile or mutter thanks.

The tree-line dropped away as the road traversed a precipitous rockface slick with water. Constructed on pillars, the road, now narrowed to little more than a metalled path, was free of the hillside and was more like a bridge than a thoroughfare. On either side were iron railings recently painted but already blotched with rust from the evening mists.

Mulrenan was further around The Peak here and the panorama was marginally changed. Below him were a few residences of the wealthy, but they were to his right. Immediately beneath him was the western end of the city, the bustling native tenement quarter where the Chinese lived. In the heat haze beyond Kowloon lay a range of hills and to his left the sea and faint blue islands.

He looked once more at his wrist watch. It was later than he had thought; he retraced his steps at a brisk pace. To be late would be to insult the expected person, a risk Mulrenan was not prepared to run.

Seated at one of the tables under the vines was a Chinese man dressed in a fashionably tailored three-piece suit. He was the only customer in the cafe, and fortunately so: had Europeans been present, he might have been obliged to leave. The only Chinese who regularly entered were baby amahs with their European charges either in big black perambulators shipped out from Britain or in local bamboo and rattan pushchairs.

Once seeing Mulrenan, the waiter was about to move the Chinese man despite his smart clothes and the fact his order of an iced coffee had only just been served, but Mulrenan sat at the same table before he could take action.

'I had wondered where you were, Mr Mulwenan.' The Chinese man's French accent was barely noticeable: his fluency was good, the product of a mission school education. 'Your arrival is just in time, for the waiter was about to ask me to leave. You coming has saved him a great loss of face.'

Mulrenan rose, draped his jacket over a chair, and sat down again. He knew well enough that he had saved the waiter more than a loss of face. Had he attempted to move this customer he would eventually have paid a considerable price. It might not have been for weeks but the time would have come one evening, somewhere in the maze of alleys and streets in Western District, when revenge would have been taken: a fist in the kidneys or a knife in the groin.

Beckoning to the lucky waiter, a discreet four paces away, Mulrenan ordered tea.

'My wristwatch does not work properly,' he explained. 'I am sorry to keep you waiting, Mr Fong.'

'It is no matter. I knew you would be here quite soon. You are, unlike your compatriots, a man of your word. Especially', he added, 'where matters of business are concerned.'

The waiter approached with a tray upon which was placed a porcelain teapot with a woven wicker handle and an eggshell china teacup. A saucer with slices of lemon upon it rattled against a jug of milk. Mulrenan felt in his pocket for some change.

'Allow me,' insisted Mr Fong. 'It is a rare occasion when I can offer to pay for a gweilo's — I am sorry — a European's tea in a Europeans' tea house.'

He smiled but Mulrenan did not.

'I am a European, that is true, and I may be a *gweilo*, but I'm not one of them. So long as we remember that . . .'

'Of course,' Fong said, but did not apologise.

One of the huge butterflies floated idly over the table, its wingspan so large and its wingbeat so firm it stirred the cigarette ash in their ashtray. Mulrenan lifted a hand towards it in the hope it might settle on him. It made no attempt to avoid his stretching fingers but did not land on them. Instead, it rose to some delicate pink blossoms overhead and, gripping one with its black legs, fed upon the nectar. Fong watched with mild curiosity.

'The butterflies are very beautiful, are they not, Mr Mulwenan? Have you any like them in Great Britain?'

'In Britain' — Mulrenan pointedly omitted the adjective — 'there are no butterflies like these. There are few beautiful things as free or as common.'

He sipped his tea. Fong drank noisily from his tall glass. A large car on the road outside ground its gears as the driver changed down to climb Mount Austin Road.

'You are a most unusual man, Mr Mulwenan.'

Fong moved his head a fraction to catch the car in the corner of his eye. He wanted to be certain it was an American car: official vehicles were of English make.

'Why?'

'Because you are British and yet you are not. You are one of the — how can I put it? — Empire builders and yet you seem to disdain that very Empire. You live within it, and profit from it, yet you also seem to want it to cease.'

The butterfly shifted to another blossom. The patio was in shadow and even such a minuscule difference in temperature slowed the insect's movements. Soon it would leave the vine blossoms and disappear into the trees for the night.

Fong continued, 'Why do you want it to fail? I do not understand.'

Mulrenan made no immediate reply. He poured more tea into his cup, adding a second slice of lemon.

'It is my way,' he answered defensively, then brought their meeting round to its purpose. 'Do you have something for me?'

This time it was Fong who made no reply. Ascertaining that the waiter was not in sight, he pulled from inside his jacket a small leather bag similar to those Mulrenan had deposited in the bank. He pushed it along the table close to the rim of the tray.

'I shall want to check them,' Mulrenan said matter-of-factly. 'May I take them away with me as usual?'

'Yes. But I shall need your decision by tomorrow evening. My principal will require completion by the end of the week and he is not . . .'

'. . . in Hong Kong. That's quite all right.'

'I was going to say,' Fong raised his glass, 'that my principal is not a patient man,' and he drank the remainder of his coffee to lend weight to his words.

'That is also not an obstacle,' Mulrenan answered, not too off-handedly, and with sufficient emphasis to indicate that he was still in command of the dealing.

The waiter headed for their table. Mulrenan calmly secreted the little bag under his hand. When the tray had been removed, he said, 'Do you have a figure in mind, Mr. Fong?'

'I am instructed to accept not less than two thousand five hundred.'

'Thank you.' Mulrenan did not allow himself to appear thrown by the sum. 'I shall be in touch in the normal way well before tomorrow evening.'

He stood up to leave, pulling his coat from the folding metal chair and snagging a button on its frame.

'You are a good friend in business, Mr Fong.'

'You are too kind,' replied the Chinese. His turn of phrase amused Mulrenan: he might have been a taipan's wife accepting a compliment on her cook-boy's excellent dinner.

5

The sedan chair stood in the roadway on its minute legs, the bases of which were carved like dragon's fists. It was a chair cannibalised from others, including a rich man's vehicle that had become woodwormed save for the mahogany legs.

Mulrenan settled into it and the two coolies hoisted the creaking poles on to their shoulders, nudging them into a comfortable position on pads of folded rags tied with twine and tucked in to their necks. They went down the Old Peak Road, a twisting and steep path that had been the only way up the mountain before the building of the Magazine Gap motor road.

The motion of the chair was not smooth. Unless the coolies kept in step the contraption bucked about, and the slope made it difficult for them to control their pace. Mulrenan gave no complaint, knowing they were doing their best, but he gripped the sides and pressed his feet against the pillars that supported the green canvas roof.

At the botanical gardens, he paid off the coolies and walked westward. He avoided going past Government House, its smartly uniformed sentries with their polished Lee Enfields sloped to the shoulder or butt-down on the concrete, its immaculate lawns and the palm trees discreetly whispering in the evening breeze like dowager duchesses.

The buildings he did pass were only slightly less galling to him. They were the homes of the rich but not necessarily the influential: those endowed with both riches and influence usually lived on top of The Peak. These houses, in the Mid-Levels, were two- or three-storeyed and sedate with deepset balconies shaded by bamboo blinds. The occupants were, to Mulrenan's mind, better than many, for although they had money they had earned it by their own endeavours. That this might have involved degrading or ruining the lives of others did not occur to him.

'Hong Kong Island's stratified according to social geology,' he had been told by Joseph Collins not long after his arrival, 'The nearer you are to the mud in the harbour the lower you are in society.'

The term 'social geology' brought a wry smile to Mulrenan's lips.

'Explain yourself,' he demanded.

'In the city,' Joseph began, 'along the crowded waterfront, squatting on the *praya* with their rickshaws or transporting tea chests from the junks moored alongside or carting nightsoil — a quaint British euphemism for human excrement. . .'

'These your own words?' Mulrenan butted in.

'Do you mind! Do you want to listen or not?' Joseph rejoined. 'Do not interrupt your guide!' He wagged his finger in the air. 'Now — where was I?'

'Excrement,' prompted Mulrenan.

'Thank you,' he said curtly.

Mulrenan smiled again as he realised there was a hidden, crudite side to Joseph's nature.

'I shall go on. There live the lowest of the low, the beggars and coolies, the orphans and the dispossessed, the stupid, and the defeated, the unlucky, the unwise and unloved. They live cheek by jowl in coolie houses, sharing a cupboard with three or four others of their own class, sleeping in shifts and earning, if they are lucky, five bucks a week for a thirteen-hour day. They pay squeeze to the foreman, rent to the landlord, bribes to the officials and fees to the street letter-writers who pen their lying, hopeful letters home to China. They smoke opium when they can get it, eat rice when they can buy it and meat or fish when they can afford it, which is seldom. They pray to whichever god they follow, that they will not be injured crossing a gangplank, or get in the way of a swinging derrick, or fall sick, for to be injured or ill is to be without work and to be without work is to starve and die.'

Mulrenan listened fascinated. He had as yet not ventured into the farther reaches of the city.

'Slightly higher up the hillside,' Joseph continued, 'are those who prey upon the coolies. Here, in cramped but less squalid conditions, exist the coolie whore pimps and their girls, the landlords, the money-lenders and the foremen, the clerks and the controllers of lesser men's destinies.

'Higher still are the small merchants, the men who own gangs of coolies and clerks, who operate shops and sell food or cloth. Here, too, live the small firm compradores . . .'

'Compradore?' queried Mulrenan.

'They are the middle-men between the European business houses and the Chinese workers, the universal fixers, the do-anything or get-anything men. They usually have large obedient families, a huge circle of friends, acquaintances and others who stand in their debt. They are the professional go-betweens. Don't you have them in Britain?'

'I think not.'

'Well, above them live the Europeans who aren't in control. In the Mid-Levels are the non-British merchants, the French from Marseilles and the Germans from Hamburg with their shipping lines, the Portuguese with trading links in Canton, Macau, Chungking and Nanking, the Americans, the Dutch with East Indies interests, the Scandinavians with their banks.

'Beyond them, towards the sky and next to God himself, are the luxurious homes of the British, the management of The Hongkong and Shanghai Bank or The Chartered Bank, those who own the hongs, the big firms like Butterfield and Swire and, the biggest of them all, Jardine and Mathieson. These companies had their vast wealth founded in the trading of opium grown in India for tea grown in China.'

Joseph was growing heated, carried away by the emotions the Irishman aroused in him.

'Slavery and corruption were their *modus operandi*. They thrived on the rape — not of women, though no doubt that entered into tiny corners of their enterprise — but of an entire civilisation.'

'We'll make an anti-colonial out of you yet, Joseph,' Mulrenan had said jokingly.

The trees overhanging the road filled suddenly with the

rushing sound of wings followed by high-pitched birdsong. Mulrenan looked up, but all he could see were black dots shifting uneasily across the beams of light between the boughs.

Less than half a mile from the palatial Government House were crowded, narrow streets, seething with humanity, in which existed the top layer of the bottom-most stratum. It was here that Mulrenan was heading.

He stopped at the corner of Hollywood Road and Lyndhurst Terrace. At the top of Peel Street a scaffolding had been erected against the side of a tenement. Within the web of bamboo poles secured together by bamboo thongs a ramp was hanging, its topmost part flattened by a casement window. In the street was a sizeable crowd, many of which were dressed entirely in white. Two or three rickshaws, decorated with gaudy paper flowers, tipped forwards on their shafts,: in one was propped a grainy portrait photograph of a Chinese man.

An overseer at the top of the ramp started shouting instructions and a glossy wooden coffin appeared through the window, to be grasped by a number of coolies who had run up the ramp at the overseer's bawled command. They carried the coffin in a din of yelled instructions and countermanding advice to the street, where it was roped to a four-wheeled handcart. Replete with corpse, the small procession set off in the direction of the nearest temple.

Halfway along Lyndhurst Terrace, Mulrenan stopped at a green-painted door and knocked. It was opened by an amah who beckoned him in.

'Missy come two min'it,' she said, indicating a chair. 'You sit.'

It was gloomy in the hallway. The furniture was sullenly heavy, beaten into immobile submission. Next to the chair, a passable copy of an upright Windsor, was a dark-stained camphorwood chest and two square rosewood chairs of a Chinese design. A European hat-stand restricted the space between them.

The amah returned, hobbling down the stairs on her tiny feet, the result of their being bound in childhood: another example, Mulrenan reflected, of inhumanity in the cause of beauty. To a Chinese, small feet were erotic.

'You come up?' she invited.

Mulrenan followed the amah to a landing from which led off a number of closed panelled doors. At the end of the landing the amah opened the last door.

The room was illuminated only by the twilight from an open window. Upon the walls hung scrolls showing sheer mountain peaks with rivers winding between them; cranes flew across misted skies, almost alive in the half-light. A Tientsin carpet covered the boards of the floor and stretched from the cane divan to a large, low bed upon which was laid a silk quilt decorated with embroidered azaleas. At the head of the bed an ornate carved panel depicted dragons fighting a victorious phoenix: their eyes were made of inlaid mother-of-pearl that glowered in the twilight. By the window stood a thin woman outlined against the evening: from below came the sounds of the street and the ivory clatter of mahjong pieces.

He dropped his coat on a stool and removed his shoes as the woman closed the shutters. A match scratched and an oil lamp glimmered before the flame caught and the glass canopy and funnel were replaced. The lamp was incongruously European in such an Oriental setting.

Barefoot, he took three steps to the woman who faced him as he crossed the carpet, the warmth of the sun still in the pile.

'You are late this evening, Sean.'

'I was busy. And my watch isn't working properly.'

He stood before her and she gazed up into his face, laughing lightly.

'That's a very weak excuse. Can't you think of one a little more original?'

Mulrenan grimaced and brushed his cream-slicked hair forward over his brow. He hunched his shoulders and let his arms swing ape-like.

'I was caught in a blizzard at the top of the mountain and the sedan chair carriers had lost their skis.'

She laughed again, just a tone more loudly.

'You have the laugh of a concubine,' he said teasingly.

'And you the avoiding answer of a man with too many lovers.'

She sat on the edge of the bed. Away from her and with the lamp shining upon her, he could see her clearly and, as he always did, looked at her without moving.

'There is no one else, Alice. You know that,' Mulrenan replied. There were times when he wondered if she meant what she spoke in fun.

'Oh, I know that. In Hong Kong, it is easy to learn of others' lovers. They say that if you sit at the Star Ferry all day for a week you meet everyone you know.'

Mulrenan liked Alice Soon because she was so similar to him. He may even have loved her, had he wanted to admit it. She shared his quick wits and sharp sense of humour: she knew what he wanted, not only in bed but in life, and her hungers and desires mirrored his own. Like him, too, she was a survivor.

Her hair was black and shone as if cut from strands of jet: when he buried his fingers in it, it was just as cool. If there were black jade or black mercury, her hair could have been made from it. Her skin was smooth, not as dark as most Chinese, but more so than a European girl, the rosy bloom replaced by a soft opacity like the thin strips in a sandal-wood fan. Her cheeks were high-boned but not prominent and her eyes darkly almond. Her hands were as delicate as a jeweller's, her fingers long, her waist curved and her breasts small but well-shaped. He could see her thigh in the slit skirt of her cheong sam: she had undone the knotted silk buttons at the top.

Taking her head in his hands, he kissed her on her cheeks, smelling scent in her hair.

'I can't stay long,' he said and sat beside her. 'My business took longer than usual. I'm supposed to be back in The Pen by seven and it's . . . .'

He looked at his watch. It was stuck at five-seventeen. Impatiently, he tapped his finger on the glass and the red wire of the second hand jerked forwards eight seconds and seized.

'Damn and blast! What time is it?'

'About half past six.'

'Well, it won't matter too much in the middle of the week, but I must be back by seven-thirty at the latest.'

She unbuttoned his shirt, slipped it off his body and knelt at his feet. He undid his trousers and she pulled them off with his underpants, piling all his clothes in the centre of the carpet.

He pushed himself back with his feet until he lay spread on the quilt. She stepped on to the bed, pulled her dress above her knees and began kneading his chest and shoulders. After a while, he rolled on to his front and she pressed and rubbed his back muscles and worked her massaging down to the cleft in his buttocks. He dozed as she moved her weight across his body.

'When shall I see you next?' she enquired almost timidly.

He woke from a semi-sleep in which not a thought had entered his head.

'Not tonight. Tomorrow night.'

'You promise?'

'Yes, I promise,' he said with a hint of resignation. He became merrier. 'And this weekend — would you like to go to the races? I actually have an invitation. It's amazing what you can pick up if you mix in the right circles.'

She instantly stopped her massage and he squirmed on to his spine and sat up, flexing his arms to return them to wakefulness and wrapping them around his knees.

'I enjoy my "new" life. Such as it is,' he mused. 'The poker is good in Hong Kong: much better than Aden or Port Said. And they're accepting me in their own way. See me as a bit of an entrepreneur, I suppose. As well as a musician. It's not the Happy Valley races — these are in the New Territories. Got the tickets from Lionel Ham. He won handsomely the night before last.'

'How can I go?' There was a quiet despair in her words. 'I'm not exactly one of the racing set. I am,' her voice broke, '*known*.'

'To hell with that. And to hell with them.' He was angry.

'They're no better nor worse than you or I. You're as near as dammit one of them, anyway. Take that dress off and you'd be . . .'

'Stark naked,' she said and cheekily lifted the hem to prove it. He could see the dark space between her thighs but ignored it and looked her straight in the eye.

'European, I was going to say. You don't have to hide all the time like some *dahnomer*.'

'I don't like that.' Now she was angered. 'I'm not some soldier's whore, some "down homer" that does his laundry and lies on her back for him when he gets tired of the company of his mates in Murray Barracks. What do you think I am? Sometimes, Sean, I — '

'You get my laundry done,' he said disarmingly.

'I do, yes. But . . . But I don't do it myself! Ah Shun does it.'

She smoothed the tight brocade dress with her hands as if smearing its pattern over her body.

'Point taken. But I'll not apologise. And you'll come to the races.'

His eyes flashed and she knew he had won and that she must surrender.

'All right,' she acquiesced. 'But I'll need a new dress. I've nothing I can wear that is the least bit suitable.'

'Go to Lane, Crawford and buy what you must,' he said dismissively.

He rose and crossed the room. The hinge on the cupboard squeaked as he opened it. He took out a freshly ironed tropical suit and a cotton shirt and casually dressed.

'I'll pay you back tomorrow night.'

'Will you show me what you collected today before you leave?'

He welcomed her curiosity. It meant she was interested in his newly-acquired business skill of which, being self-taught, he was inordinately proud. One day he hoped he might introduce her to its intricacies. She could assist him and they could operate business together.

From the dirty clothing on the floor he took out Fong's

little bag and undid the knot in the drawstring. On to his hand slid a ruby the size of a french bean. She held it between finger and thumb against the lamplight.

'Is it a good one?' she asked.

'A very good one.'

'Where did you get it?'

He paused, then decided to tell her. 'It came from China.'

It was at least a half-truth.

6

The sombre room was silent with concentration and the etiquette of poker. The curtains were drawn, the ceiling fan on its lowest setting. The men seated at the table were in shirt-sleeves, the air marbled with tobacco smoke. Those who had arrived wearing neckties or bow-ties had either removed them or loosened the knots. Mulrenan recognised two of them: one was a Black Watch tie, the other an Oxford University tie with a distinctive crest. The former had mesmerized him when its wearer entered the room. He could not believe his luck.

As he took his seat, Mulrenan mused upon the rich opportunity a kindly fate had unexpectedly given him. A British army officer would have presented a fine chance for revenge but one from the Black Watch was almost beyond dreaming: the man's regiment had done such vast damage to Ireland, had spilled so much Irish blood on the streets of Dublin. Now it was Mulrenan's turn, if only metaphorically, to draw some of the officer's in return.

A bedside light had been brought to the table, the ashtray brimfull with cigar butts and dog-ends. The German officer, whom Mulrenan had seen in the hotel lobby, was smoking thin cheroots and the scent clung to the baize of the table. Beside the ashtray were the soda syphon and two Jameson's Irish whiskey bottles, one completely empty, the other half-consumed. In the centre of the table was a heap of currency — Hong Kong and American dollars, with a smattering of sterling.

It was the German's bet. He removed the empty bottle, putting it on the carpet by his chair, and raised the stakes by two hundred Hong Kong dollars. Mulrenan, the Black Watch officer, the Oxford graduate and a young man from the Jardine and Mathieson junior mess came along, matching the stakes. The doctor raised further.

Mulrenan took careful stock of his cards: moving them only a fraction of an inch against themselves, and holding them close to his chest, he could just spy the row of straight corners. There were two red and two black. The card facing him open was the ace of spades.

The Jardine's man, after a lengthy consideration of his hand and a scrutiny of the countenances of his opponents, dropped out.

'Not for me, I fear. Got a hand like a foot.'

He closed the fan of his cards, pressing them down firmly as if afraid they might spring up and bet of their own accord.

Mulrenan glanced at him briefly: the man had two pairs. He was sure of it. His folding in his hand was cowardice in the face of a large pot, a lack of confidence in himself to carry a bluff. That, Mulrenan considered, was unusual in a Jardine's man. They were usually ruthless at cards as they had been in trade for over a century.

Gradually, the other players fell out until only Mulrenan and The Black Watch officer remained.

'Four-fifty,' Mulrenan said blankly, then, to make light of his hand, he added, 'If we could have another deal perhaps I might get five of a kind.'

The others laughed good-humouredly: they were out of the game and enjoying spectating.

'I'm with you and I'll raise you five hundred.'

The officer slid his cards on to the table so no one would see his hand and reached for his dinner jacket hanging on his chair. From it he took a pigskin wallet, his fingers leafing through the notes.

'I seem to be a little short of the ante . . .' he began, embarrassed.

'How much are you stuck for?' Mulrenan asked with a deliberately detached air.

'Two-fifty. Will you consider accepting an IOU? I know it's not really on and we said no slips, but I can meet it the day after tomorrow.'

Mulrenan gave the offer a quick thought. The man would be bound by his word even if he was a Black Watch officer. Perhaps *because* he was. An enemy, he reasoned, can always be trusted because they have been studied and are therefore predictable: it is one's friends who do the unexpected.

Yet the officer had two items Mulrenan wanted in preference to his money: his dignity, and his Swiss watch.

'I'll accept that,' he offered, indicating the man's left wrist.

The suggestion placed Mulrenan's opponent in a difficult situation. The man could hardly refuse, for to do so would hint he did not have confidence in his hand. Yet to fold now would be to lose all. His technique of playing might be undermined, his fellow gamblers learning from his hesitation. It might be also implied that his credit was not necessarily good, and that was risky in an introverted colonial society. Such information could readily travel with one to a subsequent posting. He had to agree, and promptly.

'Very well,' he said. 'But my watch is worth a good deal more than my deficit. It is gold.'

'What would you say was the value?' Mulrenan asked pleasantly. 'I'll accept your figure.'

'At least one hundred pounds.'

'Put it in at that. If you win, you simply regain your bet. If you lose, I'll give you the balance from the pot. It would seem,' he looked at the pile of money, 'as if it can stand the difference.'

'Right-o!' The officer unbuckled the leather strap and

placed the watch carefully on the money. 'And I'm raising you as I said.'

'In that case, I'll see you,' Mulrenan replied. 'I'd not want to reduce you to your underpants and vest.'

As he spoke, he smiled amiably and the others chuckled at his joke. The officer did likewise, for he had no option. He also believed, for only the third time that night, he had the winning hand.

Carefully, he picked up his cards, fanning them out slowly in his hand and spreading them on to the table, each oblong clicking crisply against the next.

'Full house. Sevens on knaves,' he declared, unable to disguise the triumph in his voice.

Mulrenan, with no show, put his cards down one at a time in quick succession. The players watched his thumb and index finger flick the cards over from his left hand. 'Four tens to the top ace,' he said.

The German sucked his breath in: the man in the Oxford tie and the doctor exchanged relieved glances. The Jardine's man clicked his tongue on the roof of his mouth.

'Well, I'll be buggered!' he exclaimed quietly, turning over a pair of eights and the two red aces.

Mulrenan felt pleased at his assessment of the man's hand.

'Beats me!' admitted the officer, disappointment and annoyance in his words. 'I thought you were bluffing, especially after the last-but-one hand. And that, I think, gentlemen, is the end of the evening for me.'

He re-knotted his tie and tucked his shirt into his waistband; leaning forward for over four hours had pulled the tails loose.

'I trust, sir, you will give me the opportunity to purchase my watch back in a few days?' he asked coolly, his formal address to a man whose name he knew indicating his grievance.

'Come on, Jock,' said the wearer of the Oxford tie. 'Accept defeat. It was a damn good game, I myself had — ' he turned over his own cards ' — three nines to the last ace.'

'And I two pairs,' added the German.

35

Mulrenan still had one item to win. 'I can give you the chance to get it back,' he said pleasantly.

The Jardine's man picked up the half-empty bottle of Jameson's and unscrewed the cap. The neck of the bottle knocked against the rim of the tumbler, ringing it. The doctor quickly touched it with his finger.

'Never let a glass chime,' he commented. 'If you do, a sailor dies. Do you have that superstition in the German navy, Herr Grass?'

'No, I have never heard of that before,' he replied, shaking his head. 'We are not like the Royal Navy. We have a different — how would you say? — traditional basis to our officers' mess.'

Taking the wrist watch from the pot and knowing his question rubbed salt into the wound of losing, Mulrenan asked, 'Does it keep good time?'

'It is a Rolex,' replied the officer indignantly. 'Of course it does.'

'In that case, it is very late. Or perhaps I should say early? One last hand?'

The consensus was they had played enough and the players prepared to leave, those still with money folding their bills into their wallets. Mulrenan stayed seated, gathering his winnings a sheaf of notes at a time, patting them into neat batches before folding them. Everyone left but the German officer who contrived to be slower in shrugging on his jacket. When only he and Mulrenan remained, he sat down again, pouring himself a whiskey.

'Before I leave, Mr Mulrenan, I wish to ask you something.'

Mulrenan was apprehensive. The German had been studying him closely, but not obviously, on several hands during the night's gaming.

'What is it?'

'Why', continued the German, 'did you do that?' He took a sip from his glass swilling the whiskey in his cheeks before swallowing it.

'Do what? I'm not sure what you mean.'

Underneath the table, Mulrenan's fingers clenched

the small jack-knife he had prised open. One never knew.

'Deal from the bottom of the pack. Shuffling in the equal amounts. Whatever you were doing. The cards are not marked and yet you arranged the deals sometimes.'

'Are you accusing me of sharping?' Mulrenan retorted with outraged bravado.

'Why should I do that?' the German said. 'You and I are the only winners this evening.' He patted his wallet through his dinner jacket. 'I just want to know why you get me to win and not these others. Or not just yourself. But maybe that is a big risk, yes? Only one winner is not good. You are certainly clever enough to take us for a cleaners.'

'A ride.'

'I'm sorry?'

' "For a ride" or "to the cleaners",' Mulrenan explained. 'One or the other.'

He poured himself an inch of whiskey, the last small cube of ice rattling in the glass: doing so hid his temporary confusion. He had not been caught out before.

'So! Yes, my English is not always of a good standard. A ride. I understand.' The German smiled. 'But you do not answer my question.'

'Did I take them? How can you be sure? Are you and I not just lucky?'

'Maybe, as I say, you needed to cover up by having more than one winner, and so you choose me. But I think not. And can I be so sure? I think so. Answer, please.'

It was nearly an order.

'Tell me, Herr Kommander, are you a good German?'

Now it was Herr Grass who was flummoxed. 'What do you mean by this?'

'Just that. Are you a good German? Are you a member of the Nazi Party? Were you in the Hitler Youth? There is a war coming, isn't there? Are you ready to defend your Fatherland?'

'Naturally. It is my duty. I am an officer in the navy of The Third Reich.'

'Then you must know.'

'So you did some cheating. I knew it!' He smirked with the pleasure of having been proved right. 'I have played often but have never seen such skilful . . . But what do you mean, "You must know"?'

Mulrenan drained his glass. The ice had already melted and given the whiskey an unpleasant taint of chlorine.

'When is your ship sailing?'

'Tomorrow. Or rather, today. This afternoon.'

'Where to?'

'To Japan.'

'I trust you'll have a safe voyage.'

'Still you do not answer me. Why do you, an Englishman, cheat your fellows and let a man you think — you know — will be at war and enemies to them win?'

'Because I don't like them.'

Mulrenan began to gather the cards, tearing them in half, a few at a time, then pitching them into the wastepaper basket by the window.

'Understand I am not English. I am Irish. My father was . . .'

'Ah! Now I see,' interrupted the German. 'You do not have to speak anything.'

'Why not? Do you really know? You are a German. Your land, throughout history, has been invaded and reinvaded. Armies have trampled upon it and tramped through it, they have fought there or they have pillaged on their way to battle. You have nursed their wounded, buried their dead, sold them grain at inflated prices and your women have no doubt sold themselves, from time to time, for a high premium.'

As he spoke, Mulrenan looked not at the German officer but at the shade over the lamp, which blurred into a distant fire of hatred.

'I'm not insulting you, Herr Grass, or the German people. These are facts and, no matter how much he might try or like to alter them, these are the things Hitler's New Order cannot change.' He sensed his companion was about to bristle at this and continued, 'And there is nothing wrong with a woman selling her gifts to soldiers: after all, she might well be the last love they ever know.'

He paused and let the last of the destroyed cards flutter into the bin: they were the Black Watch officer's three sevens and two jacks.

'Germany is used to invasion. She has learnt not to succumb to it like a beaten nation but to use it. You have drawn into yourselves the efficiency of the Teutons, the strength of the Slavs, the determination of the Huns, the patriotism of the Poles — even though you are now to subjugate it. You have the pure European blood in you, just as I have.

'But my country, The Republic of Ireland — Eire — that is different. We have been invaded only twice. The first time was when the Norsemen came and we learned, as you have learned, to fight but also to absorb. We drew in their language, their religion, their music and they thrust their sperm into our women. That made us great, just as Germany is now great.'

The German looked confused.

'The second invasion? When was this?' he asked. 'I do not know of such . . .'

'It was quieter than the Vikings who swooped ashore whooping like Red Indians, waving their battleaxes and broad swords. It did not lead to glorious battles but prolonged skirmishes in the bogs and the peat. And when was it? It has been going on for four hundred years, that invasion. And the invader is the bloody British.'

'Ah, yes. And so you get your backs by cheating them and giving the money you are winning to an enemy, and you keep some for yourself because you are also an enemy. It is an amusing idea.'

'Amusing!' Mulrenan squeezed the card-boxes into balls as he spoke. 'I don't do this out of amusement. I do it out of revenge.'

The bulb in the lampshade was no longer a filament of light but flames rising from the embers of Dublin, British bullets bouncing off the cobbles as they had when he was a boy.

'But not only revenge, I think,' commented the German.

Mulrenan calmed, and the fires of Dublin faded to a bedside light in a hotel room on the south coast of China.

'That's right. Not only revenge. I want to regain what is mine. I want to profit from those bastards, grow strong as they weaken. And this is my way . . .'

'Join your army. That way maybe you can kill some Englishmen.'

'My country is neutral. Or will be when the war comes. Ireland is small. Better we survive, all the while nagging at the British. During what they called "The Great War" it was Ireland that caused trouble when they least wanted it, when they were busy with you in the mud of France and Belgium. We drew some of them from you for a while.'

'But you were just — tst!' the German snapped his fingers and tapped his temple lightly ' — opportuniting, making the most of the situation. You did not do this for Germany or for the enemies of the British. You did it because the time was right for you.'

Mulrenan did not immediately reply. Instead he rose, pushing his chair under the table.

'Maybe. But we did it nevertheless and now it is up to me to take advantage of the British again. As you suggest, I can kill them. Of course. I can catch a drunk tommy in the street, can knife him in an alley. Or I can do what my brothers at home would do, mine a bridge in the New Territories and rub the wire over the dry cell just as the truck passes. Yet what good does that do? I kill a dozen maybe. But their place will be filled by two dozen more with a lot of loyal Ulstermen to help them. Nothing is achieved by that. And a political compromise is no use either. Ireland's already cut into thirds. Talk with the British and they agree to give you everything, then they take a bit more.

'No, the answer's not in violence or politics. It's in using the British for your own ends, show what bastards they are and be sure to let the rest of the world see it.'

He grasped one of the curtains on the window and pulled it back. The first washings of dawn were in the sky although the street below was still in near darkness.

'I must be going. I'm due back at work in six hours.'

40

'A pianoplayer has to have subtle fingers, yes?'

'Supple,' Mulrenan corrected him. 'And, yes, he does. Practice is important as well. All the exercise he can get.' He laughed briefly. 'I hope you have a good journey to Japan. And a good war when it comes.'

The German stood and clicked his heels together, offering his hand. Mulrenan accepted it and shook it firmly.

'Will you go back to Ireland when the war starts?'

'I don't know. I have matters . . . of business out here. I may stay.'

'Then be careful of the Japanese. They will be your enemy.'

'Not mine,' Mulrenan said.

'Possibly. But be careful. To the Japanese a European is a European. Already an American has died and a Danish man and a Polish dancer were recently killed in Shanghai. The men of Wang Ching-wei and his Japanese masters are behind all this. And the Chinese will be no good. They are split into many factions.' He shrugged. 'I must say I find it very muddling.'

'Confusion can be used to suit one's purpose.'

'Perhaps, yes. That is what our strategy lecturers tell to us.'

Mulrenan twisted the brass door knob, and said, 'It's not only money I want from them.' He routed in his pocket, let go of the door handle and held up his new watch. 'I've always fancied a gold Swiss timepiece.'

The German stared at him then laughed loudly. His brow crinkled in a frown of amusement and his eyes narrowed at the corners. As he laughed, Mulrenan noticed, his ears twitched in unison as if this were an artful act contrived for a cabaret in the officers' mess. It looked ridiculous and Mulrenan thought, just at that moment, how all officers were alike, be they the Black Watch or Hitler's naval marine.

'Good luck, Mr Mulrenan. I think somehow you will be a lucky man.'

Once out of the close atmosphere of the room and in the corridor, Mulrenan pitched his cheap watch into a fire bucket, screwing it into the sand beneath the cigarette butts extinguished there. He buckled the gold watch over the band of white skin where the old had rested, then, holding his arm out, he admired his new acquisition.

7

The train was standing at the platform in the Tsim Sha Tsui station at the tip of the Kowloon peninsula awaiting its allotted two dozen passengers. Each member of the party had paid twelve dollars to commission the special for the whole day.

Mulrenan had seen the streamlined, two-car special as he walked down from the Peninsula Hotel to the Star Ferry Pier: it reminded him of the helmet Spartan warriors had worn into battle — the two drivers' windows were the eye holes, the ventilation grid between them the nose bridge and the contoured drop to the spoiler just above the tracks the face guard. Even the smooth curve to the roof resembled the cranial plate of an armoured helmet and the central spotlight might have been a lady's favour, a plume of feather. The whole train was a travesty, classical design abused in the name of aerodynamics.

The blue chevron running along the side of the train lent it an impression of speed and luxury, class and clout. It was, Mulrenan mockingly thought, a fine example of colonial ostentation. It was also quite pointless. The train could not exceed thirty miles an hour, for the track forbade high speeds and the locomotive unit had a poor rate of acceleration. Yet it was polished silver, with a blue flash, and looked both sophisticated and imposing. To see it forging its way through the paddyfields and past tiny villages with red lucky placards on the houses, was to witness a real invasion. The train was incongruously named the 'Taipo Belle' after the little fishing town in the New Territories, the hinterland of Hong Kong, through which the line passed on its journey to Canton. It was not, Mulrenan considered, to be favourably compared with its half-namesake, 'The Brighton Belle'. At least, not on the outside.

Within, the compartments were luxurious, the armchairs upholstered in blue hide and the wooden surfaces french-polished. The cutlery and crockery were unique to the train. There was a smoking lounge, a cocktail bar and the car attendants wore blue livery. At the rear was an observation compartment in which passengers could gaze along the track they had just travelled, and to which they often flocked much as passengers on a ship go to the stern for a nostalgic glimpse of their immediate past.

Mulrenan crossed before the entrance to the terminus, stepping through the rank of rickshaws and coolies squatting between the shafts of their vehicles smoking and chatting. A few, far back in the rank and not expecting a hire for some time, were playing *tin kow* with paper cards. On the pavement under each man's foot was his stake of a few cents, hidden from the eyes of passing policemen. Open gambling was not permitted but rife: to stop a Chinese gambling was comparable to preventing a priest from praying.

Mulrenan stood in the shade of the station clocktower and watched the gamblers. He knew how to play the game, understood the arrangement of the cards into *tin kow* and *day paat*, but he seldom played himself. It was the game of the poor: the stakes never high enough for him. On the few occasions when he had played, he thought, studying the hands he could see, he had done so not with printed scraps of card but with worn ivory pieces like expensive Victorian dominoes.

The coolie with his back to Mulrenan won two consecutive hands and pocketed his winnings: eleven cents. He was grinning from his good fortune as he peered over his shoulder at the European and muttered incomprehensibly, displaying yellow chipped teeth in a broad smirk.

From Mulrenan's point of view, another disadvantage of *tin kow* was that it was virtually impossible to cheat. There was no way one could hide a piece up one's sleeve, for all the cards were dealt simultaneously and all had to be played. From the coolies' point of view, cheating was doubly awkward for none of them had sleeves anyway.

A ferry pulled in to the pier, the rushing of its propeller wash taking Mulrenan's attention from the game. As he left to stand by the jetty exit, he noticed the coolie's winning streak break.

The sun, not yet high enough to be scorching, warmed Alice as she walked out of the shadows. It glowed upon her skin, drawn in as if she were shaped not of flesh but of agate. She was wearing a cream dress with black piping on the seams, and carried a small black leather handbag which she did not hold as the European women held theirs. They had their forearms securely looped through the handles but Alice swung her bag jauntily by her side, and the buttons on the Kashmir wool sweater she was holding in the same hand clicked on the clasp. She stooped by the railing overlooking the flotsam-ridden waters and gazed about in search of Mulrenan.

He wove his way through the disembarking crowd towards her, jostled by coolies and amahs. As soon as she spied him, she waved gaily and came to meet him, slipping her free arm under his own.

'I'm late,' she chastised herself. 'I had to walk to the ferry. There wasn't a chair anywhere.'

'It's all right,' he replied dismissively. 'We've a quarter of an hour yet. There's no hurry. Besides, before we get the train I've something to show you.'

He led her past the rickshaw rank. The gaming had ceased, and the coolies were busy accepting passengers, setting off with their feet tearing at the road. Later in the day, had he been there, Mulrenan would have heard a sound to make his flesh creep — the slick of the soles of the coolies' feet sticking to the sun-melted tar.

By Kowloon public pier he and Alice stopped above the farthest flight of steps. It was low tide and the barnacles were visible, shut tight against the air with their beakish mouths clamped. A sampan girl not yet in her teens was plying the single oar of her frail-looking craft with childish urgency, maintaining herself parallel with the quay. Her younger sister was keeping the barnacles at bay with a short pole, on the end of which was a marlin spike. From under the sampan awning large baskets of fish were being lifted by coolies, water oozing from them as the cargo flicked and slapped. Nearby on the quay a young boy with a thin line looked on with envy. His haul consisted of four sardine-sized fish that had ceased flapping inside a tin bowl.

'Let's sit down for a minute. Over here.'

Mulrenan guided Alice towards a bench by the steps. As they approached it, an elderly Chinese with a long and straggling beard rose, folding his newspaper into a pocket. He wore the ankle-length gown that had been traditional dress for centuries. Below his wrist hung a black paper fan which he slid open to waft before his face. As he walked away his modern shoes with white spats appeared with each step from beneath his gown.

Alice sat where the old man had been, involuntarily smoothing her skirt across her knees, a habit acquired from wearing tight cheong sams.

'You look very beautiful today,' Mulrenan observed. 'Almost too beautiful . . .'

'For a singsong girl?' she added but with fun in her bitter words.

'No. For a lady.'

Across the harbour, the sky was azure except around the summit of The Peak where small clouds had collected. Mulrenan could just make out the Peak Tram pulling up the track: alongside the Royal Naval dockyard was berthed a destroyer, a wisp of smoke spiralling through its rigging.

'For my lady of today.'

'You are funny, Sean,' she teased. 'There are times when I wonder if you want me in the same room with you, never mind — ' she demurely lowered her voice ' — the same bed.' She giggled like a schoolgirl. 'But then, at other times, I feel you so want me that if I wasn't with you . . .'

'It all depends on which part of you I love at that moment.' He looked away from her, eastwards toward Causeway Bay.

45

'What do you mean? I don't understand you sometimes.'

He moved his head and stared at her with such an unexpected intensity it frightened her: the look was only there for an instant but it was sufficient. Yet she knew that in some respects it was the unexpected she liked about Mulrenan. Most of the men she had come in contact with — in what she preferred to think of now as a 'professional capacity' — had been so utterly predictable. It was not just that they always approached her in the same manner: invariably there would be a gentle knock on the door and old Ethel Morrison, her make-up neatly and not too thickly applied, would enter with a man. Sometimes he was old, sometimes not: on many occasions she hardly noticed her visitor's age and only realised it when she touched the flesh on his shoulders or the skin on his belly. But it was rather that she knew exactly how they would behave, always within certain parameters.

By and large men, she knew, were creatures of habit. The same men returned time and again and asked for her. It was not that she was necessarily good — in the early days she had been definitely mediocre — but that she was familiar. She knew how they liked to make love, how they wanted her to move, dress or behave. She knew, too, of their troubles — a boring wife, an unfaithful fiancée or mistress, the failure of a trading deal or the pressures of expatriate existence.

With Mulrenan there were no pressures, no other women, no failures. He was unpredictable. He took events as they came, and his business dealings were successful.

She had first met him when he had been a pianist on the look-out for a singer to work the midday session: it would have suited her hours of employment ideally. She auditioned for him and failed. Instead of offering her a job, he invited her to dinner.

She had expected to be dined by a musician but discovered he was more than that. If not a professional gambler he was certainly a most accomplished one. He was also a dealer in other than cards.

'What do I mean?' he interrupted her thoughts. 'I mean when I love the Chinese part of you.'

46

She was puzzled and he explained, 'I want the Chinese half of you. Badly, sometimes. But with the English part of you . . . It's different, then.'

'I can't help my parents,' she said. 'No one decides that.'

He ignored her and went on, 'Today you are Chinese, even though you have on a European dress and will be with Europeans all afternoon. Today I love the Chinese part of you.'

'Will we meet anyone I might know?' she asked hesitantly.

'Anyone who knew your mother? Possibly. But it doesn't matter. They'll not say anything, even if they think it.'

'No, not my mother. I mean anyone . . .'

'Professionally? I doubt it. It's been too long now since . . . They won't remember you from your days of employment in — Ethel Morrison's elite establishment for young ladies of correction and pleasure.' He spoke with a sharp sarcasm but softened and continued, 'You aren't in a whorehouse now. In fact . . .' he took one of his chamois leather bags from an inside pocket '. . . you will never have to return there.'

'What have you to show me?'

She was eagerly inquisitive, anxious to change the topic of conversation: reference to her days in Hong Kong's most exclusive brothel could, she knew, bring on a fit of anger in him.

He tipped the bag over her palm and from the soft leather tumbled a ring. It coruscated in the sunlight reflecting from the sea: the wake of a passing wallah-wallah boat was breaking upon the steps, the putt-putt of its motor reverberating off the railway station.

'What are the jewels?'

'An amethyst and five diamonds.'

'Will you get very much when you sell them?' she asked.

'Nothing. I'm not selling them. Not this time. The ring's for you.'

Mulrenan watched as tears welled in her eyes.

'Are you sure? It's very beautiful, and I —'

'Quite certain. Put it on.'

47

She held up her left hand and he slid the ring on to the third finger.

'I cannot take it. And, on this finger, it means we're married.'

'Wear it.' It was as much an order as a lover's wish. 'It fits you perfectly and it'll stop . . .'

'People talking?'

'Perhaps, but that's not the real reason.' He edged up his cuff and consulted the Rolex. 'Besides,' he added without feeling, 'you're not the first to get out of The Line. Even Lady Chater, it is said, served her appenticeship there before Sir Paul married her.'

'Don't!' she pleaded. 'I don't need reminding, Sean.'

She dried her cheek by dabbing at it with a brown cotton handkerchief. Any other tears were held in check by the realisation that although the ring was hers to keep and had been given with love, it was also intended to silence — or temporarily gag — gossip: Mulrenan never did anything without an ulterior motive.

'I do like it,' she said, to reassure herself as much as him. 'It's beautiful. And I love you.'

Very quickly, she kissed him on his cheek, as lightly as a sister at a family gathering. He took her hand and squeezed it gently.

'Now for the train and the races,' he said with jollity, as if the ring had been part of the day's business. 'Ready?'

8

The 'Taipo Belle' shuffled its way through the Kowloon suburbs, Alice sitting in the rear observation compartment. Beside her was a woman in her late twenties who, from her hairstyle and tight skirt, appeared to be American. She was elegantly thin with immaculate make-up, her fingernails varnished maroon to match the exact line of her lipstick.

Black mascara lined her eyes, accentuating their dark brown gleam. In the smoking lounge the men were playing brag and chatting, while in the cocktail bar the attendants mixed drinks or served coffee to their ladies.

The train left the Beacon Hill tunnel and Alice watched the view unfold. At first there was only the steep hillside covered with stunted trees and bushes in the deep green of high summer, but as the train gathered speed more of the mountainside came into view, the inland slopes of the nine Kowloon hills. A rock outcrop broke against the sky, at first only a nondescript pile of boulders but, as the train continued, it took on form and shape. It had been a long time since Alice had last been to the New Territories and seen the sad outline of Amah Rock.

'Excuse me,' her fellow passenger said, leaning across and stretching out her hand as a child might to draw attention.

Alice, deep in her own thoughts, did not realise the woman was addressing her.

'Excuse me,' the woman repeated. 'That rock up there. What is it? A statue?'

Alice was taken aback, surprised to be addressed: she had considered herself somehow apart from the other passengers.

'In a manner of speaking, yes', she replied hastily. 'It is called Mong Fu Shek or Amah Rock because it looks like a Chinese woman carrying a baby on her back.'

'Thank you.'

The train reached the seashore and slowed for a bridge over a creek, by a hamlet of stone houses with low-pitched, tiled roofs. A buffalo was wallowing nearby and, where a footpath crossed the line, a woman in the loose black jacket and trousers of rural peasants waited. She was a Hakka, her head-dress a circular flat plate of rattan from the edges of which hung a black curtain. On her back, strapped tightly in a brightly coloured sling, an infant slept, its head lolling and its weight causing the chest thongs of the sling to bite into the flesh around the woman's breasts.

'Like that,' said Alice and pointed to the peasant,

continuing, 'Women who would like to have a baby but cannot, go to the rock in the hope it will bring them fertility. There is a word — *hsien* — which means "immortal spirit". Up by the rock is said to live a *hsien* who will help the childless.'

'You are very knowledgeable about such things,' complimented the woman.

'I was born here. My father was . . .'

Alice stopped in time. To admit on the 'Taipo Belle', en route to the Fanling Hunt and Race Club, that she was a Eurasian was tantamount to social suicide. Once exposed she would be politely excluded from the company, unspoken-to except by Mulrenan until the train returned in the evening and she melted back into the twilight of the lower strata of The Peak. Not that she supposed Mulrenan would speak much to her anyway: he would be busy establishing contacts, arranging a game, backing the horses and drinking.

'There is a story behind the rock,' she went on, covering her incompleted sentence. 'Would you like to hear it?'

The young woman nodded, moving nearer to Alice as the train clattered over a set of points.

'I'm not too clear about it,' Alice began when the clamour of the wheels subsided. 'Because I've heard several versions. But once upon a time there was a poor woman who married a fisherman. Every day, when her chores were done, she walked up the hill with her baby on her back to watch for her husband's sampan. One day he did not return. Refusing to believe he was drowned, she continued to climb the hill daily to watch for him. For a whole lunar year she kept her vigil. Then the gods, taking pity and admiring her faithfulness, lifted her and the baby off the mountain and into the shadowlands where her husband lived. In her place they built a monument to her love.'

'That's stupid,' exclaimed the young woman.

Alice's anger rose. It might only be a superstitious folk story, but it was a part of her heritage. Her thoughts must have shown on her face, for the young woman said, 'I mean, it was foolish of the woman to keep on going up there.

Faithfulness and love are one thing but — every day! No man's worth that much, surely!'

Alice laughed. 'You may be right,' she replied. 'I might almost agree with you. Maybe not totally.' She glanced quickly at her left hand.

A moment later one of the attendants entered from the smoking lounge with a bottle of champagne in an ice bucket and a single glass. He placed it on the low table in the centre of the compartment and uncorked the bottle, filling the glass.

'Bubbles! Aren't the men kind? Another glass, please, boy', the young woman ordered, adding, 'You will share this with me, won't you?'

'Thank you. I'd like that very much.'

'I should introduce myself,' said the woman, smiling. 'I am Irina Popescu.'

'Is that an American name?' Alice asked.

'My! No, certainly not. Do I sound American? Maybe just a little. It comes from living in America, I expect. Or with Americans.'

'I am Alice.' She did not give her surname. 'Soon' would give her away.

The attendant returned with a second glass into which he poured the champagne, screwing the bottle back into the ice and draping a white napkin around the green glass neck.

'Who are you with, Alice? No — let me guess. Either Captain Horwood or Sean Mulrenan. And I think the latter. Am I right?'

'How did you know?' Alice was amazed.

'Simple deduction. They're the only two bachelors, and Captain Horwood isn't handsome enough to attract someone as pretty as you.'

There was no rancour in her bluntness and Alice blushed, sipping her champagne to cover it.

'My husband's a Romanian. I am a Russian — what they call a White Russian down here. We have come from Harbin by way of Shanghai. Things are getting hot up there.' She smiled at her own Americanism.

The Japanese, Alice knew from the *South China Morning Post*, were playing cat-and-mouse with the Americans in

China and, where the Russians were concerned, there was virtually no diplomatic contact. Border conflicts in Mongolia and Manchoukuo were commonplace. Chinese politics were in traditional upheaval.

'As a Romanian, surely you're safe.'

'Not really. To the Japanese or their allies, a European is a foreigner. Besides, though I've a Romanian husband now, my last husband was an American, so I have three nationalities, Romanian, American, Russian. None is too useful in an emergency.'

Her words betrayed her immediate past: something had happened to drive her and her husband to Hong Kong but what it was Alice dared not ask. Irina Popescu looked hardly old enough to have been married twice.

The train followed the coastline so closely the rails were supported for sections by girders on low trestle bridges above the sands or muds of tiny inlets and coves. The hills were forested right up to the track. In the black shadows under the trees and creepers, broad-leafed succulents and dark bushes threatened. On the placid sea the sunlight glinted: by a rocky island offshore drifted a small fleet of fishing sampans from which men were casting nets. Beyond, a cargo junk in full sail was making for the open sea.

Crossing the mouth of a little river, the train began to brake and the attendant returned to close the windows. Inshore appeared a dense mass of sampans, coastal and ocean-going junks and flat, punt-like vessels. About the periphery of this log-jam of craft, passenger sampans were being rowed.

'This is Tai Po,' Alice informed Irina.

The fishing town was not large and in the yards of the houses hung frames bearing tens of thousands of fish desiccating and bleaching in the sun, the pungent stink permeating the carriage. In the narrow streets coolies carried vegetables and fish on shoulder poles, a few transporting their wares in heavy wheelbarrows with solid wooden wheels. Over the rooftops fluttered garish triangular flags with serrated borders.

'They're temple flags,' Alice said, seeing Irina catch sight of them.

The train rumbled over another river and into a long valley of paddyfields and hamlets. Now the hills were only partly forested: where there were no trees the slopes were covered with browning grass. The fields of vegetables were emerald green but the rice was ripening. As they passed another hamlet with a temple, a single, modest, red flag flying over it, Alice pointed out the threshing platform being swept clear of debris by an old man with a twig broom.

Somehow, sharing the sights with Irina, Alice felt a companionship growing between them: it was not what she had expected from a passenger on the 'Taipo Belle'.

9

The Kwanti Course, a mile down the road to Sha Tau Kok and the border with China, was advertised as 'a Home-side country steeplechase course'. Within the constraints of Oriental possibility and colonial ingenuity, this was a fair description. The sound of a regimental band could be heard issuing from the far side of two huge marquees. The marquees were uncommon, however: most of the shelter was provided by thatched matsheds. The rails were constructed of three-inch-wide bamboo nailed to the uprights, but the sides to the jumps were timbered and painted white. The treeless hills behind might have been downland or the Malverns — or the Quantocks had those looking at them screwed their eyes half-closed. Yet the jockeys wore silk hooped shirts and some of the ladies flamboyant hats.

'Join us for a drink?' asked Vincent Delderton, who had given them a lift to the course in his Riley. He was a portly man in his mid-fifties wearing a sharkskin suit and a boater.

'Later, if we may,' Mulrenan replied. 'Want to get a peek at the odds.'

Alice was relieved: she had not enjoyed Delderton's wife and her prying questions. There was nothing worse, she reflected, than a middle-aged wife on the scent of scandal. They walked towards the large board by the bookmakers advertising in big red and black letters 'Double Event Totalisator For The Long Odds'.

'Who was that woman you were talking to on the train?' Mulrenan enquired.

Alice told him and, for a moment, he was thoughtful. When he spoke again it was on a totally different subject.

'How will you bet, Alice?' he asked, handing her a race card.

'I don't know,' she said. 'I've never bet on horses before —on anything very much, come to that. My mother used to play mahjong with her cronies but I never really took it in.'

There was no harm in mentioning her mother's penchant for the game. It was not unusual for European women to play, for it had come into vogue a few years before and she had spoken in the past tense. All the same, her comment drew a rapid glance from a middle-aged matron standing next to her.

To allay any suspicion, Alice added, not too loudly yet not too softly, 'All that business about the north and south wind tiles and the three dragons tiles: it's as bad as the Japanese flower cards — wild-boar-with-clover and paulownia with phoenix. It's so complicated.'

The woman butted in, 'I could not agree with you more, my dear. Dominoes for ladies, my husband calls them.'

Mulrenan smiled obligingly. He admired the skill with which Alice had avoided a possible *faux pas*. Her ability to live by her wits, as he did, was a common bond between them. In fact Alice abhorred lying, even in self-defence, but this was no longer a real lie, somehow. It was part and parcel of social activity.

Alice knew how to play mahjong from having learned it in The Line with the girls. It had helped to while away the time between customers, between 'the good gentlemen', as

Ethel Morrison, the buxom White Russian madam of the best bordello had called them even behind their backs. Alice had not, it was true, gambled at the table except for petty stakes. Her mother had gambled heavily and, as an adroit player, had seldom lost. Her cronies, however, had been her servants, the seamstress from Wanchai and the wife of a Eurasian policeman. Had that been known, Mulrenan and Alice would have been obliged to forego the 'Taipo Belle', catching instead the evening train from Canton to Hong Kong, crowded with peasants and live-stock, shopkeepers, fidgetting children, amahs and coolies.

They walked on, into the crowd gathered around the viewing enclosure. All the jockeys were Europeans who, in the normal course of the week, would have been business-men in the hongs or their sons or, in a few cases, their daughters. They wore different colours, as was obligatory under the Hong Kong Jockey Club and British National Hunt by-laws, hard riding hats buckled under their chins, jodhpurs and riding boots. They might have been at some grand gymkhana back home in the United Kingdom had it not been for the low, partly-wooded hills in the back-ground, the quaint architecture of a distant village and the far-off waving paddies.

The horses, however, had this been a British meeting, would have been different. A shire steeplechase would have entered tall horses with majestic countenances. The Kwan-ti mounts were not as elevated in their equine society as their riders were in the human one. They were mostly ponies from northern China, noted for speed and stamina rather than finesse. Most had failed to run well in Shanghai and had been exported to Hong Kong to serve as polo ponies in Causeway Bay. When not required for a chukka, they raced.

The names of the ponies were curiously English: *Go Far*, *Piccadilly* and *The Bodger* stood next to *Sally's Darling*, *Bal-moral* and *High-Jump*. All had Chinese mafoos, stable boys who groomed, fed and cossetted them as if they were Aintree winners: no European child was better looked after by its amah.

'Any take your fancy?' Mulrenan said, running a rolled gold propelling pencil down his card. The pencil was a new acquisition.

'What do you suggest? They're just horses to me.'

'Ponies,' he corrected her. 'Chinese ponies. Pure bred from beyond Peking, I dare say.' He stopped and ticked two names on his card.

'Those two: the top one in preference, or both if you like. One will come first for certain. Ignore the odds. I know they're long on that one, but back it.'

'Will you?'

'Maybe, maybe not. Do you have some money?'

'A little.'

'It's no use going to the race with a little.' He removed three one-hundred dollar bills from his wallet and gave them to her. 'Expect to lose,' he told her. 'I'll not expect it back.'

She thanked him, surprised at his generosity. He had never given her so much hard cash before.

'May fortune smile upon your head and baptise you with the light of the devil.'

He spoke with an exaggerated Irish accent, so broad she did not understand; she giggled and he showed her how to place a bet.

The horse she chose was a white pony called *Dunbar's Madam*. It looked a sturdy, plucky animal ridden by a girl in her teens sporting red and green hoops. When they closed the odds were 9 to 1. Alice put fifty dollars to win. *Dunbar's Madam* began well but finished a poor third.

'Never mind,' Mulrenan advised. 'You'll win on the next. Once you pick up the form . . .'

'The form?'

'Racing term,' he replied knowledgeably. 'How they're running, which mounts are at the peak of fitness. Which are *on form*, as they say. You'll soon get the hang of it.'

A girl with bobbed hair and wearing a narrow, cream silk dress pushed between then, her scarlet varnished nails showing like talons against the material. She was with a young RAF officer who was nurturing his first moustache, ostentatiously fingering the ends as if to encourage them to grow: the girl was prattling to him about a pony called *Pick-me-up*.

'When you've got the knack,' Mulrenan continued, glaring with annoyance at the couple, 'you'll be able to choose a winner nine times out of ten. Just like any gamble — when you can assess the length of the odds you can bank on them. Even the gee-gees.'

'Gee-gees?'

'The equine creatures of steeplechasing persuasion,' he answered, again in mock Irish, and this time Alice laughed gaily.

She studied the card and chose an outsider at 15 to 1. She extravagantly placed one hundred dollars to win, her risk-taking Chinese mentality overruling her English caution. She had no reason for deciding to bank on this particular animal except that its name appealed to her. It was one of the few ponies to have an Oriental-sounding name: *Miss Macao*.

The rider was given on the card as Master Stanley Hartley. Alice looked for the horse in the paddock and soon found it, an example of docility, the reins held loosely by a mafoo.

'You ready, Stan?'

Alice turned to see a boy adjusting the strap on his riding hat. He was stockily built but pale-skinned and when he walked he had a pronounced limp.

His father received the reins, the mafoo giving the boy the necessary assistance into the saddle by going down on all fours and allowing the lad to clamber on to his back.

'Just do your best, son. Remember what I told you. Keep away from the fence.'

'Yes, father,' the boy replied. 'I will. Do you think anyone's bet on me?'

'Never you mind that.'

The mafoo took hold of the leather strap running along the pony's cheek and led it towards the exit. As the pony passed by, Alice, close to the paddock rail, leaned forward.

'I've bet on you, Stanley,' she said.

57

The boy looked startled, then concerned. 'Thank you, madam. Thank you very much indeed.'

The race was a short six furlongs; as the flag dropped, *Miss Macao* was the last away in a field of eight. By the third fence, however, she was up to fifth but appeared to be making no ground against the leaders.

'Which have you backed?' Mulrenan asked. 'The one I told you to?' He had left her for a few minutes to talk to an acquaintance.

'No! I chose *Miss Macao*. But I can't see her now.'

He squinted through his binoculars. Suddenly, the commentator who was giving a running account of the race over an echoing tannoy became agitated.

'There's been a mix-up at the fifth,' he reported. 'Two horses are down. It's...it's... No! Three down. All mounts and jockeys up. It's now a race between *Cocksure* and *Miss Macao*. They're neck and neck as they come to the seventh. There's nothing in it.'

The crowd, having been silenced at the news of the falls, for a rider had recently broken his pelvis, sighed then began to cheer and shout.

'Into the last turn.' The commentator continued feverishly, 'it's *Miss Macao* from *Cocksure*. *Miss Macao* from *Cocksure*. They're drawing level. There's nothing in it! *Miss Macao* and *Cocksure*. *Miss Macao* and *Cocksure*!'

Alice heard no more. She closed her hands over her ears to press out the sound. Mulrenan shook her arm, pulling her hand away from her head.

'By a nose!' he exclaimed. 'By a bloody nose!' He chortled and put his arm around her shoulder. 'Well done! Now.' he grew serious, 'to collect. Fifteen hundred bucks. Plus your stake. Don't spend it all at once.'

'Picture time!' exclaimed a man in the panama hat, as they were standing drinking in a lull between races. He chivvied them together. 'Come on, Sean old boy! Out you come. And your pretty lady. Haven't we met somewhere before, my dear?' he asked, taking Alice's elbow.

'I don't think so,' she replied but she knew him. He had visited her, just the once, when she was a 'girl of The Line.'

He had been slimmer then: now his paunch hung over his belt and his face was florid. She tried to recall how he had performed in bed or what his preferences had been, but there was nothing to remember: he had not been exceptional either in his fornication or in his subsequent gift-making.

'Super! Now get yourselves in a group!'

As everyone shuffled closer, the former client suddenly recognised Alice. She could tell from the sharp stare he cast in her direction that his memory had cleared. Unable to resist the temptation, she cheekily winked at him and he rapidly averted his eyes.

In the crush, a tall man wearing a pith helmet pressed against Alice and trod on her foot.

'I say, I do apologise. Most clumsy of me . . .'

'Face in shadow! Get your hat off, Duggie!' bawled the photographer.

As he removed his helmet, tucking it under his arm, the man introduced himself.

'Douglas Birchett. I do hope you're alright,' he added. 'Most clumsy of me.'

'How do you do,' Alice answered. 'And I'm fine.'

She had often seen Birchett in The Line; his favourite was an Australian, Minnie, a girl with auburn hair, shapely legs and dimples on her buttocks at the spot where a man's hands fitted.

The photographer twisted the catches on his camera and unfolded the bellows, at the same time flicking over the prismatic viewfinder.

As the camera levelled on her, Alice remembered: Birchett was an inspector in the Wanchai Division of the Hong Kong police.

Pressing the camera to his chest, the photographer said, 'Look jolly, for pete's sake! It's not a funeral.'

He snapped the shutter and it clicked loudly.

'Now it's my turn.' He handed the camera to the policeman. 'You just look through here, get us in the middle and — bingo! Stand by that tuft of grass there: distance the same.'

As he joined the group, someone took the place of the

policeman beside Alice. It was Irina Popescu, her arrival as unexpected and as startling as her words on the train.

'I love photos,' she whispered. 'They capture the most delicious of moments. Are you winning?'

'Yes,' Alice confided.

'A lot? Do tell!'

'Quite . . .'

'Super! When the kindly policeman's done, you must come over to the beer tent!'

Alice was amazed Irina knew Birchett for a policeman and asked her how she could tell.

'Anywhere in the world, you can pick *them* out.' She nudged Alice. 'Especially girls like us . . .'

'I say! Keep still you two. Come on then! Snap away!' the owner of the camera ordered merrily.

'Can't seem to catch you. Hold on! Got it!' Birchett replaced his pith helmet on his head, casting a shadow over the viewfinder. 'That's better. Cheddar cheese, you lot, cheddar cheese!'

'Would you mind taking one of us together?' Irina asked Birchett as the group split up. 'Just for my album?'

'Not at all, my dear. A pleasure.'

Alice put her hands behind her back, but he remarked that she looked like a suspect, so she let them loose by her side. Irina was holding a glass of champagne.

'I'll send you a print,' Irina promised as she smiled at the policeman.

Alice had no outstanding luck during the remainder of the afternoon and eventually spent her time watching the ponies rather than backing them. Twice she spied Stanley Hartley leaning on the rails and shifting his weight from foot to foot but she overcame the impulse to speak to him. It was not, she knew, 'done.'

As the race card for the day ended, Mulrenan walked with Alice to the Deldertons' grey Riley and they were driven back to the station. On the way, Margaret Delderton prattled about the friends she had met and gossiped about those she had not.

As they stood on the platform at Fanling, she asked Alice, 'Did you win?'

The twilight was settling into the folds of the hills, the scents of woodsmoke, charcoal and night blossoms filling the air.

'Yes, I did.'

'Jolly good! I won three hundred and fifty dollars myself. And you . . .?'

'One thousand seven hundred,' Alice responded, trying not to sound smug.

Mulrenan, overhearing their conversation, gave Alice a quick look and raised his eyebrows approvingly. Now she was, he considered, joined with him in putting down the accursed British.

10

It was a cool, still morning, the sky grey with high altitude clouds through which the sun was struggling to shine. Here and there patches of faint blue showed: it would be warm later. During the night it had rained and the foliage of the hillside dripped and clicked as if it were alive. In the stone gutter at the side of the road ran a fast-flowing rivulet which plunged down an iron grid. Mulrenan heard it gurgling as he passed.

He had alighted from the omnibus at the junction, deciding to walk the last mile into Repulse Bay. After the rattling and creaking of metal and wood, the sound of the trees and insects was an almost physical pleasure.

He did not walk quickly. It was only half-past ten and he was not required until noon. He planned to have an hour in which to swim, shower and change into the clothes kept for him in the Repulse Bay Hotel.

He enjoyed his moments of solitude. He did not have to be isolated; he could as readily be by himself in a crowded nightclub. He just needed to be left alone so that he could withdraw into the deeper recesses of himself, to think and dream, plan and hope. He did not necessarily have to be idle. He could be swimming, in the cinema, walking on the hills or through the streets — even playing the piano.

Below the road, between it and the sea, was one of the new buildings that were appearing in the colony. They were peculiar, original, self-indulgent structures put up by those with money to spend and little idea of what to spend it on. Constructed by a Chinese millionaire called Mr Eu, this particular example had a square, churchlike tower, a crennellated flat roof, high surrounding walls, an imposing wrought-iron gate and a separate building with a cupola on top. It looked like a hybrid between a Rhine valley fortress and a Georgian stable block. A plaque on one of the gate pillars bore its name — *Eucliff*.

It was an incongruous and ugly place, borrowing nothing from the beauty of Chinese architecture. Its owner also had a house on the lower levels of The Peak which he had named *Euston*. Mulrenan wondered if the man knew that the namesake of his luxurious, status-symbol home was a sooty railway terminus.

He felt a familiar anger rise inside him. *Eucliff* was a good example of how the Chinese were being corrupted, their culture eroded, their countryside altered by speculative land deals. It was the same wherever the British went. India, Africa, Malaya, China: whatever they saw, they changed — as if that was the natural way of things. They did not learn the local languages except in order to teach the natives English. They built their churches and imported their own god and tried to subvert the local deities. They eradicated customs without having anything better with which to replace them. They brought their own business practices which they expected to be adopted, their own laws to be obeyed, their own merchandise to be purchased. They even brought their own diseases of influenza and gonorrhoea to add to the local scourges. When they could not get their own way with the natives they ruled by division, pitting tribe against tribe, clan against clan, religion against religion: when that failed, they brought in their troops and their gunboats.

He turned into Beach Road. Where the concrete steps gave on to the sands, he paused, sat on a low stone wall and removed his shoes and socks. The tide was in and the sand cool under his bare soles. Out to sea, the sun had broken through and Lamma Island was a dark silhouette above a sparkle of light on the waves. It reminded him of his childhood, the islands of southern Eire with rocky inlets and verdant hilly shores.

Just as the British had abused Hong Kong so had they, long before, done the same evil to his own land. Indeed, what the British were doing to this fragment of southern China, he thought angrily, they had first perfected in Ireland.

The beach was deserted except for coolies cleaning out the matsheds, raking the sand smooth, filling the square buckets in each with dousing water. An urchin was thrusting litter into a basket he dragged behind him along the sand, the cane ribs snagging on ridges formed by the wind: it left a scar like that of a beached turtle. The urchin's sister dusted dry sand from the canvas seats and scrubbed at wooden tables in the matsheds.

Mulrenan walked at the water's edge. The tide was about to turn and the sea had an air of expectancy about it.

He had heard it all in school. The master in Dublin had pressed history into his boys. He was a Jesuit and, as he strode about the dingy classroom, the long black sleeves of his soutane would hiss in the air and stroke the hair and faces of the boys.

It had begun, he taught them in his slow droning voice, with Henry II of England, the first Englishman to fear Ireland as a potential base for enemies. That fear, born perhaps of the Viking raids upon the western coasts of England, had fuelled the national apprehension ever since. Henry VIII, the fat king on page 138 of their textbook whom Mulrenan despised, had added enmity to this worry by taking six wives and turning against the Catholics. Next, his red-headed daughter, Elizabeth — whom they misguidedly called 'Good Queen Bess' — had tightened her grip on Ireland. The Protestant Scots were encouraged to settle in Ulster and, within a hundred years, the Catholics had been ousted from their farms and homes. After came William III, the Protestant king who rid Britain of James II, the true Catholic, at the Battle of the Boyne. The Catholics were forbidden to buy their own land, disenfranchised, excluded from the professions or from marrying Protestants. Then came the Act of Union: Ireland was to be a part of England, as Wales had become, and Scotland. The king in Windsor Castle was the ruler. There followed the Fenians, and Mulrenan's first, all-important hero.

When he was a boy, Mulrenan had had Charles Stewart Parnell as his idol. Some of his peers worshipped stars of the silent movies, others famous inventors or flying aces: a few worshipped sportsmen. He loved Parnell. In a frame by his bed an engraving cut from a magazine showed Parnell being ejected from the House of Commons for disrupting parliamentary business. In the picture, Parnell walked nonchalantly down the centre of the chamber, his left hand in his pocket. Around him, members of the House waved their fists at him, shook their top hats at him, grimaced through their pompous whiskers. Sean's father had taken the picture to a framer for his birthday; his mother had silently disapproved of it. She further suppressed her displeasure with a tight-lipped smile when she discovered, in her husband's Bible, a photograph of Arthur Griffith, the Sinn Fein leader. It annoyed her more when she saw the similarity of appearance between him and her husband.

Mulrenan's paternal grandfather had been Patrick Mulrenan, a fisherman from Kinsale. He and his wife, Edna O'Foley, had eked out a living with a single-sailed boat and a few nets; of their four sons two had drowned before their twentieth birthdays. They had enough to eat and to buy yarn to repair the nets. They could clothe themselves and had a roof rented from an English landlord who, because of his permanent absenteeism and a genial estate manager called O'Neill, seldom raised the rents beyond their means.

When David and Matthew were lost within months of each other the kick went out of old Mulrenan's step. He sold the boat and advised his other two sons to go to Dublin or

Belfast and seek work in the docks or the shipyards. They knew enough about the construction and repair of small craft to fashion one from a standing tree. He had hoped they would gain employment making lifeboats for the new steamships.

John Mulrenan went to Belfast. For a year he sent home regular letters; then they stopped. Four months later, a money order for three guineas arrived in the post. Sixty-three English shillings was deemed by the management to be the worth of the life of John Arthur Mulrenan, shipwright, killed when a derrick broke loose and the steel hawsers whipped back, ripping his chest apart. A complaint to the shipyard was met with refusal: the rate was three guineas for a death by accident, five if the victim was maimed, not killed.

Patrick and Edna Mulrenan were broken: one son left of four, and he in self-imposed exile.

For Jimmy Mulrenan, the youngest son, had betrayed his family by marrying Daphne Hastings. She lived in a tall house on the front at Ramsey in the Isle of Man with her mother, three servants and an invalid father who was prescribed sea air and ozone for his arthritis. She laughed prettily and often, had auburn hair and hazel eyes. Her biggest fault was that she was English. His parents voiced the doubt that she was worth as much as three guineas.

Jimmy proposed to her not so much out of love as out of need. She had what he wanted: social position, and a small but acceptable fortune. And she was infatuated with him.

They thus had nothing in common except desire: he wanted what she could offer and she wanted him. That he was Irish and a Catholic from working-class stock and she English and Anglican with a comfortable middle-class upbringing did not come into it.

Jimmy Mulrenan knew, once married to her, it would be for life. Rome would not permit a divorce: neither, if on different, social grounds, would she. Once she was his, he would settle down to an ordinary and secure life. He need not worry what the sea did except to the paint on the window frames and what the wind wreaked on the slates of the roof. Most of what he needed she would provide, and what she could not he would find elsewhere.

They were wed in the tiny, ancient church at The Cronk, where Vikings had landed and St Patrick himself might have prayed. After the ceremony he set about planning his life, building his support for the newly-reborn Irish Republican Brotherhood, bedding the occasional young girl in Liverpool where he travelled on business: Daphne Mulrenan, on inheriting her father's money, bought Jimmy into a chandler's firm in Ramsey which he expanded with his charm, his sense of humour and his dogged determination to rid the company of his two English partners.

Their only son was Sean, born after two daughters, Marianne and Victoria. As he grew older, the boy followed his father in every way. Like him, he was stocky — muscular, even. He had the same firm face, high brow and wiry, curly hair. His shoulders were not broad but strong: he had the build of the brawler but the looks of a prince. They sent him off to school in Dublin. There he grew distant from his mother and the British who had valued his uncle in guineas.

When Daphne Mulrenan died he did not cry. The Jesuit schoolmaster commiserated and understood.

'That's right, Sean. Don't you fret. Be strong, as strong as Ireland, for you've the whole of the blood of the Republic behind you.'

Two years later, when Sean Mulrenan was sixteen, his father died. The loss was felt almost as deeply by the Republican cause as it was by Sean: the steady flow of rifles from Liverpool dried up temporarily. Jimmy was buried in Kinsale, alongside his parents. His wife had been interred in a family vault in Somerset, but only her daughters had attended her funeral. The couple were apart in death as they had been in life.

An elderly, anonymous man in gold-rimmed glasses and a well-tailored suit had approached the son after the service: his attempts at persuasion, at which he had quietly persisted all through the wake, were lost on the would-be Republican. Sean had politely declined to take up where his father had left off. He wanted to get away, escape his past and think. As Ireland needed to be free so did he: he was not yet ready stolidly to serve a cause. He wanted to live a bit first, see the world, for such an opportunity had never come to his family. Yet he had dreamed of striking a blow for the cause whenever the chance arose. He had not abandoned his beliefs, just postponed them.

Lost to himself, Mulrenan had walked far past the Lido where he was to play that afternoon and was almost at the rocks. A coolie struggled past him, two heavy panniers of water at each end of his bamboo pole. His feet dug into the sand and he wheezed as he walked. Mulrenan looked at him: he was an old man, his collarbones prominent and his fingers, where they gripped the pole, yellowed by opium smoke. Offshore a small naked boy fished from a bobbing sampan.

'There but for the grace of God go I,' he said to himself as the Chinese boy landed a tiny fish, its scales flicking in the sun.

Yet for Mulrenan there was no God: at least, there was no god in heaven. His deities were secular.

11

A typhoon had closed fast upon the coast during the night, whipping the harbour into waves, swamping sampans and soaking coolies on the lower deck of the Star Ferry. At around nine pm the Number 5 warning was hoisted at the Royal Observatory and had been a signal for those who were not at home to return there. Mulrenan had recently moved out of his small flat in Tsim Sha Tsui to live with Alice, and so had to cross the harbour.

In the hotel he had been playing light classical pieces and popular tunes from recent musicals which meant that the painted charioteers had been ignored. The maitre d'hotel of The Rose Room had decided as 'The Five' was raised he would serve no more meals; there were few guests dining in any case. Timid residents were in their rooms or the bars and those who were adventurous had gone out, despite warnings, to see what a typhoon was like. The waiters were dismissed and everyone knew business would not return to normal for forty-eight hours at least.

Mulrenan walked in squally rain to the pier and managed to board a ferry back to the island. It had been bucking and lurching against the timber piles, the whole jetty squealing and vibrating as the craft rubbed against it or the waves struck it from beneath. The gangway, attached to the ferry rather than the quay, was scraping across the landing platform and Mulrenan had to be nimble-footed to get on to it. Once aboard, he chose to stand near where the funnel passed through the deck. There would be less motion amidships and less spray. The mid-harbour wind would be fierce enough to drive spume through the edges of the window frames on the enclosed central cabin of the first class deck. As the wind was easterly, he faced west. He felt somehow more secure this way, even though the darkness was more threatening in the face of the typhoon.

The mooring ropes were cast off and the ferry began to make headway, steering for Causeway Bay at the far end of the harbour because the pilot knew he would be forced back to the spot at which he was hoping to arrive. Empty of the running and deck lights of any sort of shipping, the harbour itself appeared lifeless. The ocean-going steamers had long since left port to ride out the storm at sea. All the junks and sampans, the lighters and wallah-wallah boats and company launches had sought refuge behind the breakwaters of the typhoon shelters where they were crammed side by side, an homogeneous clot acres across. Any craft that had not reached the safety of the shelters was doomed. Even beaching a craft, unless in a tiny, protected cove in the New Territories, was pointless. The waves would seek it out and pick at it, take it apart as a crab might gradually dissect a corpse.

The eight-minute, usual crossing of the harbour was

stretched into more than twenty minutes of buffeting, pitching and rolling, the instability of the craft increased by the passengers who, as the vessel approached the pier, mustered at the gangway giving the deck an awkward list. Eventually, the ferry docked on the island and Mulrenan, his legs unsteady, followed the anxious crowd ashore. Even the pier was shifting in the wind and running tide.

The rain, which had begun to fall consistently, came in bigger drops and felt somehow wetter than rain in Europe, harder than an Irish shower.

Mulrenan would have preferred hailing a sedan chair but there was none left to be hired, and he was faced with the alternatives of remaining where he was until a chair returned or walking to Lyndhurst Terrace and receiving a drenching in the process. The long queue for sedan chairs made the decision for him.

It was dangerous to walk, he knew. Tiles, broken window glass, electricity and telephone cables, lengths of twisted bamboo scaffolding or shop signs might at any moment drift by horizontally on a gust. The street lights only succeeded in illuminating the area immediately below them. As he made his way through the streets the wind snagged on his mackintosh and snatched at his hair. Rain seeped down his collar and his shoes soon filled with water. Had he been carrying an umbrella it would have been blown inside-out within seconds.

By the corner of one of the steep streets he paused, looking up to check his direction. Sure enough, he had passed the right turning. The centre of the street he was on was constructed of a stone base, with raised ridges every foot or so. The houses on either side, because of the sharp incline up which they were built, had been erected on wedges of stone seeming to lean backwards, lazing against the hillside. In deep gutters torrents of water rushed cascading from the mountain behind.

With his eyes to the ground to pace his steps according to the ridges, Mulrenan watched as various debris hurtled by — leaves and twigs, the head of a broom, some scraps of cloth, then a kitten, obviously dead. Its head was lolled by the rapid currents. He paused in his ascent, catching his breath, watching its progress down the sluice. At a small drop in the gutter, now a waterfall, it was projected into the air for a little way before splashing down and careering on towards the harbour.

The houses around were uncharacteristically neat. The small wrought-iron balconies were stripped of their usual wooden laundry rods, potted azaleas and kumquat bushes, rickety chairs and bamboo cages of songbirds. The shutters were tight-closed, some boarded with planks and the silvered sides of tea chests, all nailed to the frames. From the steps of the houses anything moveable — bamboo coolie poles, wooden buckets, baskets for the carriage of fish or Chinese cabbage or live poultry, lengths of timber, hawkers' stalls and tables — had been taken inside. Even the red notices glued to the doorposts for luck, for good health and wealth, for the blessing of a new-born son or a recent marriage, had been shredded to tatters by the wind, the black calligraphy on each reduced to a tawdry smear of ink and crimson dye.

As he turned into Alice's street and started to climb, the wind was deflected by buildings. Nearer the top it was a consolidated force, not yet the full typhoon blast but strong enough to spray the water along Hollywood Road from the puddles that had gathered where the drain grids were choked with leaves, sodden paper and twigs. His feet crunched over a shattered window pane, the broken fragments of glass cracking like hard snow.

In the more powerful gusts, minute pellets of grit stung his face and he kept his eyes to a squint. Above him, on the mountainside, the wind was exercising itself in the wooded slopes and he could hear the threshing of the foliage.

He reached Alice's house without harm. Her amah opened the door a crack before widening it to allow him in, slamming it quickly behind him. In just those few seconds the rain drove in and mottled the floorboards.

By two am, the Number 8 signal had been raised.

Mulrenan woke just after dawn, his body sticky with sweat.

He swung his legs under the mosquito net and flung its flimsy curtaining on to the ceiling frame.

'Did you have a nightmare?' Alice asked.

'A sort of nightmare,' he admitted, standing. 'It was nothing.'

She sat up, rubbing her arms, the sheet slipping loose from her shoulders.

'All dreams mean something . . .' she began but he interrupted her.

'That's bosh!'

Outside the house, the storm was at its height. Mulrenan moved to the window, his torso silhouetted against a faint, unearthly light, sombre and heavy. As Alice watched him, he opened the window and reached for the catch on the shutters. A blast of air whistled into the room. It was warm and moist, a sickly force the temperature of blankets after love-making. It had the same clammy feeling, as if trying to adhere to all it brushed against.

The daylight was military olive in colour. The clouds were low on The Peak and curtains of rain lashed across the space between the wrought-iron balcony and the building behind. It did not curve into the room, for the angle of the wall and the strength with which it was blowing kept it away, sending it on to the stonework of the other building. It drifted across it in ripples, splattering at the lines of mortar. He closed the shutters but left the windows ajar.

'How is it?'

'Still from the east,' he reported, gazing down at her on their bed. 'The eye's yet to get here.'

In the morbid light of dawn, Alice's pale skin shone with a faint but determined light, as if she were luminous. The darker aureoles of her breasts were exaggerated by the paleness of her body.

'You look very beautiful,' he said but he did not move towards her.

'You look very strong,' she replied. 'Against the gale.'

He took her seriously.

'Sometimes I feel strong, powerful enough to — do anything. At other times, I feel drained. Empty. I felt that way the other day at the Lido, walking along the beach. I felt hollowed out. Yet, a few minutes later, I was strong again. Within myself. It was strange. Sometimes I like feeling strange . . .'

There was a clattering outside the window. Mulrenan peered through the shutters. A wooden chair had blown on to the roof of the building opposite and was breaking up.

He stretched, his back muscles easing and tightening.

'One day,' he prophesied, his thoughts going off at a tangent, 'I'll be really strange and stay in the Pen. — as a guest. And the other guests will . . .'

She giggled. There was a quiet knock on the door and as he moved his head she stopped: he was still quite serious. Mulrenan pulled a blue silk dressing gown over his shoulders and tied the sash around his waist.

The amah entered carrying a black lacquered tray upon which were two Chinese cups, a porcelain pot decorated with garish dragons which seemed to dance in the half-light and, looking most out of place, a European plate with shortbread biscuits fanned upon it. As soon as she entered the aroma of jasmine tea filled the room.

'Cho-san,' Alice greeted their servant and Mulrenan repeated the words before Alice continued in Cantonese, so rapidly he quickly lost the drift.

The amah answered, bowed slightly and left, closing the door behind her.

'Ah Shun says the radio predicts the eye will reach us in mid-morning. The Number 10 is up. It will be a direct hit. There is much flooding in the New Territories and some junks have sunk at Tuen Mun. Several people have been drowned. Of course, all offices are shut and the ferries have not run since ten last night. You must have caught one of the last.'

He sat on the bed with her as she poured the tea. He slurped it, cooling it in the Chinese fashion, then lay back against the pillows. The forecast meant he could spend the whole day with Alice: a luxury. It was not often musicians of his kind could expect such good fortune. Like whores and criminals, he thought, they work at night.

'You made love very well last night,' she whispered, running her forefinger along his thigh where the flesh showed through a fold in the dressing gown. 'Was it good for you?'

He swung his legs off the bed, pulling the gown about him and thrusting his arms through the sleeves.

'Don't talk like that! You're not a tart, even if you do live in The Line.'

'What *was* The Line. This street has not been that way for some time now. The American girl moved business to Happy Valley.' Alice refilled her cup. 'I get very fed up with you always talking like this. It is all right for you. You live almost as a bachelor, like the men in the Jardine mess or Bank mess. You could move out of here any time you wanted. For me, I'm nothing without you. I have no money of my own. You pay for Ah Shun, for the rent here. If I want clothes, or food, you buy them. If I fall sick, you pay my doctor. When I . . .'

She had avoided his eyes as she spoke but glancing at them she saw the anger beginning to rise. It was best, she knew, to keep quiet at times and this outburst had been unwise. For once she had lost herself to her thoughts: she could not risk upsetting him. If she had been pure-bred Chinese it would not have been so bad. A European would gladly keep her as he might a pet but, being half-English, she was somehow taboo, not quite acceptable even as a concubine.

Her silence brought no response. He glowered and put his tea cup down with deliberate slowness. She thought for a moment he was going to strike her: he had, almost, the last time she had been outspoken. Instead, he switched off the overhead fan and opened the windows a little wider.

'The wind is dying a fraction,' he said. 'The eye'll be here sooner.'

In the brief passage of a typhoon there comes a time when matters stand still, when an inner calm develops that cannot be breached or altered except by the passing of the hours. For Mulrenan, similar periods of calm came only at irregular intervals. He felt them when he had succeeded. It did not matter at what he had done well or the form or magnitude of his success. It might be a winning hand in a poker game, the flash of a pair of ears past the finishing post at Happy Valley or Kwanti. It might be settling a good deal, holding a fine stone, depositing another chamois leather bag in the vaults. It might be the comparative success of surviving another day. It came upon him when he slept with Alice.

Yet he feared it. Success was inevitably followed by the vacant sense of failure. Like a piece of music, 'The Black and Tan Fantasy', his moods rose and fell, plunged low or lifted high like the plaintive wail of a clarinet. His temper was the same: it could flare, sometimes terrifying him, then could as readily lie dormant. But it would always reappear, and then control him.

He recognised the typhoon as if it were a person with whom he shared something intangible and intimate.

12

Mulrenan walked: the ferries, the Peak Tram and the buses were operating to their schedules, but there was still a shortage of rickshaws and sedan chairs. He had been excused the lunchtime session on account of the typhoon; a piece of debris, blown inland from the railway sidings opposite the hotel, had smashed the windows of The Rose Room. Within minutes the floor was awash, the walls besmirched with grit, leaves and rubbish.

The restaurant to which he had been told to come was not an establishment where one would normally have discovered a European in the middle of the day. When business was to be discussed with small firms which had no compradore system, or when Chinese staff had invited one of their European superiors to a luncheon in his honour, then there were restaurants to cater for such an inter-racial gathering. Most, however, provided for one race or the other.

Fong, Mulrenan saw, was seated at a table in the corner with two other Chinese. As he approached the table, the men with Fong stood up and, without looking at the new arrival, discreetly left. A waiter hovered nearby in case he was required to eject the foreigner. The other diners paid them no attention.

'Mr Mulwenan, good morning. Please sit down. The typhoon was most severe. I hope you were not affected by it?'

'Good morning, Mr Fong. Thank you. And only in that our meeting was postponed. I'm sorry for that.'

'The weather belongs to the gods,' Fong said. 'It matters not.'

The waiter was signalled and brought a bowl, a pair of chopsticks and two side-dishes of sauce. A second waiter handed Mulrenan a hot scented flannel with which he wiped his face. It felt as if he were removing layers of congealed skin. He returned the flannel, the waiter accepting it from him with a pair of small wooden tongs.

'You notice how the waiter is cautious of you? Here, it is the reverse of your Peak Cafe, is it not? What a strange world when men of business cannot meet unhindered by etiquette.'

Mulrenan answered, laughing, 'Now it is your turn to save my embarrassment.'

'It is indeed good', observed Fong, 'to remove the perspiration and dirt from the face. Those gods are not being kind today.'

Mulrenan politely laughed again but, seeing Fong's wonder at his mirth, added, 'That is very amusing. It is the British who always talk of the weather, not the Chinese. They have better things to speak about. As have we.'

Fong did not accept this as an immediate hint to start discussing business. It was not his way. But Mulrenan knew he was westernised enough to appreciate his remark.

A girl in her teens was making her way between the tables. Around her neck hung a tray supported by a broad band of webbing like an army belt but with steel instead of brass buckles. She could — had she been European, dressed in a skirt instead of baggy trousers, with a lace hanky in her hair and carrying a torch — have been vending ices in a Dublin cinema. She was pretty, and obviously Cantonese, for her cheekbones were high but not prominent and her eyes, less narrowed than those of the northern Chinese, were dark and utterly expressionless. Her black hair, tied in a bunch, shone not with health but with steam rising from her tray. She was calling out loudly like a street hawker.

'A beautiful girl,' Fong said, guessing the thoughts running in Mulrenan's head. 'I am sure she could make much more money in Wanchai or Western District than she does here. Perhaps someone should offer a price to the restaurant owner. Maybe you?'

Mulrenan was briefly amused. 'Not for me. I have a woman, as you well know.'

'Yes. You are lucky, to have a girl who is part Chinese. That way you can see the goodness of all her past — she is a European like you but she has all the . . .' he searched for the word he wanted, failed to find it and continued '. . . fine points of a Chinese girl. She can fit into your world and yet she brings with her the devotion of a Chinese lady.'

'Also all the bad points,' Mulrenan remarked.

Changing the subject, Fong said, 'Of course, this girl is *mui tsai*.'

'I thought that was no longer done,' Mulrenan said. He was not shocked but surprised. 'Isn't slavery over now, especially for children?'

'In theory,' Fong answered. 'Since the various committees have been talking about it, it has grown less, but is still widespread. You cannot destroy tradition so easily. If you stop the buying of *mui tsai*, where will the concubines come from? How will poor families in China survive? A daughter is of no use, not like a son. Better she is sold and does some good for her parents.'

'She'll end up a whore ,' Mulrenan commented.

'That is not so bad. Better than be dead. Besides, it is right for a woman to serve a man. It is honourable for her. It is only dishonourable when the man treats her badly in return. It is the duty of men to protect women.'

The logic of the argument seemed so simple and yet simultaneously so convoluted Mulrenan chose to pursue it no further. The girl had arrived at their table.

'You will have some *dim sum*? It is very well made here.' Fong beckoned to the girl, indicating their two bowls. Mulrenan noticed Fong's bowl was clean: he had yet to eat. The two men who had departed upon his arrival must have been either henchmen or messengers.

Two dumplings about the size of tennis balls were placed in Mulrenan's bowl. He gave the girl thanks in Cantonese but she seemed not to hear, going on her rounds without acknowledging him.

Mulrenan used both his hands to halve the dumplings, scissoring the chopsticks. He had lived in Hong Kong long enough to know many of the tricks at Chinese meals. As the doughy coverings split apart, a pungent aroma of herbs wafted up. Inside were cubes of pork. He picked a piece up, dipped it in the soy sauce and ate it. It was tender and delicious.

Fong peered at Mulrenan out of the corner of his eye. When he had eaten his own dumplings, he put down his chopsticks, leaning them on a little rest by his bowl.

'You like Chinese food?'

'Indeed I do. There is an old saying, "When in Rome, do as the Romans do." I believe in that.'

Fong chuckled. 'We also have a saying, "If you wish to think like a tree then you must bear leaves on your branches." You are more Chinese than any European I know. Even those they call the "old China hands". Perhaps your lady helps you.'

Mulrenan made no immediate reply. Whenever he considered Alice, it was the Chinese in her he loved, giving him pleasure and companionship: her hair, her skin, her fine bone structure, her quiet kindness and her serious, innocent adoration. He knew too it was the English in her he despised, that gave her the tenacity by which she clung to him, the quirks of character which so annoyed and frustrated him.

Fong was right. Alice had taught him much: whatever he knew of the Chinese way of life he had gleaned from her, learned at her side. He had first grappled with the language under her tuition, and it was she who had shown him how to use chopsticks, when to use a spoon, how to handle his rice bowl to his mouth rather than bend forward to it. It was she who had first shown him how to make love in the Chinese manner, slowly and with the finesses of pressing and touching, of teasing the mind as well as the senses, as if love and sex were not merely functions of living but aspects of an ancient art, requiring as much practice as calligraphy or painting.

Fong's voice broke into his thoughts. 'I have some not good news for you. I must leave Hong Kong. I am going next week. You will not see me again.' Noticing the concern on Mulrenan's face, he went on, 'You need not have any worries. Business, for you, will continue.'

'Where are you going?'

'To China. To Nanking. But I am not staying there for more than one month. After, I am going to Burma. Perhaps to Hanoi . . .'

'What on earth for? What can you find in Burma or Indochina? They're jungle, mountains and nothing else.'

'A big war is coming to China. The trouble in Europe will be war very soon. You know that. Everyone think so. The Priminister of Great Britain' — he pronounced it as one word — 'is a fool. He think he can have peace with Germany. He cannot. The Germans are for you what the Japanese are for us. They want to rule. All through history in China, the Japanese have been our enemy. All the time they want to own China. For a long time now, as you know, they have been stitching China up.'

He waved his hand to draw the attention of another *dim sum* girl who had entered from the steam-filled cavern of the kitchen.

It was decidedly comical to hear a Chinese mobster in a restaurant in Hong Kong talking as if he were a New York bootlegger chatting in a speak-easy off Fifth Avenue. Nevertheless, Mulrenan showed no sign of amusement: it was not decorum that silenced him but profound anxiety. If Fong was beating a hasty retreat into China and beyond, it could mean one of several things, none of them pleasing. For Fong to quit when he was well ahead implied he had reasonably assessed or knew of matters concerning the war in China most others did not realise.

There was every possibility Fong was a marked man. The arabesques and intrigues surrounding Chinese life, could make a corpse of a well-established and successful businessman at any time. Somewhere in the struggle for supremacy in the Oriental underworld of assassination, thievery, politics and commercial chicanery, Fong had surely trodden on toes he should have side-stepped.

Perhaps, Mulrenan wondered, Fong's IOUs had been called in. These would not have involved money or material possessions but obligations. A favour done for him long ago was now being claimed with interest. On the other hand, his benefactor, his patron, might have been affected and his imminent flight was but a knock-on effect down through the ranks of criminality.

'So!' Fong bit into his second serving of *dim sum*. 'I will go soon. And this will affect you, for we shall not be doing business. However,' he continued, aware of Mulrenan's worries, 'you will not need to worry, for I have someone else to deal with you. He is not so expert, but he is good and eager.'

'I'm sad you feel you must leave.'

'It is the way,' Fong shrugged in a most un-Chinese manner. 'Maybe it will be for the best. The gods have ways of bending us as the wind shapes trees by the seashore. If we do not bend, when the wind is stronger we break.'

'Why Burma? Will the Japanese not . . .?'

'The Japanese. I am not afraid of them. Their idea of a South East Asia Co-Prosperity Plan is only a clever name for conquest. They will not reach where I am going. My leader will . . .'

So that was it: now Mulrenan knew. Fong was somehow tied up with one of the old Chinese warlords, and as he was pulling in his horns so Fong had to do likewise. Rumours of certain warlords withdrawing to western Yunan, beyond K'unming, to the upper Mekong River system, to Kachin and south-western Szechwan had been rife for several years. The inner turmoil of China was splitting the ruling class into factions, the Nationalists and the Communists, the ideologists and the sheer greedy.

He owed much to Fong. When playing the piano had begun to pall, when the salary from the Peninsula Hotel became insufficient for his needs or his ambitions, when he at last accepted that playing poker was not a reliable source of income, Mulrenan had sought a new channel into which to steer his energies. Fong, whom he had met by chance when watching a mahjong game in the hope of assessing whether it was worth his time learning, had provided him with a timely and lucrative alternative. It had been just as well. Mahjong was too complex, too slow and, besides, Mulrenan did not want to fleece the local Chinese — and only European wives took to the game, and then as a social rather than a serious, gaming sport.

Theirs was a merger of similar interests. Fong had needed a regular buyer for his gemstones and Mulrenan agreed to take the risk. Few would suspect Mulrenan of being a fence for a Chinese mobster and he had European contacts through which he could dispose of the goods. By handling the gemstones, Mulrenan legitimised them, laundering them from the Chinese underworld into the respectable society of the Europeans.

In the process, Fong taught Mulrenan the rudiments of the gemstone trade. His knowledge was not vast, but it was a sound foundation. Mulrenan was quick to learn and eager to apply his knowledge. At first, the local Chinese jewellers were amused by his avid interest. When he started to produce high quality stones for them to recut or set, their attitude changed — from that of mild humour to one of respect, and a curiosity he was careful never to satisfy.

In his own way, Mulrenan was grateful to Fong, but was not sure how he might express it. They had never been more than business associates: Mulrenan had never sought Fong's friendship and the Chinese had certainly never offered it.

80

'You are silent,' Fong observed. 'And I think you understand now. We all of us have masters and my master needs me.'

'Will you return?'

'Who can tell which way the tide will run when the sea is disturbed?' Fong replied enigmatically.

A party of four Chinese men were preparing to sit at an adjacent table. They were elderly and dressed in the long silk robes many younger Chinese, like Fong, had cast off for Western dress. One of the men, with watery eyes, had a fingernail at least four inches long, a sign he had never engaged in manual work. He eased his coat off his shoulders and was about to hand it to a waiter when he caught Fong's gaze. In an instant, something passed between them, some transmission of mutual recognition: the old man, averting his eyes, guided his party to another table.

'For you, the jewels will stop for a while,' Fong said in a lowered voice. 'Do you read the Shanghai newspapers?'

'Sometimes. Why do you ask?'

'In June, on the seventeenth day, a man was killed in Shanghai. His name was Kao Lee-sung. He was also known as Mo-bee Ah-kung. Have you heard of him?'

Mulrenan nodded. Kao was an underworld ringleader in the Western Outside Roads region of the city, a criminal of no small repute who had well-established political connections in high places in two of the main camps in the power struggle to control China, the pro-Nationalists and the pro-Japanese.

'He was killed in Shanghai,' Fong repeated, 'as he was leaving a singsong house in Swatow Road. His bodyguards were badly hurt. From him, or from his men, came the gems you have been buying. His organisation is a little upset now but is returning to normal. There is a new leader but he has decided to leave Shanghai. At first he went to Hangchow but now he is in Foochow. He has a young man in Hong Kong who will do the business for you instead of me. Do you want to meet him?'

'Certainly,' Mulrenan said.

He expected Fong to give him an address or slip a folded

piece of paper across the table. Instead, he looked across the room: a young man at a far table stood up and, brushing past the *dim sum* girls, came towards them. He was wearing a pair of grey trousers, an open-necked shirt with the sleeves rolled up to his elbows and scuffed brown shoes obviously discarded by their previous, European owner. He might have been a household servant.

'Mr Mulwrenan,' Fong introduced them, attempting for once to pronounce Mulrenan's name correctly and almost succeeding. 'This is Leung Tse-tung.'

The young man bowed very slightly, accepting Fong's offer of a chair and sat down with them.

'How you doo-ing,' he said.

'His English speaking is not too good. But he can understand you and I think you will understand him.'

Mulrenan smiled encouragingly to the young man. He could not yet have been in his twenties.

'He was educated in a Christian mission school but has forgotten much of what he learned.'

'I do you lumber one ok-ay,' Leung said. 'Lo ploblum.'

'No,' Fong corrected him. 'Nn — oh.'

'Nn-oh ploblum,' Leung repeated and all three of them laughed.

'He has his first delivery for you. It is a good stone. See what you think of it. And him.' Fong gestured with a slight flick of his wrist and, from a twist of cloth, Leung produced a gemstone which he held close to the table. It glittered in the light of a wall-mounted lamp.

It was a sapphire, dazzlingly blue and quite large. He moved it gently with his fingers so it caught more of the light.

'Sevung-harf cullut,' Leung said. 'Good kwa-lee-tee stong flom Ceylong.'

He passed it to Mulrenan in its bed of cloth. It was a fine stone, well cut but dirty on the underside: it plainly came from a ring. The gold mounting would have been melted down long since, within hours of the robbery.

'He has a price in mind?'

'Yes,' said Fong. 'He knows the price. He has been taking lessons.'

'Same arrangement?' Mulrenan questioned.

'Same. But not the same place. He cannot be seen in the cafe on The Peak. He does not, as you can see, have the same tailor as I do.'

They decided upon a mutually agreeable rendezvous the next day, and the price. Leung rose, shook Mulrenan's hand in such a manner that suggested he was unused to such behaviour, and left. As he made his way between the tables, Mulrenan noticed how his head moved slightly from side to side, observing the diners, watching for danger. He was clearly a natural for the work Mulrenan hoped would lie ahead.

Fong also rose to leave.

'Maybe we shall meet again.'

'Thank you for your — your help,' Mulrenan said.

'No help,' Fong replied. 'Business.'

13

As the Peak Tram bounced and swayed gently on the end of its cable, two British naval officers waited on the step for the elastic motion to reduce before they boarded. Both were in their 'Number Ones', replete with braid and sword, the brass and gold glinting in the May Road station lights. The bell rang and the tram recommenced its ascent. Above, up the steepest incline of the track, Mulrenan could see the headlamp of the descending car.

'Are we late?' Alice asked.

They had not left Lyndhurst Terrace until after seven and, not being able to find two sedan chairs, had walked to the Peak Tram station at Kennedy Road.

Mulrenan looked at the Rolex. He could easily have afforded to buy himself a new, even better watch but he had not; he preferred to retain the Rolex because it reminded him of the win and the detested British officer. Whenever he checked the time, the memory of the previous owner asking for a chance to regain it fleetingly formed in his mind's eye.

'We're in good time. The invitation was seven-thirty for eight.' He lowered his voice. 'So long as we're first off the tram.'

To ensure they were, they had taken seats by the forward door and, as the track levelled to approach the top terminus, Mulrenan stood, holding the rear bar of their seat. As soon as the tram slowed to walking pace he stepped on to the platform and started for the exit. Two other Europeans, dressed in dinner jackets, followed him with equally brisk strides. By the time Alice reached the road outside the Peak Cafe, Mulrenan had secured two sedan chairs, one for himself and one for her.

The balmy mountain air was warm and smooth, moths frantically congregating around the lamp outside the terminus building. After the muggy heat of the city and their walk to the station, it was paradisiacal to feel a breeze rising from the sea and to inhale the night flowers. The station lamp flickered as the engines commenced to purr and run: the tram was beginning its downward journey. The flicker gave the moths a frenzied appearance, the sharp pulses of the rays freezing the rapid strokes of their wings.

When a strong breeze momentarily blew from the thin bamboos beyond the cafe, where the mountain sloped sharply away in forest, the moths were joined by a ghost. Alice watched its arrival and was filled instantly with a mixture of wonderment and a strange, foreboding darkness which unaccountably pierced her, making her suck her breath sharply.

As it passed, she realised the ghost was not a spirit. It was a moon moth with a wingspan greater than the spread of her fingers. Its flight was not jerky and frenetic like the smaller moths but slow and languid. Its forewings were curved, coming to a point above its head: the tails on the hind wings drooped stiffly, wavered out of synchronisation with the lazy beats of the wings.

With no apparent reason except perhaps that it was bored with the company of the lesser creatures of its world, the moth glided away from the light and settled upon the roof of the sedan chair beside Alice. It landed soundlessly near her face, unlike butterflies which can be heard in flight. One of the sedan chair carriers, standing between the rear shafts of the vehicle, pulled a rag from his waistline to swat the moth away. She raised her hand.

'M'ho!' she exclaimed, adding less loudly for fear it might disturb the moth, 'No. Leave it.'

She drew her face closer to it. The wings of the moth were a luminous creamy green, with white drifted into the colouring: the most accomplished artist could never have achieved such a perfect blend of tones and shades. Its body was the size of her thumb, its eyes mottled grey, bearing the dazed, vacant look of nocturnal insects. Its feathered antennae and its tongue, coiled like a clock-spring, tested the air and the doped canvas of the sedan chair canopy. Its legs were as stout as electric wire.

As it shivered before her eyes, the scales of its wings and the fur of its body shimmered, drawing the lamplight until it seemed as if the moth were the source of illumination. She would not have been surprised if the other moths had fluttered around this god of their universe, paying their homage.

'Come along,' Mulrenan touched her elbow, 'or we shall be late.'

Despite its beauty, the moth was loathsome: its exquisite form and unearthly colouring suggested it might conceal some unknown danger or terrible disease. The moth lifted into flight and Alice started, her head jerking back. The draught of its wings fanned her cheek. It did not seek the lamp but returned to the forest.

She sat upright in her sedan chair as it swung along Findlay Road. Over the shoulders of the front carrier she could see the polished woodwork of Mulrenan's chair glistening in the beam of a dim street light.

She tried to remember what a moon moth signified. She had been told. Her mother, one of her aunts, a childhood amah or another servant — someone had given her the details once.

The chairs crossed the junction with Plantation Road, entered Severn Road and turned up a pathway. She noticed the corner no more than she had the glittering panorama of the city, the harbour and the peninsula of Kowloon spread beneath her, the scintillating lights on the sea, the whole tableau presented as if on a cleverly designed stage, with a dark backdrop of hills and ranges of mountains silvered in the moonlight. She had not even noticed the moon.

At the top of the path was a grand house in the terraced gardens of which were thick Chinese candles guttering on bamboo stakes. Looking towards The Peak, Alice saw it had dressed itself in the only cloud in the whole sky upon which the starlight and moonlight played with an intensity so beautiful it prompted her to tears. She was awed and terrified simultaneously.

The sedan chair was lowered to the ground and she stepped from it. She spoke briefly in Cantonese to one of the carriers.

'What does it mean? The moon moth? I have forgotten.'

The carrier looked at his feet, embarrassed to be drawn into conversation with a woman of position. She repeated her question.

'No can do,' he said, speaking in broken English as if not sure if he was addressing a Chinese or a European.

'You tell me,' she demanded. 'You tell me. Now.'

'No can do,' he muttered again.

Mulrenan was at her side, paying off the carriers. They bowed their heads to him as they received their fee and a tip.

'Now,' he said, mimicking an English upper-crust accent, 'for a jolly good evening, what!'

As she took his arm and was guided up the steps towards two servants waiting to show them into the house, she cast a quick glance backward. Mulrenan's sedan chair had disappeared down the path but her own was where it had halted. The carriers, standing shoulder to shoulder in the night, their sweating skin glossed by the light of the candles, were watching her intensely.

'You look a little pale,' Mrs Antrobus remarked as they

were introduced. 'Would you care for a glass of water? It can be awfully exhausting coming up on the tram. Sometimes, the mountain air — after the atmosphere in Central — makes one feel a little peaky.'

'I shall be all right, thank you,' Alice replied, smiling. 'I saw a large moth by the terminus and . . .'

'Beastly things!' Mrs Antrobus exclaimed. 'Ugly, furry bodies covered with mould. I can't stand them. Anyway — I'm sure after you've met a few people and had a drink you'll feel much, much better. And we are dining at nine. Right!' She scanned the room into which she had led Alice. 'Let's see — to whom can we introduce you?'

She did not understand about the moth: Alice hardly expected her to. She was British, and superstition for her was limited to the number thirteen and not walking under ladders. If superstition it was. For Alice, it was more a belief, a firm acceptance of nature governing men, not vice versa.

The sitting room was vast. At one end was a replica Adam fireplace, the grate filled with an Indian peacock-feather fan. On the mantle ticked a brass clock in a flawless glass dome, its movement controlled by a counterbalanced wheel. On either side were Ming vases on rosewood pedestals. The furniture consisted of large sofas upholstered in beige satin upon which had been strewn silk cushions embroidered with orchids. Before each was a long, low table made of rosewood and inlaid with ivory scenes from classical Chinese tales. Five armchairs were arranged about so the seating formed a semi-circle before the fireplace. Upon the walls were Victorian watercolours of seascapes in ornate gold-leafed frames and, on the broad pillars between the french windows opening to a terrace hung Chinese scrolls. The room was painted in a deep cream both warmly inviting and coolly appropriate. Before a mahogany drinks cabinet stood the Number One houseboy, as much a part of the fittings as the sofas or the clock.

Charles Antrobus stepped forward to greet his guests.

'Sean,' he said to Mulrenan, extending his hand. 'How grand of you to come. Jolly good to see you.'

He turned to his wife and Alice caught the conspiratorial half-wink from Mulrenan.

'This is Alice, dear,' Mrs Antrobus said.

Accepting her offered hand, Antrobus pressed it softly as one might a rare fruit, testing for ripeness.

Antrobus had been worried about Mulrenan's companion. Everyone acquainted with Mulrenan knew he had a Eurasian woman but few had met her. He was not in the habit of taking her with him unless they were in large crowds. At the races or the yacht club on Kellett Island, at the Hong Kong Cricket Club, at the Foreign Correspondents' Club in Robinson Road: there he might be seen with a young woman, but observers could never be certain quite which one was his. He did not stay by her side yet nor did he ignore her. He just let her be.

Having invited Mulrenan and partner to dinner, Antrobus had afterwards been concerned as to what he might have let himself in for; his wife shared his thoughts. He was, therefore, relieved that Alice appeared far more European than she did Chinese. Indeed, wearing an evening dress and with her hair permed in the latest fashion, with the sides curled and trimmed, she could be passed off as British — if one put out of mind the deep brown of her eyes, the lustre of her hair and the smoothness of her skin.

It was not that Charles Antrobus minded: he had lived in the colony for over twenty years, having been sent out during the Great War to mind his company's holdings should the Germans further develop this sphere of interests in the Far East. By 1925, he had parted from his employers and established his own business, exporting tea and silk. The firm expanded into the jade and timber trades and he became a taipan. He did business with Chinese merchants, compradores, even coastal trading junk captains and he did not bother himself with racial distinctions and social divisions.

Yet as an important businessman he had a social position to maintain. Although he had invited into his house business associates whom he knew consorted with girls from the better bordellos in Happy Valley, he knew in advance their ladies would be European or Australian. Likewise, Chinese guests who visited him accompanied by a concubine did not jeopardise his standing. However, no European with a Chinese mistress was thoroughly acceptable. They were considered to have 'gone native' and that was not right.

In Mulrenan's case, however, Antrobus was prepared to make an exception, for the Irishman had something he badly wanted.

There were ten guests for dinner. None approached Antrobus's age of fifty-two. The nearest in years was a tall, angular man with prematurely grey hair and a hard-line jaw. He was introduced as Mr Norris, the representative of a Canadian life assurance company: like many of his Canadian forebears, he was a Scot and bore a trace of the Highlands in his accent. His wife was a short, dumpy and pleasant-looking woman who smiled at Alice, patting the cushion next to her.

'Come and sit by me, my dear.'

She shifted along the sofa a token inch or two. From her fair pink skin it was obvious she and her husband were newcomers to Hong Kong.

Alice was handed a gin and tonic by the houseboy, a slice of fresh lemon floating on a bed of crushed ice. Whenever she visited the homes of Europeans Alice was ill at ease with the servants. She did not consider her own, Ah Shun, as such. She and the amah had lived together for many years and were friends, had been since her childhood: they were more like two spinster sisters than employer and employee.

With the Chinese servants of well-to-do Europeans she felt irrationally out of place, wanting to help them. It was illogical: they regarded her as they would anyone who had succeeded, be they Chinese or British. Yet she feared they saw a part of themselves in her, knew her for what she had been — a singsong girl, if a classy one.

'Where do you live, my dear? And do call me Pauline.'

Mrs Norris's question was not meant searchingly, as it might have been from a resident more accustomed to the form, social standing being immediately assessable from an address.

89

'We live in the mid-levels,' Mulrenan interjected, balancing himself on the arm of the sofa. 'Not far from Government House. Prefer it there. I like to be close to the heart of business.'

'For you, that means close to the Chinese,' Antrobus observed. 'Old Sean here's a dab hand at dealing. If he was Chinese, he'd be the best compradore on the coast south of Amoy. If you want it, he'll fix it. Won't you, Sean?'

Mulrenan smiled obligingly. He objected to the word 'fix': he was reluctant to appear a spiv, a wide boy. Respectability was vital to survival.

'What exactly do you do?' asked a man sitting on the farthest sofa, by the french windows.

Derek Glanville was known to Mulrenan. They had met on two occasions, neither of them precisely social ones. The first had been a blackjack game in which Glanville had lost heavily and the second had been in the security office of the Hongkong and Shanghai Bank. Mulrenan was there on one of his regular visits to the safe deposit department when Glanville had entered with a senior clerk from his office. They had barely spoken apart from passing the time of day but Glanville had caught a glimpse of the contents of Mulrenan's deposit box. The box was no longer the small metal cube the bank had provided in Mulrenan's early days. He now had a steel trunk delivered on a trolley, requiring two burly bank messengers to lift it.

The private room was being redecorated and Mulrenan had to open his box in the office. The bullion bar had been sufficient to set Glanville's mind racing and his curiosity burning: he vowed not to play with Mulrenan again. Men with that much power and cash were born winners.

'Import-export,' Mulrenan said casually.

It was a classification to cover anything from gun-running to selling Bibles. But Glanville was not to be so easily put off.

'Yes, but of what?'

'Frankly, anything,' Mulrenan answered disarmingly. 'Anything legal, that is. If you want something and it's to be had, I'll get it. If I can. I'd certainly do my best. I'm the archetypal middleman.'

The joke at himself set Glanville at a disadvantage and Mulrenan was quick to seize the initiative.

'What line of work are you in? I don't think you told me when we met previously.'

'I didn't know you two were acquainted,' Glanville's wife exclaimed. 'Where did you meet? You should have invited Mr and Mrs Mulrenan over to see us. We live near Magazine Gap — a small house on the right hand side of the road as you go towards town. Just before you get to the sharp bend above the hairpin with May Road. Do you know it? We have a palm tree by the gate.'

Glanville put a stop to his wife's prattle by saying, 'I doubt it. There are a lot of palm trees about. And we've only met in passing.'

'What do you do, Mr Glanville?' Pauline Norris asked.

'A medical importers,' his wife blurted. 'The head office is in London but they have branches all over the world. We came out in '34 when they expanded. At first, we were in New Delhi for eight months, then Penang, but they were only temporary.'

As she paused to draw breath, Mulrenan said thoughfully, 'Medicine. Do you deal in vaccines as well as ordinary drugs?'

Glanville nodded and raised his tumbler of whisky to his lips.

'Smallpox?'

'Yes.'

'I would gladly purchase a stock from you now,' Mulrenan offered. 'Ideally, I need fifteen thousand doses.'

Despite his dislike for Mulrenan, Glanville knew the man could pay without delay — and it would be cash or a local bank draft. And business, after all, was business.

'I could get hold of that many doses in a week or ten days. Not cheap, I'm afraid.'

'I'm sure we could come to an arrangement,' Mulrenan replied. 'I'll give you a ring on Monday. Perhaps a spot of tiffin . . .'

There was a faint click as the brass door-handle was twisted and a servant admitted the last two dinner guests.

91

One was a handsome man in his forties with slicked black hair, his dinner suit immaculately pressed yet his black patent leather shoes a little dusty. He wore a silk bow tie. On the index finger of his right hand was a large ring with a cut carnelian mounted in a thick shank of red gold. By his side was Irina Popescu.

The men rose as the couple entered and introductions were made. When Alice was introduced, Irina Popescu walked around the sofa, lifted her up by her hands and kissed her on both cheeks.

'It has been a long time since we met. I remember it well. It was on that incredibly grotesque train going to the races. It must have been at the start of the season. Yes,' she added emphatically, 'it *was* the start of the season.'

She sat down next to Alice and the conversations swelled once more. Mulrenan and Glanville went on to the terrace, the Norrises entered into conversation with another couple present, a Mr and Mrs Burroughs. The Antrobuses spoke with Irina's consort and Barbara Glanville.

'How are you, Alice?'

Alice was flattered. 'You remembered my name,' she exclaimed.

'I remember names easily,' Irina replied, her voice close and personal, 'especially when they belong to such beautiful women. Tell me. Are you happier now than on the train? You were very sad then.'

'Was I?'

'Oh, yes. Very sad. I could tell. But we are all sad from time to time. It is the men that do it to us, make us laugh or cry. It is their way.'

'I am happier now,' Alice assured her.

'That is so good.' Irina was genuinely pleased. 'Is Sean treating you better?'

'Well, I . . .' Alice stammered.

'I know,' Irina said confidingly. 'I know all about him and about you. You and I are very alike, you know. You are part Chinese and I am Russian. They don't know how to take us, don't know where they stand with us. That is why they treat us so — how shall I put it? — guardedly. We worry them. We are — unclassifiable. The British — and that includes the Irish, so Sean's no excuse — like to have everything in its little compartment. Like books in a bookshop. "A nation of shopkeepers": that's what Napoleon called them. He was right. They are superb traders and they have to be orderly thinkers to be so successful. So — everything in its place. Including us, the odd ones.'

She laughed, so appealingly it set Alice giggling.

'I had never quite seen it that way.'

'Of course you did not! You are partly British and therefore partly blind to it.' Irina accepted a tumbler from the houseboy and leaned a little closer. 'Your surname is Soon. That is good. It might be English but it is also Chinese. Take my advice, my darling. Keep it. Or,' she took a long sip of her drink, 'are you married now?'

'No,' Alice reported, trusting Irina's discretion. 'We are not married.'

'I detect a little disappointment in your voice,' said Irina astutely. 'Do not be. But if you do marry him — or anyone — keep your Chinese name. It will be better for you.'

'As good as Popescu?' Alice asked. There was laughter in her words now.

Irina put her fingers to Alice's lips 'Shush! I am now Irina Boyd.'

'Boyd?'

'Much soap has gone under the wedding ring since we met.'

'How many names do you have?' Alice enquired suddenly.

'Oh, you are funny! And so — do you know what the Scottish say?'

'Yes,' said Alice. 'They say "canny".'

'You see!' Irina exploded, her sudden loudness stopping Burroughs in mid-sentence. 'Just as I said. Keep it up!' Then she lowered her voice and said conspiratorially, 'Four!'

The Number One houseboy came into the room, spoke to Mrs Antrobus then hit a handbell with a tiny gavel.

'Right-o!' exclaimed Antrobus, rising and slapping his

hands together. 'Dinner is ready. Do come along through. And bring your glasses with you.' He looked to his wife. 'You lead the way, Dotty?'

Alice was seated between Burroughs and Glanville. The former, a King's Counsel, talked of piracy, telling her of a recent case he had prosecuted, of the crew of a junk who had boarded a Russian-owned coaster and had not only been repulsed but subsequently chased by their would-be victims, blasted with rifle fire and captured. Glanville talked of cholera and smallpox epidemics raging in central China, of typhoid in Formosa, of the wonders of aspirin and the usefulness of small quantities of opium administered under a doctor's regime. He expressed a desire to branch into surgical instruments and hospital equipment. Of the two men, Alice deemed the King's Counsel the more interesting.

The meal was of eight courses, served with vintage champagne, and, by the time they finished eating and the men had gone off on their own to Antrobus's study, Alice was feeling tired and light-headed.

The women sat on the terrace. The night was still and warm, the perfume of night flowers drifting on the thermals lifting from the city. The candles had gone out but the servants had placed oil lamps around the garden, the wicks turned low to discourage moths. The moon had set and the sky was a riot of stars.

Antrobus had skilfully turned the dinner-table conversation away from the war but the women, seated under the starlight with coffee cups and brandy goblets, were no longer to be held in check.

'What do you think will happen?' Barbara Glanville asked, voicing the thoughts of several of the women present.

'I think,' replied Mrs Antrobus, 'and speaking as the oldest of us here, though I don't wish to advertise the fact' — they laughed amiably '— that we've nothing to worry about. The Germans will stay put in Europe and try to invade the UK. Of course, they won't succeed. Winnie said we'll fight them on the beaches and, by George, we will. They'll be too overstretched to fight out here. Be like the last war: they'll slog it out in Europe and the Mediterranean. Even India's too far. And too pro-British, for all the politicking that's going on for home rule. As for the Chinese, they're too disorganised to fight even themselves: Chiang Kai-shek on one hand, that Japanese-backed fellow, the Communists under Mao whatsisname, the warlords and the triads and the gangsters. As for the Japanese themselves: too few of them. Island race. Finite numbers.'

'Don't you think we've anything to fear from the Japanese, then?'

'No. Our biggest worry — Charles feels so, anyway — won't be an actual war with bullets but the effects the war will have on the economy. We might survive if China had something to export to the war — though lord knows what! — and we can export it. We can be the middlemen. Just what we've always been really. Sean,' she looked sideways at Alice, 'will be all right, for example. He is adaptable in business. The thing is,' she continued, 'most of us can't actually make anything, can we? No manufacturing industry. No,' she picked up the mat from under her glass and batted an insect crawling on the arm of her chair, 'I think we are in for hard times but I don't think we need be afraid. After all, we've always pulled through, haven't we?'

'You are so sure of yourselves,' Irina commented, addressing no one in particular.

'What do you mean by that?' Pauline Norris asked brusquely.

'I don't mean it as an insult,' Irina explained. 'I simply mean the British are so certain, as if the future was theirs. I think . . .' Her voice faded.

'What do you think?' Barbara Glanville enquired, also on the defensive. 'I'm sure we'd all like to know.'

'I think we shall have a war. Here. In the Far East. I think the Japanese — I think it's only a matter of time, and that is running out.'

'What makes you so sure?'

'Talk.' said Irina. 'Only talk. But I have seen invasions: they are in my blood, a part of my heritage. I am English now, but I was born a Russian. I can sense when there's a conqueror in the air and I sense one now. The Japanese are only staying their hand because it suits them. When they are ready . . .'

'An island race,' Mrs Antrobus repeated, as if to prove her point. 'Finite resources.'

'Are the British not an island race?' Alice said. 'And look what they've achieved. A huge empire, the greatest ever built.'

'But, my dear, the Japanese . . .' Mrs Antrobus said with polite exasperation.

'There are more Japanese,' Irina announced, 'than there are British. And they are to be feared. Whose navies helped train their navy? The American and the British. Upon whose armies is their own based? The German and British. Why, look at Japanese lorries. I've seen them in China. They are copies of American ones. So are their cars, their bicycles. The Japanese are very clever. They borrow the best of all they see and mould it into their own. And they have the one thing that forges national success.'

'And what's that?'

'The biggest single thing we need to fear,' Irina advised. 'Fanaticism.'

'Never tangle with fanatics!' retorted Antrobus.

He had come on to the terrace, a drift of cigar smoke lingering in the doorway behind him.

'Mind if we join you now, ladies?'

The men walked through the french windows and the houseboy and his assistant busied themselves filling and handing round glasses. Mulrenan stood by Alice's chair as the others were talking.

'Missy of the house okay?' he asked, bending to her ear.

She nodded and said, 'We were talking about the war.'

'So were we,' he told her. 'They think they're safe but they're not. It's on its way.'

Antrobus sidled up to Mulrenan, an ivory-handled cutter in his hand. He snipped the root of a new Havana cigar, and placed the instrument on the arm of the chair.

'Fancy a walk round the garden, Sean?' he suggested. 'Fine view from the far end, by the traveller's palm'.

'Gladly, Charlie,' Mulrenan replied.

Alice watched as the two men sauntered off, brandy goblets in hand. Antrobus's cigar glowed amid the night foliage.

Out of sight of the house, behind a hibiscus bush, Antrobus halted.

'Have you got it on you, Sean?'

'I have,' Mulrenan said but made no move to reach into his jacket.

'I can let you have the money tonight. It's in the house.'

Antrobus was keen to see what Mulrenan had brought, as previously arranged. He also wanted no one to know he had bought it.

'Twenty-five thousand Hong Kong.'

'That's what we agreed, Sean. Do I get to see it?'

Mulrenan produced one of his chamois leather bags. He handed his brandy glass to Antrobus and untied the bag, letting the contents tip into his hand. Antrobus balanced their brandies on a low stone wall, then stubbed out his cigar.

'May I?'

Mulrenan dropped the gem gently into the other man's hand.

'My God, Sean!' Antrobus exclaimed. 'It's certainly a beauty.'

'Burmese,' Mulrenan informed him. 'Pigeon's blood red, they call it. The best red for a ruby. Trap cut, as you requested. A little smaller than you wanted at 22.6 carats, but the biggest I've got in such a fine colour.'

'Did you get it from Burma?'

Taking up his glass, Mulrenan sipped the last of his drink and said, 'Very good brandy, Charles.'

'Fine champagne,' Antrobus answered, accepting the compliment on his cellar as an avoidance of his enquiry.

There could be few greater personal pleasures, Mulrenan considered, than standing on the property of a wealthy man, inhaling his expensive Havana tobacco smoke, drinking his very best cognac and at the same time selling him, at well over the market price, a gemstone of above average but by no means excellent quality.

Antrobus, as Mulrenan knew well from previous conversations, was ignorant of gems. A ruby was merely a translucent red stone to him, for which one had to pay a high sum and for which a woman would give much in order to pin it to her breast or hang it round her neck.

The delight for Mulrenan was that Antrobus would be more than annoyed if he discovered he was being duped. A man of ruthless business acumen, he was for ever on the watch for an easy killing, a smooth operation which would bring in good profits for minimal capital outlay. That others suffered under his contracts concerned him not: that was part of the process as far as he was concerned. Until, of course, the tables were turned and then, as rumour had reported it to Mulrenan, he was as vicious as a cornered mongoose.

The beauty of this transaction was that Antrobus would not find out that he had been taken for a fool. He trusted Mulrenan in much the same manner one thief trusts another. Mulrenan was aware of his position and used it. Yet, to be certain of protecting himself from being found out, which could ruin his status with others in Antrobus's circle, he covered himself with an artful trick he had successfully employed with others.

'A pendant or a ring?' he enquired.

'Pendant,' Antrobus replied, rolling the stone between finger and thumb. 'It's a bit too big for a ring, don't you think? Look a bit gauche, eh?'

'Yes,' Mulrenan readily agreed. 'A pendant with a heavy-ish clasp setting. Rose gold, not the yellowy Chinese gold.'

'Too right! Don't want it to look common.'

'I know a jeweller who'd do a very fine job. Over on Kowloon-side. Runs a damn good workshop and has done a fair bit for me over the past months. Won't skimp on the product: no silver hidden under the mounting. Bit pricey, of course . . .'

'If you pay peanuts, you get monkeys,' Antrobus observed. 'Give me his name before you go, will you?'

Mulrenan nodded obligingly. In the morning, he mentally noted, he must slip over to Ah Lo, tip him off the work would be coming in, arrange his percentage of the price and assure the jeweller that Antrobus wouldn't know gold from brass. The ruby would be set in a heavy pendant with a gold-plated silver backing.

From the hillside came the curt call of a muntjac deer: it coughed like the bark of a fox. There was a rustling of leaves in the undergrowth at the farthest end of the wall and a hibiscus bush swayed violently.

'The little beggars often gather around here,' Antrobus said. 'A naturalist chum of mine says it's a latrine site for them. Can I have the little bag, too?'

Without speaking, Mulrenan gave it to him, marvelling as he did so at the perspicacity of the miniature deer.

'Do you know what the Sanskrit writers called the ruby? "Ratnaraj" or "ratnanayaka" — the King of Stones.' Antrobus was showing off. 'It is said to protect the health and if immersed in water its inner fire will make the liquid boil.

'They also say that he who wears rubies cannot be wounded by spear or gun. I'd not recommend you to try it in the near future, Charles.'

'I'll give you the money before you leave,' Antrobus said. 'Now, I think, we'd best rejoin the others.'

'I hope your wife likes it,' Mulrenan ventured.

'Not a word, old boy, if you don't mind,' Antrobus requested. 'It's not actually for her. Get my drift?'

Alice knew of Mulrenan's deal and wondered if Antrobus would like the stone. She also wondered, with the shrewdness of a woman, for whom the ruby was a gift. At that price it would not be for a concubine and he would not dare to give it to another's wife or daughter: that left only an occupant of the American madam's cathouse in Happy Valley. Alice had heard of a very beautiful Danish girl there.

'Ten cents for your thoughts,' a voice whispered loudly in her ear.

99

It was Burroughs's wife. She was much younger than her husband, perhaps half his age, and not much older than Alice. She had auburn hair, and her eyes sparkled even in the light from the oil lanterns burning in the garden. She was never motionless, but not in the sense of one who fidgets: she was graceful in her movements like a bird. Her hands were never still, and seemed continually to move as if weaving spells or invisible silk. She had not conversed with Alice all evening, but Alice had watched her from time to time with fascination.

'I think a penny's a little inappropriate in Hong Kong. And one cent's far too little value for a thought,' Burroughs's wife continued. 'Perhaps one should say a dollar for your thoughts but then, for many of those here, that would be rather overdoing it, don't you think?'

Her cheeky grin indicated she was making fun of their fellow guests rather than criticising them.

'Mine are perhaps one cent ones,' Alice said.

'At least you keep them to yourself. My name's Chrissie. Burroughs. I'm actually Audrey Christabel but the first one sounds like an Anglo-Saxon saint — one of those two-bladed-axe-swinging harridans — and the second like a character from "Peter Pan". Or a racehorse. So I'm Chris to my husband and Chrissie to my chums. You're Alice Soon.'

Alice was so surprised she made no reply. She was grateful Chrissie Burroughs had kept her voice down.

'Don't worry so. I'm not going to tell. I think it's silly — no, I think it's unjust — you should be treated this way. They are stuck up, aren't they?'

Alice just nodded. 'How do you know me?' she asked.

'Well, I don't. But a friend of a friend — it's a long story.'

There was a raucous rattle of laughter from the men and genteel shrieks of amusement from the women at the other end of the terrace.

'Evidently,' Chrissie remarked, 'someone has finally cracked a passable joke. Aren't I being bitchy?'

'Not really,' Alice replied, warming to her. 'I think you're really being rather truthful.'

'I didn't really want to chat with you about them, anyway,' Chrissie said, adding mysteriously, 'I've actually got a message for you.'

'A message?' Alice was intrigued. 'From whom?'

'Your half-brother.'

'Alec?' Alice whispered. She felt dizzy, putting out her hand for the arm of the chair. She missed and Chrissie took hold of her.

'I'm sorry. I didn't mean to startle you. Are you all right?'

'Yes.' Gathering herself, Alice added after a pause, 'Where is he?'

'In Hong Kong. He arrived last month and tried to trace you but without any luck. He asked me if I knew you and, of course, I didn't, but I knew of you through . . . how can I put it? — a common acquaintance. From the past. Heard of you as Sean's . . .'

'Mistress.'

Uttering the word, saying it aloud, jarred her.

'I don't think I'd have put it quite so plainly,' said Chrissie, 'but if that's how you see it . . .'

'How would you put it?'

'I don't quite know. I'm not sure how I regarded myself when I was in your shoes.'

She winked and Alice was immediately put at her ease. The camaraderie that exists between concubines, between ladies of fashion — even between downright whores — is often closer than family ties could ever be. It occurred to Alice she had seen the news of a King's Counsel's wife having been drowned the year before at Shek-O beach. She had gone swimming too far out and it was supposed either the heavy undertow or a shark had taken her. Within a few months the KC had remarried, his choice of bride causing a stir in both legal and social circles: it was said he had first met her when she appeared before the Bench in a public order fracas over a sum of money and a junior naval officer from a visiting destroyer. He was involved in a case in the next court at the time. Alice thought — with a twinge of envy — how fortunate Chrissie was to have landed such

101

respectability, so quickly and with such apparent ease.

The best means by which to find a lost soul in a city like Hong Kong was not to ask the police, search the city hall records or start thumbing through hotel registers. The most efficient means was to request a search by the underworld, for a thief can be found by other thieves, a priest by other priests, a lunatic by madmen and a mistress by another courtesan.

'Where is he? What's he doing?'

'I think I'd better let him tell you. But he's working for The Chartered Bank. He thought you might have had a bank account and could be discovered through it . . .'

'I share Sean's.'

'I know. But I didn't tell him because I didn't want to cause trouble for you. He said for me to ask you to phone him at the bank. Any morning before ten. He wants to meet you.'

For the remainder of the evening, Alice brooded on Chrissie Burroughs' message: in her mind she was concocting the various forms which her meeting with her half-brother might take. None of them was in the least way pleasurable. She had known some day they would meet again, but she had always either looked upon the event with dread or thrust it to the back of her mind by deliberately thinking of more immediate and unpleasant matters.

When spoken to by Chrissie or Irina, Antrobus or one of the others who drew her into their conversations, Alice responded, joining in their discussions and laughing at their jokes but the sparkle had left her. Mulrenan noticed this but gave it no thought until after the party had broken up and those going down on the late night, reserved tram had taken to their sedan chairs.

Mulrenan and Alice took the first chair to arrive and, as they waited for the others to reach the upper terminus, he remarked, 'You're very silent all of a sudden. Did you have a bit of trouble, after all?'

His question broke into her reverie.

'No.' She rubbed her eyes. 'Nothing happened: they didn't know me. Not really,' she added as an afterthought.

'I'm just tired, that's all.'

She hoped her excuse did not ring hollow and looked at Mulrenan's face. She need not have worried. He was too pleased with his sale of the ruby. When the bank opened, he'd pay the money in and buy gold.

The mist swirled about them, calming the activity of the moths around the lamp by the entrance to the ticket barrier. She remembered then the moon moth, and shivered.

14

Mulrenan locked the car and walked through the trees towards the shore. For several miles he had kept to a cart track, at places narrowed to just the width of the Ford. Finally the gradient became too steep and, fearful he would not be able to turn the car, he had stopped in a clearing by a ruined house overgrown with creepers and screened by luxuriant bushes. He backed the V8 in so he could drive clear away.

Not far from where he left the car the track became a wide pathway, the slope of the hillside increasing markedly until he was obliged to walk faster, his calf muscles straining. He was unused to such vigorous exercise and made a mental note to improve his stamina. At the foot of the incline the path met another running at right angles and leading towards the headland in a parallel course to the coastline.

Mulrenan paused, unfolding the map he was carrying. With his nail he marked the spot where he had left the car and gazed about to get his bearings. If the sketch map was correct there should be a dead tree trunk two hundred yards to his left. He set off counting his paces, the sun beating down on the trees over his head. Birds flew ahead of him, squawking or cheeping news of his arrival. As he walked he wondered how long it had been since a tiger had last been spotted in the wilder parts of the New Territories.

The path was evidently not much used, at least by human traffic. Where the sun was able to penetrate the branches the grass grew a foot tall and, where a stream trickled across the path, Mulrenan saw in the mud the prints of a wild pig. These made him even more cautious: humans he could cope with but wild pigs, with their short curved tusks, were another matter.

His preoccupation made him lose count of his steps but he found the dead tree trunk where he expected. Beside it was a faint pathway going through the undergrowth towards the shore. Unless he had been looking for a path he could easily have missed it. He forced his way downwards, hearing as he went the hushing sound of waves upon pebbles.

After reaching a stand of thick bamboo he was forced to detour and, as he did so, he heard a click made neither by an insect nor his feet upon a dry bamboo stem. It was metallic and unnatural.

He stopped to listen, staring around but seeing only a few yards into the thick forest. Insects were scratching and sawing their noises, the birds singing or alarming at him. After a few minutes of his hair prickling, he was still not convinced he had misheard the sound or that he had caused it himself, and he proceeded warily.

The undergrowth ended abruptly at the top of a ten-foot rocky drop to a pebble-strewn beach. Going down on his haunches, Mulrenan slid over the rock, looking quickly from left to right. The beach was deserted. All that moved was the hot breeze in the trees, the wavelets and a cormorant soaring overhead, spying for fish. As he watched the bird it banked, folded its wings, pointed its beak and rocketed into the sea. Within seconds it was back on the surface, a fish thrashing in its beak. It lifted off the water and flew away, gulping the fish in mid-flight. When Mulrenan looked along the beach again he saw two Chinese standing halfway between the water and the tree-line.

His shoes crunching on the pebbles, Mulrenan

awkwardly walked towards them whilst they, in bare feet, easily came towards him.

'Goo' ahftarnoon, Mista' Muw'enan,' Leung greeted him. 'You ge' here fine aw'ight.'

'A good map,' Mulrenan praised him. 'Not hard to follow.'

''Is name Wu,' Leung said, indicating his companion. 'He got w'at you wan'.'

Wu was of coarse and unsavoury appearance. He was taller than most southern Chinese, muscular rather than leanly strong like the local people. He wore the customary black loose trousers of the peasantry, with the waistband folded over but, in his case, additionally fastened by a belt into which was thrust a Chinese-style short sword in a lacquer scabbard. Around his head he wore a sweatband of green cloth and his chest, which was hairless, was bare and bronzed. For such a large man he had surprisingly small hands. If the Chinese had children's pantomimes, Mulrenan thought, this man would be a comic pirate. In real life he was just an ordinary one.

Aware of the etiquette involved, and certain now the metallic click had been the snap of a safety catch, Mulrenan gave the pirate a slight bow, which was exaggeratedly returned.

'He got w'at you wan'.' Leung repeated. 'You wan' see?'

'Of course. Where is it?'

It was plain the man did not have the merchandise on him.

Wu, without taking his eyes off Mulrenan's face — which was unnerving since the Chinese did not stare, for to do so was considered impolite — signalled in the air with his fist. From the trees three more men appeared, two carrying between them a small box. All three had rifles slung across their shoulders: Mulrenan recognized the guns as standard Japanese army weapons.

Lowering the box, they flexed their shoulders to ease them of the weight. Apart from Leung's few words with Mulrenan no one had spoken, but now Wu gave a curt order in an incomprehensible dialect. The two porters lifted the box into the shade of an overhanging tree.

The faded stencil on the lid stated the contents had been ammunition of American manufacture. The box was painted khaki and had metal strengtheners on the corners.

'You got w'at he wan'?' Leung asked.

Mulrenan sat on a boulder in the shadow of the tree.

'Yes. In my car. Up topside.' He jerked his thumb in the direction of the saddle between the two hills above the beach. 'Got plenty. Now you open box.'

Wu bent over and pulled up the catches. One of his henchmen lifted the lid and removed a layer of straw packing. Inside were two ingots of gold and an oblong package.

'Two more goal undah st'aw,' Leung said. 'You opung udder one.'

Feeling under the straw, Mulrenan confirmed the presence of two extra bars. He picked up one of the topmost and studied it. It weighed approximately the correct amount but he was not too bothered: Leung knew if he cheated Mulrenan the latter would be very quick to report him to the topee-wearing Anti-Piracy Guard. The mint marks were correct: American. What Mulrenan did not want was the smelted mish-mash of stolen jewellery. He wanted only fine gold. As he looked at the other three bars he tried to remember when the last American ship had been hit by pirates.

'You wan' know w'ere dis come f'om?' Leung was eager to dispel any doubts. 'Not from shipside. Come f'om Nanking. Ame'ican soyjar paying Wed Chinees soyjar in goo' kwa-lee-tee goal.'

Mulrenan had heard as much: despite their antagonism towards Communist ideology the Yanks were paying the way for the Communist guerillas as well as the Nationalist forces of Generalissimo Chiang Kai-shek. Like all doubtful gamblers, he thought, they were backing both horses to place and win.

'I looksee in package now,' Mulrenan said, picking it out of the straw. With his penknife he cut the twine that bound the tar paper wrapping.

Inside was a crudely carpentered wooden box filled with light brown sawdust. He poked about in the shavings with his finger, a scent rising from the box which he knew to be the aroma of sandalwood. Wherever the sawdust had come from, it had been swept up from the floor of a wood-carver's premises. He lifted what he found from the sawdust, blew the items clean and placed them upon the lid of the ammunition box.

'I weigh them,' he informed Leung and the pirates. From his jacket he produced a small bakelite case containing his delicate set of jewellers' scales. Holding these in one hand he placed each of the stones on the scales, balancing them against little brass weights.

There were six stones in the box: a seventeen-carat cross-cut ruby, not as red as the one he had sold to Antrobus the week before; two cornflower-blue sapphires with a milky lustre suggesting they were of Kashmiri origin — one was just over eighteen carats, the other twenty-eight; of the remaining stones one was a pretty and not very valuable violet-blue fibrolite of Burmese origin and another was a magnificent alexandrite of fifty-seven and a quarter carats. It was bluish rather than verdant green and Mulrenan knew instantly it was a Russian stone.

The last of the stones was smaller than all the others. He assumed it was a white Zircon from Siam, possibly a Japanese white topaz and of no great value. When weighed, it came out at exactly twenty-two carats. As he saw it swinging on the balance, he began to have doubts. It was cut in a style called 'cushion-shaped brilliant' and the sun, bouncing off the sea and shining through the leaves overhead sparkled in it. He realised then it was a diamond and was quick to hide his excitement: the pirate was watching hawklike to size up his reactions.

'Here got two ruby so-so-good. One stone call fibrolite' — he held it out for inspection and Wu looked closely at it: as he did so, Mulrenan knew he was ignorant of the gems — 'one good quality alexandrite. This best number-one stone.'

Leung translated and the pirate grinned, his chipped and

yellowed teeth like old ivory knife handles.

'This one,' Mulrenan concluded, 'white topaz. Good stone, not much cash. Only so-so.'

'Price sti'l good?'

Mulrenan put on a show of indifference. The prearranged price was all right but he had expected more, he said. He would not argue because the gold was fine, but he hoped they would do better next time.

'You take topside to car. We do business.'

'Mus' be chop-chop,' Leung demanded.

Mulrenan readily agreed. The longer they parleyed, the more chance there was of a patrol boat turning into the bay.

He returned the gems to the sandalwood shavings, wrapped the twine around the box and gripped it firmly in his left hand. Wu replaced the ammunition box lid and slapped the catches down. His henchmen heaved it off the ground and set out a different way from that Mulrenan had taken. He realised that they had made him take a longer route so they could ensure he was alone. The trickiest part of their meeting would be at the Ford. Once in possession of payment they might turn on him and Leung, who was after all only the go-between.

For some minutes as they climbed the pathway to the track Mulrenan did not speak. Partly he wanted to save his breath and partly he was preparing himself for trouble.

They reached the car and Mulrenan unlocked the boot. While the pirates inspected the contents he placed the gems in the glove compartment, giving himself two free hands: one would fend off blows, the other was for the small ladies' pistol he had in his trouser pocket.

'We tek,' said Leung.

Mulrenan read out the contents list of the boot, badly pronouncing the Cantonese Alice had translated into the alphabet. He went methodically down the list — bandages, morphine capsules and three hypodermic syringes with needles, cholera and smallpox vaccine, two thousand rounds of 9 millimetre, one thousand of .303, two blocks of opium from the Hong Kong government store and six thousand crisp Hong Kong dollars still in their bank bands.

The pirates unloaded and checked the items.

When they were done, Mulrenan bowed. Now was the moment for the pirate and his three cohorts to make their move, but they did not. Wu returned his bow and the two pirates who had carried the gold loaded it into the car boot. The pirates picked up the cases of cartridges and set off down the pathway. The third brigand carried the first of the medical supplies. Leung spoke to Wu then to Mulrenan.

'Captin Wu say you go now. I see you Kowloon-side two day.'

Mulrenan bowed again, all the while keeping his eyes on Wu.

'Good! Kowloon-side in two days, then,' he confirmed as he straightened. 'You watch out for yourself.'

'I do!' Leung replied. 'Ve'y good looksee for me. For my backside.'

Mulrenan twisted the ignition key and rammed the car into first gear. It swung on to the track and he began the two-mile jolt back to the metalled road.

As he drove down the hill towards the airport at Kai Tak he began to hum. By the time he reached the vehicular ferry pier in Yau Ma Tei he was whistling. The diamond was superb, his previous biggest being a mere five carats. It would be the centrepiece of his collection.

15

At the doorway to the temple precinct, Alice paused. She was reluctant to enter, afraid she might be taken for an inquisitive European rather than a serious devotee. She regretted not having put on a *cheong sam*: her skirt and blouse were conspicuous.

It had been a long while since she had last visited a temple. Regular attendance was not required, as in a Christian church. There were no weekly services to attend, only occasional ceremonies at which participation was not essential. Once in a while it was sensible to pay a visit — and a few cents or dollars, depending on one's means — but the convenience of Oriental gods was that none expected to see worshippers unless they had a specific and pressing need.

The courtyard was busy. The astrologers and fortune-tellers were besieged: there was a major race meeting in the offing and advice from the spirit world was as sought after as tips from the mafoos. Around the gateway were stalls selling amulets and incense, fruit and sweetmeats. Nearby was a group of coolies gambling with two fighting crickets; a few feet away future contestants were chirruping in miniscule bamboo cages.

Within the temple, in the shadows and incense haze, several coolie women were making offerings before the goddess. Their shoulders were protected by squares of hessian which, when they moved, drifted cement dust on to the flagstones and prayer mats.

Alice was not concerned with the fortune-tellers or the goddess, with her moulded plaster army of heavenly followers and demons. She did not want advice but knowledge, and she knew from whom to obtain it.

Behind the temple was a smaller courtyard. It was paved with cracked slabs and, in a corner against the ancient stone wall that surrounded the sacred ground there was an incinerator made from tar drums beaten flat. Assorted rubbish — rotted gilt altar rails and several broken lamps and urns — were piled next to the incinerator awaiting collection by the garbage coolies who would sell the wood for kindling. A lean-to had been constructed against the mildewed wall out of pieces of wood and cloth and it was to this Alice wended her way.

From the cracks in the flimsy structure eddied a faint blue smoke, disappearing where it met a beam of sunlight cast between the roofs of two adjacent buildings. Alice had not visited this person before and had only come to hear of her through Ah Shun whose sister had recommended a consultation. Not knowing quite what to expect, Alice

110

knocked on the roof of the hovel, at its tallest not five feet high.

A crone stuck her head out from between the two lengths of sacking which served as a door.

'Good afternoon, madam,' Alice greeted her in Cantonese, with the politeness she had been told the old woman expected.

The response was a grunt followed by a curt, 'What do you want?'

'Your advice,' said Alice. 'Your interpretation of an omen.'

The old woman brushed the sacking aside and staggered into the sunlight. She was crippled and bent, her hair matted and her skin unwashed; she was dressed in rags that would have shamed a coolie working the docks, but her fingernails were long.

'Why does a foreign devil's woman want to know such things?' was her next question.

'I am Chinese,' Alice responded indignantly.

This was greeted by another grunt of disbelief and annoyance.

'I did not ask you for your parents' names,' the hag replied bluntly. 'I said you were a foreigner's woman.' Alice made no comment but prised apart the clasp of her handbag.

'Twenty-five cents!' said the crone with finality, indicating she was not prepared to discuss terms.

Alice held up a blue dollar bill between her fingers.

'A moth coloured like the moon,' she said quietly.

'With thin green lines on its wings?'

'Yes.'

'Were its feelers like fern leaves?'

'Yes.'

'Was its body furry as a rat's?'

'Yes.'

'What did the moon moth do?'

In detail, Alice recounted her experience. The old woman pondered for over a minute. Birds twittered in a gnarled tree growing against the temple wall and, in a nearby tenement, a child started crying.

'The moth can mean but one thing. For some it is a sign of much wealth and wisdom. For you it is a warning.'

With trepidation, Alice waited for the old woman to continue but she did not. To encourage her, Alice held out the dollar bill.

'All of this if you tell me everything.'

'It is good you did not kill it,' the woman began, warming to her task and the possibility of a whole dollar. 'White moths are the souls of the dead. It is unlucky to kill them. They are not ill-omened — like the big brown moth with windows in its wings through which devils can look — but bring messages. The way this one came to you, and stayed by you, is lucky. It will remember you saved it from death.'

She paused for effect. Information imparted rapidly earned less than that strung out over ten minutes. The longer the telling, the greater the credence and the larger the reward.

'Be warned of things that fly and settle not like birds or butterflies which alight quickly. You must beware of things that fly by gliding. By night they are worse than by day. In the sunlight, you must heed them. At night, you must drive them away. But do not kill them or try to harm them. If you do, they will harm you and those you love.'

Alice handed over the dollar bill. The woman held it to the sun to check the watermark then rustled the paper between her fingers. A whole dollar for her knowledge was rare: it might just be counterfeit.

'If you leave them well alone, they will work for you, rid you of those things you do not like or no longer want. In this way, they can make you rich and wealthy and give you much. Even a son, perhaps . . .'

'What if I touch a moon moth?'

'Rub your hands with seaweed picked at the low-water mark. I can sell you some . . . One dollar.'

Thanking her, but without taking up the offer of the seaweed, Alice left the temple and walked slowly home along Hollywood Road, considering her confusing and contradictory information. At an apothecary's shop she purchased, as a precaution, a linen bag of herbs. The hand-written label claimed the contents would drive insects away. Little moths attracted to lamps were allowable. They did not glide. Only the big ones flew barely moving their wings.

16

Alice dreaded the meeting. She had mixed feelings about her elder half-brother which time had both dulled and confused. Although she had only seen him during the long school holidays of his teenage years she had grown to like and then to love him. When he had returned to the Far East she had hoped they would become firm friends, bonded by fraternal love; but Alec Cowley had not responded. With the death of her parents — and his mother — she had felt alone and afraid and had turned to him. But he had ignored her pleas for help.

Being Eurasian with a Chinese father, she had taken the only course she could see open to her at the time. Quite how she had slipped into the life of a courtesan she could not remember clearly. Her first guide had been a middle-aged man working for one of the hongs. He had been a former acquaintance of her mother and had given her love, protection, money and a roof over her head until his wife had found out and threatened to talk first to his employers, secondly to her friends and thirdly to a solicitor unless he repaired his way. True to form, he did: an enraged spouse bent on revenge, a career with a hong and a concubine in Kennedy Town did not mix.

The rain was warm, the huge drops frequent but not pelting, splashing upon the ground, the first to fall leaving radiated blots on the stones. As they hit the roof of her sedan chair they thumped hollowly. Through a gap in the curtain Alice watched the water bounce off the front carrier's flat hat.

By the time she reached the building in which Alec lived the rain had eased. Ah Shun paid off the two chairs and Alice entered the porch, knocking upon the varnished panel which bore his business card in a chromium-plated frame.

The door was opened by Alec himself. He was shorter than she remembered, and his trimmed blonde hair had been whitened by the sun, but his eyes were just as piercingly blue. His skin was more tanned than she could recall and he had a bushy, masculine moustache. His mouth was a thin line, his lips without colour. He stepped aside and ushered her into his lounge. There was an awkward silence.

'Will you sit down?' were the first words he spoke.

She sat in an uncomfortable leather armchair she knew had once been his father's: it was in good condition and she realised he must have had it in a cold store for years. As she bent to place her handbag on the floor beside it, the smell of saddle soap rose from the hide. By her face the polished studs down the front of the arms shone dully.

'You haven't changed very much,' she said weakly. 'You look very well.'

'Quite surprisingly, I'd say. Malaya is not exactly Cheltenham — a health spa,' he added.

She realised he had explained the reference, assuming she, being not fully English, would miss it, and that stung her. Any normal brother would have given her a hug and a peck on the cheek, as they did in the films — as they did in real life.

'You're with the bank here now?' she asked needlessly.

'I've been promoted and am likely to stay here for a good few years. If all goes well.'

Alec made his last sentence take on a meaning she was unable to misconstrue. He saw in her a means by which things might not 'go well'.

He rang the bell by the small fireplace. Almost immediately the door to the kitchen opened and an elderly amah came shuffling in. She placed a tea tray on a bamboo table and promptly left.

'My houseboy's mother. I keep her on as a supernumary. Do you take milk or lemon? It's Indian tea.'

'Milk, please.'

She felt cowed, insignificant. Everything he said, even the type of tea he served, seemed antagonistic.

While he poured she gazed around the room. It was spartan. There were no niceties, no frills or ornamentation. The furniture was heavy and plain, a mixture of solid European-made pieces, like the armchair and the dining-room table by the window, and cheap local imitations or makeshift pieces like the tray table. There were two pictures on the wall, one a large, poorly executed painting of the spires of Oxford in a clumsy frame, the other a long thin photograph of the entire pupil and teaching body of Alec's public school. Somewhere, she thought, in that blur of puerile faces was his own, glowering at her over the years. The dining-room table was strewn with papers and manila folders: obviously, he brought a good deal of office work home.

Handing her a cup and saucer, he said, 'I hope you are keeping well?'

'Yes.'

'I'm sorry I seldom replied to your letters. Pressure of work.'

It had been at least five years since she had stopped writing to him. His silence had finally broken her will to correspond. Now he was speaking as if a lapse of only a few months was involved.

'When Mother died I seemed to want to be alone,' he explained. 'Life's not been good to either of us.'

Alice noticed how he referred to their mother in abstract terms. There was no possessive pronoun to show they were talking of his mother, their joint parent.

'Especially not to me,' she said, hoping she sounded reproachful.

'I've never really had a home I could look back to for safety,' he said, ignoring her implications. 'When my father died I believed I was cheated of it somehow. That was increased when Mother went and ' — his momentary pause spoke more than words could have done — 'married your father. It was a great shock to me suddenly to have another

115

father. And a Chinese one.'

'My father,' she answered with pride, 'offered you his love. He wanted to look after you. It was you inheriting so much of your father's money in trust, for your education, giving you a degree of independence, that really upset things.'

'He gave me nothing else,' he retorted fiercely, balancing his cup and saucer in one shaking hand. 'Your father gave me no financial help when the money began to run short. Mother did. Granny paid up with money sent by Mother.'

'The money originated from my father,' Alice said, defending not only her father but also, she felt, herself. 'He transferred it through my mother. She had no money of her own. They sent all they had. That was why, in the last years, they were so hard up. You have no idea what they — both of them — sacrificed for you to carry on in your school.'

She wanted to say the sacrifice had been made at her expense, too.

'He could have sent it himself.'

'Would you have accepted it? You were,' she decided to risk it, 'you *are* awfully stubborn sometimes.'

'Am I?' Alec replied. He stood up and walked to the window. Rain was sheeting across the façade of the Peninsula Hotel. A squall was blotting out the clock tower on the railway station. To the right, Kowloon Bay was clear. The sky overhead was lighter and it appeared the weather was breaking. There would be a moist and humid end to the afternoon.

'I don't want to speak to you about the past,' he said, not facing her but the window and the table laden with documents, balance sheets and loan certificates, 'but about the present. In particular about the piano-player Mulrenan.'

'Sean?'

'Do you know who — do you know what he is?'

'Yes, I do.'

'He's a crook.'

She could see as well as hear Alec's temper rising, for his ears were turning pink.

'A downright bloody crook,' he continued. 'A thief, a wheeler-dealer with no scruples. He's a con-man and an out-and-out bounder.'

She stifled a grin at his last description and wondered if he would next accuse Mulrenan of being a cad.

'He doesn't mind whom he hurts or how deeply. He despises everyone and tramples on those who get in his way. He's only a nightclub pianist made good. And he's Irish.'

'Half-Irish,' she corrected him. 'His mother was English.'

'Makes no difference,' Alec dismissed her. 'He's still a crook. He's nothing better than a gangster and you're no better than a gangster's moll.'

She felt the blood drain from her cheeks, to return with a rush. Now she was furious, with the suppressed anger all Chinese have bottled up within them.

Putting her tea cup on the floor, she stood up and said to his back, 'How dare you, you pompous little man! You dare criticise him and you dare degrade me? Where were you when I — as you would no doubt put it — turned to whoring for a living? You were already in a bank, in Malaya, earning a steady salary. You didn't send a wreath to your own mother's funeral, let alone your stepfather's. You didn't write to see how I was. You didn't offer to help me. You ignored me. I didn't even get a telegram of condolence.'

He turned to face her and she involuntarily stepped back, kicking her cup over. Tea spilled on to the varnished floorboards.

'I wasn't good enough for you.' she continued. 'You, the high-and-mighty bank man rising fast through a world of ledgers and figures, playing with other people's money. Now you think you're in a fix. You've come back to Hong Kong where you find your half-sister's a tart living with a criminal, and it might rock your selfish boat.'

The rattle of the spilling cup had been heard in the kitchen, along with the rest of their conversation. The door opened and the houseboy appeared with a cloth and bowl.

'Get out!' Alec roared. 'I told you to stay in your quarters. Get out, damn you!'

The houseboy scuttled off. Alec waited until he could hear the outer kitchen door close before he spoke.

'You think so? I could — ' he began to threaten.

The interruption had calmed her a little, given her time to consider her tactics. She still felt aggrieved and angry, was eager to continue her attack.

'You could what?' she brazened. 'Have Sean arrested? Throw him in Stanley jail? He has more powerful friends than you think. Have me arrested? I don't think so.

'Consider this, too. Why do you think I've not already ruined things for you? I need only let slip at one of the parties I go to with Sean that you're my half-brother, that your mother married a Chinese after your father's death, and you'll be marked by them and that'll be your end. Your father dying bravely in the war in France, and gaining The Military Cross, won't make a jot of difference. And why have I kept silent? Because I love you. You are my sole relative. Only a half-brother, and not much of a brother, but all I've got. In you I see our mother. Not just "Mother" or "your mother" but *ours*.

'I know you hate me, resent me. You always have. You don't just miss your father, even now you're a man, but your mother, too. She didn't betray you by remarrying. Even a Chinese. She gave you competition in the shape of my father. And me. And you couldn't — you can't — bear it.'

'If you tell anyone . . .' he threatened.

'Chrissie Burroughs knows.'

'I can trust her.'

'Why?' Alice asked. 'Have you slept with her? Before the old man wed her?'

For a moment she thought Alec would slap her. His hand rose level with his chest and opened out but he lowered it again and she knew her statement had hit the mark.

They were silent for some minutes. He sat in his chair again, withdrew into himself and brooded on his own thoughts just as he had as a boy. She could remember the times when he went out early in the morning, sometimes even before the servants were stirring, and did not return until late in the evening. She had asked him once where he went and what he did. He replied he spent the day walking through the streets or taking to the paths on the hills behind Kowloon. He claimed to have walked long distances, to the coast beyond Ma On Shan or to Port Shelter. She had not known whether to believe him but one day he took their Brownie camera and later he showed her photographs of Sha Tin taken from across the inlet on which the village stood. When she asked him what he did when he walked so far he replied that he thought; when questioned about his thoughts he would make no answer but would scowl and glare at his feet in the embarrassed, angry ways boys of his age seemed to have.

'Mother let me down,' he said quietly, breaking their silence. 'She badly let me down.'

'What do you mean?'

'When we were young — you were nearly five and I was ten and about to go back home to school — do you remember? Mother used to say to your father, "Look at them. Alec and Alice. What a pretty pair!" Always me and you. She even rolled the words together. "Alecunalis." She took away . . . She let me down.'

'She was only looking at her children. Mothers do that. They love each equally. Even if they have different fathers.'

'Him,' Alec said bitterly. 'He wasn't a real father. He was a Chinese.'

It was then Alice realised the dilemma her mother's second marriage must have caused Alec. Before the Great War, he had been a member of the ruling classes, living in a house on The Peak, with his own servant and toys made specially for him. His own mafoo groomed his own pony. His family had their own sedan chairs with their own coolies. When his father had died he had to leave the heights of the mountain and move lower down.

His stepfather had a house below Magazine Gap, fewer servants and no sedan chairs. When the pony died it was not replaced. He was not mocked or ignored when he began attending school in Kowloon but he was, in subtle ways,

119

treated differently. The teacher glanced at him in an odd manner and the other pupils seldom invited him to their homes. He did not go to birthday or Christmas parties, to beach outings and picnics. Alec had gone from being a ruler to one of the ruled. His mother now associated with the class which had previously provided the servants. It was intolerable to him, even though, when she married, he had been only four years old.

'Mother went native,' he said, his voice low with passion, pain and undisguised disgust. 'That your father was a Christian Chinese was merely fortuitous. That he was reasonably well off was sheer luck. She was never very practical about money. It still remains she married out of her class, out of her race.'

His remark wounded Alice. She knew he regarded her as an inferior who, by circumstance, was jumped up beyond her place. She was not part English in his eyes. She was Chinese. A chink, a Wanchai tart. Better in a *cheong sam* than a decent skirt. What he really hated, she realised, was that she was a part of him, his blood and flesh in her.

'You hate me because I'm the result of that union,' she said, putting her empty cup on the saucer and setting it on the tray.

Involuntarily, she sat down so he need not look up at her. She wanted him to see her concern for him.

'We can't be blamed for what our parents did,' she went on. 'We are presented with our lives and must make the best of them.'

'That's what I'm trying to do!' He turned on her with a fury he was finding difficult to contain. 'Only you and your sugar-daddy are ruining it.'

'Don't be so ridiculous!' she exclaimed. 'How on earth can we be harming you? So far as we both are aware, only you and I and Chrissie Burroughs know of the connection.'

'You're jeopardising it. Your lothario has only to get a grudge against me and — puff!' He snapped his fingers like a magician. 'It'll be all over Hong Kong like the smell of a *nullah*.'

'He won't,' she said with a calm assurance. 'I won't let him.'

120

'You won't let him! What the hell has it to do with you?'

'If I ask him not to, he won't.'

Alec glared at her, his dislike for her narrowing his sharp blue eyes.

'You expect him to listen to you, take notice of the wishes of his whore?'

She flinched then said, quietly, 'Your trouble is you don't know the world. You have lived in your protected school, in your protective bank, and you don't know what it's like outside. You think the worst thing in the world is to have a half-Chinese sister who might let out the secret. A secret, I might add, some people must already know. There are people here who knew our mother before she remarried, and just because you've hidden in an English school and a Malayan business house doesn't mean they've forgotten. But that's by the way.'

He leaned back theatrically in his chair, linked his fingers in his lap and started to tap his thumbs together. He fixed his eyes on her like a headmaster annoyed with the repeated excuses of a miscreant pupil.

'Sean will listen to me. I know that because he knows I love him' — Alec snorted at this — 'and he loves me, in his way.

'You see, in the real world, where you have to fend for yourself and not be cossetted by parents and employers, you learn the art of survival. I have learned that. I have had to. I've not had Sean all the while, you know. If I look back on it, I've fucked' — it was his turn to flinch: such words were not a part of his vocabulary — 'some of the best Englishmen in Hong Kong. And a few from Singapore. Maybe,' she added from devilment, 'a few from your bank. Maybe high officials, men with influence.'

She saw from his face that he was keeping up with her insinuations. She watched as the doubt crept over him that perhaps he was where he was now because of his half-sister's pillow-talk.

'In my kind of life, Alec, more than in yours, you need insurance. I have that insurance. It's knowledge. No,' she too now leaned back in her armchair, 'Sean will listen. If I want him to.'

There was utter silence in the room. The sun had cut through the cloudy sky and the verandah, upon which geraniums were growing in green-glazed pots, was flooded with light. The sun striking the tiles drew a faint wisp of steam which was rising where the floor was warming and drying.

'You see, Alec,' she continued, 'if you had kept quiet about your return I might not have known of you being here. As it is, now I do. I am also made aware of your intense jealousy of Sean and his success, your hatred of me and your disrespectful attitude towards your mother and my father. Or their memory. In China,' she knew her next words would hit him hard, 'it is not right for a child to be disrespectful of its parents. Especially a firstborn son.'

It was then Alec must have known she had the best of him. His discomfort clearly increased at her next words.

'Sean and I aren't staying much longer in Hong Kong. As I said, if you hadn't sent me your message I mightn't have discovered you were here. We're moving to Macau in nine weeks.'

Alec made no comment. He sat in his armchair, morose and despodent. The meeting had gone badly awry.

'It's not that I don't love you, not that I dislike you,' he said defensively. 'I'm just worried, that's all. You know the way things are, how people talk. Even Sir Robert Ho Tung himself is a Eurasian but there's still . . . I have to maintain . . . I'm in the yacht club, joined the Volunteer Defence Force, am up for membership of the Hong Kong Club . . .'

She gazed at him. His head was lowered and he was staring at his shoes. She felt almost guilty she had won.

The leather armchair creaked as she leaned down to pick up her handbag from the floor, then stood to leave.

At the door he said, 'I'm sorry I caused you . . .' Yet no other words came.

'When you need me,' she told him, 'I'll help you, though I don't expect that occasion will arise. I don't believe you'll let it. But should it, remember I am of your family. I don't bear you any ill will, Alec. I just feel very sorry for you.'

She could not have been more damning, and he knew it.

Doing Bizniz

1

The rickshaw coolies struggled up the slope from the Rua Praia do Bom Parto to the hotel and stopped, bathed in sweat, at the main entrance. There were few hills in Macau up which they would willingly pull their loads. More usually, passengers took sedan chairs but Mulrenan, prepared to pay a higher than normal tip, had hired rickshaws.

An old, colonial building, the Bela Vista Hotel was constructed in the fashion of well-to-do merchants' town houses in Lisbon or Oporto. In keeping with its name, the hotel possessed one of the finest panoramas in Macau. Flanked by trees, there was beneath the main verandah a terrace upon which a smooth, stone dance floor was surrounded by a white-washed balustrade, beyond which was a drop to a road along an embankment and the sea. Two miles away rose the low island of Taipa and, yet further away, the larger island of Coloane. Above the hotel, on the summit of Colina da Penha, was the Bishop's residence and the Penha Church.

Mulrenan, handsome and debonair, stepped from his rickshaw and took Alice's hand. He was wearing a cream suit with a dark blue shirt. His jacket was unbuttoned, his belt and brown shoes glistening in the lamplight shining from the lobby. Only as he bent to lift her evening bag from the rickshaw seat did she catch a fleeting glimpse of the equally brown and polished butt of a small revolver in a holster behind his left hip.

He paid the rickshaws off, the coolies bowing at the generosity of his *kumshaw*. It was equivalent to half the fare:

the usual tip was ten per cent.

Halting on the bottom step of the hotel entrance, he gazed down into her eyes. She had not lifted her foot off the square stone paving of the road and was even smaller against him than usual.

'One thing you must always remember,' he said authoritatively, replacing his wallet. 'It's best to be in with everyone. Not only the governor's men and the administrators, the police and the businessmen but also with the coolies. Those below you. You never know when you may need them. The next time we're caught in the rain and want a rickshaw, one of those coolies will see us. They won't oblige simply in the hope of another large tip: they'll help because the last tip was great. One day, when you or I are down on our luck, they'll carry us for nothing. A tip is not an act of gratitude, it's a contract for future considerations.'

From within the hotel wafted the music of a string quartet, the waltz increasing in volume as they ascended the steps.

'Strauss — the young one,' Mulrenan commented. ' "Wine, Women and Song": typical that such a vacuous musician should turn such masculine subjects into sentimental rubbish!'

Alice had not visited the Bela Vista and the grandeur of the hotel filled her with a joyful excitement. Mulrenan had been there on a number of occasions — he had even played the piano one night at the request of the owner and those with whom he was dining. The regular musician had been down with malaria, one of the scourges of the Pearl River estuary.

At the top of the steps was the foyer from which a staircase with filigree wrought iron bannisters wound upwards to a landing, its ceiling supported by classical pillars. The first floor was only a little higher than the foyer and had a balustrade along the corridors. The entrance appeared like a picture Alice had seen in a magazine of the inner court of an Italian renaissance house only neater, more compact. The walls and ceiling were white, the archways and pillars picked out in ochre. Upon stands, green glazed pots held

126

deep green palm fronds. The electric lights were extinguished — by design or one of the regular power failures — and the entire scene was illuminated by thick candles like those found on altars. To the left was the reception desk and the door of the restaurant and bar.

'Senhor Mulrenan, good evening,' the proprietor's son greeted them. 'It is good to see you once more. How are you keeping?'

'I'm well. Thank you.'

'We have your table, senhor, the usual one. By the window. Also, as you requested, we have reserved you a table for two by the dance floor. For later.'

'Magnificent!' Mulrenan exclaimed and stepped forwards. His every move, Alice noted, was full of confidence in his success. To him, a good table in the best restaurant was proof that he was at the top.

The restaurant was candlelit and close. The fans overhead swung slowly, so the candle flames danced but did not die. Upon the tables, most of which were already occupied, crystal glittered and the moving silver of cutlery and raised glasses captured pinpoints of light and cast them on to the walls. Many of the diners were Europeans, the majority of them Portuguese, but there were a few Chinese present as guests. The former wore evening dress, the men in dinner jackets or evening suits and their women in silk: the latter were dressed in classical Chinese costume, the women in demure ankle-length *cheong sams* and the men clad in the long cotton robes of the official, decorated with authoritorial cloth buttons and silk cuffs.

As she walked between the tables, Alice was acutely aware of her own silk dress as it rustled like dry bamboo leaves in a cool breeze. The music on the terrace had stopped and, in its absence, she was certain the noise of her dress was drawing attention. Several men glanced at her, their eyes momentarily lingering before returning to their partners.

She had not attended many functions with Mulrenan since they had moved from Hong Kong. He preferred her to stay in the house, Ah Shun seeing to the purchasing of food and clothes. He told Alice he wanted the house to be lived in, never to seem empty. It was important, he said, for appearances. He was loath even to leave the amah as a substitute.

But then, one night after they had lived in Macau for some weeks, he had slept restlessly and, in the early hours, woken and — as silently as he could — dressed and left the house. Her mind seethed with curiosity. She longed to follow him yet did not dare risk discovery. He was gone until just before first light, returning to shuffle and scrape about in the next room for well over an hour. He finally crept back into the bed and she, feigning sleep, felt his skin hot and his hands rough upon her side. As his body cooled it grew clammy, like a corpse sweating after death.

From that surreptitious night onwards, he ceased insisting Alice stay in the house. He began to take her to parties in the homes of his Portuguese and Chinese acquaintances, to see a performance of 'Don Giovanni' at the Teatro Dom Pedro V, to the gambling rooms in the Cental Hotel and to restaurants.

Whenever they visited the Central Hotel, Mulrenan's delight in gambling was overwhelming, but the gaming scared her for she became so wrapped up in it, so involved that she sensed she was losing control of herself. He often claimed she was his luck, his charm.

'Well, Beautiful Cloverleaf,' he said one evening, inventing an Oriental sounding name for her, 'how do we bet? Give us a touch of the "Miss Macaos" .'

'Red seven,' she advised for the colour and the number were both very lucky for the Chinese: but he chastised her.

'No! Be serious!'

'Manque then. Or black seventeen.'

When the wheel spun, Mulrenan's excitement was intense. A suppressed energy burned in him. The backs of his hands steeled and his cheek muscles set.

If they won he congratulated her: if a loss was incurred, he accepted the blame.

'Gambling is a drug,' she warned after the evening's

gaming and a run of heavy winning.

'Like religion,' he replied.

'What do you mean?'

' "Religion is the opium of the people." Karl Marx.'

'Then gambling is another sort of poppy. You must beware of it or it will destroy you.'

'All my life is a gamble,' Mulrenan answered. 'That's why I do what I do, why I like it. So long as the odds are loaded my way and the luck holds . . .'

'And if it doesn't?'

'It will, so long as I have my Precious Shamrock by my side.'

As well as his companion and mistress, Alice was a social decoration and a talisman: it was difficult for her at such times not to share in his boundless optimism.

Mulrenan grew eager to show her off, to introduce her as his woman. He was never seen with another and it was assumed he had no other, so people believed she was his wife. She called herself Alice Mulrenan when it was appropriate and had done so without asking his permission. He did not react the first time she gave the name and so she believed he either was indifferent to her airs and graces or secretly cared and liked them.

Much to Alice's surprise and pleasure, Mulrenan was a changed man in Macau. In Hong Kong, he had always been on edge, always angry at those British with whom he dealt and towards whom he was privately contemptuous if outwardly overflowing with bonhomie. His temper remained on a short fuse. He had been offhand with her, carelessly — even deliberately — cruel in his remarks, selfish when they made love and generous only when there were others to witness it. She held dear in her memory that afternoon before the races when he had given her the amethyst and diamond ring. It had been the nearest he had come to showing her love, a deeper emotion than dull hatred or dismissive contempt.

As she sat down at the table in the candlelight, a waiter holding her chair, she remembered what he had said that day, how he loved the Chinese in her, but when the English blood presented itself . . . perhaps, she thought, in Macau where there were far fewer British, she did not remind him so much of them.

Mulrenan put aside the wine list and opened the menu, surveying it with a cursory but critical eye.

'What will you have, Alice?' he asked and he started to read the list of those dishes he thought she would prefer.

It occurred to her, as his voice pronounced the Portuguese names, how she would be so happy if, instead of always using her first name, he would sometimes call her 'darling' or 'dearest' or even 'dear' but he did not, not even when they slept together.

'I'll have whatever you have,' she said. 'And the same to drink but not a whisky first.'

'You're not adventurous enough,' he scolded her. 'You've got to take risks. Avoid the known all the time. If you don't step out you'll never learn, never progress. Why not have the bacalhau?'

'No,' she answered, then added cautiously, 'What is it?'

'It's fish,' he said noncommittally, hoping she would agree without asking how it was prepared.

'No,' she repeated. 'I'll have what you eat.'

He was tempted, as a teasing punishment, to order the Goanese chicken which was cooked in red chillies but that would have punished himself, too. He ordered instead lobster soup followed by grilled rabbit. The wine he requested, with a large scotch, was a bottle of Mateus Rosé, chilled and light of taste as well as colour, the label depicting a Portuguese villa similar to many of the older Macanese houses. When it was poured into glasses, it reminded him of the delicate pink of Japanese rose quartz, especially one stone that had passed through his hands during their last weeks in Hong Kong. It was virtually unclouded. Antrobus had bought it for his wife.

They talked only of everyday matters as they ate. Mulrenan had tutored her in how to speak in public, and of what to speak. They discussed the war in Europe, but only briefly, and the progress of the Japanese through China in a little more detail. She told him about a Somerset Maugham novel she had recently read called 'The Painted Veil', set in Hong Kong and China.

'It's ever so sad when Walter goes,' Alice reported. 'His last words were "The dog it was that died." He was the poor wretched dog.'

Mulrenan had no time for the fantasy of emotion. Facts were of more interest, more importance.

'There're plenty to fit that description,' he said. 'You only have to look around you. What did he die of?'

'Cholera,' she answered.

'Not surprising,' was his reply.

They did not discuss gold or gemstones. Or the British. When she wondered about the weather and the possibility of a storm, he chided her for mentioning an English topic.

When they had eaten and cups of coffee were placed before them, he leaned back in his chair and unbuttoned his jacket. She noticed he was careful not to let it hang loose and away from his body on the left side.

'You are very pretty tonight, Alice,' he complimented her. 'Did you enjoy the meal?'

She nodded, sipping her coffee. It was strong and black, hot and sweet and scorched her tongue. To relieve the pain she drank from a glass of iced water served with the coffee.

As she put down her glass, he leaned across the table, smiled and said very quietly, 'Find me a green zircon about ten carats.'

'Now?' she asked incredulously.

'Yes,' he commanded and he leaned away from her, taking up his cup as if he had just whispered a lover's line to her or reached for his coffee.

'May I have a liqueur?' she said.

He moved round in his chair to the right, his left arm automatically holding his jacket in to his waist. The maitre d'hotel caught his eye and Alice watched as he approached.

'What would madam like?'

She looked casually around as if thinking, then replied, 'A benedictine, please.'

'One benedictine, one cognac, please,' Mulrenan said.

As the maitre d'hotel took their empty wine bottle with him towards the bar, Alice said quietly, 'There isn't one. But there is, I think, a green tourmaline of about the same size.'

'Well done!' he congratulated her, keeping his voice quiet. 'You're dead right. Magna cut, too.'

'Marquise cut,' she corrected him. 'You're thinking of the lady by the door to the balcony. I'm talking about the one with the man in the dinner jacket with the bow tie that's coming undone.'

Mulrenan used the arrival of the liqueurs to cover his glancing. When the waiter had left, he chortled.

'You're learning, Alice. By God! You're learning.'

'I'm trying.'

Mulrenan had been tutoring Alice in the judging of gems. For a fortnight, they had sat together for two hours every evening as he conducted a course in practical gemology. He had given her stones to handle, to study, to analyse, weigh and value. He had instructed her in the various methods of shaping different stones until she was conversant with such terms as 'flat convex cabochon', 'Ceylon cut' or 'scissors cut with truncated corners.' She could differentiate between a cross facet and a star facet, understood what a culet was: refraction and birefringence, the Mohs scale and density entered her vocabulary and she discovered that a topaz could be not only yellow but also pink, blue and colourless and that which appeared at first to be a ruby might be a red spinel, a red zircon, a red tourmaline — also called a rubellite — or a garnet.

It pleased Mulrenan that she was not only an avid but also an accomplished pupil, quick to acquire knowledge and adept at using it, her continuing education obtained as and when he bought new varieties of stones.

On the terrace, the string quartet was tuning up once more and Mulrenan stood, eased her chair from under her, and they went out on to the verandah.

Around the dance floor below them the tables were decorated with coloured clothes and thin candles inside glass holders. Another waltz commenced and a dozen couples were soon gliding to and fro across the smooth stone.

On the sea between the hotel and Taipa, sharp pricks of light bobbed and reflected off the water from the sampans of night fishermen, each attracting fish as a street lamp does moths. As if attempting to mimic the dancers and the fishermen, the sky beyond Coloane flickered with heat lightning.

'Do you know,' Mulrenan said, 'this hotel is built on the site of a castle?'

She shook her head.

'It is. There was a fort constructed here in 1622. It was called The Bom Parto Fortress. Seven years later, the Portuguese built another one around the headland there,' he pointed to where Barra Hill sloped to the sea, 'to protect the Porto Interior. I suppose this one fell into disrepair. I can't understand why they built it in the first place. The obvious spot was at Barra Point.'

'To protect the bay here?' she suggested.

'Maybe,' he replied, 'but this was never the real harbour.'

He spoke with conviction, utter certainty, as if seventeenth century military strategy was a topic in which he was learned. His confidence, Alice knew, came not from knowledge but from bluff. So much of his life was based upon bravado, carrying off a deal by sheer artful effrontery. In some ways, she loved him for this adventure in which he allowed her a share: in other ways, she was frightened by it. Life was so fragile and impermanent yet he regarded it with such nonchalance that she was sometimes filled with a sudden, fleeting yet terrible apprehension. Always lurking at the back of her mind was the fear that when something went wrong it would do so catastrophically.

Later, they danced together for the first time since they had left Hong Kong and she enjoyed their wicked abandon, while half the world was at war. It was after midnight when two rickshaws took them home.

2

The house Mulrenan bought was a typical Macanese building on the corner of Rua dos Curtidores and Rua do Patane. It was two storeys high with a balcony running the two sides facing the street: the railings were alternate wrought iron bars and curlicues, supporting eight iron rods that held up the narrow, gutterless roof. When it rained, water streamed on to the balcony and either spattered down into the street or seeped under the doors which were shuttered and painted light blue. The rooms were spacious, tall and cool in the summer heat but promising to be chilly in winter. The building had a gable with a stucco plaster pattern borrowed from classical Greek architecture. It was a building that could have been transported from the side streets of Lisbon, stone by stone and tile by tile, to be reconstructed on the South China coast by a homesick trader now two hundred years in his grave.

In choosing the house, Mulrenan had been careful. It was not a grand residence like some available for one with his money, yet nor was it a humble abode. It was respectable but not ostentatious, suggesting only a modicum of wealth. It was ideal for his purposes, giving him a sound background and placing him a cut above the other expatriates.

As soon as the war in Europe had been declared, a number of enemy nationals fled from Hong Kong to Macau. Wary of British colonial reaction, the Germans had gone first to be followed by a few Austrians and Italians. As the months of 1941 passed and the Japanese inexorably pushed their forces deeper in China, others began to feel Hong Kong might not be so secure, and they too began to move. The Germans and the Italians had long since travelled on, overland from Macau through China, Mongolia and Siberia towards Europe, or eastwards across the Pacific. Their vacated houses and apartments were quickly occupied by those with neutral, 'Third National' passports: the Irish, the Portuguese and Portuguese Chinese in Hong Kong, the Russians and those whose homelands had been overrun — the Poles and Czechs, Romanians and Hungarians. They were joined by the wealthy Chinese and Indians who held British passports. Most of the latter only used Macau as the Germans had, as a springboard for home, but the remainder stayed.

Many of those electing to settle in Macau, for the time being at least as they told themselves and each other, believed they were just immigrants. In fact, however, the Portuguese enclave presented them with Hobson's choice: they could either stay there as refugees or return to Europe and be refugees at home. But they would not accept they were refugees for that carried the stigma with which their nations had been branded, off and on, for centuries.

As for Mulrenan, he was definitely not a refugee. He was not on the run. He was merely transferring his business activities to a new and, he hoped, more profitable arena.

Mulrenan had purchased the building as it stood, with the furniture and fittings, from a Chinese who had bought it from a Portuguese who had bought it back from the German to whom he had sold it only six months before. Its value had trebled in less than a year. Mulrenan paid for it indirectly in gold coin. He had not wanted the vendor to realise he was in the possession of a large quantity of gold, not to mention gemstones, so he sold the gold through a compradore to a dealer in Hong Kong who credited his account at the Hongkong and Shanghai Bank. From there he had transferred the money by draft to the vendor's Portuguese-owned bank in the Avenida Almeida Ribeiro. He hinted, as he collected the deeds, that the transaction left him somewhat stretched, information he knew would soon be common knowledge. It was never wise as a newcomer, he told Alice, to appear well-heeled: if one gave such an impression, the spongers and the greedy would be on the scent in hours.

His canny business sense saw that he purchased the entire house, including the ground floor. He and Alice lived upstairs and used three rooms downstairs, one as living quarters for Ah Shun, one as a kitchen and one as a storeroom into which they crammed all they had brought with them that would not fit in their apartment. Chairs, a table, sealed tea chests full of odds and ends liberally scattered with camphor balls, bundles and packages were fitted piecemeal into the room until it was impossible to enter without first removing something. A fourth room, opening onto the street, Mulrenan rented out as a shop.

They had sold some of the furniture that had come with the house but Alice had insisted they retain those items that suited the building. For the first few days of their occupation, she and Ah Shun, with the help of a boy hired from the rank of coolies that lined up in the street every day hoping for employment, moved chairs and beds, couches and divans, tables and chests to and fro between the echoing rooms, the walls bare and the floorboards uncarpeted, up and down the narrow unlit staircase.

It was on the afternoon of the third day when Alice finally believed matters were in order, that she had a home once more, one in which she and Mulrenan were partners. The upheaval of sorting and arranging had robbed her of the realisation that this was, indeed, their first joint home.

Opening the shutters on the room she had chosen for their bedroom, she stepped on to the balcony. The sun blazed, the shadow of the roof cutting across her toes as if drawn by a sharp knife. The heat and humidity of the day struck her and caught her breath.

The street below, Rua do Patane, was not as busy as in the morning. Most of the coolies had departed either to work or to console themselves with opium or to sleep under the shade of the trees in the squares of the city or along the waterfront of the Porto Interior or the Praia Grande. Several foodstalls were set up in the narrow shade of the wall opposite and the owners were cooking over charcoal braziers. The steam carried the sickly aroma of burning sugar.

In the middle of the street, a dog scavenged in a pile of refuse, an infant watching it with the bemused smile of an

136

innocent. The child stood with its hands on its hips in a defiant stance but, as soon as the dog turned, saw the child, assumed a threat to its ownership of the rubbish and snarled, its lips drawing back from its teeth, the infant stepped back, paused then fled into a low doorway, screaming for its mother. Alice could see the cheeks of the child's bottom through the traditional hole slit in the seat of its little trousers.

To the left was the main artery of Rua Coelho do Amaral. A few cars went by slowly, a rickshaw piled high with flat rattan baskets full of ducks being laboriously tugged out of their path by a pair of coolies dressed in ragged shorts. Cyclists pedalled past, their bells jangling. Pedestrians and other coolies with loads suspended from poles weaved in and out of each other, those most heavily burdened cursing and cajoling those less weighed-down into allowing them straight passage. Dogs went purposefully about their business. Cats huddled in corners to arch and spit at them as they neared. Overhead, small grey doves fluttered from the eaves of the buildings to the branches of the trees over the wall.

In contrast to the activity and squalor in the street, the world beyond the wall opposite the house was silent. It was the cemetery in which the Protestants of Roman Catholic Macau were buried, the graves well-tended and surrounded by trees that shaded them. Two terraces on a gentle slope were lined with tombs. The headstones were austere yet reduced to softness by the dappled light. The coolness of the place attracted Alice and, closing the shutters behind her, she changed from her baggy servant-like trousers and smock into a European dress.

The shadows of the trees in the small town square by the entrance to the cemetery were thronged with the prone bodies of the unlucky coolies. At the curb, half a dozen were tossing coins; even their poverty did not prevent their incorrigible desire to gamble, to let the fates take command and give to them what their own plans and determination did not. Alice threaded her way between them, stepping carefully.

Beside the cemetery an archway led to a small chapel. Alice pushed open the heavy door. The air inside was moist, heated by the sun burning upon the tiled roof. The pews gleamed silently and the brass cross on the altar shimmered in the heat. Alice slowly walked to the lectern upon which squatted a fat, dull Bible bound in cracking leather. Opening it, she saw fragments of the binding break off and drift to the floor.

'May I be of some assistance, my child?'

Alice was startled, dropping the cover of the Bible. The book thumped shut, an eddy of dust blowing out to dance and hang in the air.

'I'm sorry, I had not meant to make you jump.'

The priest was a tall, thin man in his fifties with a sallow complexion and long limbs. He was wearing a black suit and a priest's collar around the inside of which he was rubbing his finger.

'The terrible thing with being a man of the cloth,' he said, sitting down in the front pew, 'is the collar. In England, it is no bother at all, but once beyond Calais . . . The blessed things have to be starched and, once the weather is hot, they chafe so. I honestly believe the Good Lord personally invented these collars to remind His followers of the everyday agony of their calling.'

Alice made no reply. She felt guilty to have been caught unawares and was annoyed at herself for not having noticed the priest's arrival. Mulrenan had taught her to be alert. One never knew when a quick wit might save one's life.

'Rev. Prickett,' he introduced himself, pronouncing the abbreviation rather than the complete honorific. 'Formerly of the China Inland Mission, now local vicar in Christ to the Anglican populace hereabouts.'

'Alice . . .' she paused, chose truthfulness. '. . . Soon. I have come to live in a house overlooking the graveyard. From my window, I can see into it.'

'Many people come in here out of curiosity,' the priest replied. 'It's the same the world over, I find. Rural parish churchyards in Sussex, mission grounds in Yunan, burial places in Uganda; always the same. There is an attraction the Christian dead offer to those living, even those of other faiths.'

He mopped his brow with a frayed, linen handkerchief already limp with absorbed perspiration.

'I like to think,' he continued, 'it is the promise of the life everlasting that attracts the heathen thither, but I suspect that's not it. In truth, I suspect they come out of innate curiosity to see what is carved upon the headstones. We Christians have such a quaint habit in the epitaph. How it must confuse the Hindus who cremate their dead and the Taoists who worship them. And the Buddhists . . . Are you a Buddhist?'

'Not really. I'm not anything, when I think about it.'

'Everyone must have a god,' replied the priest. He rose from the pew, pushing down with his hands upon his knees to give himself leverage. He walked by and, with his sopping handkerchief, caringly dusted the brass cross on the altar.

'Does the god have to be a deity?' Alice asked. 'For me, life is my god.'

She was surprised at her own words, wondered where they had come from, what crevice deep inside herself had harboured them unknown so that now they could come out shockingly to a man whom she did not know and towards whom she felt nothing but a mild pity that he should be exiled far from home in the middle of a war and could afford only one soiled handkerchief.

A bird flew into the nave, squawked once and glided through the hot air to settle upon the shade of one of the electric lights hanging on a single flex. It was a dull brown bird the size of a thrush. The priest, catching its flight in the corner of his eye, squinted at the creature. Alice tried to guess whether he would welcome it to his church or shoo it out before it squirted lime across the pews.

The priest did nothing. He watched the bird intently for a moment, then continued to speak.

'There!' he exclaimed. 'You do have a god. Everyone has, somewhere in themselves. Yours is the most important god for the young. Jesus Christ himself was life to his

139

disciples. When He was crucified, they felt a part of themselves had died and when He was resurrected, new life coursed through them and they went their ways with renewed faith and energy to spread the teachings of their master. To worship life is indeed worthy.'

He lifted the Bible off the lectern and wiped it with his handkerchief, his sweat smearing the desiccated leather.

'Tell me. Why did you come into the graveyard?'

'I've not been there yet. I stopped in here and . . .'

'You must go there, then. I should not detain you. The path is down the side of the church. Do mind the steps for they tend to be mossy and terribly slippery.'

'Thank you — I will. I came because it looked cool and peaceful from my balcony.'

'Indeed.'

The priest flapped his handkerchief to try to dislodge the dust from it. The linen snapped in the air like a tiny whip, alarming the bird which chattered nervously. A fine spray fanned from the handkerchief and marked the tiled floor. When the priest stroked his brow again, he smeared himself with dust.

'Death is cool and peaceful,' he said, his eyes serious, 'even when it is won in chaos, fire and torment. We are entering a time of chaos, fire and torment. Both of us,' he added.

'Yes,' Alice agreed. 'I think we are.'

The priest folded his square of linen, walked past her and, as he reached the door, called back to her, his voice strangely powerful.

'One thing, Miss Soon,' he advised her, 'is to be sure that those closest to you have a god. Be sure also that it is a god of love, not a god that feeds itself on hatred. I'm sure you know what I mean.'

She narrowed her eyes at the oblong dazzle of sunlight in the door. Suddenly the priest was gone. Overhead, the bird ceased its chatter and flew straight for the day, its wings hardly beating, ducking under the lintel as it escaped into the heat. For a moment, its flight resembled that of a large moth.

Alice ran to the church door, stumbling as she caught sight of the path into the graveyard. It was deserted. She ran back to the archway. It was only a two minute walk to the house but it seemed to take much longer. She weakened and leaned upon the wall. The strong sun made her scalp sore through her black hair and blood throbbed behind her eyes.

Ah Shun saw her staggering in the street and, fearful she had been attacked, rushed out as quickly as her once-bound feet would let her to assist her mistress, calling for the boy to fetch cold water. Yet there was no bruise to soothe, no cut to dab.

3

The shop beneath the apartment was rented by a herbalist. He was a man who looked, as elderly Chinese do, far beyond his fifty-five years. He wore the traditional gown of a learned man and, although he kept his hair unplaited, he allowed himself a long, straggling beard. His hands were bony, as if the flesh had drained from the knuckles to leave bare ivory. One of his thumbnails was three inches long and horny with ridges, suggesting that each one, like the rings of a tortoise's shell, told of a year survived.

Upon his shelves in the gloomy room he kept an assortment of bottled potions, packets of herbs and spices, organic powders in twists of paper and inorganic pastes in little ebony boxes with sliding lids. Wizened strips of unrecognisable plant and animal matter hung from hooks screwed into the beams: some were so old they bore a coating of soot from the oil lamps. A pair of Chinese scales with weights shaped like fish lay on the table and, on shelves above the old man's chair in the corner was a row of grimy, much-consulted almanacs, herbalist's volumes and, incongruously and inauspiciously, an out-dated copy of Black's *Book of Poisons*.

On warm nights when Mulrenan was away, Alice was afraid of someone breaking in and slept with the balcony shutters closed and the ceiling fan on — if the electricity supply was functioning. Mulrenan's privacy might work in the opposite direction from that which he intended: a man who is private must have secrets. Or so it might be construed. It could enter into the head of a local burglar, of which there were not a few, to find out for himself.

It was during the warm nights of autumn, with the shutters closed, that Alice lay with the multitude of scents from the shop wafting up through the floorboards. The odours and aromas were friendly and soothing, yet simultaneously threatening and overpowering. On some nights they gave her a headache while on others they seemed to drift her into sleep: sometimes they would keep her awake with their pungency or they would be so delicate she would be hard put to catch them on the air.

The perfumes which did worm their way through the floorboards depended upon the last customer of the day. Whatever bottle, box or packet the old man last opened would be the predominant scent.

When she was bored, Alice would watch the customers arriving at the shop, surveying them from the balcony. The old man did a brisk trade throughout the day, sometimes not even being afforded the time to close for an hour at noon.

His clients divided into four main categories, regardless of sex. There were those who walked purposefully along Rua Do Patane from Rua Coelho Do Amaral, straight into the shop, stayed a few minutes then left just as purposefully: they were often well-dressed and, from the hum of their conversation, well-educated. Then there were those who came from the same direction but paused at the top of the street to glance in their purses or feel their pockets: they would approach the shop quite deliberately, the conversation would last longer and carry the tones of gentle bargaining. They would leave firmly holding their purchases. These people were seldom well-dressed but they were not the poorest.

The third group were poor — general coolies, wash-amahs and sew-sew amahs, waiters from the cafes, steve-dores from the docks on the Porto Interior and the Bacia Sul Do Patane, rickshaw and sedan chair coolies, even beggars. They did not approach the shop from the main thoroughfare but came by way of the alleyways and Rua Dos Curtidores: they clutched their money and bargained fiercely. When they left, never empty-handed, they some-times used their medicine immediately, with desperation or evident yet eager loathing.

Yet these were all ordinary people, from ordinary sta-tions of life and opportunity. The fourth category were not and it was this group which fascinated Alice.

They represented all classes of humanity save the poorest. Some were dressed richly in plain silk or brocades. One or two came in covered sedan chairs or rickshaws as far as the top of the street, where they dismounted, dismissing their coolies to walk the last few steps. Others wore com-monplace clothing. Some were young women and some old men: some were bent and some walked upright: some looked perfectly healthy and a few sickly. What they all had in common was an uncertainty, a furtiveness, a reluctance to approach or enter the shop, and yet a driving force thrust them on. After they had entered the shop, the old man invariably closed the door and their consultations lasted longer than those of all the other patrons. Their conversa-tions never clearly penetrated the floorboards to Alice's ears and they never haggled over the charges levied. They accepted them, paid them and left as they had arrived, secretively and yet, in truth, as obviously as if they had advertised.

It was to Mulrenan's advantage to have the old man use the shop. He opened his premises seven days a week, ignoring Sundays but not Buddhist festivals, and was therefore almost always present. If people entered the apartment, he would know, their footfalls creaking the boards, their movements traceable. In one or two places, the lights from above sparkled through chinks in the shop ceiling. If the apartment was unoccupied the old man would spend the night in his shop to act as a watchman as well as a tenant. For such an arrangement, his rent was well below the market rate.

'He's a good old boy,' Mulrenan frequently told Alice. 'He keeps himself to himself but he's friendly in his own way and you never know when you might need a doctor. His sort of doctor.'

The arrangement was another instance of Mulrenan storing up favours. As for Alice, she was sceptical of the old man's medicine and expressed her mistrust.

'Right!' Mulrenan agreed. 'Some of it's quackery. Whoever heard of rhinoceros horn making for virility! That's just sympathetic magic. The horn is rigid and curved so the penis will follow suit. Rubbish! But what about ginseng and ginger, belladonna and willow? They work. Some of it's actually sound medicine.'

He was right. An extract of willow had cured Alice's terrible headaches after her encounter with the vanishing priest. On helping Alice into bed, Ah Shun had gone straight down the stairs, her tiny bare feet clapping on the steps, and into the herbalist where, shooing out a customer, she had nervously explained her alarm.

The herbalist had immediately shut the shop and brought some powder upstairs with him. He mixed it with warm milk and Alice drank it back in one draught. It was bittersweet yet as soon as she had swallowed it she relaxed, the tension in her head diminishing. She knew her eyes were open — she could feel the hard scrape of the old man's long thumbnail on her brow — but then they grew heavy. She slipped into a blackness against which, at first, blacker shapes flew and glided but they soon departed and she was emptied of everything.

For some days, Alice was weak. The herbalist sent remedies which she swallowed and, gradually, her strength returned. During this time, Mulrenan arrived home, spent two days with her and mysteriously left again. He explained his absence as concerning business.

Whilst Mulrenan was away Alice, without even Ah Shun knowing, methodically searched the whole of their apartment. Mulrenan had a secret: she wanted to know it. He always had one part of himself he never opened to inspection. She wanted to be aware of it, not necessarily to share in it for that would be to ask too much of their relationship, but at least to understand it and therefore to know where she stood with him.

From time to time, he told her as much as he clearly thought would satisfy her feminine curiosity. He gave her the details of a few of his business dealings, coached her further in gemology and let her into the whereabouts of what he called his crystal assets, by which he meant gems and a quantity of hard cash in a number of currencies. She knew, however, this was only a front, to appease her thirst for knowledge.

Of all his arts, putting up a front was his most accomplished. It was his stock-in-trade, developed because it was also at times his only means of survival.

'Give a man a gold coin,' Mulrenan would say, 'and he'll never suspect you of stealing all his silver ones.'

Yet it hurt her that he would not take her into his complete trust. Business matters were not beyond her: as any one-time whore knew, the ability to wheel and deal under pressure of emotion, getting the best payment possible whilst at the same instant not jeopardising the transaction, was a basic skill.

She had learnt that early on in Ethel Morrison's bordello, from a New Zealand girl already eighteen months in The Line who was singularly unattractive but knew how to play men. She was subservient and delicate, quiet and compliant in the bedrooms but after the customer had left, she was mercenary about him in the crudest of ways.

Alice asked her once about a 'trick' who had seemed a charming and pleasant man, considerate and gentle. She had heard them cooing and coupling through the wall.

'Him?' the New Zealander had replied, her accent coarse and masculine. 'He was nothing. No bloody clue. Didn't even aim right. He was the second variety.'

'What do you mean?'

'I tell you. There's two types, Alice. Dollars and dames,

145

and cents and cunts. He was the second. No money, no bloody idea.'

Alice was shocked, determined from that moment she would not regard their visitors in such a cruel light.

The difference, she knew, lay between the Oriental attitude of service towards men and the European attitude towards the servicing of men. She was certain she would not slip into the latter. In this way, she kept her charm and her womanhood even if she did compromise her body, and being in Ethel's house gave her the opportunity of mixing only with the best: sailors under the rank of first officer never appeared there, no bankers under the rank of senior teller or civil servants less than a grade two administrative officer. The only males to enter the establishment under those ranks were the sons of those above them, introduced by their fathers as if visiting The Line was a ritual of attaining manhood like killing a lion bare-handed.

Some of her 'tricks' had taken her fully into their confidence: broken hearts, cuckolded spouses, widowers, homesick bachelors, bored husbands — they all passed through her bed. Financial problems, bereavements, deceit, sorrow, desperation mingled in her mind with thin, wiry, tanned bodies and flabby, ignored, lily-fleshed bodies, young and pliable bodies and firm, muscular bodies. She could never put problems to faces: rarely, after she had started to socialise with Mulrenan, could she put a situation to the face of a man whom she met at a party or a dance. She could tell whom she had met before: they averted their eyes as soon as they saw her but, during the evening, she would notice them casting furtive, anxious or longing glances at her from behind their wives or their fiancees, their dance-cards, or menus.

These strangers had entrusted her with their deepest secrets and she only a girl in The Line. Her lover, with whom she lived and supposedly shared everything, kept his deepest secrets from her.

During her convalescence, Alice became gradually more angry within herself. She began to find reasons why she should be allowed to share in every aspect of their lives together and the more she considered these, the more upset she became until she felt she had to act. To confront Mulrenan with her feelings was unthinkable. He would easily dismiss them and her: that she could not risk. She needed him and he knew it. She was not so sure he needed her as much. Perhaps a man with secrets needed no one.

Alice knew already, because Mulrenan had shown her, of two secret hiding places. One was beneath a loose floor-board. The kitchen ceiling below was plastered and Mulrenan had constructed a tin-lined cradle that hung between the joists. In this he kept only money, with American dollars, pounds sterling and Indian rupees predominating. The other hiding place was a hollow drilled into the thick middle leg on the right hand side — his side — of their bed. In this were stored gemstones of average to good quality.

On the day of her search, Ah Shun having gone to the market to buy rice and fish, Alice unscrewed the leg. The dozen chamois leather bags were full: emeralds, amethysts, sapphires of which two were blue star sapphires of at least ten carats each, a fine ruby of about five carats and several small but good quality diamonds. Other gems of lesser but still worthwhile value included a demantoid, some aquamarines and a three carat heliodor.

As she replaced the stones in their bags, Alice wondered where the really good ones were hidden. Mulrenan had a bank deposit box in Macau but he regarded it as insecure. Official as well as unofficial eyes could peer into it at the drop of a few patacas in the correct palm. Somewhere there had to be the better quality gems, the bigger diamonds and the large emeralds, one of which she had been shown. It was, at the very least, a fourteen carat stone and of the purest colour with no obvious inclusions and few to be discovered with a powerful lens. At the time of acquiring the jewel, Mulrenan had said he had never come across the like of it before. She knew he had not sold it. It was too valuable to let go at an unprepared moment: it was, as he called the best examples, one of his insurance stones.

Returning the bags to the leg of the bed, Alice sat on the sheets and scanned her eyes around the room. She was certain the hiding place was not in their bedroom: had it been she would have seen Mulrenan going to it in the early hours when he returned from his nocturnal meetings. Nevertheless, she studied all the possibilities before she went into the main living room.

The furniture was substantial but she was sure Mulrenan would not risk the best quality stones in any movable object. If something could be moved, it could be stolen, even something as large as the carved camphorwood chest they had brought from Hong Kong.

Perching herself on the edge of the chest, Alice scanned the room. None of the furniture looked to have been shifted more than a few inches and that would have been done by Ah Shun sweeping the floor and scattering camphor in the corners to mount a counter attack against the cockroaches. Several floorboards were loose: when she tested them, not one yielded to her gentle pushing or cautious prising. Beneath most of them, in any case, was the ceiling of herbalist's shop which was not boarded or plastered. The few pictures that hung on the wall would not disguise a niche: that would be too simple. There were no convenient ventilator bricks.

With a growing eagerness but simultaneous frustration, Alice searched elsewhere. The kitchen produced nothing and the room in which they stored their unused possessions was too chock-a-block to offer an accessible hiding place. Even the simple, squat Oriental lavatory with its hole in the ground and two grooved stones on either side for one's feet, gave no opportunity for a secure secret place.

Finally admitting defeat, Alice went into the kitchen and tipped several handfuls of charcoal on to the stove, placing a copper kettle on the hob. From a tin-lined caddy she took three level spoonfuls of jasmine tea, dropping them into a porcelain pot with a translucent rice pattern design. She watched absent-mindedly as the dry flakes tumbled into the void. Already, she was tired from her search. Her illness still took a toll and, as lonely housewives do, she started to talk to herself.

'I wonder where you've put them,' she said, addressing

an image of Mulrenan in the teapot. 'You've put them here somewhere. They're too good to chance in the bank. Even in the yard . . .'

She went out into the small courtyard. The sun was obscured by a huge cumulus cloud. The welcome shade made her less uncomfortable. Standing with her arms hanging by her side, she surveyed the cobbles and flags. It was inconceivable any of them had been shifted — or could be — by one man in a hurry.

The kettle was boiling. She emptied it into the pot, took a handleless Chinese cup with glazed bamboo stalks decorating its sides and slowly climbed the stairs to the living room. She put the teapot on a folded cloth spread on the table and poured herself a drink.

'Diamonds!' she said aloud to the cushions as she lay back on the divan. 'And emeralds. And sapphires. Amethysts. Rubies. Tourmaline and topaz. Pearls and peridot.'

Her fingers smarted from the hot cup and she quickly put it on the floor, rubbing her fingers into the palm of her other hand to dissipate the pain.

'That hurt!'

There was a sound from beneath and she could hear a strident voice asking the herbalist for a prescription against sores on the tongue. The demand was followed by a quieter reply and then ensued a conversation in semi-whispers.

'Emerald, amethyst, pearl and peridot; topaz, turquoise, opal and onyx; ruby . . .'

Alice paused, searching for another gem that might complete the rhythm of her verse. It was then she saw it.

For a moment, she just stared, dumbfounded by Mulrenan's cleverness and just as surprised at herself for not having realised it from the start. When she stood up, the cup of tea was knocked over, the liquid rivering across the floorboard and disappearing down a crack.

Hanging on the wall, above the camphorwood chest they had brought from Lyndhurst Terrace, was a shrine. It was no bigger than a shoe box and coloured bright red with a frame decorated with arabesques of gold paint. On the back was pasted a garish picture of the household god Ah Shun had chosen to protect them and, on the narrow shelf in front was a pot of sand from which poked three red splinters, the remains of burnt joss-sticks. On the side of the box-like altar had been pinned two thin sheaves of paper money for the god to spend in the afterworld.

Carefully, so as not to upset the pot of sand belonging to the god, Alice lifted the shrine off its nail, placing it on the camphorwood chest. As she had expected, behind it was a faint outline in the plaster. With a razor blade, she slit the edge of the square and levered the plaster loose.

Mulrenan had kept the original plaster as a tile which he could replace after every visit to the niche. Behind it was hollowed a cavity extending behind the lath and plaster to either side of the entrance. To get her arm in, Alice had to stand on the chest.

The jewels were there as she had anticipated. The emeralds — there were four over eight carats — and the diamonds were in their bags. Some very good pearls were hidden next to them with a rich blue aquamarine of at least six carats, unusually fashioned in an elaborate rosette cut. In a small box filled with sandalwood shavings, Alice discovered over thirty uncut emeralds one of them the size of the end joint of her thumb. What she had not expected to find was the seven half-ingots of fine gold, each of them wrapped in cloth and with a Swiss assay certificate tied to it with cotton thread, the four small bars of platinum, the thirty-eight British gold sovereigns — each of them dated 1899 and bearing the head of the ageing Queen Victoria — the nine Mexican gold dollars and the fifty-odd other assorted gold coins from Britain, France, Germany and Holland. There was even a small Roman aureus with an emperor's head bearing a laurel crown on the reverse.

One by one she removed the items, looked at them closely then replaced them in exactly the position in which they had been resting.

To replace the plaster tile was not difficult. All she had to do was repeat what Mulrenan had done: press it into place and seal the cracks with dampened rice flour. The weight of the little shrine would hold the tile in place while the paste dried, a process that would not take long in the hot weather and with the dry plaster around the entrance absorbing most of the moisture.

Just as she was stepping down from the chest to go to the kitchen for the flour jar, there was an urgent knocking on the downstairs door. Alice's heart missed a beat then raced. The blood in her neck hurried to find her brain, prepare it against fear.

'Missy!' a hoarse voice cried. 'Missy! Quick! Quick!'

She slid the tile behind the chest and rapidly re-hung the shrine in place over the hole.

'Missy!'

It was the herbalist's voice. He spoke to her in pidgin English even though he knew she could speak Cantonese.

She descended the stairs and pulled the door open to find the man peering at her with a worried face, the shoulder of his jacket marked with a dark wet stain. At the sight of her, his screwed-up cheeks relaxed a little.

'What do you want, Mr Chou?' she asked, disguising her nervousness with a stern front.

'Shui,' he said. 'Watah cum downside. Hot watah. You aw-wite?'

For a moment she was confused then she laughed delicately, relief flushing through her.

'I am fine,' she said. 'I spilt my tea.'

'Flow and woof no ve'y good,' he commented, rubbing his shoulder.

'No,' she replied. 'I'm sorry. I hope your jacket . . . Do give it to me. My amah will wash it for you.'

The old man bowed.

'It aw-wite,' he repeated. 'No wuwwy, Missy.'

At ten that evening, Mulrenan returned. He kissed her as she lay in bed, supposedly dozing. The oil lamp was low and he could not see the fear touching her eyes. She lay quite still, fighting to remain awake. At two am, she felt him climb out of bed. He was gone for thirty minutes. When he came back, he said nothing but, as usual, turned on to his side and rested his hand on her breast. She tried not to let him sense the sigh she gradually released.

4

'All of southern China is made for piracy,' Dr Alvarez told Mulrenan as he lay in the dentist's chair waiting for the cocaine to work. 'It has been an area of pirates and brigands since the time of the famous Marco Polo. They used to prey upon fishing junks and trading boats. In the sixteenth century, when the Arabs traded as far as China, the pirates attacked their dhows. There was much killing. It is in the chronicles.' He smiled benignly and pressed his finger on Mulrenan's cheek. 'Do you feel this?'

'Yes.'

'A minute or two more. Perhaps,' he returned to his historical treatise, 'even the famous Sinbad fought in these waters.'

'How do you know so much?' Mulrenan asked, his words a little garbled as he was losing the use of his tongue.

Alvarez was an expert at one-sided discussion. He had to be. As a dentist, his fellow conversationalists were often obliged to remain mute or, like swans, only mew a reply of assertion or denial, agreement or argument.

'Mister Mulrenan,' he replied, 'I have lived in Macau since 1921. Where are we? July? Yes! Twenty years to the month. I arrived just ahead of a big typhoon. In all that time, I have made a study of China. It is a fascinating country, do you not think?'

He again prodded Mulrenan's cheek with his index finger.

'Do you still feel anything?'

'A bi',' said Mulrenan.

'We'll wait a little longer. Yes, I have studied the history of China and especially of Macau. Do you know *Historic Macau* by Carlos Augusto Montalto de Jesus? No? He is my hero, my boyhood giant. There was a man! Born in Hong Kong in 1864 — no, I lie — 1863, he knew China, understood China. You would have liked him. He too was not fond of the British.'

The cocaine had taken effect and Alvarez began to scratch at Mulrenan's tooth with one of his implements, a thin piece of stainless steel with a bent point mounted in the tip.

' 'ow 'as 'ah?' Mulrenan asked.

'A little wider, please. Well, there was a story — quite true — that he argued one day with a Scottish man with whom he was employed in one of the hongs . . . this won't hurt.'

Mulrenan grunted and winced.

'And he did not like him,' Alvarez continued, 'so he emptied an inkpot over the man's head. Then he walked out and never returned. Of course, no one would give him a job after that. But he survived, all over the world. He lived well. Sometimes. Sometimes not. And he wrote his book. In it, he is sometimes very critical of the British in China. And the Portuguese. You must read it. The 1926 edition is the best but that is very rare. Very rare, indeed. The Macanese authorities burned it publically. Yet there are a few copies . . . The 1902 is enough. I can lend you mine.'

' 'ank you,' said Mulrenan.

'I am going to use the drill now. It will not take long, I assure you, Five minutes.'

Mulrenan watched as Alvarez fitted a burr into the drill. It was exactly the same as the kind goldsmiths used.

'Anyway, I digress, as they say,' Alvarez went on, pressing his foot on a floor pedal to confirm that the drill was plugged in. 'Now we enter five minutes of risk,' he said jovially. 'Now we want no power cut.'

The drill whirred as the cables spun round their pulleys, humming as the slack was taken up.

'Piracy. Yes. All the south coast of China is a gift to pirates. Lots of little islands to hide behind. Or on. Hold still, please. Many coves and rocky bays in which to weather. Many little beaches to land upon and thousands of tiny villages in which to live as fishermen. Lots of local people to rob when the seas are rough. Nowadays, with steamers sailing the coast, the pickings are much richer. Of course, the flow has dropped a bit since the war in Europe and, of course, since the British in Hong Kong set up their pirate patrols. But it still goes on. There. Rinse your mouth, please.'

Mulrenan swilled the antiseptic water round his mouth, a trickle of it dribbling down his lip and on to the bib protecting his shirt. He spat the noxious liquid into an enamel bucket and leaned back.

'You must be very careful when you sail in the estuary,' Alvarez warned him. 'Pirates exist all along the shores. If they know of you heading to Canton — you may not need my services again!'

Mulrenan gave as much of a laugh as the circumstances permitted. It came out of his throat as a strangled gargle of saliva and powdered dentine. Even with his mouth numb and aching, he could afford a little humour. The pirates and the brigands, the Nationalists of Generalissimo Chiang Kai-shek and the Communists of Mao Tse-tung, would not touch him. They needed — even relied upon — his services.

5

'What'll you drink? I've a mature scotch or a new bottle of Gilbey's London gin. And a bottle of the finest goddam bourbon to leak out of Kentucky. None of your Liffey's grape, I'm afraid.'

'A gin, if I may,' Mulrenan requested, shifting the cushion behind himself to one side. 'Have you any tonic?'

'Sure thing.'

Davis Corrigan pressed a stubby finger on the bell and his houseboy appeared at the door carrying a silver salver bearing a bottle of tonic water, a soda syphon and a jug of ice. A small dish of sliced limes stood beside the jug.

'War or no war, standards have simply got to be maintained,' he commented, his plainly New York accent struggling to resemble a British colonial voice. ' 'Specially where it concerns good ol'-fashioned booze. Is it true the British invented quinine' — he pronounced it kwee-nine — 'tonic water . . .'

'. . . to counteract malaria? It's true. In India. The drug tasted foul, so they invented a way to get it down without upsetting the mouth. Never under-estimate British ingenuity.'

'Nor Irish artfulness,' Corrigan said, pouring out a liberal measure of bourbon into one tumbler and gin into the other. 'Lime 'n' ice?'

'Please.'

'Inch of tonic?'

Mulrenan nodded and said, 'When are the girls due back?'

'Half-seven. Give or take a psalm or two.'

Corrigan was not anti-Christian: he was, in his own words, 'a god-fearin' man from the east', by which he meant the eastern USA rather than the world beyond Suez. However, he was anti-Papist with little time for the Church of Rome which he summed up as 'a convocation of candles and clowns' because, he explained, they burnt a lot of the former and dressed like the latter. His dislike of the Roman church was the one major difference he allowed between himself and his Chinese wife, a devout Roman Catholic for whom the war was a mixed blessing: it brought her to Macau, the resting place of the most important relic of St François Xavier. It was with determination honed on the whetstone of Protestant belief that he avoided accompanying his wife to her devotions.

Yet as Macau filled with refugees and the streets became dangerous, he worried about his wife going abroad after dark and mentioned his dilemma to Mulrenan: he was damned if he would go with her to evening Mass but apprehensive when she ventured out alone. Alice immediately offered to accompany May Corrigan and the offer was gratefully accepted.

They went, twice a week, to one of the many Macanese

churches and, while May attended a service, Alice would either sit at the rear of the nave or leave the building and take refreshment in a nearby cafe.

The services aroused her curiosity not in Christ and his religion so much as in the language. Mass was spoken in Latin and she was fascinated much as a child is with a newly discovered, long and unpronounceable word. The prayers were magical chants, the music and psalms with their responses strange and moving.

After the service, as they walked towards the Corrigans' house in the twilight, May asked Alice if she would not consider converting to the faith.

'I don't think so,' Alice replied. 'I prefer a family of gods from whom I can choose the correct one as the need arises.'

'Christ covers all the eventualities,' May said, not piously but practically.

'My mother was a Christian,' Alice answered, not to be moved. 'My father was a Buddhist as much as he was anything — at least, he believed in the teachings of the Lord Buddha even if he ate meat — and I suppose I've fallen between the two stools. I don't think I'm ready to think about clambering up on one or the other.'

'When you do,' May said, 'let me know. I'd be more than pleased to attend your christening. You are, Alice, a very *Christian* person.'

'What do you mean?'

'You're good,' she answered simply.

'I wasn't once, by your standards.'

'Repented!' exclaimed May Corrigan. 'And by good, I mean kind and loving, not necessarily moral. Morality isn't religion. Not always.'

'If there was more light in this street,' Alice said, as their footsteps echoed off the walls of the houses and courtyards, 'you'd see me blushing.'

'I'm glad. It shows you're ready to make the move.'

Ahead in a doorway of the dark street there was a scuffling. They stepped over the gutter to avoid it. Their men had warned them of getting involved.

From Corrigan's window, across the water, Mulrenan

could see the Hong Kong ferry materialising from the sea mist that had settled around midday and had yet to lift. The ship was late. From its funnel, it left a streak of black smoke neither dispersing nor drifting but hanging in the air like a dirty flaw in an opal.

'To the Irish,' suggested Corrigan. 'Long may they have the tenacity to survive and the temerity to kick British asses.'

'To the Irish,' Mulrenan agreed.

He sipped from his glass and the tang of the lime smarted a cut on his upper lip made when his razor had slipped that morning. He sucked at the tiny wound.

'You know what today is?' Corrigan asked.

Mulrenan thought and said, 'December 7th, isn't it?'

'Anything else?'

'Alice informed me this afternoon — according to your wife — that it was the feast day of St Ambrose. He of the Athanasian Creed. Hence our two ladies being absent as we see down the sun. Wherever it is in the fog.'

'St Ambrose's Day: yup! It's also my birthday. Fifty today. Half one goddam whole century.'

'You should have said,' Mulrenan exclaimed. 'We'd have brought you a present. Here's to you and fifty more.'

'God forbid! By then I'm sure to be well past it. What can be worse than being a hundred! No dames. Doctors keeping the bottle screwed tight. Boiled rice and fish twice a day. Pissing your pants. As for a present: thanks for the thought, Sean old pal. But what in hell's name do you get for a man who's fifty, got a beautiful broad from Shanghai and lives on the coast of China with such a view of an evening.'

He swept his hand and glass of whiskey across the vista of Taipa Island, the mist and the fishing fleet of sampans making for the ocean. From somewhere in the town, a single church bell was dolefully tolling, the mist flattening the chime and dropping it into the water.

'The best gift I could've gotten, I've — gotten. You here with the two ladies off to their devotions and we left to ours.' He raised his glass again. 'To future years,' he suggested.

'To *your* future years, Davis,' Mulrenan qualified and

157

they drained their glasses.

As Corrigan refilled them, Mulrenan stood and leaned his hands on the balcony wall. In a palm tree below the house, a brightly-coloured bird was picking at a fruit. The ferry, slowing to round Barra Point and steering a careful course through the sampans, belched out a larger cloud of soot and dense smoke.

'Do you think there'll be a war out here?'

'Bet my last buck on it,' Corrigan said after a moment's deliberation. 'It might be the Chinese against the Chinese or an up-grading of the Chinese and the Japanese set-to. Might even be the Chinese against the Foreign Devils — another Boxer Rising all over, except for Boxer read Commic.'

He put Mulrenan's tumbler on the wall and leaned back luxuriously in a woven bamboo chair under the standard lamp, also made of bamboo, a thick post with a bamboo strip shade.

'What do you make of the Communists, Davis?'

'The Commies? They'll win. Sure as hell's hot, they'll win. One day. Not yet. But China's in the shit, Sean. Right in it. It's riddled with corruption, in total chaos and split right down the middle. Some want this guy Mao Tse-tung to win, some want Chiang Kai-shek. Some want it to stay in upheaval because that way they can milk it. As for the foreigners, they don't know what they want. On the surface, the British and the French — and ourselves of the Stars 'n' Stripes — want a republic led by Chiang Kay-Ess. Under it, no one knows. Chungking crawls with foreigners yet we are, at the same time and unbeknownst to all, backing the Mao Brigade. Ever wondered where the Communists get the ammo for the guns you slip them?'

Mulrenan made no answer but, turning round, grinned and rested his elbows on the verandah wall, leaning like a Cagney wise-guy.

'Guns?' he said. 'Come on, will ya? I ain't no goddam gangster.'

Corrigan laughed.

'Not bad, not bad at all. For an Irishman who ain't never

seen Chicago. But you do let 'em have a few, from time to time. So word has it.'

'Words can never be trusted,' Mulrenan observed.

The twilight was deepening and, in the mist, the sampans were lighting their oil lamps. A few had even commenced fishing now the last ferry was in harbour. Mulrenan could hear the splash of water as the fishermen's cormorants dived for the catch.

'That war . . .' he started.

'Forget it. Macau'll be safer than the Vatican itself. Portugal's been neutral since Columbus. So's blessed Eire, come to that. The US of A is keeping out of it, save giving the British a few out-of-date battleships and a lot of slaps on the back. We'll be A1 OK!'

'What of the civilian population? Won't they —'

'The Chinese?' Corrigan interrupted. 'No sweat! They'll not rise up against us here. Macau's a haven, as you can see. Everyone scared witless in Hong Kong has moved here. Or those who see the way the wind blows for a profit.' He winked at Mulrenan and made a squawking noise with his tongue. 'No sweat!'

'What I mean is, once the mainland's a war zone, what will happen here? A siege? Will Macau be cut off, starved out? Everything the place lives on comes from China. If there's nothing there . . .'

'Sure. Things might get tight. But Lisbon's not going to neglect the place and it'll be the only neutral ground east of Goa. In a war, neutral areas are needed as meeting places, trading houses, information centres. It might get tough here, but it's not going to cave in. It's in nobody's interest to close it down completely.'

The houseboy appeared on the verandah carrying a shallow wooden dish of Japanese rice crackers.

'What time missy an' young missy come back church?' he enquired.

'Half past seven,' Corrigan replied. 'Okay supper nine o'clock?'

'Yes, master,' the houseboy confirmed.

'One good thing about the proximity of the Japs is that

159

we get these dainty little biscuit jobs. Try one, will you? The little green bits sticking to the sides are seaweed.' He laughed. 'Damn me! What the hell do we have to fear from a race who has barely a member over five-six high and who eat seaweed and goddam raw fish!'

Mulrenan picked up one of the crackers. It tasted salty in the way soya sauce did. There was a delicate tang underlying the saltiness, a hint of the smell of the seashore. The baked rice flour in the centre was light and tasted of nothing.

'You know, Davis, I think the Japs're a deal more cunning than we grant them. We've seen them bulldoze through China. Scorched earth policies, grind the Chinese down, but behind it all there is a distinct plan, no matter how crazy we may think it. Remember their emperor is more than that — he's a damned demi-god to them. Soldiers will do things for their god they'd never do for their benighted comrades.'

At that moment, the electricity supply fused. The houselights around the Baia da Praia Grande were extinguished but not all at once. The power ebbed from them in sequence so Mulrenan could see, over the space of five seconds, how the supply failure was travelling round the bay like a sheet of darkness being drawn over the buildings. Just as the last windows in the last houses went out, the houseboy and amah arrived carrying globed glass oil lamps. After a moment's milling hesitation, the moths and midges which had been on the lampshade began to head for the lamps and the geckos that had been preying upon them shifted station to the new, softer shadows around the flames.

'Look at 'em go,' said Corrigan, pointing his glass at the ceiling. 'Zig-zaggin' over the plaster. Upside-down, too. Now see! Those lizards are like the East, wouldn't you say? They're versatile. They accommodate. That's why they are so goddam successful. Been around for millions of years. Descended from dinosaurs.'

'Yes, we live in an adaptable society here. But they have standards lower than ours — different, anyway — and they take the rough with the smooth. You know the expression

— "easy come, easy go." That's not my way. Once I get up there I want to stay. That's what motivates me. You too. The drive to strive . . .'

'That's good! I like it! Make a yankee doodle dandy of you yet, Sean. "Drive to strive." Must remember that one.'

Mulrenan was sometimes annoyed by Corrigan's flippancy, his reducing of the serious to levels of banality, but he knew that under the facetious exterior was a man harder than sword-steel and just as sharp: the man's jokery simply stemmed from the Irish blood in him. One hundred years of American life, since his Protestant grandfather had emigrated from Londonderry, had only slightly diluted his sheer Irish joy in being alive.

'Besides,' Mulrenan added, joining in his friend's humour, 'I think I'd be wary of any nation that can produce something as subtle as these crackers. One taste changes into the next in mid-mouth and the body of the thing has no flavour at all.'

'Exactly! You got it!'

The electric light flickered. Out at sea, the mist was flattening. A half-moon was rising through grey wraiths over the horizon, its silvery glow competing with the fishermen and their lanterns.

'I hear the Japs're building up their forces near Waichow,' Corrigan said. 'Don't know how much truth there is in it. One can never tell. My informant got it from a rice merchant.'

'I noticed several Japanese ships making for Canton when I was last sailing past Fuyong. One was riding at anchor, awaiting a river pilot. Do you think they'll push further into China?'

'Who the hell can tell? I doubt a holy prophet could figure that one out.'

When Alice and May returned from church, they were holding hands like schoolgirls. Alice's eyes were pinkrimmed as if she had been smoking opium, and May's face powder was smudged. Mulrenan kissed Alice on the cheek as she stepped through the faint light of the oil lamps. He could smell Corrigan's despised holy incense in her hair.

May Corrigan sat without speaking. She was at least ten years older than Alice: her skin was still smooth and her eyes sparkled with fire but her hair had lost the lustre young Chinese women are so proud of and the backs of her hands were lined.

'Gin, Baby?' asked Corrigan. She nodded to her husband. 'And for you, Alice?'

'Yes,' said Alice in a detached voice, 'gin. Thank you.'

'What's wrong, Alice?'

Standing by her side, Mulrenan could feel a coldness surrounding her, an almost physical drop in temperature. As he placed his hand on hers he found it to be icy. She made no attempt to remove her hand from under his but she made no sign of wanting to grasp it. It was as if that part of her was lifeless, unrelated to her.

'We were coming past St Augustine's,' May started but then said no more, as if that were enough information for the men to be able to divine the rest of the story.

Corrigan passed both of them a glass of gin with fresh lime juice, a twist of peel hanging in the colourless liquid. Alice sniffed at her glass but May took a stiff drink.

Corrigan prompted her.

'Then?'

'It was misty,' said Alice.

'And there was a scuffling,' May said, her words charged with misery. 'A voice called "Oh, God! Help!" clearly, in English.' She emptied her glass and held it up but Corrigan made no move to refill it. She went on, 'It was dark because of the failure but there were some coolies with lanterns and one with a bundle of temple candles.'

Alice slipped her hand from under Mulrenan's and rubbed absent-mindedly at a raw scarlet weal on her forearm. It was livid, even in the lamplight. She saw Mulrenan was looking at it.

'The wax,' she explained indifferently, 'from the candles. They spit.'

'We went to investigate . . .' May continued.

'Jesus H. Christ! That's plain dumb!' Corrigan exploded with exasperation. 'How many times have I told you . . .'

162

'What else could we do?' his wife retorted. 'We couldn't do nothing!'

'It was Irina Boyd,' Alice said quietly. 'She was lying on the ground by the edge of the cobbles. Her leg was bent under . . . I didn't know she was here. Maybe she'd been to our house and . . .'

Alice looked at the sampan fleet. Following her gaze, Mulrenan saw the boats had drifted farther out and the lights were less sharp in the moonlight.

'Her throat had been cut,' said May bleakly. 'She was gurgling just a little, but she was already dead. She had no pulse.'

Alice started to sob. Mulrenan put his arm around her but she did not yield to him, allow him to draw her close.

'When I felt for her pulse . . . her fingers had been chopped off. For the rings.'

Alice dropped her glass. It hit the parapet but instead of breaking, bounced off and rustled as it fell through the branches of the bougainvillaea below.

'The coolies picked her up and carried her to that hospital near the old fortress,' May said, 'but it would have been no use.'

Corrigan went to the telephone but there was no reply. Mulrenan decided there and then to employ a bodyguard for himself and Alice and to obtain a pistol for her to keep in the house.

When they returned home, Alice could not sleep. She stayed awake, Mulrenan by her side, sitting with a blanket draped around her shoulders. It was cold outside and the house, in common with many of the old Portuguese properties, was draughty.

The motive for Irina Boyd's murder had been robbery. The police had received a tip-off within hours of her death but the assassins had escaped out of Macau and were well into China before dawn. They had, it appeared, chanced upon her walking alone in Rua Sao Paulo, had followed her past St Dominic's Church and were obviously wondering how they might attack her when the power failure happened. She had tried to run but they had caught up with her.

163

At first, Alice took her friend's death badly, the hurt increased by the fact that she had not known of her being in Macau and by the fear she might somehow have contributed to the murder by not being at home. As the hours passed, however, she accepted the death philosophically, agreeing with Mulrenan's stoical comment that it was foolish to be out alone after dark. He criticised Irina's husband, not knowing that Boyd had elected to remain in Hong Kong, sending her away as a safety precaution.

In the morning, Mulrenan visited the coolie ranks on the quays of the Porto Interior to find a bodyguard. Whilst walking in Rua das Estalagens, he heard of the bombing of Pearl Harbour.

6

Coolies jostled with disembarking passengers, scrabbling to carry baggage or fetch rickshaws. Touts offered non-existent hotel rooms and rented accommodation. Friends and relations pushed through to loved ones as they descended the gangplank. Every passenger was laden with suitcases, wicker baskets, parcels secured with string, boxes and belongings compressed into bundles tied into blankets or sheets, even canvas sacks with 'Royal Mail' stencilled on the sides. Children staggered under luggage as heavy as themselves. Mulrenan watched one young woman, a baby strapped to her back, stumble down the gangway with a roll of bedding jammed between the infant's head and her shoulderblades. The baby had averted its face so it could breathe; it was imperturbably sleeping, its arms dangling free like those of a puppet.

The passengers were of all classes. A few were Europeans, dressed in suits or tweed skirts and jackets, accompanied by one or two servants: yet even the master and missy carried bags and bulky packages. Most were Chinese, young and old, poor and well-to-do. The men wore cheap trousers and coats or expensive, ankle-length padded silk gowns and their womenfolk wore loose-fitting cotton pants and smocks or brocades under costly overcoats of American or British cut. Often even the better-off were wearing as much as they could, and, despite the chill wind, many people were sweating with exertion and worry. Some of the children wore two or three pairs of trousers, even two padded jackets.

As he watched from across the Rua das Lorchas, Mulrenan noticed the one trademark of the refugee on everyone. Somewhere in their mass of baggage there was one piece more precious than the rest: if the worst came to the worst, all could be lost except for that one bag or parcel, box or case. Women clutched theirs close to their sides; men held theirs tightly in their fists; children hugged theirs. They might contain jewels, money or a prized toy — it did not matter. Each was the most treasured possession, which no coolie or rickshaw driver was allowed to touch.

Gradually, the crowd dispersed. The rickshaws vanished into the side streets carrying luggage, the owners walking by the vehicles rather than in them. The coolies settled down to await the next ferry from Hong Kong. The schedules were being ignored: as soon as its passengers had gone ashore and the ship had refuelled, it sailed on its return journey. With the Japanese forces pushing towards Kowloon, as many as could made this escape to Macau.

Almost the last passenger off the ferry was a young Chinese man dressed in traditional clothes. He carried only a much-scratched leather briefcase and an equally well-worn leather suitcase. As he reached the bottom of the gangplank, he placed the case upon the stones of the quay, raising his left hand and snapping his fingers at a coolie squatting by a bollard. The coolie, realising his good fortune, jumped up and bent to lift the suitcase. The young Chinese stopped him and, instead, spoke to him. The coolie, a surprised look on his face, walked quickly away.

Mulrenan followed the coolie, overtaking him in the Travessa Caldeira.

'You!' he ordered in Cantonese. 'You have a message for me?'

The coolie stopped and spun round.

'Yat chat chat,' he ventured in a bemused voice, offering only a number to Mulrenan by way of introduction, as he had been instructed.

'Ho!' exclaimed Mulrenan and he gave the coolie one pataca. 'You lo spik or . .,' he said in pidgin English, leaving the threat unspoken and the coolie in a state of clear understanding.

Returning to the dock, Mulrenan stood where the young Chinese could see him. Once he had caught his eye, Mulrenan lifted his right hand level with the front of his chest and raised three of his fingers together to touch his shirt.

The Chinese took a circuitous route through the streets, Mulrenan following him at a distance to a point halfway along Rua de Afonso de Albuquerque where he paused outside a shop doorway to wipe his nose with a handkerchief, a very westernised action: most Chinese regarded handkerchiefs as insanitary.

Mulrenan entered the tea shop opposite and slowly drank a single cup of jasmine tea. Having paid he crossed the road. The building resembled that in which he and Alice lived, except the shop beneath was occupied by a vegetable seller. Evening was falling and, under the glare of a hissing petromax lamp, the shopkeeper was offering a Chinese cabbage to a young woman dressed in black trousers. As Mulrenan passed, the woman tipped her head to the shopkeeper who tugged on a piece of string hanging down the wall from a small hole in the ceiling above some sacks of beans.

Mulrenan climbed the stairs and knocked on a door. It was opened by a middle-aged Chinese woman. She said nothing but ushered him in to a room where the young Chinese was sitting sipping hot water from a glass. The room was illuminated by an ornate oil lamp with a red crystal reservoir, its green shade making the man appear more sallow than he was. Mulrenan thought how he must

166

be a creature of the night, of the darkness; his skin was pale like a houseplant that is given no sun.

Bowing, Mulrenan offered his hand. The Chinese youth accepted it without standing, shaking it weakly.

'You like some hot water, Mista Mu'wenan? Tonight not ve'y good for you lungs. Some cold in air coming f'om China.'

'Thank you, no,' said Mulrenan.

'Okay. You sit, p'ease.'

A chair was produced for Mulrenan by another man whom he had not seen and who must have been behind the door. Accepting the seat, he twisted his head. Behind him stood Leung.

'Hewwo,' he said, grinning. 'Long time no see. You good?'

'I'm fine. How are you? I had heard . . .'

'I fine, too. Wuk long time Kowloon City side, go into China. Wuk long time Weichow side. Get lo' of expewience. Get talking Inglish beta, too.' He smirked and suggested, 'We talk Inglish now.'

'Indeed, you have,' Mulrenan complimented him. 'And we will if . . .'

He looked to the other man who was blowing on his tumbler of hot water having wrapped the glass in a flannel to prevent his fingers from scorching. The steam dissipated in the darker reaches of the ceiling.

He had lived long enough in the East to know the more you compliment and prevaricate with good manners the sooner the business end of the meeting arrives and the easier it is to clinch a deal to satisfy everyone with a minimum of argument and bandying of prices.

'How you lady?'

'Very well, thank you.'

'I hear she not so good one day back. She faw iwl goin' f'om church. Not so good.'

Mulrenan hid his emotions: he had suspected they were being watched, studied from afar. That would have been only natural.

'Are you supp'ised, Mista Muwenan?' the other Chinese

asked. 'Nefer mind. So long as you know we keep good watch on you. For you safety. Some peepul no like you, want you to leave Macau. You makin' too much money, buy too much.'

'Is Mista Yip,' Leung explained. 'He . . .' he had obviously been practising the word for some time for it came out perfectly, '. . . liaison officer for Chinese Army.'

Mulrenan was about to ask which army when Yip answered his thought.

'I fight in the glo'ious army of liberation, Chinese Peepul's Army. It my job to clean all Japanese and all Nationalist sodjers from China. My g'eat leader,' he added, as if to be certain he had clarified matters, 'Mao Tse-tung.'

'May you have good fortune in your struggle to free your people,' Mulrenan said tactfully.

'Good luck, yes!' He laughed. 'But a'so need somet'ing of you, Mista Muwenan. So far you got plenty gun and medicine for us. My leader in Kwangtung province ve'y g'ateful. Now want one mo' t'ing.'

'If I can be of help, you know I will.'

Yip put his glass down on the table under the oil lamp. The wisps of steam wove through the shade, changing colour as they went. Mulrenan had once seen a magic act do that with a prism: the steam had turned into a floating rainbow.

'You can. But we no pay you. Not in cash. We pay you in ki'ness.'

Mulrenan knew when he was backed in to a corner. He could not refuse. To do so would bring about too great a series of risks.

'Of course,' he replied, putting a brave face on it. 'As we say, for old times' sake. I'm sure I'd be pleased to do you a favour.'

'M'koi,' Yip said and he smiled faintly.

He beckoned to Leung and whispered to him in Cantonese so rapidly that Mulrenan, straining to hear, could not catch even the gist of his words.

The woman, hearing the conversation change from English, entered the room with bowls of tea. Having served

these — the two Chinese men not breaking off to acknowledge her — she took from under the tray a fat manila
envelope tied with string.

Mulrenan sipped at his tea noisily, in the best of manners.

Yip ceased talking and gave the envelope to Mulrenan,
saying, 'You take dis. Opung now.'

He pulled the string at the end of the package, slit open
the flap with his thumb nail and removed a small photograph.

'Who is this?'

It was an ill-focussed photograph of an Oriental man
seating himself in a rickshaw. His face was partly downcast
and in shadow. Pedestrians on the pavement behind the
rickshaw were blurred by their own movement.

'That Fukui.'

Being none the better for this information, Mulrenan
enquired further.

'He Japanese consul in Macau. You no see him?'

Mulrenan had heard of him but had never met or seen
him. He shook his head.

'No matter. Opung more.'

There was a rectangle of paper in the envelope, with a
brief line of European writing on it.

'You see Fukui one day, you go to here' — he pointed to
the paper in Mulrenan's hand — 'an' you ask for Mista
Sum. Eve'y time you see Fukui go to Mista Sum.'

'Is that all?'

'Yes,' said Leung.

'We no pay you,' Yip reiterated. 'But you want some
time some big job by us, we do it.'

It was dark when he left the house. The vegetable seller
had shut his shop and the streets were deserted. A bitter
wind was blowing from the north and cut into him as he
turned out of Travesso dos Bombeiros. He paused in the lee
of a closed food stall to fasten his coat collar.

As he snapped the button, he thought he heard a sound
behind him. It was a dull noise like a soft footfall on a
wooden surface. He spun round. The street was dimly-lit

but empty. The sound came again, no nearer yet no farther away. He listened intently, the wind whistling in the telephone and electricity wires overhead, rattling pieces of paper along the cobbles and bricks of the road surface. Again, the sound reached him. It was quite a few moments before he realised it was distant heavy artillery fire.

7

Alice was trembling when Mulrenan arrived home. He had told her he would be back by seven and it was already past nine when he knocked on the door at the foot of the stairs and Ah Shun let him in, checking his identity through a peephole and murmuring to the bodyguard.

Mulrenan was certain he could look after himself. It was Alice he was convinced was at risk. The Communists had been keeping an eye on them and if they had been able to learn so much then Mulrenan hated to think what information a determined opponent would be able to glean.

It was the opposition that concerned him: the spies of the secret society bosses, the Nationalist Army officers who were as greedy and corrupt as the gangsters, the pirates and the common thugs, all in the same great game and vying against each other.

In the green corner, thought Mulrenan, in the emerald colours of Beloved Ireland, we have Sean Mulrenan, weighing in at just over three quarters of a million Hong Kong dollars and a reputation as a dealer in gems and cure-alls.

He knew he was the odd one out, the only European in an otherwise exclusively Oriental domain: and the single foreign devil was doing as well as — and in some cases, a good deal better than — those who had a family tradition, sometimes even a village tradition in the running of crime, the master-minding of crime or the ingenuities of crime.

He did not have an army of henchmen to guard his back, followers bound to him by blood oath and the allegiance of revenge. It was Mulrenan's considered opinion, the more men you had, the more the chance of spies, traitors and ambitious bastards. A single man, he believed, fared better for as long as his nerves held and his reflexes remained as sharp as those of a mongoose.

However, he acknowledged that everyone had a weak spot. It might be a muscle in his cheek that betrayed him when he was excited, angry or worried. It might have been a predilection for good brandy or under-age girls, opium or other men's wives. It might have been a blind spot over his right shoulder. Whatever his Achilles heel, there would be someone whose job it was to probe and pry until he discovered it. In Mulrenan's case, the weakness was not hard to find: it was his mistress, the pretty ex-singsong girl, Alice Soon. If you cannot hurt a man's body, he knew, his pride or his wallet, strike at his loved ones.

It was on this course Mulrenan's thoughts were running when he hired Ts'o Sau-tak, a sturdily-built man in his early twenties with powerful, stocky legs and rock-hard biceps even when they were unflexed. Although he had recently taken a local name, he was not a local man but hailed from Shanghai where he had worked first as a boy coolie on the waterfront and later as a deckhand on a coastal freighter. This job had not been to his liking; nor had the Glaswegian captain and the Geordie chief engineer. On his third voyage, when the coaster was docked in Foochow, the deckhand had gone ashore, spoken to a few acquaintances in a tea house and passed on details of the ship's manifest and course.

Two nights later, off the coast between Tungshan and Swatow, he had gone below to the engine room and prised open a tool chest. With a huge wrench, he had smashed first the engine room artificer over the crown of his head and then the governor spinning on top of the engine. He had no idea what his action would do, but as the governor was the quickest moving part he could see he assumed it was important. After that, he hid in a locker.

As soon as the governor went, the chief engineer sensed something was drastically wrong and rushed down the companionway just in time to see a drive shaft bearing burst. Pandemonium broke out. The ship hove to and dropped anchor. The deckhand remained in the locker until he heard the gentle rub of timber against the steel hull plates of the coaster. Then he climbed out of the locker, made his way unseen to the sterncastle and threw overboard the five ropes he had previously tied to the rail. Within fifteen minutes, the British officers were dead, the Chinese crew in the port lifeboat rowing hard for the shore four miles away. The pirates looted the ship and set fire to it. For the deckhand, after that, a change of name had seemed advisable.

'What's the matter?' Mulrenan asked as he saw Alice shivering. 'Have you caught something?'

'No,' she replied, hesitantly.

'Is Ts'o about? I didn't see him when I came in.'

A corner of the kitchen had been set aside for the bodyguard and a folding camp bed provided. He was grateful: it was a considerable improvement on his previous accommodation, a shallow dip in the ground behind a stone wall near the border gate with China. T'so was an inveterate gambler and signally unsuccessful. No money he acquired stayed with him longer than half a day.

'Yes. He's awake because I heard him speak when you knocked but he keeps quiet. He says he'll be more effective that way.'

Mulrenan eased himself onto the divan, stretching his feet towards a tall black metal Valor stove standing in the middle of the room. The flames of its circular wick flickered behind the red mica window near the base.

'You know,' he said, 'those stoves remind me of pillar-boxes — boxes you post letters in.'

The dense smell of burning paraffin filled the room and gave it a warm, homely snugness. The window and door frames had been lined or jammed with strips of cloth and paper to exclude the wind.

'Alice? What's the matter, then?'

He held his hands up to her and she took one of them.

'Oh, Sean,' she half-whispered, a solemn despair in her voice. 'That noise. Like summer thunder.'

'It's gunfire,' he said. 'Hong Kong. The Japanese are attacking. It'll all be over by . . ,' he pondered the date, '. . . by Christmas Day, I'd say.'

She shuddered as a spasm of anxiety passed through her.

'You needn't worry,' he consoled her. 'We'll be alright here in Macau. Safe as houses.' He smiled reassuringly. 'They'll not attack a neutral state.'

He glanced up at her. Huge tears rolled over her cheeks, dropping to the collar of her lined and padded gown.

'Come,' he ordered kindly and, pulling on her hand, caused her to step to him and sit upon his knees like a child with its father. He put his arm about her waist and pulled her head downwards, kissing her hair. He seemed genuinely concerned.

Alice felt his chin rasp on her forehead. His lips, when they brushed against her brow, were dry. With his hand, he stroked her thigh and gently rubbed her arm through the thick material of her sleeve.

She made no immediate response but, after a few minutes in which neither of them spoke, she kissed him on his cheek, her tears smearing his skin and leaving a cold trace on his twelve-hour stubble. When she spoke, it was just one word.

'Alec,' she said, despairingly.

'What of him?' asked Mulrenan.

'He's in Hong Kong.'

'No,' he replied, 'he's in Singapore or Kuala Lumpur. The Japs haven't got that far yet. After this little lot, Singapore'll be warned and they'll all get out.'

'No,' she said again.

'Yes,' he comforted her.

'He's in Hong Kong. I saw him.'

'You were mistaken,' Mulrenan said. 'I often see people in the street and think they're so-and-so. But then they're not.'

'You don't understand. I met him, talked with him. I

173

wanted to tell you but I couldn't . . .'

Mulrenan put his hand on the arm of the chair and started to rise. She slid from his knees onto her feet, like a cat being discarded from an uncaring lap. She circled the stove: like a cat, some instinct told her to move to safety.

Quietly, through clenching teeth, he said, 'I told you never to see him. Never! Not ever!'

His fury mounting, Mulrenan crossed the room to the camphorwood chest under the altar to the fung shui. Behind him, a sandalwood joss-stick wisped its thin column of smoke into the air, counteracting the paraffin.

'He was afraid,' she said, timidly.

'I bet he was,' Mulrenan sneered. 'Afraid for his own skin. Afraid some cunt in the fucking Hongkong Bank or fucking Jardine's or fucking Butterfield and Swire would find out his half-Chink sister was shacked up with Sean Mulrenan, the Anglo-Irish pianist turned mobster.'

Alice was shocked both by his sudden and uncharacteristic foul language and his astute guess at how their conversation had gone.

'And I'm right. Aren't I?'

'Yes,' she admitted.

For a few moments, Mulrenan stood stock still, his face expressionless, his arms hanging by his side. His head filled with a rushing noise like water plunging over a fall: hidden within it was a high-pitched whine. Illogically, he wondered if he was possessed by a banshee.

His thoughts grew confused with a loathing he could not at that moment comprehend and an anger he was unable either to suppress or accept. It was as if something had gained control over him and he was immediately afraid. His fear, swirling like a dense smoke under his abhorrence and rage, was for his own sanity. As a poker player, he understood the need to hold the upper hand: now he was in possession of a pair of twos, while his anger or its master held a royal flush.

Suddenly, he slammed his open hand down on the camphorwood chest and spun at her like a Tai Chi boxer, his arms flailing bewilderingly yet with complete coordination. She was stunned into inactivity by the speed with which he moved. One of his fists, shaped like a blade, jabbed for her stomach and her hands instinctively went down to protect her soft belly but, no sooner were they down than his other hand hit her on the cheek with such force her head rammed to one side and the pain scorched through her as if it was the heat of his palm as much as its strength that had shattered her nerves. She lost her balance and fell to the floor, thrusting out her arm. Her wrist pressed against the Valor stove: she whimpered, drew it away, and stumbled to lie on the floor.

From the corner of her eye, she saw the polished toecap of his shoe streaking towards her side. She was defenceless. She could do nothing. Yet the foot halted in mid-air as if it had hit an invisible barrier. It stopped so abruptly the turn-up on the trouser leg above it swung on forward before falling back against the shin. Slowly, the shoe was lowered to the floor. She did not see it as part of Mulrenan but as an inanimate object, some kind of missile hurled at her by a stranger.

Her hand slipped on the floor, scraping splinters from the wood. Alice raised herself on to one elbow. Turning her eyes upwards, she saw Mulrenan staring down at her. His face was ashen, made more ghostly by the glow of the stove and the lamplight. She thought he was going to pass out, quickly realising that if he did he would fall upon her. She rolled away from him, using her legs to help twist the rest of her body. Once clear, she sat up.

He did not keel over nor did he lean on anything for support. His hands, returning to his sides, twitched as if trying to rid themselves of a sticky and loathsome substance.

Gradually, partly from weakness and partly from the fear that a movement on her part would attract him — much as motion, no matter how tiny, gathers the immediate attention of a poisonous snake — Alice got to her feet. When she thought it safe, she stepped slowly backwards towards the bedroom door.

As her fingers grasped the handle, he spoke to her in an

undertone she could barely hear and yet the words were clear with the deliberation of the speech of a teacher hoping his lesson was well learnt.

'Never see him again. Do not write to him, communicate with him in any way. Do not associate with his friends. Keep away from him altogether.'

He did not need to add any threat or hint of punishment. She knew every syllable he uttered carried the full conviction of what he believed to be fully justified hatred.

As she lay in bed, the lamp burning low, Alice tried to think what it was her half-brother had done to engender such animosity. Alec had had no business dealings with Mulrenan: he did not work for a firm with which Mulrenan had connections, did not mix in the same social circles, did not have anything to do with him. She tried to recall if they had even met, but her mind was confused.

There was nothing, so far as she could see, that would make Mulrenan jealous of Alec. Mulrenan lived a life of excitement and was — as she knew from the cache behind the altar — very wealthy, whereas Alec worked long hours in a boring office.

She remembered, as if to draw her mind away from the turmoil, how he had once told her of an inter-mess ragging in which the 'boys from our place' had raided the mess of another hong and 'liberated' a mounted boar's head one of the other hong's number had lanced when pig-sticking near Meerut. They had returned to their mess with the trophy which they dressed in a party hat and hung over the entrance to their billiard room. In retaliation, the owners of the trophy made a reciprocal night raid during which they not only recaptured the boar's head but smeared the insides of all the shoes of their sleeping enemies, which had been left outside their rooms for polishing, with the red ink Chinese scribes used in pads for their ivory seals and chops. Everyone unknowingly put their shoes on in the morning, and the result was that, by the time tiffin came around, with the sweat and activity of walking, the ink had soaked through and everyone's feet were indelibly stained crimson. Alec had thought it was all a huge joke and revelled in the retelling of it and, although she had laughed at his story, Alice had done so only to avoid embarrassing him. She had really thought it very infantile.

In all of this, she could find nothing to cause more than distaste or contempt on Mulrenan's part: and contempt rarely bred deep-seated hatred.

After a while, she could hear Mulrenan moving about in the next room. There was a scraping sound for a while followed by silence. Twice, he called quietly down the stairs to Ts'o and each time they held a quiet, short discussion at the door, none of which she could pick up but which filled her with apprehension. Ts'o left but returned a few minutes later, though he said little. Presumably, she thought, her bodyguard — which she had accepted that she might require now Mulrenan was rich — would now be her prison guard.

Later, after a period of silence during which she dozed fitfully, she heard Mulrenan pacing the living room. He was muttering to himself, his voice rising and falling unintelligibly as if he was taking two parts in an argument. She wondered if the second role was that of her half-brother, then her Chinese instinct suggested that, perhaps, Mulrenan was possessed by a devil and was fighting with it. If he was, she reasoned, the outcome might go to either combatant: devils had strong magics when dealing with weak souls.

Just before dawn, he came into their bedroom, knocking on the door before opening it.

'Come in,' she whispered. It still hurt her mouth to speak.

He was carrying the oil lamp from the main room. It was newly-filled with oil and had had a new wick fitted so the yellow flame, though small, was bright and inappropriately cheerful. She realised Ts'o had been ordered to deal with the lamp, giving the lie to her apprehensive thoughts.

Mulrenan closed the door, holding the lamp so he could see her face but shielding the flame from her eyes with his hand. At first, he said nothing but stared at her as if surprised she was still there.

177

He pulled over the chair upon which she had draped her clothes and sat down, creasing the material. He still held the lamp.

'In the morning,' he said. 'I'll go down and get something from the old man.'

Her face stung where it touched the pillow and, for a moment, she was glad they used European pillows rather than the hard, lacquered papier maché Chinese variety.

'Why?' she asked.

A pained expression entered his eyes. 'Because I love you,' he said, adding as a qualification, 'very much. Very much indeed.'

A man who confesses to love when he is in the wrong is one whose soul is unguarded. Alice knew this and was about to use it against him, accusing while she had the upper hand, but as quickly as she saw her opportunity she let it go. She did not have it in her to press home her advantage.

Except obliquely. Deniably. By implication.

'Can you give me the mirror?' she requested.

He put the oil lamp on the floor by the bed and reached across for a small mirror framed in tortoiseshell lying on the dressing table. He gave it to her and she leaned on one elbow to gaze at herself. Her cheek had not swollen but it was light mauve and blue from a large bruise stretching unevenly from her cheekbone to her jaw.

'Is it tender?' he asked pointlessly.

She pressed her finger against the bruise: where it touched, the skin went white but filled with blood as soon as she released the pressure.

'Yes. Quite.'

'I'm sorry,' he said after a long silence.

He made no move to draw closer to her but sat, leaning forward, his arms on his knees. He appeared so dejected she instantly felt sympathy for him.

'I shall be all right,' she said. 'It's only a bruise.'

She raised her hand again to touch the wound and he saw the red stripe on her wrist.

'What is that?' he asked.

She saw what he was looking at and explained, 'The stove. I pressed my hand upon the stove. It doesn't hurt as much . . . It's not so bad.'

'I'll get something for that, too. From the old man.'

She lay back on the pillow, pulling the blankets up to her neck. The day was breaking outside and a cold dawn wind was draughting into the room, despite the wadges of cloth and strips of paper. She thought about Mulrenan's visit to the herbalist, what category of conversation it would fit into as she listened through the floor.

She dozed but when she awoke again, Mulrenan was still by her bedside. The grey early light was washing into the room through one window from which he had swung aside the shutters. It was windy outside and the glass was rattling. By the bed was a tray upon which was a copper pot of tea and two cups. Under the pot was a spirit flame keeping it simmering.

Mulrenan helped her to sit up, pushing cushions behind her and propping her head on one he held against the end of the bed. His hands were strong and comforting but she could only think of how hard and quickly they could strike, of the other man who dwelt behind the concerned eyes now surveying her bruised cheek.

'Will you have something to drink?'

She shook her head.

'Something else?'

'No.'

They lapsed once more into silence. Alice watched thin veils of dust blow past the window. There had been little rain for several weeks and the streets were dry and bleak. The cold weather had driven the beggars into hiding and the coolies passed by dressed in sacking and paper over their scanty short trousers and vests.

A knock sounded on the door. Ah Shun entered with a stone bottle filled with hot water and wrapped in a length of flannel. She avoided her master and spoke softly to Alice as she tugged free the blankets and inserted the bottle. Alice replied and Ah Shun left, returning shortly with a bowl of small Chinese biscuit-like cakes. Each was yellow and oval with a serrated edge like a coin and embossed with red characters.

Alice smiled her thanks and said to Mulrenan, 'These are very dry. Maybe now I'll have some tea.'

He had been sitting bent over, staring at the floor. Her pointedly speaking to Ah Shun rather than to him had put him in his place. Now the opportunity to do something for her had arisen he moved with alacrity, pouring the tea into one of the porcelain cups.

'Do you mind if I have one, too?' he requested.

She considered this for a moment before replying, absent-mindedly, 'Of course not. Do.'

They continued to sit in silence, sipping their tea. She was determined not to start a conversation: she had nothing to say to him. She felt empty, drained of either love or hate.

'I am sorry,' he repeated.

'I understand,' she said. 'At least, I think I understand. As much as I can. I know you hate' — she was suddenly wary of even using her half-brother's name — 'him though I can't tell why. He's never done anything to you. To us. He has kept away.'

'It's not him I hate,' Mulrenan said, 'but what he is.'

'That's the same thing.'

'No. It's not. It's not the same thing at all. It's very different.'

There was another interruption. Ts'o entered the room and gave two small packages to Mulrenan. Each was wrapped in broad, green leaves secured with twisted bamboo slivers tied in a bow as neatly as if it was silk ribbon. With the packages was a piece of paper covered with scrawly, child-like characters clumsily written with a black-inked brush. She recognised the herbalist's hand. Mulrenan had been down to his shop while she slept.

Mulrenan said nothing and Ts'o left the room walking backwards, as if in the presence of royalty. Perhaps, Alice thought, he would be careful, now he had seen how his master treated his woman, not to turn his back on Mulrenan.

He undid the packages. In one was a grey paste smelling faintly of almonds. In the other was a white powder with brown flecks in it. He read the paper.

'You smear the ointment on the bruise,' he said then reading on added, 'but don't rub it in. Just leave it. The powder you sprinkle on the burn and bandage over it.'

He offered the ointment to Alice but she waved it aside, saying, 'Later. I don't want it now. It will mark the pillowcase. I'll put it on when I get up.'

She finished her tea, refused another cup and, reaching under the blankets, eased herself up a little higher.

'A man, what he is, it's the same thing,' she said again.

'Yes, to you I suppose it is,' he admitted. 'Yet it isn't to me. You see, I really do hate Alec simply for what he is.'

'A clerk?' She expressed surprise. 'How can you hate a mere clerk? That's all he is. He just might one day be a manager, even a director — a powerful man, a taipan — but I don't think so and I don't think you do, either. He's so average. He works hard and plays — he's like a boy, no matter what his age is. He can't offer you a threat. You are much more than him. So much more.'

'Yes, I am,' Mulrenan agreed, no conceit in his voice. 'What I hate about him isn't his job or his position. He can never touch me. What I so hate is . . .'

He rose to his feet and gazed out of the window. Past him she saw that the trees in the cemetery were waving and the dust was eddying in the street. Through the railings of the verandah she caught sight of a Portuguese soldier in a smart uniform, a negro from Mozambique, walking by with his head hunched into his shoulders and his hand before his eyes. He was wearing an overcoat too long for him. It flapped in the wind which was rippling the tight curls of his hair. Had it been September, warm and humid, there might have been a typhoon approaching but this was blowing not from the sea but from the land and it was carrying on its back the central Chinese winter.

'. . . what I so hate is that he is English.'

'So are you,' she observed. 'So am I.'

181

Mulrenan left the window and stood at the end of the bed. His hands grasped the rail and she could feel him shaking, gently vibrating the bed with his suppressed anger and frustration.

His face was tense, every muscle strained even though he was not grimacing or leering but simply staring ahead at a point on the wall above her.

It was then she realised he was weak, and understood what that weakness was and how it undermined his soul.

Never before had it occurred to her that he had such a failing. Of course, she had appreciated his faults and had learnt to accept them, assimilate them into their relationship, but she had always seen him as strong. He was, she had considered, a confident man: hard-nosed in his business dealings, determined and successful. Yet, beneath this veneer of self-assurance there was a flaw in his character which had caused him to hit her, to hate her half-brother, and to despise the British.

Mulrenan could not, she now saw, truly love.

Something within him forbade him to feel love: she wondered if he believed such an emotion was a weakness in itself to be avoided and she was saddened by the thought. Yet she also realised, in the very same instant, she would never be able to convince him otherwise.

She felt strangely secure. He would not hit her again. He would not dare. Any rage surging in him now was not directed at her. It would be elsewhere, at Alec, at the whole world. She did not care. She was safe, had gone through the tempest of his anger and survived.

'I am not.' he said emphatically, his knuckles whitening. 'I may be many things. I may be a gangster in the eyes of some, a thief, a gun-runner, a friend of pirates: I've been called all those by people jealous of me. They still need me, though. But English I am not and nor are you.'

Alice replied, 'My mother was English.'

'And your father Chinese. Does that make you English? Does that make you Chinese? No. It makes you neither. Certainly not one or the other. And me? My father was Irish and my mother . . .'

'English. And so the same applies to you.'

'Yes,' he replied, 'but you are what you feel yourself to be. I can't be English. I've seen what they've done to Ireland. To my country. Destroyed it. Divided it, stolen the best land for themselves, forced the common Irishman and woman into starvation and emigration.'

'To your half-country.'

'No!' His voice rose but he quickly controlled it. 'I am Irish. By bad luck, I've English blood in me, but I ignore it. It's a flaw. Like having malaria. I'm not ill all the time but the disease is there, erupting every now and then and, when it does, I fight it.'

She looked at him standing by her feet and was filled with pity: yet it was not compassion born of love but more something she might feel towards a stranger or an animal being maltreated in the street.

'The English,' she argued, 'or at least the British, and that includes the Irish, have done the same to my country. If I can call China my country. They've used it, invaded it, made millions of us slaves to opium so that they could gain trade. But I don't hate them. I know they are still men, simply doing what men always have done. We Chinese have invaded Japan, Korea, Manchuria over the centuries. We have fought from region to region. It is the way of people.'

She stretched her hand to the leaf-wrapped ointment he had put on the bedside table, scooping some on to her fingers. She sniffed it and spread it gently across her bruise as if applying a delicate cosmetic. Mulrenan, anticipating her needs, opened a drawer and brought out a handkerchief on which she wiped her fingers clean.

'The Chinese have murdered the English, too,' she continued. 'Think of the guerrillas in what Europeans call the Boxer Rising. They thought they were doing good. Perhaps they were. But I no more hate the Chinese for killing the English than I do the English for degrading the Chinese. Those peoples are not in me. I am myself. I control my own fears and hates, my own destiny as much as I can. I do not allow myself to be influenced by such thoughts.'

Her hands had risen to her small breasts, pressing in on them as if the argument she offered was bursting from her and she was trying to keep it in herself where it might remain pure, unsullied, her own possession.

Mulrenan did not immediately answer. At length he said, 'For you it's easy. You can be detached. That part of you which is the Chinese is inscrutable.'

He seemed to realise the cliché in what he had said and laughed ruefully. She laughed with him. The first tenuous strand of reconciliation was woven.

'You know what I mean,' he went on, to justify himself. 'You've that fatalistic inner calm. You can put things aside or into perspective. I can't. I'm not half-Chinese but half-Irish and the Irish are Celtic and have the Celtic anger, that . . . Do you know what "Celtic" is?'

She smiled and said, 'No. I don't. But I can guess.'

Mulrenan moved around the end of the bed and sat on the edge of the mattress by her feet. It was hard where the wooden frame pressed through the kapok and blankets. He shifted to make himself more comfortable and she moved her legs aside to give him space.

'I hate that part of me that's English,' he confessed suddenly, staring at his hands where they spread out on his thighs.

'Why? What is the point?'

'The point!' he exclaimed. 'Dear god! If I knew the point I'd do something about it.'

There was an awful anguish in his words and his voice took on a more Irish accent than she'd heard him use in many, many months.

'You can do nothing about your Englishness. You can't deny your birthright. We none of us chose our parents,' she said.

'I know. That's the terrible part of it.'

The anguish was replaced by a tone of defeat. She touched his arm. He looked at her then grasped her hand as if it could pull him from the suffocating quicksand of himself. His fingers tightened on her wrist and on the burn from the stove. She gave a cry. He let go of her, horrified to have caused more pain, even in error.

There were tears in her eyes and he said quickly, 'I'm sorry. I didn't think of your burn.'

'It's not why I'm crying,' she whispered. 'I shouldn't have mentioned Alec. I should have kept quiet. It was just the gunfire . . .'

Through their fighting and the night, through the wind, they had forgotten the distant rumble of heavy artillery.

Together, they listened. The wind was whining in the cracks. The pane of glass rattled in the frame. Grit tapped upon the window.

'I can't hear it now,' she said.

'They'll not open fire until they can see. It's very early.'

'I am still afraid. For him. Despite everything.'

'Don't be,' he tried to reassure her. 'He'll be alright. The British Navy'll sail up from Singapore. They've big ships down there; battleships like "Prince of Wales" and "Repulse", destroyers and frigates, maybe an aircraft carrier. If the navy don't get here, Hong Kong's an island. Easily defended. Think of those fortresses with their big guns built on Hong Kong-side. Above the university, at Lei Yue Mun. Think of the fortress the British have made of Stonecutters Island. He'll be alright. If the worst comes to the worst, they'll evacuate.'

He fell silent, lost in private thoughts.

'Sean.'

He returned to her from his reverie.

'I love you,' she said. 'The English and the Irish.'

Yet no sooner had she spoken than a doubt began to form.

He lifted her burnt hand to his lips and kissed it, pressing his lips lightly on the scar. It was weeping and his lips were wettened by the straw-yellow fluid oozing from the wound. There was, he noticed, an area of ragged pinpricks on her palm.

'Splinters,' she explained as he rubbed them enquiringly with his fingers.

'I love you, too. And I'm sorry — most terribly sorry —

for what I've done to you. I don't know . . .' He stopped speaking, his eyes fastening on her own and moving from one to the other. 'Yes, I do know. You see, Alice, I love the Chinese in you, and I hate the English in myself. And therefore I hate the English in you. That's why I can't abide him. Alec,' he added, unnecessarily. 'I regard him as a part of you I'd drive out like the Chinese do spirits from in front of the moon at the August festival. But beating drums and gongs and firecrackers won't exorcise him.'

'Nor will violence,' she said.

He stood up and tucked in his shirt which had slipped from the waist of his trousers. She realised he was wearing the same clothes as he had returned home in the evening before.

'I have to go out. Ah Shun will fetch everything you want. Don't let her leave the house. I want her with you, to nurse you, get you whatever you want. If you need anything from outside, send Ts'o. I'll tell him.'

She saw that he wanted to kiss her but felt guilty, so she asked him to and, tugging his sleeve, pulled him within her reach.

'I can forget all this if you can,' she told him. 'It's maybe not my place to say it but — I forgive you, Sean.'

His expression, already serious, became more grave.

'It is your place,' he said humbly. 'I'll make it up to you. Somehow. I promise that.'

Ah Shun brought a light meal of steamed fish and rice at noon which Alice, famished, ate quickly whilst seated at the table in her padded gown. When the bowls were cleared away and she had wiped her mouth on a hot face cloth, Alice called Ts'o and ordered him to go to the stationers' shop near the Central Hotel in Avenida Almeida Ribeiro and purchase two thick notebooks bound in marbled board. He was also to buy a pen, a box of steel nibs and a pot of Stephen's blue-black ink. He was instructed to make certain it was a bottle with a tight fitting screw top and, inside the neck, an angled glass divider that acted as a reservoir: she did not want to have to keep an inkwell. Ts'o could not understand what she meant about the bottle: with a pencil stub, she drew him a diagram on a piece of paper. At the same time, she requested of her amah she go to the fishermen's stalls on the quay and obtain a big grouper at least two catties in weight. If that was not possible, she was to buy as many individual fish as would make up the weight. She intended, she said, to have a feast when Mulrenan returned that evening: while the amah was out, she would draw up a list of other shopping needed.

As soon as the bodyguard and the servant had left, Alice quickly drew up a list of delicacies. That scribbled down, she went into the bedroom, opened the remaining shutters and, with a sharp knife usually used to butcher meat or decapitate hens, began to hollow out her own secret hiding place at floor level, behind a section of loose skirting panel.

It took her several hours. When Ts'o returned, she sent him on another errand: the shopping list kept the amah busy for the rest of the afternoon.

The stonework was firm and she had to scrape away the mortar to shift each block. At some stage, the wall had been repaired with bricks which crumbled. She had to build a wooden lintel and side props, pilfered from a broken chair in the firewood box in the courtyard, to stop the aged bricks caving in. She hid the bricks, dust and mortar chips in the space beneath the floorboards.

After Ts'o had delivered the notebooks, matters were easier, for she now had their size and the hidey-hole was intended for these as well as any treasures she might acquire in the future. Mulrenan knew of her other hiding place in which she stored important papers; of this one she wanted him to remain completely ignorant.

By five o'clock, the task was completed. Alice stood back to check the skirting appeared un-tampered with: a few touches to the panel and the deft blowing away of dust ingrained into the flooring was all that was needed. She tapped the wood with her foot. The length of folded cloth tacked on the back muffled any hollow thud.

Her work done, she sat on the bed, crossing her legs and balancing the first of the notebooks on her ankles. She fitted the first nib into the pen, dipped it in the ink, tapped it on the rim of the bottle and wrote:

December 23/41

I have decided to keep a diary from this day on. It will not be just a document of events and deeds, happenings and parties and social chit-chat.

She lowered the nib too far in to the ink and her next letter blotted as if it was the result of the penmanship of a clumsy schoolgirl.

I get little of those. It will be a book of thoughts and ideas.

She dipped the pen into the ink for a third time and continued to write, her hand unsteady.

Last night, we heard gunfire from the east. I think Hong Kong is falling to the Japanese. I fear for Alec's safety.

She started a new line.

Sean hit me.

She stopped writing and watched the words dry. Somehow, by putting them on paper, the events they documented became divorced from her. The ink removed the recent memory to a distant place.

It was only just in time that Alice managed to hide the embryonic diary. She was inserting the skirting board into the grooves cut to receive it when she heard Mulrenan's voice through the floor, passing the time of day with the herbalist. Within minutes, he was mounting the stairs, calling to Ah Shun to bring hot water. For her part, the amah was fully occupied cooking the fish and it was Ts'o who filled the enamel jug from the kettle on the hob.

Mulrenan was still unsure of the kind of reception he might get from Alice.

He knew he had been lying about Hong Kong's safety. If

the Japanese mounted a concerted attack, the island was doomed. There were a number of divisions of tested and tried Japanese troops in Kwangtung Province: that he knew from his trips up the Pearl River estuary and his contacts with the Communists. Their supply lines were no more than twenty miles long whereas the British supply line stretched to Singapore. The big gun batteries on The Peak were positioned to repel a sea-borne assault. The Japanese were coming from the landward side. Hong Kong had had it.

As soon as he entered the main room, Alice came through from the bedroom and kissed him lightly on the cheek, reaching up on tiptoe like a daughter to her father. On her hand he saw there were the browny stains of iodine solution dabbed where, he assumed, the splinters from the floor had pierced her skin. He was not to know she had acquired these additional cuts during the afternoon.

'There's something special for you tonight,' she said with as much false feminine guile as she could muster. He enjoyed it when she was coquettish.

'What?'

'You'll see. If you can't smell it.'

He sniffed the air and, as he did so Ts'o opened the door with the water jug. The aroma of deep-frying fish and spice blew into the room as strongly as smoke.

As he washed his hands and face, she sat nearby studying his back. Under his shirt, the muscles moved with a set pattern as if there passed through his flesh, at every move, a tremor or series of waves each ordered and depending upon the other for life. It was like watching ripples spreading across a pond.

'The house is warm,' he complimented her. 'It's bitter outside. The wind's dropped yet it's still cold. They say it'll get warmer, though.'

'Any news from Hong Kong?' she ventured.

'Some. I've had several messages via the Reds inland from Shum Chun. The Japanese've occupied the New Territories and most of Kowloon. They've landed on the island — at the eastern end — and there's fighting on the

189

southern shore by Aberdeen. The Japanese control Lamma Island. There's a rumour the Stanley peninsula is holding out, but it can't stay for long. The British're outnumbered ten to one, some say. Others twenty to one. There's even rumour of surrender.'

Despite the knowledge that his information was scaring Alice, he could not help feeling a sense of vicarious triumph as if he, somehow, had aided and abetted this defeat. He considered it was good news, the timely doling out by the omniscient fates of just desserts.

'I've kept the stove alight all day,' she said, changing the subject completely, wanting to force out of her brain all his war news, replace it with banalities.

From the chest beneath the household altar, Mulrenan lifted a bottle of brandy. He poured two generous measures in to delicate cups intended for rice wine not cognac.

'Will you accept a small gift from me?' he asked. 'It's meant only as a small part of my apologies,' he added, cautious in case she thought he believed he could eradicate his lost temper and her pain easily, with one present.

'Yes. What is it?'

She gave her reply as much enthusiasm as she could, holding out her hand.

Often she had seen such chamois leather bags, with their black or brown drawstrings like the laces from ladies' shoes. The contents of this one, however, exceeded by a considerable margin anything which had tumbled out in the past.

In her palm was a single gemstone. The lamps had been lit whilst Mulrenan had been washing and their light pierced the stone and was magically fractured and magnified.

'What is it?' he questioned her. 'Have you learnt your lessons?'

'Of course,' she chided him. 'Give me a glass.'

Mulrenan gave her a watchmaker's glass and, holding the stone close to the lens under the full white glare of the hissing petromax lamp, her shadow cast darkly on the ceiling, she studied it, revolving it in her fingers. Finally, after a thorough examination, she removed the glass from her eye and spoke, unable to disguise her pleasure.

'Is this for me?'

'Yes. I'll get it mounted in gold. As a ring?' he suggested.

'Yes, please.'

She was thrilled by it.

'But what is it, Alice?'

'It's a blue sapphire, a Kashmiri one. It's that — what do they call it? — cornflower blue. Very few inclusions. In fact, only one I can see readily with the glass. It also has the milky quality suggesting a stone from Kashmir, from the 1880s. It's oval, trap cut. It's huge, too. For what it is. Seven carats?' she guessed.

'Bravo!' he exclaimed. 'You're right in every detail completely. Except the weight. It's 7.91 carats, so eight as near as dammit.'

'Where did you get it from?' she enquired.

She knew it was not from his secret stock behind the all-guarding shrine. She was well aware of what was in there and it was her intention, quite soon, to take an inventory: it was a decision she made whilst burrowing her own niche.

'That's a secret,' he said. 'But I only bought it today. I've known of its existence for several weeks but no one was prepared to offer on it. It's too big. So I did, in the end. It's yours.' He swallowed the brandy in one gulp. 'If you give it me back, I'll take it to the goldsmith in the morning.'

'No,' she said after a moment's thought. 'I think I'd rather keep it like this. It's so beautiful.'

He was a little disappointed at her decision but was in no position to complain. It would have pleased him for her to have worn it when they went out together but, knowing the recent history of the gem, he decided perhaps it was just as well she preferred to preserve it unset.

8

The fan tan table was about five feet square and well-worn in the centre where years of sorting and counting by sweating hands had smoothed the dark wood and given it a lustre no polish could achieve. Leaning away from the surface, his fingers linked behind his head and his back arched to relieve the dull ache at the base of his spine, Mulrenan considered how that stain represented so many millions of beans, so many tens of thousands of dashed hopes and so many moments of exhilaration or despair.

The banker called the next game and Mulrenan placed three patacas' worth of chips on the two and five on the four. Four had been lucky for him that evening, perhaps because the corner of the table into which was carved the character for four, an oblong with two lines in it giving it the appearance of a crude window with draped curtains, was opposite from him and the act of leaning across gave him good fortune. The other gamblers, all of them Chinese, placed their bets and the banker, who was working for the house, dipped his hand into a brass bowl full of red beans and dropped fistsful of these into the centre of the table. With a small ivory, strigil-like rake he divided the beans into groups of four, the punters checking carefully to ensure no error.

Mulrenan did not bother to watch. The banker had nothing to gain by miscounting for he took ten per cent of the stakes regardless of whoever won.

The last of the beans were sorted: there were two left over therefore those who had bet on the two corner were the winners. Mulrenan shared the winnings with an elderly Chinese man who had watery eyes and an unsteady hand. He was sitting next to Mulrenan and had about himself a faint, dry smell like that of an antique shop or a secondhand book stall.

Another game commenced and, once more, Mulrenan backed the four but ignored the other corners. This time, as on a number of occasions that evening, the beans were sorted to leave no remainder: therefore the four corner won. Mulrenan took the stakes from all the corners after the banker had cut out the house share.

Feeling in his pocket, Mulrenan realised he was having a very good run. His initial bank of one hundred patacas had grown into nearly one thousand: he did not need to count the chips for experience told him how much he had made on the evening.

He looked at the Rolex. It was just past midnight and he smiled as he remembered its former owner, wondering where the man would be now. Probably dead in Hong Kong.

He stepped away from the table, his space quickly occupied by a young woman dressed in a chocolate brown *cheong sam*. As she sat in his seat, he watched the material stretch across her thighs and buttocks, pressing the flesh in. Many of the players stood around the table and seats were only for agile first comers.

The large room was crowded. Smoke hung about the ceiling, the smell a mingling of perspiration and tobacco. The fans revolved slowly. It was surprisingly not as hot as he might have expected and, as he neared the door, Mulrenan felt the chill of the winter touch his hands and face. The cold spell was continuing.

As he buttoned his coat about him, a voice over his shoulder said, 'Excuse me, sir.'

It was a cultured voice suggesting it had been given a good education outside China. It had, in just three words, a propriety about it, a politeness neither subservient nor oppressive. It was the voice of one man speaking to an equal. For that reason, it surprised Mulrenan and he turned to find the old man from the fan tan table.

'You dropped this,' said the old man, holding out a silver Yard-o-lead propelling pencil. 'It slipped from your pocket as you were placing your last bet. It's never good to play across the table for these things can happen. Though for you I see the four has been an auspicious number.'

'Thank you,' Mulrenan said, receiving the pencil and taken aback at the man's honesty. 'And yes, four has been my number tonight.'

'I, too, have not lost this evening, though I have not made the kind of profit you have achieved. You would seem to have the best gambling man's inheritance: it is not to be counted in chips or coin but in unbankables such as a fair share of good fortune. But a gambler needs much more than luck, wouldn't you say? A gambler's best assets are his cash reserve, good luck and a degree of anger. Perhaps that's why you're such a fine gambler.' He paused to fumble with the cloth fastenings on his gown. 'May I walk with you, Mr Mulrenan?'

Mulrenan agreed, said he would be delighted, but was immediately on his guard. A stranger who knows one's name without being introduced is a man of whom to be wary.

'My name is Tsang. Frederick Tsang, but my friends inevitably call me Freddy. Do follow suit.' Unusually, for the Chinese did not often laugh in the outward manner of Europeans, he chuckled and added, 'Not an inappropriate metaphor bearing in mind that we have only just left a house of cards.'

'Do you live nearby?' Mulrenan enquired. 'Perhaps I might walk some of the way to your home? Or perhaps we might find a tea house still open? It is a freezing night and it's not wise to walk alone these days.'

'In fact,' Tsang answered, 'I do not live in Macau but in Canton. Here, I am staying with an old friend. Or, to be more truthful, I am staying in his house while he is away. Family business in China.' He put his hands into the sleeves of his gown and hugged his arms into his stomach. 'I doubt we shall find a teahouse open at this hour. But I would be honoured if you would take a glass of something in my present residence.'

Accepting, Mulrenan knew the man must have spent the past five hours building up to this moment, preparing his invitation. Folding his fingers around the butt of the small pistol in the pocket of his overcoat gave Mulrenan confidence. He was glad he had not been drinking during the evening. He might need his quick reflexes. Perhaps he had not dropped the pencil at all.

The chill wind precluded conversation but they did not have far to go. Tsang was lodging in a small house at the end of a narrow court off Rua do Monte, under the shadow of the Old Monte Fortress with its dull bronze cannon poking through the crenellations in the walls from which grew weeds that now, in the winter months, were reduced to brown tufts of rustling dead leaves and stalks. The house was approached discreetly, through a gate tucked away behind a courtyard in which there was a well of the kind often found in Italian piazzas. The well was boarded-over and pots of barren earth awaiting seedlings lined the rim.

Knocking on the door, Tsang waited as bolts were drawn and the latch snapped. As he and Mulrenan entered, a heavily built manservant with a shaven head and big hands offered to help Mulrenan with his coat but he removed it himself, slipping the pistol surreptitiously into his jacket pocket.

'Please,' Tsang indicated a half-open door, giving it a gentle push, 'come in and sit down. Make yourself comfortable.'

The room into which Mulrenan was ushered was luxuriously furnished in the traditional Chinese style. The furniture was solidly made of dark rosewood, the broad chairs square with carved sides, the seats padded with quilted brocade and plain silk cushions. It was not furniture upon which anyone could be comfortable for it was designed to suit a strict code of etiquette and formality. Upon the floor a large, patterned Tientsin carpet covered the boards; the walls were hung with painted scenes of the mist-wraithed Kweilin hills and tapestries of slender egrets or plump finches balancing upon blade-leafed bamboo canes or twigs laden with apple-blossom.

A small table with legs bowed like those of a well-bred English bulldog was produced and set in the centre of the room. Cups were brought in on a tray along with a slender vase-like vessel filled with hot rice wine.

'Mei jow,' Tsang said, their not having spoken since sitting down. 'Do you like it? But, of course, you do. How can you not after living in China for so many years. It is usually served with food, as you know, but I see no harm in taking it on its own on such a raw night. Or perhaps you would prefer a brandy?'

Tsang raised his hand to beckon the man servant, but he had left the room quietly upon his slippered feet.

'I'd prefer the wine,' Mulrenan said and, receiving his cup, raised it saying, 'Yum sing.'

It was the common Chinese form of 'cheers' or 'down the hatch'. He hoped this might give Tsang the impression he was off his guard.

It was soon evident the ploy did not work for Tsang continued, 'Yum sing. I find rice wine a joy only acquired with time. Too many years living outside China has given me some particularly un-Oriental tastes.'

'Where have you lived?' Mulrenan asked, not sipping his wine until he saw Tsang partake of his own. The Chinese were pastmasters at mickey finns and Mulrenan had seen a few swallowed in his time.

'In England, mostly. It's where I picked up the name Freddy. At Oxford. I was an undergraduate there, at Merton College, in the early years of the century. Reading medicine. Do you know Oxford?'

'I've played the piano there a few times. The Randolph Hotel, the Mitre. Do you know those?' Mulrenan rejoined.

'Yes, indeed I do,' Tsang replied. 'I've spent a pleasurable evening in the former. I expect,' he refilled his cup and passed the container to Mulrenan, 'with the war it is a little shoddier now. It will have lost some of its former glory. But I doubt if that will concern you very much, will it?'

'Not a great deal.' Mulrenan decided to play a trump card in the game of their conversation. 'As you must know, I'm no lover of the British.'

'Indeed not.' Tsang looked meditatively at the painting hanging on the wall opposite him. For a moment he seemed far away in his thoughts, then he said, 'Your anti-British emotions are not unknown to us, Mr Mulrenan. And I can sympathise with that point of view — even if others cannot. I understand also that, despite your opinions of the British, you are at present considering doing them a great service — perhaps I should say favour? — in their war effort.'

Mulrenan helped himself to the rice wine and took another sip before answering, the tart perfume of the wine catching in his nostrils.

'I'm not quite sure I know what you're getting at,' he said truthfully but politely and with enough force, he hoped, to imply he was not pleased with such a prying invasion of his activities.

'Fukui? Do you know him?'

'Not really. He's the Japanese consul — that's common knowledge — but I don't know him. I've never met him though I've seen him about, of course.'

'You've met him socially, perhaps?' Tsang hinted.

'No. Not at all. He's not one to mix in my circles.'

Tsang laughed quietly.

'Quite. He's not one to know many pirates except, possibly, as their torturer. A particularly unsavoury race, the Japanese . . .'

Mulrenan thought of the irony in the statement: the Chinese were not novices at the arts of painful persuasion.

'. . . And you report his movements to the Communist guerillas?'

Mulrenan drained his cup.

'What makes you think that, Freddy?' he asked, with an appropriate stress of polite sarcasm on the name. 'I'm known to the Communists; that's true. And as you seem to know so much about me, I'm sure you also know I'm a businessman not a soldier. I deal . . .'

'In guns, medicines and medical supplies, gemstones, precious metals; yes.'

'Are you implying I'm some sort of agent provocateur?'

'Not at all. I know exactly what you are, Mr Mulrenan. I also know it is your bidding to report Fukui's movements to Mr Sum.'

'What are . . .' Mulrenan began, but Tsang lifted his hand, his finger upright in an admonishing point.

'Do not deny it. I am merely testing you. You seem to hold firm to your friends.' His finger lowered to the table between them. 'Do refill your cup.'

Mulrenan declined and Tsang helped himself to the last of the wine.

'I am aware of your request to report on Fukui for I am — in a manner of speaking — Mr Sum's superior. And it worries us — me, that is — that I understand he has heard nothing from you for a while.'

'That's correct,' Mulrenan admitted.

He had not sent word to Sum for a fortnight partly because he had not seen Fukui and partly because he was tiring of leaving messages which seemed to him to be of little import. To simply state he had spotted the Japanese walking in the street struck him as pointless and he said as much to Tsang.

'Good. I was afraid perhaps you were having second thoughts, were worried that by spying on the consul you would be assisting the British. After all, his downfall would be of advantage to the British and, if it was traced to you, might compromise your neutrality. I'm sure you realise that the Japanese have a fairly large sphere of influence in Macau . . .'

Mulrenan grunted agreement. It was well-known the Japanese had more than a hand in the operation of Macau despite the Portuguese administration.

'But,' Tsang continued, 'we have had need of your reports, no matter how trivial they have appeared. They were a test of you.'

Tsang looked back at the scroll then shifted his gaze directly into Mulrenan's face.

'It may well be, in the not-too-distant future, we will want you to do something more for us. You will not be paid. Yip was right when he told you that. But we shall do you a huge favour shortly afterwards.'

'You sound like a prophet,' Mulrenan interrupted.

'I am, Mr Mulrenan. In this instance, I am.' He put his

wine cup on the tray. 'Tell me, in your travels and dealings, have you ever killed?'

Mulrenan made no reply.

'No matter. If you have to, you will. I know this. We are alike, you and I. Men of the world. I save lives as a doctor, but I take lives as a warrior: that's the dichotomy of my world, much as your dichotomy is your mixed blood. And now, I'm afraid, I must attend to some — how can I put it? — paperwork before I sleep.'

Taking the hint, Mulrenan rose and said, 'I may be capable of many things, Mr Tsang — and you no doubt know them all . . .'

'Say nothing. You'll be hearing from me.'

He opened the door and Mulrenan saw the man servant standing guard by it: he was returning a Bowie knife to the scabbard on his belt.

'How ingenious is the Oriental mind!' Tsang exclaimed, recognising Mulrenan's appreciation of the sentry. 'As you well know, ingenuity is increased with a foreign education or, in your case, breeding.'

Mulrenan shuffled himself into his coat and gripped Tsang's offered hand.

'Let me advise you, as a friend,' Tsang remarked as Mulrenan stepped into the courtyard, 'Fan tan is a foolish game for a serious gambler. You cannot win large sums except by strokes of considerable good fortune and only in a game with high stakes. Stick to poker or backgammon or chemin de fer. Your best bets are made on gemstones, though. Especially good sapphires.

'And be warned: there are those of more than one persuasion who would like to see you . . . *removed* I think is an accurate word to use.' He pointed to Mulrenan's pocket. 'And you are well advised to carry a pistol: Macau is not, as you have said, the safe place it was. Ask the British Consul. Or the Japanese!'

It was with an acceptance of the inevitable that Mulrenan bade Tsang goodnight. He would hear from him again, with an instruction he would be bound to obey to the letter. There was, he thought, no avoiding it and he walked home quickly, taking care to mind his back so that nothing more than the winter wind penetrated his coat.

9

The temple forecourt was empty except for a young boy sweeping the litter of spent joss-sticks into a dustpan fashioned from the corner of a plywood tea chest and a woman who was pulling them out of the huge bronze urn, the incense burner positioned in the centre of the yard, to throw them heedlessly on to the flagstones. A tree overhanging the low wall had shed most of its leaves which were smouldering in a pile by the arched gateway. As Alice watched, the boy tipped the contents of his dustpan onto the leaves, a dense cloud of incense smoke infiltrating the barren branches.

She had purchased a packet of the chrome yellow joss-sticks the day before and now before the urn, removed the gaily printed wrapping of red, gold and silver characters, dragons and arabesques. Beside the urn was an oily flame burning in a small lantern with a cracked glass door. Holding the joss-sticks in a bunch in her right hand, Alice opened the door and revolved the bundle in the flame, protecting it from the wind with her left. When the incense was alight, she held the sticks in her two hands and bowed three times towards the temple entrance, waving them up and down so the glow on the ends flared and faded. She then lifted them, ramming the red spokes of the lower ends into the damp sand and grey ash in the urn. The flames on the joss-sticks were extinguished by a gust and the ends smoked into the sky.

Alice watched for a few moments how the smoke rose a few inches and was then whipped away by the wind as it surged round the eaves of the temple roof.

Normally, the portico to the temple would have been

thronged but on this harsh day it was abandoned. The person whom she had come to see would, in weather like this, be inside the temple, sitting just within the door.

The wind tugging at her European style coat, beneath the lower hem of which her Chinese-style trouser legs looked most quaint, Alice crossed the forecourt and climbed the steps to the main temple door.

The interior was gloomy, the ceiling hung with banners and huge coils of incense glowing in the semi-darkness like the cigarettes of a silent heavenly host. A red candle burnt in a holder to one side of the image of the god. He was seated between pillars of wood painted crimson and gold, up which carved gilt dragons clawed their way, his own body gaudily be-decked in godly clothing and pressed with gold leaf. His stark eyes stared, his lips half-smiling and half-grimacing. Like the very best gods, he was ambiguous. He might be laughing or he might be sneering. It depended on the worshipper's point of view.

Before the altar was a table bearing a bowl of sweetmeats, the sugar coating glossy in the light of two small candles. More joss-sticks smoked in pots, their smoke mingling near the ceiling with that from the coils so that the peak of the roof was obscured by a blue haze. The cold draught entering through the door kept the fog of incense high up: Alice would otherwise have felt her eyes stinging.

On a low stool by the doorway squatted the fortune teller. He was an old man dressed in a grubby padded coat, the sleeves of which were too long and had been rolled up, and a pair of baggy trousers. Beneath these, as out of place as Alice's trousers under her coat, appeared a pair of cast-off Portuguese army boots. He was eating a bowl of plain rice.

Without being asked, he handed Alice a bamboo cylinder in which were loosely packed thirty or forty slivers of wood, each delicately decorated. She bowed before the altar, knelt and started to gently shake the cylinder. Gradually, some of the wooden rods began to rise. She continued until, finally, one fell out of the cylinder onto the floor. She picked it up and returned the cylinder to the old man who, putting it aside, took the one that had fallen and, peering at it, consulted an almanac.

He still did not speak. Alice was a little concerned at his silence but was also aware his apparent reticence was a part of the proceedings. It lent mystery to what she believed was a simple divination of the truth.

'You would like another method, too?' she was asked, the old man's Cantonese mumbled and indistinct.

'Yes.'

From her pocket she took some coins. The old man accepted them, dropping them into a box under his stool. They thumped on the wood. He had not had many recent customers.

In a recess nearby was a cage containing a pure white finch with pink legs and a red beak. It was huddled on its perch, its feathers fluffed for warmth. Between the cage bars was jammed a cuttlefish skeleton at which the bird had been pecking.

On the floor, next to the cage, the old man smoothed out a line of well-thumbed cards, face down. From under his stool he produced a sardine tin which he rattled. The finch shuffled its feathers. The old man slid the cage door up and the little bird hopped out, surveyed the line of cards, picked one up in its beak, dropped it on the floor and chirped once. The old man opened a makeshift lid on the tin and the bird helped itself to seed before hopping back into the cage. The old man slid the door shut and returned the cage to its dark niche.

Once again, the fortune teller consulted his almanac before pronouncing what the sticks and the bird had shown to him, Alice having to pay close attention to his blurred articulation.

'You are a queen as yet to be crowned,' he began, 'but before your coronation there will be much strife and trouble in your nation. You will suffer much in the day but your evening will be blessed with a glorious sunset and your remaining days will be warm. A great joy will come to you in the form of a son. But he will be your only child whom you must guard against common devils. You will lose what you want, and you will gain much you do not want but time will show these treasures to be more valuable than what you have lost. And you must beware of those that fly. Your destiny is set and you can do nothing to alter it. Yours is not just a common course but a fate decreed by the gods.'

'Is this good or bad?'

'Good, mostly good. But you may think it bad.'

Alice questioned the old man further but he was unable to suggest any other interpretation. The stick and the bird were irrefutable.

As she rode home in a rickshaw, the hood up to protect her from the weather and the gaze of passers-by, for her bruised cheek was still lurid, Alice considered the fortune teller's prophecies, searching in her mind for the inaccuracies. All fortune tellers promised a son, if not three or four: it was almost obligatory. And the vagueness of the predictions made possible several alternatives. What most scared Alice was the advice to beware of those that fly.

10

From time to time, Chinese visitors came to the house in Rua dos Curtidores. For the most part, they were former acquaintances of Alice, her parents or Ah Shun. Only a few were known to Mulrenan or his contacts. Some of them were making for relatives in Kwangtung Province: others had nowhere to go, preferring the instability of travelling to the insecurity of struggling to make a living in occupied Hong Kong. They all used the house as a stopping-off point for a square meal, exchanging a bowl of rice and fish for the news or information they carried. Alice gave them a little money, usually without Mulrenan's knowledge, while his contacts within the fishing fleet made their onward journey easier, at a price.

The Japanese were less active the further one travelled

west. That bottom, left hand corner of China, as Mulrenan put it, was not of particular interest to them. They occupied it but, by and large, they were not bothered with such an unstrategic area of a huge country. They were too busy with their conquests in Malaya, Burma and the Philippines.

The information Mulrenan received might have been of great interest to Freddy Tsang — but he kept it to himself. The British, also, could have used it, but Mulrenan was determined they too should remain ignorant of all he knew or heard. His neutrality was one of his most treasured possessions: heeding Tsang's advice, he would not risk it.

The news that filtered through to Macau by radio and by word of mouth from fishermen, pirates, partisans and refugees was not good. The Imperial Japanese Army had overrun the colonial British in Malaya, the Dutch in the Dutch East Indies, the Americans in The Philippines. Borneo, Sarawak, Brunei, Luzon: all were lost under the Japanese leather tabi and all the tiniest lagoons and atolls of the entire western Pacific seemed to be under Japanese occupation.

In Hong Kong, matters were reportedly grim. From information Alice gleaned, she had to accept that what was left of her home had been looted and was occupied by two Japanese NCOs and their Chinese ladies. Food was scarce. The Japanese were cruel overlords: killings were common, the black market thriving, the streets dangerous after dark. The Japanese were also reputed to be catching and eating all the wild monkeys: gunfire in the hills at night was as likely to be a party of primate-hunting Japanese as a clandestine group of Japanese-hunting partisans.

All the non-neutral nationals and most of the Indian population had been imprisoned: some Chinese and Eurasians also. The prisons in which they were held were situated all over the colony: the military barracks at Sham Shui Po was a huge internment centre as was another barracks in Argyle Street. At Ma Tau Kok a compound held those Indian troops who would not turn against their British masters. On Hong Kong island, His Majesty's Prison at Stanley and a nearby school formed the internment centre for European civilians. The Japanese barber from the Hong Kong Hotel was now promoted to the rank of a Lieutenant Commander and appointed commandant of Stanley prisoner-of-war camp: he had, in Alice's thoughts, gone from cutting hair to throats.

The Japanese, although historically despising the Chinese and loathing the British whom they furthermore regarded as cowards for having surrendered — a true warrior would rather fall on his own sword than wave a white flag and capitulate — gave themselves the airs and graces of the colonial power they had vanquished. They availed themselves of the best houses on The Peak, took over the Peninsula Hotel as it stood, with its entire Chinese staff, and renamed it Toa Hotel, meaning the East Asia Hotel, with Mr Takesiro Toki as manager. European food was offered on the menu alongside Chinese dishes and sukiyaki or tempura. Afternoon tea was served in the lobby, tiffin in the dining rooms and even dancing took place, although the Japanese regarded such activity as being appropriate only to geishas.

'I wonder if the old joanna is still there,' Mulrenan mused one afternoon.

Alice was serving fried rice to a middle-aged Chinese couple. By their chairs were two bundles of possessions, all they could carry, wrapped round in sheets knotted at the corners, looking like huge *dim sum* dumplings.

'Are you thinking of going back to play?' she teased. 'Selections from "The Mikado"? I don't think "Lagasaki" or "Honeysuckle Rose" will be much appreciated. "Wild Man Blues" perhaps?'

Mulrenan laughed with her.

'I don't think so,' he said, 'though there may well be some rich pickings to be found among a few of them. They must have looted their way through southern China, not to mention the strong boxes in the bank vaults. I'd give an arm and a leg to see what a few of those contained.'

'Not possible,' wryly put in one of their temporary guests.

David Yuen, a clerk in one of the Hong Kong shipping

205

companies, had lost his job now free trade had ceased. He had once worked for Alice's father and she accepted the responsibility she knew her father would have wanted her to take, of looking after a one-time employee.

'What do you mean?'

'The Japanese, Mr Mulrenan, have taken over The Hongkong and Shanghai Bank and are running it with the cooperation — reluctant cooperation, I must say — of a team of the senior British officials. Some say these men are secretly ruining the Japanese monetary system, others that they are traitors and others that they are merely guarding the real wealth of the bank by hiding it or maintaining the book-keeping at a low level. Apparently some of the bank deposit boxes have disappeared but not into the hands of the Japanese.'

'They'll be caught,' Mulrenan predicted with finality. 'It'll only be a matter of time.'

'Maybe not. The Japanese managers are quite ignorant of the procedures of western banking.'

The rice was barely fried. Animal fat, lard or oil were becoming a scarce commodity. Fish was available but meat, especially pork and beef, had all but vanished: poultry was becoming uncommon and even the supply of dogs, traditionally eaten in the winter, had dwindled.

'It surprises me in a way,' Mulrenan said, changing the subject but retaining the information safely in his memory, 'that the Indians — and a lot of the local Chinese, come to that — don't take sides with the Japanese. The British've occupied parts of China and all of India for centuries, exploiting and demeaning the native population. Even now, in India, there's a fierce independence struggle beginning.'

'History,' explained David Yuen. 'The Japanese are as much a colonial power as the British. Even worse. I can see your point of view but look at what the Chinese have gained from the British — trade, a sense of stability in some areas, individual opportunity. I am an example of that. If the British had not been in Hong Kong, I should be a coolie or working in the paddyfields. Instead, I am well educated,

can speak the most important international language —
and a little of the second most important, French. I have
been given a position of importance in a foreign company
. . .'

Mulrenan opened his mouth to cut Yuen off, but the
Chinese continued.

'No, wait. Please. Because I am Chinese I know I am not
a senior partner in my firm, nor will I ever be. But that is
how it is. It is the way of things. And if I worked for a
Japanese company, I would be an office boy at the very
best.'

He picked up his rice bowl and shovelled a little of the
contents into his mouth with his chopsticks.

'Excuse me,' he apologised, 'but I am very hungry. We
both are. It is some days since we ate a proper meal.'

His wife, who did not speak English, was silent. She had
not touched her bowl until she saw her husband eating.
Once begun, however, she did not stop.

'Do eat,' Alice said, repeating herself in Cantonese.

'But also talk,' said Yuen.

He removed a fish bone from his mouth with his chopsticks, dropping it into a side dish before going on.

'The British have fought and killed Chinese, but only to
protect their own national interests. They have never invaded China with an army, slaughtering and raping and
destroying. The Japanese have. For many hundreds of
years. There is a good British saying which I always find
amusing, especially as a Chinese who dislikes malevolent
spirits. It is "Better the devil you know than the devil you
do not know." ' He smiled. 'That is a very wise saying . . .
where the Japanese are concerned — well, I am familiar
with both devils and I am sure I know which I prefer.'

Mulrenan made no reply. Encapsulated in David Yuen's
argument was the Oriental ability to make the best of a bad
job. A starving Chinese man was grateful he was not a
starving Chinese dog. But Mulrenan was not Chinese; he
was Irish and he was damned if he would ever compromise.

11

The months dragged by and news leaking out of Hong Kong lessened or took on the air of the improbable to such an extent that those eager to receive it were left according to their character, either terribly worried, utterly confused or faintly hopeful. Reports of food shortages, petrol rationing and racketeering mingled with rumours of massacres, political kidnapping and murder, atrocities against Chinese women, the starvation of prisoners and the rampant spread of typhoid and cholera.

In Macau, life was marginally easier. The miniscule colony was respected as neutral territory although the Japanese maintained a large presence. Their troops and the Kempetai, their secret police, openly paraded in the streets, publicly drank in the bars and privately whored in the brothels. They spied on the British consul and his small staff, kept a more than watchful eye on other enemy nationals and expatriate Hong Kong Chinese and Portuguese, censored the mail as soon as it crossed into China and eavesdropped on radio transmissions.

In essence, the Japanese blockaded Macau. The ferry to Hong Kong operated a limited service but passes required for travel were hard to come by: the roads through China were guarded and patrolled and, if a traveller escaped detection by the Japanese they were just as likely to fall foul of the Nationalist or Communist armies working behind Japanese lines. There was no air transport at all. The big PAA seaplanes which had swooped down into the Porto Exterior of Macau before the war no longer appeared: occasionally, a Japanese military seaplane might arrive. Aircraft flew over Macau — Zero fighters, bombers, cargo aircraft heading for refuelling in Hong Kong en route from the Malayan and Burmese theatres of war to Okinawa or Shanghai and then Tokyo or Yokohama. Sometimes, aircraft passed over at a considerable altitude leaving white wakes behind them which the hot summer sun quickly dissipated in the high, thin air. There was speculation as to which side these aircraft belonged. No one dreamt, in the summer of 1942, that they were in fact American reconnaissance flights.

It was a harsh existence for the poor and not much better for those with little money coming in to their money belts. For the well-to-do there was little change, with parties to attend, the theatre to visit, social gatherings and church services.

Yet shortages soon developed. Food crowds formed in which the poor and the servants of the wealthy stood for hours. Once food was made available, the crowds surged forwards, pushing and jostling, slanging and complaining and shouting. New cloth grew scarce and no amount of money, neither patacas, Nationalist Chinese currency nor even Hong Kong dollars could purchase so much as a metre.

The best restaurants remained open. The grill in the Central Hotel, where the gamblers congregated on the off-chance lady luck might improve their wartime lot, continued to serve Portuguese and Chinese dishes and the American Restaurant in Avenida Almeida Ribeiro ironically grew in popularity with the senior Japanese officers. The Hotel Riviera on the waterfront of the Rua da Praia Grande, in which the British consul maintained his office, kept its reputation for fine food. Generally, however, standards slowly fell, good ingredients being replaced first with those of lesser quality, then with substitutes. Stringy wild mushrooms were used in lieu of straw mushrooms, bamboo shoots were gritty and fibrous, potatoes — when they appeared — were small and yellowish, meat all but disappeared and seafood dishes entered the menus in their stead. Shellfish were rare and crabs and lobsters no longer served except as soup in which very small specimens were boiled.

In the Central Hotel music was still played in the evenings. At the Bela Vista, the dance floor was re-opened in the spring, Mulrenan playing the guest spots at the piano in both establishments. He did not accept payment: it was better to have a favour owed than a sum of money.

Business for Mulrenan in the spring and early summer months of 1942 was brisk and profitable. There was always a market for the commodities in which he was now dealing. His earlier trading, as he called it, had dried up when the increased isolation of Macau prevented him from obtaining guns and medical supplies. Piracy fell off, too, with the reduction of coastal trade and the ever-present fear of retaliation by the Japanese, ruthless in their revenge against any community harbouring men whose ideas were contrary to the principles of the Japanese plan of South-East Asian co-prosperity. Mulrenan's concept of co-prosperity was somewhat different.

Macau was filled to saturation point with refugees. It was like a prison, overcrowded but well-guarded within by the Portuguese Chinese policemen and without by the Imperial Japanese Army. Through Lisbon, the various governments of those nationals seeking refuge sent financial aid: those who received none were willingly, if meagrely, assisted by the Portuguese.

Income had to be supplemented by whatever means came to hand. As employment was largely out of the question this involved the selling, bit by bit, of heirlooms, jewellery and such possessions as might be valuable. It was not long before Mulrenan was known as the man to approach for a quick cash sale.

Mulrenan was available for consultation every day between ten and noon in a small teashop in Rua do Barao. He had chosen this venue because it was easily protected. There was no rear exit for the back of the premises gave on to a tiny yard, totally enclosed with very high walls topped by broken glass. The street outside the teahouse was narrow: no one could approach without being plainly seen. An arrangement was struck with the proprietor that Mulrenan had the use of the same table every weekday, one against the wall behind the door. Ts'o sat at another facing the door, accompanied by one or other of his friends whom he sub-contracted, in true Oriental entreprenurial fashion but with Mulrenan's approval, as a deputy. The teashop owner provided fresh tea for each visitor. He would accept payment only in Nationalist Chinese currency, believing he was backing the eventual winners of China's civil chaos.

Mulrenan's clients were as varied as the items he purchased. Jewellery was common and he preferred this because he understood it. Objects in gold or silver ranged from fountain pens to ink stands or cigarette cases. Ornaments made of ivory or jade were also presented to him and he accepted these but invariably offered a low price which, despite considerable haggling, he would not raise. He was not so sure of himself in assessing such goods and storing them was difficult. Fortunately, a few of the senior Japanese who visited Macau and several financially secure Macanese purchased *objets d'art*. As Mulrenan's retail prices were low — he expected at the most to make only twenty percent profit on jade statuettes and snuff bottles, grave-jade carvings and carved discs — he was able to maintain a rapid turnover. He regarded the antiques as secondary to his primary trading in gems.

12

The European child had shaken him.

Many of Mulrenan's clients wanted to talk about themselves, in great detail, before coming to the point, the sale of their wristwatch or ring. Mulrenan realised coming to him was the equivalent in their own home countries of going to the pawnshop; this was not something someone of their standing would usually do — they would under normal circumstances send a servant. They were embarrassed, flustered, annoyed with themselves and the world, even afraid of what they were doing. At first he attempted to cut their conversation short but he quickly learnt that if he listened apparently sympathetically, and gave them twenty minutes of his time, he would obtain what they were selling more easily and at a better price. Listening to them fostered a feeling of trust. He, too, was a European: he would see them all right, would not cheat them. And Mulrenan, camouflaging his ruthless boredom with their stories, cheated them nevertheless. Especially if they were, in some way, connected to the English.

It was usual for women to seek him out to sell the family's belongings. Either they were living on their own, their menfolk dead or captured, and therefore had no one reliable to represent them, or it was reasoned that a woman would incur more sympathy. A man in similar circumstances presented a preconceived image of thoroughness and masculine determination, and was more likely to be argued with.

In the event, Mulrenan found the women far harder drivers of bargains than the few men who approached him. Within them was an instinctive animal will to survive and guard their loved ones: they were quite as devious as he was himself, and he found handling them a challenge.

They sometimes offered him more than simply a precious stone or a jade figurine. Those under thirty-five would offer themselves, promising to pander to his every sexual whim. They were prepared to procure for him other women — and also their gems. If he guaranteed them so many patacas a week or so many Hong Kong dollars a month, they would be his agents, his mistresses, his whores for hiring out or personal use. One — a Belgian woman in her mid-twenties — suggested she would provide whatever she could that he wanted in exchange for three catties of rice and a catty of fish per week. Mulrenan noted, with interest, that no men put their wives forward.

If business was quiet, Ts'o would rise from his seat to walk up and down the street outside, from the bend by the tailor's shop to the junction with Rua San Jose. He did this partly to ensure the coast was clear of known adversaries and partly to see if there were any would-be customers lingering while they plucked up the courage to part with some much-loved bauble. He had learnt a little English and Portuguese and was able to guide them towards Mulrenan much as a trawl guides fish towards the funnel of the net.

In the Travessa Chan Loc, Ts'o saw the European boy. He was wearing a pair of long black trousers with ragged hems at his ankles where they met his scuffed brown shoes. His white shirt was without a collar and the sports blazer he wore had been taken in to fit him but the stitchwork had obviously been done by a hand very unused to sewing. The tucks were uneven and crooked and the lapels were the original adult size. The child's hands and face were clean, however, his fair hair brushed and combed. Perhaps nine or ten years old, he was such an unusual sight that Ts'o approached him.

'Heww-ow. You speek Ingleesh?' he asked.

The boy looked nonplussed and Ts'o repeated his question in pidgin Portuguese.

'I can speak English,' replied the boy, somewhat indignantly.

'Wat you wan' here? No goot place for smaw' boy.'

'I want to see Mister Mullan,' his voice wavered uncertainly over the name, 'but I can't find him.'

'You com. I show you. He nam Mista Mu'*weng-ung*.'

At the teashop, Ts'o held open the door for the boy to enter.

'He wan' see you,' Ts'o reported and sat down next to his deputy, a small Chinese with a stubble haircut and powerful arms and legs projecting from a podgy torso.

'And what can I do for you?' Mulrenan asked patronisingly.

The boy sat opposite Mulrenan across the wooden table, hoisting himself onto the chair with his hands. Mulrenan, more out of amusement than decorum, requested another cup of tea as if the boy was a new client.

'Are you Mister Mulrenan who buys things?' the boy enquired. He was experienced enough in the interpretation of pidgin English to work out T'so's mispronunciation.

'Yes, I am, to be sure.'

The boy's composure fascinated Mulrenan. He was

more self-possessed and in command of himself than any of the previous visitors who had come over the months.

'My name is Philip Haversham.' He raised his right hand over the edge of the table and Mulrenan shook it. The boy's grip, for the size of his hand, was firm and decided.

'How do you do, Master Haversham.'

'Fine, thank you,' he answered.

The tea was brought to the table by a Chinese lad not much older than the person he was serving. Mulrenan watched with detached humour as the one poured out the beverage for the other who, knowing his position, thanked him in Cantonese, using the formal style.

'Have you something for me?' Mulrenan prompted. He wondered if perhaps the boy wanted to sell a toy car made of lead or a clockwork soldier with the key missing.

'My mother, Patricia Jane Haversham, is not very well otherwise she would come herself. Instead, she has to stay in bed and has sent me. She wants me to sell you this.'

From his blazer pocket he produced a small package rolled in crumpled tissue paper and folded around with an old manila envelope bearing several British stamps and an address in Hong Kong. Mulrenan smoothed the envelope flat and opened the wrapping.

It contained a diamond and emerald ring, the setting in rose gold. The diamond was fashioned in a round, brilliant cut and was quite plainly a Jager or blue white stone of the finest quality. Mulrenan guessed it was about five carats. It was surrounded by three one carat, step cut, leaf-green emeralds. In between the emeralds were smaller, but high quality, diamonds.

'My mother wants a good price,' the boy said when Mulrenan had completed his examination of the ring.

'We'll talk about the price in a minute,' Mulrenan told him. 'First, a few questions: where do you come from?'

'I was born in Bromley, in Kent, in England on June 3rd, 1932. My father is an accountant in private practice and my mother is . . .' He was lost as to how to describe his mother.

'Where do you live?'

'At 21, Plantation Road, The Peak.'

'I mean where do you live now?'

'We live in Rua de Pedro Nolasco Da Silva, near the hospital. My father is fighting the Nipponese in Hong Kong.'

The hell he is, thought Mulrenan. The chances were the boy's father was dead or dying in one of the camps. He must have been a civilian volunteer and, according to rumour, they had not fared well in the battle for Hong Kong.

'What is wrong with your mother?'

'She is ill,' the boy answered noncommittally. 'I don't know what with but she's sick a lot and her mouth bleeds.'

'How much are you expecting for the ring?'

'My mother says she wants at least five thousand patacas and it must be in cash. She says no cheques and no kind.'

'Four thousand five hundred,' Mulrenan said, not so much to get a better price but to discover what the boy would do.

He thought for a moment and replied, 'Four thousand eight-fifty. Not a cent less.'

'Four seven fifty,' Mulrenan rejoined.

'That diamond is a top quality stone, Mr Mulrenan,' the boy reminded him. 'In normal times it would be worth at least four times my price. These are not normal times. I accept that. Four eight.'

Mulrenan fell back into his chair and roared with laughter. Ts'o had been following the proceedings with suppressed mirth, translating the action as best he could for the benefit of his assistant thug and the other customers in the teashop: they too laughed raucously. The boy retained his composure.

'I don't see what's so funny about it,' he said indignantly when Mulrenan's laughter reduced itself to a prolonged chuckle.

'It's not every day a young chap like you strikes such a hard bargain,' Mulrenan said, taking his wallet from his coat and counting out the money, the boy watching his fingers and counting silently with him, his lips moving as the notes landed on the table.

'This is a lot of money, Master Haversham,' Mulrenan

reminded the boy. 'Do you think you'll be alright walking through the streets with it?'

'I'll run.'

'You might trip. There are lots of robbers about. They know you might have a lot of money when you leave here. I think it would be best,' he nodded to Ts'o, 'if one of my men escorted you home.'

'Thank you, Mr Mulrenan. I'm most grateful.'

They shook hands again like schoolboys confirming a playground pact.

'Tell me,' Mulrenan asked as he rolled the notes into the manila envelope and handed them to Ts'o to carry, 'are you an only child or do you have a brother or sister?'

'I've a sister called Angela,' then, knowingly, he added, 'but she's not for sale.'

13

The government office was dusty and hot, the desk before which Mulrenan was seated piled high with papers some of which, at the base of stack, had coatings of dust upon them. On the wall hung a calendar with a photograph of the cloister of the Jeronimos monastery at Belem, near Lisbon. It was an appropriate illustration, for the building had been financed by trading in the East and its architecture, though thoroughly Portuguese, subtly suggested Oriental influences. Mulrenan wondered as he awaited his interview if the very room he was in had once seen the monks' money pass through it.

The wall decorated by the calendar was peeling, the plaster bare in places with hairline cracks radiating from the window sill like lines from an old man's eyes: it was as if the window had spent centuries squinting at the tropical sun. The ceiling beams were pitted, splitting and worm-riddled. As he glanced round the room, Mulrenan saw a two-inch-long, rich-brown cockroach scuttle from behind a wooden filing cupboard to disappear into a crack in the skirting. The insect was as glossy as french-polished walnut veneer.

A portly man entered the room, a cardboard file in his hands, the cover heavily scrawled upon and bearing a mass of red and blue rubber stamp marks. He wore a stained white suit and brogues and a panama hat which he dropped onto the pile of papers before sitting down in the officious way civil servants have, regardless of the nationality of their masters. A cloud of dust eddied from under the sweat-soaked brim.

He did not speak but produced from a drawer a pair of round, steel-rimmed spectacles which he balanced on the bulbous end of his nose.

'Mister Mulrenan,' the Portuguese official began, peering over his glasses and not introducing himself, 'it is good of you to come.'

Before Mulrenan could reply, a Chinese clerk came in and switched the ceiling fan on. It gathered speed, creaking and swaying.

'Excellent! Excellent!' the man burbled and he seemed about to clap his hands with glee. 'The electricity has returned. It is so warm today.'

He opened the file and extracted a sheet of flimsy pink paper. As he did so his demeanour changed from that of a bumbling official to that of a man wielding power.

'Now, your papers, please,' he requested, an edge to his voice.

Mulrenan handed his Irish passport across the dust and unsettled business. The official flicked through it and began to question him.

'You were resident in Hong Kong?'

'Yes.'

'From when were you resident — ah, yes! I have it here.' He pointed to the relevant entry with a podgy index finger. 'And you came to Macau — here! Yes! How did you travel?'

'On the ferry from Hong Kong.'

217

'Direct?'

'Yes.'

'Not via Canton?'

'No.'

'Why did you not return to Irey-land? You departed from Hong Kong a long time before the Japanese attacked.'

Mulrenan had rehearsed those questions he thought would be most probably put to him.

'I expected them to attack sooner.'

'Why?'

'I had heard rumours in China when on business there.'

'What exactly is your business? Your passport states you are a musician.'

'Import-export,' Mulrenan replied.

'Of what.'

'General trading. Cloth, medical supplies, bicycles . . .'

'Guns and opium?' interrupted the official.

'I know what opium does to men,' Mulrenan answered sharply.

The official smiled and said, 'And guns?'

'I know what they do, too.'

'How do you now make your living in Macau?'

'Trading.'

'In what?'

'Jewellery and gemstones.'

Mulrenan knew it was useless to deny it. The official knew the answers to most of the questions: posing them was a formality.

'What do you do with your purchases?'

'Trade. Resell.'

'To whom?'

'Those who will buy.'

'And gold? Silver?'

'I am not a metal dealer,' Mulrenan said. 'I do not understand the gold and silver business. That is best left to bankers.'

'Quite so! Quite so! There are others with specialist knowledge, as you say. It is better to leave them to their own affairs.'

At that moment, Mulrenan realised the interview had been called not only to check his citizenship but also to make sure he was keeping within the bounds of his own business. It was evident the official was anxious to confirm that he was not dabbling in gold dealing. Someone else was more than likely seeking to corner that market and they had the political muscle to ensure success.

'What do you do,' the official continued, 'with the gold from your jewellery? Some of what you buy must be made of silver or gold.'

This was not a question Mulrenan had expected, but he was ready for it.

'I crush it and usually buy things with it.'

'Buy what?'

The official's tone betrayed a hint of increased interest.

'Food, clothing, oil for the lamps — we live off it.'

'You also use money. Where is your money kept? You do not have a bank account.'

'You must be mistaken,' Mulrenan retorted. 'I do have an account.'

His interrogator shuffled the papers in the file, extracting another pink sheet. Mulrenan had avoided his trap: that he maintained the account only for appearances would escape the official: most of Mulrenan's money was elsewhere, secreted away from the prying eyes of curious civil servants.

'Of course. I had forgotten. I think I was confusing you with . . . You know how it is. One man to keep up with so much work!'

He held his hands up in a gesture of resignation to the burden of officialdom and Mulrenan smilingly nodded agreement.

'Your papers seem in order. But I must remind you, as a neutral resident and a refugee, of the obligations you have to remain within the laws of Portugal. Here is not British Hong Kong.'

The threat was veiled but Mulrenan, being a man of threats, was quick to recognise it. He was being warned. He was not to try to become a gold dealer.

'I understand.'

'Of course, we can hardly expel you!' the official admitted jovially. 'There is nowhere we can send you — except into the hands of the Japanese!'

He laughed at his own joke and Mulrenan joined him but he knew, under the humour, it was a fact. If the Portuguese felt it expedient, the Japanese could have him.

14

Alice knew nothing of the boy or his sick mother until a month later when she saw the child walking in a short procession behind a four-wheeled trolley, rather like an expensive perambulator with curving steel suspension leafsprings, upon which was balanced a tar-painted coffin. The boy was not crying, which was what had drawn her attention: otherwise, the procession would have been but one of many to wend this way past the house.

The weather was tropically hot with high humidity and fair weather clouds suggesting rain but, in fact, merely hung in the sky by the gods to mock and tease.

In the summer months, funerals were held as soon as possible after death for the condition of the corpse very rapidly deteriorated. As soon as *rigor mortis* was positively set in to the flesh the priest began his work. The sexton and his coolies would have started digging as soon as the last breath hissed. For them, gouging out a six foot oblong in the ground was work demanding regular breaks and the consumption of much water. What the soil did not drain from them the sun did.

The funeral procession was very short. It consisted of the boy with a young priest guiding him, his hand on his shoulder, two coolies pushing the coffin and two amahs in black trousers and starched white smocks, their black hair greased and combed backwards, cut square at the nape and pinned at the sides, just above the ears, with bone clips.

From the top of the long, wide flight of steps leading to the lower terrace of the graveyard, Alice watched the proceedings from the shade of a frangipani tree. The trolley bumped over the low steps, its wheels muffled by the moss. The scent of the blossoms made her heady with joy, for such is the perfume of the heavenly tree, yet her heart was immeasurably saddened by the scene before her.

When the brief service was concluded at the graveside, the amahs bowed to the boy and he presented them each with a bright red lucky money envelope. They left him then and, as they passed Alice, they were silent but glanced at her and she saw they were crying in the quiet, private way the Chinese have. The coolies were shovelling the earth into the grave when the boy and the priest began their slow climb up the steps. The latter was evidently greatly moved but the former was stepping by his side with a stoical acceptance of his lot that would have seemed strange in a man five times his age.

The priest and the boy drew level with Alice and, as they went by, she overheard a brief snatch of their conversation: what she heard so affected her, made her so curious, she walked behind them to listen further.

'Do you have any money, Philip?' the priest asked.

'Yes, vicar,' the boy replied as if he was thirty years old and standing outside the lych gate of a parish church in rural England. 'I've enough for the journey, I'm certain. Enough for myself and my guide, in any case. And I do have some unrealised assets.'

'What are those?'

'I have some of my mother's jewellery. We sold the best piece to pay for the doctor for Angela and medicine for mother. And our rent. And to buy food for ourselves and the amahs, of course. But there are still some pieces left and a few of them are quite good. There are a few ornaments too, but I don't think they are very valuable.'

'You will get help, of course,' the priest said. 'Some of the other English here have made a few small donations and Mr Reeves, the consul, will have some money for you from the government.'

'I've met him, I think.' The boy scratched his ear thoughtfully and Alice thought it looked like a habit he was mimicking from his absent father. 'Isn't he that rather nice man with fairish curly hair and glasses?'

'Yes, he is.'

'I met him at that hotel. He bought me a soft drink just before Angela died, when mother was very poorly.'

He spoke as if the recent deaths were far off in the past, as if the mists of time and the Pearl River estuary were already blurring his memory and, if he was fortunate, would continue to do so for the rest of his life.

They reached the entrance to the cemetery, the archway by the church into which Alice had not dared to venture since her inauspicious meeting with the other priest and the bird, both of whom she believed were spirits sent to torment her.

'How will you dispose of the jewellery?' the priest asked.

'That's quite easy,' said the boy. 'There's an Irishman here who buys it. He bought the ring we sold. His price was low but fairly good considering what must be the state of the market. I don't expect he'll give me much more for the rest than twice the price of the ring but that should be sufficient to get me through to Calcutta and I'm sure my Uncle Brian there will sub me for the rest of my journey home.'

The priest was struggling to contain himself; bishops warn their shepherds not to get involved with the flock, instruction well-learned, but there are always those cases where human compassion and the love of God spills out. He checked his tears.

'You are a very brave little boy, Philip,' he said. 'I wish you all the luck in the world and I'm sure Jesus Christ will travel with you not only until you reach home but throughout the remainder of your years.'

'I don't think I'm brave. I'm simply presented with a fay-a-come-plee.'

'Fait accompli,' said the priest. 'Do you know what that means?'

'Yes,' the boy answered confidently. 'It means I've been

222

dropped in the creek without an oar and I've got to learn to paddle my own canoe. My father told me that.'

Under different circumstances, the priest would have been highly amused by such a retort. He again laid his hand on the boy's shoulder.

'I must just put away a few things in the church. Will you wait and I'll walk home with you?'

'No, thank you. I'll walk by myself. I have to pack my case.'

'It will be dangerous, Philip . . .'

'I know that, vicar. I've got to go beyond Canton to Luichow then to Guiyang and on to Chungking. I've been shown it on a map. It is over six hundred miles and we've to walk and ride bicycles and ponies and sleep in the fields. But I'm most afraid of the mozzies.'

'The what!'

'Mozzies. Mosquitoes. I get awfully bitten on picnics. I've bought some ointment from a Chinese doctor but it smells foul.' He felt in his pocket and produced a small glass jar from which he tugged the cork, holding it up for the priest to sniff.

'It is rather pungent,' he admitted.

'Maybe,' the boy suggested, 'it's the smell that drives them away.'

'I'm sure you'll make it,' the priest said encouragingly. 'The people who are taking you are trustworthy and used to this sort of job. Number 50 is Chinese but he's also a Canadian and you can trust him fully. Remember you must never tell his name to anyone. And I'll see you before you leave.'

'I hope so. And thank you for the funeral. It was very nice.'

Alice followed the boy and caught up with him at the end of Rua Tomas Vieira. She called to him to stop and he turned round whilst at the same time accelerating his step. When he saw he was being addressed by a lady in a European skirt and blouse he halted.

'Yes?' he asked defensively.

'My name is Alice Soon,' she introduced herself, 'and I

223

was in the graveyard. I'm so sorry about your mummy.'

It seemed to her that 'mother' was too harsh a word and, now that she had spoken to the boy, she was at a loss as to what to say next.

'Did you know my mother? I don't think we've met, have we?'

'No, I did not know her and we have not met.'

'I am Philip Haversham,' the boy said formally.

'May I walk with you, Philip?'

'Certainly. I should like that. I'm going to my house to pack my case and then I'm moving to the Hotel Riviera.'

Already, Alice thought, it was no longer 'our' house but *his*.

They walked slowly along the street side by side, the young woman and the old little boy.

'Are you leaving Macau?'

'Yes. In a few days, I think,' he responded. 'I have just been told to get ready so I don't know the exact date. I expect they have to wait until the Japanese are busy.'

'Will you be sorry to go?'

'In some ways I will. I'll be leaving a very interesting town and, of course, whilst I've been here there has been no school. That's been fun although I know I shall have to catch up later. And I shall be leaving my sister and . . .'

His face was serious yet somehow bleak and drained of thought. Down one cheek rolled one fat tear. Each step he took jarred it a little lower until, finally, it slipped from his jaw and made a dark blot upon the collar of his blazer. As it fell it briefly caught the sunlight.

'You should cry, Philip,' she said softly. 'If you cry all the pain gets washed out.'

'I know,' the boy whispered. 'But somehow I can't. It wouldn't do. Not here, in the street.'

One of the nearby tea-houses was formerly a small restaurant which had, with the food shortages, reduced its fare to tea and sweetmeats with, if customers were fortunate, *dim sum* at the middle of the day. Alice had been to the restaurant before and remembered the dining room was divided into latticed cubicles.

224

Steering the boy into the restaurant, she summoned a waiter and was shown to an empty cubicle where they sat opposite each other at a polished table. The establishment was serving tea only but Alice ordered someone be sent out for a bottle of soda water: she was not concerned where they got it nor what they paid for it.

'That's very kind of you, ordering a soda water. I'm not very fond of jasmine tea.'

The boy's understanding of her fluent and rapid Cantonese conversation with the waiter surprised Alice and she said so.

'I picked it up from our servants. It's not a difficult language to learn to speak. Of course, I can't write it at all, though I can read a little. I can recognise a few characters like the one for shop and for man. And the numbers. They're quite easy because the first three are one, two or three lines. Four is so distinctive and five looks a bit like the character for man. And set signs are easy to work out like bus-stop and tram-stop, hotel or ferry pier.'

He suddenly stopped talking and Alice, who had not been listening to his chatter, grew attentive again.

The boy was crying. He was not sobbing or even breathing awkwardly. His shoulders did not heave and his head did not drop. His hands were still on the table, clenched together as if in determined prayer. His eyes were closed and between the lashes seeped tears which ran down his cheeks and on to the polished wood where they stayed like raindrops on a burnished metal plate, the meniscus bent in, the drops remaining separate.

Alice moved beside the boy, putting her arm around him, drawing him closer. He did not resist yet he did not at once accept her. His hands relaxed on the table. Once up to her side though, he pressed his face into her breasts and she felt his damp skin against her own through the light material of her blouse. She held his head close to herself and stroked his hair which tousled against her shoulder. The tears kept coming silently.

Eventually, the waiter approached their table with the tea and a glass of soda water. She nodded her thanks and

225

he, embarrassed, unloaded his black lacquered tray and left them alone.

The boy leaned into Alice for a quarter of an hour, pressing into her like a man walking into a strong wind. At last, his hands took to life once more and he pushed himself upright on the table, his sleeves spreading his tears across the surface. He looked at them guiltily for a moment, as if only now realising they were his and, talking his handkerchief from his pocket, mopped them up.

'I am sorry,' he apologised. 'But I think you were correct. I do feel a little less sad now.'

His objective point of view, his analysis of himself and his grief, affected Alice more deeply than his crying. She could say nothing.

'It is very, very kind of you,' he said. 'I don't know anyone else I could go to, really. Joy has been very good to me and mother but she is a friend and I feel awful . . . But now you are a friend . . .'

'I'm glad you think of me as a friend, Philip.'

'I was always told never to impose upon friends,' he continued. 'You can rely on them, but not impose on them. That's different. My father,' he spoke with pride in his words, 'says one should only impose upon servants and officials because that's what they are paid for.'

'Who is Joy?'

'Joy is Mrs Wilson who works with Mr Reeves at the consulate. She's very kindly and is going to look after me until William . . .'

He remembered the priest's warning he should never mention the name and he stopped himself just in time.

Alice handed him his glass of soda water to which a little sugar syrup had been added. She sipped her tea which was now lukewarm.

'I had better be going,' the boy said. 'I have to pack and I must get the last of mother's jewellery to the Irishman.' He gazed about the restaurant, found no clock and asked, 'Do you have the time, please?'

'It's just after eleven.'

'Then I really must be going. They might worry where I

am.' He stood up, smoothing the nap on his collar where his tears had raised the cloth. He held out his hand, saying, 'Thank you once again very, very much indeed. I shall always think of you as a friend.'

Alice took his hand but she held it rather than shook it.

'I want you to have this,' she said and she pressed into his palm a roll of Hong Kong dollars. She had no idea how much was in it. The notes might be ones or they might be tens folded over. Mulrenan had given it to her and she had not yet removed the paper band holding the money in a tight wad.

'I couldn't, really!' the boy exclaimed.

'You must! I can't tell you why, but you must. You are a very good boy and I'm sure your mother and father — and Angela — would be very proud of you. You are being very brave and you must accept all the help your friends give you.'

'Angela was my sister. Now she's dead, too.'

For a moment Alice believed he was going to cry again. A faraway stare came into his eyes but it was soon gone and with it, Alice thought, an album of childhood memories was instantly erased or tucked away where they could do no harm.

'Please. Take this. It's but a small gift.'

'It seems to be quite a lot,' said the boy. 'Are you sure you can spare it?'

'I'm quite sure. Take it.'

She realised she was pleading, almost begging him to accept the money.

'I must be going,' said the boy. 'I must catch the Irishman before he closes his business for the day.'

Alice let go of his hand, the roll of notes protruding from either side of it.

He peered at the money then thrust it hard down into his trouser pocket as boys do when they want to be certain what they are carrying is safe. Quickly, taking Alice by surprise, he stepped closer to her and bent over, kissing her on her cheek.

'Thank you,' he said. 'I'm only a stranger really but I think I love you.'

Then he ran from the shop, no longer a man before his time but a little, flummoxed boy.

15

'Such a view!' Tsang commented, leaning against the breach of the cannon. 'From here, for centuries, Portuguese soldiers have surveyed the coasts of our China and calculated the range of their powder.'

He turned and gazed across the Porto Interior towards a Japanese gunboat lying at anchor fifty yards off the quay. From the buildings below rose the smoke of evening cooking fires. Beyond the blue of the distant hills a hazy summer sun was sinking, the shadows of the battlements lengthening over the scrubby grass poking through the crevices in the flagstones.

'I wonder,' he said thoughtfully, 'if a five kilo cannonball, shot at this minute, could reach that craft.'

In the setting sun, the red Japanese disc fluttering from the stern mast on the gunboat took fire.

'I doubt it,' Alice replied. 'They say these guns are useless now.'

Tsang laughed quietly at her practical opinion.

'You are right, of course. If a charge was put in them now, they'd explode. The bronze is flawed and pitted.'

He scratched his fingernail along the metal by the touch-hole which was blocked with rust and grit. It rasped on the pockmarks and dents.

'Only birds nest in them now, not flames.'

As if to prove his point there was a sound from the mouth of the next cannon along the parapet and a bird took to flight from the gun's maw, dipping low over Tsang's house beneath the fortress.

'Are matters well in hand, Freddy?' Alice enquired.

'Yes. It's all arranged,' Tsang answered. 'We'll be ready

to move when the moment comes. It's just a matter of timing. So much depends on timing.'

She looked out across the roofs of Macau. The smoke was thicker now. From the direction of the barracks there sounded a bugle and, from one of the churches, a dull bell was booming.

'Do you know Donne?' Tsang asked.

'Oh, yes! My mother read him to me when I was girl. It's quite cliche now. *For whom the bell tolls* . . . Do you read Hemingway?'

'I keep clear of popular novelists,' Tsang replied with a haughtiness that amused her.

'You should read his latest. He writes of humans — real humans — caught in lives they cannot control.'

'Like us, my dear?'

'In a way . . .'

'Can you quote me Donne's lines?' Tsang said.

'No, I can't.'

' "Any man's death diminishes me," ' he quoted, ' "because I am involved in Mankind; And therefore never send to know for whom the bell tolls; it tolls for thee." Perhaps that bell is ringing for you. Or for me.'

'Or for him,' she said softly.

'Perhaps for him,' Tsang agreed.

The twilight deepened for the sun had disappeared behind the hills. The scent of woodsmoke drifted on the rising breeze.

'There is another section of the same poem that might apply,' Tsang said. ' "No man is an Island, entire of itself; every man is a piece of the Continent, a part of the main." '

'Poor Sean,' she said sadly, but Tsang made no reply.

16

Mulrenan had expected and feared it, but when the time came he was nonetheless taken aback. He had lived as any man does whose livelihood depends on good fortune and fair trading weather: he enjoyed the luck and light winds but when the clouds began to gather he tried not to heed them. It was only when the rain of bad luck actually started to fall that he saw he was without adequate cover. What really surprised him was the speed with which the end came.

On the Monday, the little boy who had sold him the diamond and emerald ring over a month before reappeared in the tea-house with a jewellery case under his arm. It was a poorly-made box of wood inlaid with triangles of bone and Mulrenan did not expect much from it.

'I wish to sell you the remainder of my mother's jewellery,' the boy said after shaking hands, sitting down at the table and nodding politely but in a superior manner to Ts'o.

'What brings on this sudden sale?' Mulrenan enquired, adding, 'Don't you know to sell everything at once floods the market and lowers the price? It would be better if you let things go bit by bit.'

'I'm well aware of that, Mr Mulrenan.' He looked Mulrenan up and down as if sizing-up the coming deal. 'However, I'm left with no option.'

The boy pushed the box across the table between the empty bowls. Overhead, flies buzzed and settled on the ceiling, joined all the while by others escaping from the burning sunlight outside. From a darker corner of the room, behind Ts'o and his side-kick, drifted the sweet smoke of opium.

As he laid his hands upon the box, curious as to what it

might contain, he involuntarily flicked his head and furrowed his brow to drive an equally curious fly from his forehead.

'You may open the box, Mr Mulrenan,' the boy said.

Mulrenan saw a tiny key projecting from a miniscule lock, twisted it and lifted the lid. The contents were wrapped individually in tissue paper, each held in its own felt-lined compartment in a closely-fitting tray.

As he unfolded the wrappings and laid the pieces on the table, Mulrenan became aware that in this box he had hit a mine of valuable gems and high quality metal. After he had removed seven or eight articles, he signalled to Ts'o who came to the table. Receiving a curt order, Ts'o called the tea-house proprietor and gave him some money. The only other customers, at a table in the centre of the room, were obliged to leave. The door was shut and barred. As the metal rod fell into the slots across the door frame, and the flies' entry was sealed, the boy grew edgy.

'Don't worry,' Mulrenan told him. 'It's not to lock you in. It's to lock anybody else out.'

An electric bulb snapped on overhead, casting hard shadows on the table but scintillating off the stones, the silver, the platinum and the gold which ranged from nine to twenty-two carat.

When the box was empty Mulrenan sat back and surveyed the goods. Practically every precious stone was represented: diamonds — though none as good as the one in the ring — blue, green, pink and violet sapphires, emeralds, rubies, white opals, one high quality alexandrite. Lesser, semi-precious stones he recognised included yellow topazes and heliodors, amethysts, garnets and peridots. From beneath the tray he lifted two strings of natural pearls; one consisted of equally sized pearls and the other of pearls graduated in size to one almost half an inch across.

As Mulrenan lifted the pearls, the boy observed, 'That big one is very valuable. My father bought it in Fiji for my mother's twenty-fifth birthday.'

'Yes, it is,' Mulrenan replied, 'but this necklace of similarly sized pearls is far more valuable: they are equally sized and matching in lustre and therefore rarer.'

'They were to be Angela's when she was twenty-one,' the boy commented. 'She's gone now so it won't matter.'

'You want to sell the lot, do you?'

'I'm afraid so,' said the boy, a little ruefully.

'How much do you expect?' Mulrenan prompted.

The boy wasn't going to fall for such an easy trick.

'I would rather hear your offer, Mr Mulrenan.'

For several minutes, Mulrenan pretended to be assessing the worth of each item, picking it up, turning it over in the light, admiring the beauty of the stones, the settings and the sheer value. This display was all a sham: he had already decided a price based upon his available cash reserve, his possible immediate resale of the lesser gems and his determination to get the better of the English, even if they were represented by a mere boy.

'Twenty-seven thousand five hundred patacas,' he said at last, assuming a long-sounding figure would impress the boy.

Now it was the boy who sat back. Until this point, he had been eagerly leaning forward over the table on his elbows.

'Mr Mulrenan,' he said, 'what is in front of you is all I have in the world. My mother and sister have died and my father is probably a prisoner-of-war. I have to fend for myself until I can get back to England. I shall have no inheritance because we lost everything when Hong Kong surrendered. You will have to do better as your first offer.'

Where Mulrenan had laughed at the boy on his first visit to the tea-house, he now grew silent. This slip of a lad was as shrewd as he was — if not more so — and he begrudgingly admired him.

Certain the boy was spinning him a yarn, Mulrenan replied rather sternly, 'I'm afraid thirty thousand is the highest I can go.'

'In that case,' the boy answered, 'I'm sorry.'

He got to his feet and commenced re-wrapping the jewellery.

Mulrenan let him do so. In a few minutes, he was sure, the boy would try to reopen negotiations. He was disappointed when the tray was filled and the boy was laying the strings of pearls into the bottom of the case. It was plain he either meant it or was an adept at bluffing.

'What do you feel to be the worth?'

Mulrenan phrased the question in such a tone as to give the impression he was no longer seeking to buy, just interested for purely academic reasons.

'I've given it a good deal of thought,' the boy said, 'and I think a figure around fifty thousand Hong Kong dollars. I know what the original prices were because I've seen my parents' insurance policy where they're listed.'

He closed the box, turned the key and put it in his pocket after rolling his handkerchief around it. Mulrenan noticed the handkerchief was unlaundered: the boy was on his own now.

'I'll say goodbye, then.'

The boy glanced over his shoulder at the tea-house owner.

'Hoi moon,' he requested.

The Chinese started to unbar the door.

Mulrenan was obliged to make a hasty decision. He wanted the case, could resell some of the contents fairly quickly but only, if he was lucky, up to the figure he had offered. The remainder would be dead stock and he would show no profit on the day. On the other hand, the alexandrite alone was worth having, not to mention the matching pearls and several other items. He was also concerned what Ts'o might think. He had never seen a transaction refused at the whim of the vendor: such an act might suggest a weakness in Mulrenan's abilities or financial background and, as he knew only too well, in the world of the rat, he with the biggest tail and the loudest squeak rules the nest.

'If you have proof of the original values, I might raise my price,' he tendered.

'How much?' the boy said bluntly.

'Sit down and we'll discuss it.'

It did not take long. The boy began with his original demand and Mulrenan beat him down in three moves to forty-four which the boy accepted on condition he could

233

keep one piece back. He would not name the item he wanted: he told Mulrenan quite openly he was reluctant to let this information go in case the Irishman decided to include it in their deal on the assumption it was somehow valuable. He assured him it was not one of the prime gems.

The deal finalised, Mulrenan started to count out a mixture of Hong Kong dollars and patacas.

'I think I stipulated Hong Kong dollars only,' the boy pointed out as Mulrenan thumbed the notes.

'It'll take me some time to get together so much money in just one currency,' Mulrenan replied, continuing to count.

'Hong Kong dollars or no deal,' the boy said abruptly. 'It must be Hong Kong dollars. Patacas are of no use to me.'

'It'll take a day at least.'

'You have two hours, Mr Mulrenan. That's all I can allow. I'll wait here if you like, with your servant. Or you can meet me in the Hotel Riviera or send him.'

'It's not possible.' Mulrenan pulled back his shirt cuff to view the Rolex. The association the wristwatch usually prompted was, he considered, just a little soured in the present circumstances. 'The bank will not be open.'

'I'm sure, Mr Mulrenan, you have your reserves in safer places than a bank.'

It was not with any degree of humour Mulrenan laughed. He was of two minds whether or not to abandon the deal and kill the arrogant child instead. It would be easy, but might lead back to him even if Ts'o hired a thug for the task. Macau was a tiny place in which rumours, gossip, counter-rumouurs, lies and the steely truth reverberated like earth tremors.

'Very well,' he decided. 'Hong Kong dollars. *Mostly.* You'll have to have some other currencies as well. I've not so much in just the one.'

'What others?'

'It will be a mixture of sterling, American dollars, French francs and German marks.'

'No French or German money, please,' said the boy after a few moments of deliberation. 'But I'll take all the sterling and bucks you can afford in perference to Hong Kong dollars. I think the immediately pre-war exchange rate would be appropriate.'

This was no suggestion but a veiled demand and Mulrenan knew it. The boy was no fool. For a ten-year-old he was astonishingly au fait with the commercial mind. In adult life, Mulrenan knew, he would be a nasty adversary.

'Ts'o will bring the money to . . .' Mulrenan called across to his bodyguard and briefly discussed instructions for the handover '. . . the bench under the tree on the Praia Grande opposite the hotel. There's a seat by the rickshaw stand. Will four o'clock be all right?'

'Two-thirty,' said the boy. 'And he's to wait while I go in and count it. I'll give him the jewellery then. Except for the one I want to keep.'

Now it was Mulrenan's turn to stipulate demands.

'Take it out now and I shall seal the box. If the seal is broken when Ts'o arrives, he'll not complete.'

'If you feel you can't trust me . . .' Yet the boy was obviously not hurt by Mulrenan's implication. 'Very well.'

He unlocked the box, rummaging about in it and feeling through the tissue. Eventually, he removed a package, put it on the table, relocked the case and gave Mulrenan the key.

'You should still have the box sealed,' he said. 'I may have another key.' The sarcasm in his voice was, for a child, biting. 'And you had better check to see the piece I'm keeping.'

Mulrenan tore off the tissue. Inside was a brooch of silver. It was two inches long and the metal had been worked into the shape of a flower with three leaves. The centre of the blossom was a miniature blue enamelled painting of a windmill. The pin was bent and did not fasten properly. Of all the objects in the box, this was one of the very few Mulrenan had decided, when sorting through the contents, to discard.

'This is worthless,' he said, unable to resist a comment. 'You should chose again. Perhaps the tourmaline and rock crystal bracelet or the agate cameo brooch?' He opened the lid, removed the bracelet and locked it again.

'The value isn't in dollars, Mr Mulrenan. That brooch was my aunty's and she gave it to my mother, and she gave it to my sister. Now it's mine. I expect I'll give it away one day.' He stood up again but did not proffer his hand. 'Two-thirty,' he said, repeating the time in Cantonese to Ts'o.

Mulrenan felt again a begrudging admiration for this English boy.

'Master Haversham,' he said, 'please accept this as well as a token of — as a gift from one businessman to another.'

Mulrenan held out the bracelet and the boy accepted it.

'Thank you. That's most generous of you. Goodbye.'

The door was unbarred and the boy left with the case tucked under his arm.

Damn, Mulrenan swore to himself when the boy was already out of sight round the corner of the street. He had forgotten to tie the case round with twine and seal it with wax and a chop.

It was as well Mulrenan had bought the dead woman's jewellery. The next day, business was not good. A Chinese woman approached him with a set of jade and gold bangles which he bought for a small sum. As she left, another woman — an amah — offered him a silver tea caddy which he had to refuse. Scrap metal was not his line, he told her. On the Wednesday, a Dutch woman sold him a pair of turquoise earrings and a matching ring for thirty patacas: she had sobbed at the very low price but accepted it. That afternoon, a White Russian girl in her late teens sold him two gold coins bearing the head of Tsar Nicholas set into a brooch: she also offered to 'fok wif you.' He refused her clumsy soliciting, paid her a very low price and prized the coins out of their mounting. They were of more use to him as coin than ornament.

On Thursday and Friday, no one came to him.

On Saturday, he sent Ts'o out to discover who was out-pricing him.

No one was. The market had dried up. The refugees were out of belongings.

236

In the early hours, Mulrenan crept from their bed. Alice was fast asleep: of that he had made sure.

Deftly, he cut the plaster behind the altar and sorted through his hoard, classifying the stones into groups according to type, weight and quality. He arranged in piles the various gold coins. Where the gems were far superior to the mountings, he carefully bent open the claws or rub-over settings, tossing the metal aside to be melted down.

He could not find it in his heart to break up four pieces. One was the boy's diamond and emerald ring: the others were a diamond pendant, a short necklace of rubies and diamonds and a pink sapphire and diamond brooch.

When he finished his work, he studied each group of stones closely, picking out the finest three of each sort and placing them, with the coins and complete pieces, in one bag. The remaining stones he grouped together and placed in separate bags. Everything was then packed back into the recess. With the plaster smoothed over and the altar returned to its hook, he put all the metal into a small sack.

The following evening, the sack went by rickshaw to a blacksmith, Mulrenan travelling with it, Ts'o and his deputy following along behind in another. The gold, silver and platinum were formed into half kilogram ingots then rolled thin enough to be bent. The blacksmith was given a block of gold and two of silver for his labours and to keep his mouth shut. Ts'o and his deputy received half an ingot of gold each. Mulrenan took the remainder back to the house and hid it above the plaster of the ceiling in the bedroom. Although he did not inform Alice of his actions, she knew exactly what he had done.

Mulrenan and Alice were sitting on the balcony of the house in the late evening. She was drinking cold tea and he a much-diluted scotch. Supplies were running low. The street was busy with pedestrians and rickshaws, some loaded with effigies as the Chinese were preparing for the festival of the hungry ghosts. Although they appeared heavy, the effigies were not, as the easy step of the rickshaw coolies gave testimony. Some were so large they had to be tied into the seats with twine. They swayed precariously as the rickshaws turned the corner into Rua Do Patane and ran over the drain which cut across the street.

The effigies were not of people or gods, but of earthly goods. There were four-storey mansions with green roofs and red brick walls, tree-like objects hung with fake banknotes printed with incredible values: a dust-devil whisking up the hot street tore a few notes free and lifted them up past the balcony. Mulrenan caught one. It was for ten million patacas. Other effigies paraded below the verandah were of bicycles and motor cars, chairs, tables and beds, cooking stoves, chests labelled with the Chinese character for gold, European and traditional suits of clothing or dresses and an airplane with a single, nose-mounted propeller which spun with the forward motion of the rickshaw. And there was multi-coloured food, covering the full range of fruits from paw-paws to oranges, loquats to lychees. There were roast pigs and huge fish. Some were larger than life. Everything was made of painted paper stretched across split bamboo frames.

A hundred yards down Rua Do Patane, opposite a hovel used by a shoe mender, a woman stood in the shadow of the cemetery wall with a paper house before her on the ground. She was a small woman, shrunk by age, the mock building as tall as she and just as frail. She tottered into the cobbler's stall and reappeared with a paper chest on top of which lay a paper bicycle. She seemed to struggle as if the pretend objects had a pretend weight which she was obliged to acknowledge.

These placed next to the paper house, she struck a match on a cobblestone, igniting a corner of the flimsy building, squatting down like a woodsman by a camp-fire. She stoked the flames with a bit of stick and, when the building was almost consumed, added the chest and cycle. The flames reddened the wall, thin smoke drifting along the street.

'Money burning for the ancestors,' Mulrenan observed, passing the ten million pataca note to Alice. 'What we could do with a real one.'

The note was printed in English with the words "Hell's Bank Note" embossed in yellow.

'They'll be doing well in heaven or hell this week,' Mulrenan went on. 'All over China, the ancestors must be waiting for their annual food supply and new wardrobes of the latest fashions.'

'You shouldn't mock. The dead are good to them. They believe their ancestors watch over them and guard their welfare. It's wrong not to show reverence for ancestors. People know they are what they are because of their forebears.'

'Serves them right,' Mulrenan retorted. 'If they think a man is what he is because of his father, then more fool them. A man is what he makes of himself.'

Listening to him, Alice knew from the manner in which he spoke he did not entirely believe his words. He thought he knew what he was and how he came to be himself.

'I met a boy the other day to prove the rule,' he continued. 'A ten-year-old or thereabouts. A mere lad. English. His name was Philip Haversham.'

Alice felt her heart tug, a lurch upsetting her pulse for a moment.

'His mother and sister had died. His father seems to have copped it in Hong Kong. He came to me first some weeks ago with an extraordinarily fine diamond which I bought for a good price. His mother was alive then and sent him with it. I never saw her.'

He reached to the boards by his chair where there was a jug covered by a square of butter muslin. He added a further inch of water to his already weak whisky, ekeing it out.

'She died and he brought the rest of her jewellery to sell off. I bought the lot. Some of it was rubbish, the stones generally not very good but there were a few really superb bits and pieces. You should have seen him bargaining! Like an old pro at an auction. Raising his price, fixing terms, agreeing a sum, shaking hands on it. Now he was making something of himself. His past had nothing to do with it. I had to admire him . . .'

The old woman's offering to her departed souls had finished burning. Smouldering tatters of paper lifted on the breeze, winking with red, fading strands of fire in the gathering darkness.

'Time we had a light out here.'

Calling Ah Shun, Alice had an oil lamp brought out and put by the jug.

'How much did you pay, Sean?'

'A good bit. I struck a hard deal and the boy had underpriced himself but it still took a lot. I've recouped some of it and I'll get a bit more yet . . . it shouldn't leave us short for long. A fortnight at the most.'

'How could you cheat a child?' Alice remonstrated, instantly anxious at her rash question. Yet she had to say something in defence of the boy who had so affected her, for whom she had so fleetingly felt such sympathy, love even.

'Cheat! I didn't cheat him. It was business. He gave a good account of himself. Beside, he was English and that's an end to it.'

'If he was English, how could you even slightly admire him?'

Mulrenan was silent.

'If you condemn him for being English, you're condemning him because of his ancestors — yet you say ancestors count for nothing.'

Again, Mulrenan held his peace.

Alice, too, judged it best to keep silent now, for her thoughts were consolidating along lines she had been considering for weeks.

She no longer loved Mulrenan, no longer wanted him near. He had served his purpose, had brought her out of the servitude of The Line, had fed and clothed her, had loved her in his misanthropic way: he had saved her from living either in penury or in a Japanese-occupied Hong Kong where she would have been incarcerated or killed — or reduced to whoring once more. Now she was safe from all that, and he was redundant.

It was not just his distant cruelty and arrogance that had driven her from him. She could no longer abide his hatred, his continual desire to debase his self-appointed enemies: for, as much as he demeaned them so he demeaned himself and, by association, her.

There had been those times when she had gladly helped him at his shabby business, assisting him to assess the value of gems. She had also spotted for him those men in his social circle who were potential customers — she knew, from her past, who had a rocky marriage and a concubine, hungry for gifts, hidden away in Happy Valley or Kennedy Town.

On one occasion, she had even surreptitiously inspected an unlocked jewel case for him. She had been shown in to the bedroom of a house to which they had been invited for the evening: ostensibly, she had wanted to repair a torn nylon stocking which her fingernail had deliberately laddered. On their return to Lyndhurst Terrace, she had reported her discoveries to Mulrenan and, predictably, the house had been ransacked over the Chinese New Year a few weeks later, while the owners were in the New Territories and servants absent on their annual festival holiday.

She had felt no shame then: it had been an act of bravado, a sealing of their relationship. She was truly joining in his life.

Yet over the months since they had moved to Macau, Alice had felt a deep shame slinking up on her. It had come insidiously, like a disease which disfigures so slowly that no one notices it until, one day, it is gruesomely apparent. This conversation about the boy had brought her to her senses, showing how the sickness engendered by his passion for hating had crept upon her.

With a certainty which excited her by its firmness, Alice knew she wanted to be rid of Mulrenan. It was not just a matter of having him out of her house and her life. She wanted him far away, so removed as to be utterly out of touch. She wanted him, more than anything else and regardless of the consequences, out of Macau.

19

In the centre, the shelf had warped under the weight of books and ground-glass-stoppered jars filled with achromatic powders or the dried, shapeless fragments of mysterious roots and barks. None bore a name, only a number on a label, and not one of the books had a spine, each bound by string sewn through the margins.

On top of a glass-fronted cabinet, into which had been etched and stained a red cross, resided in a state of theatrical rage, its mouth opened in a mute but threatening mime, a stuffed baby crocodile. Inside the cabinet, arranged on different levels of thick, bluish glass was a collection of medical instruments. Some were polished, some bore traces of rust. None, Alice was certain, was sterilised. The room smelled musty but curiously pleasant and encouragingly friendly. It was only a little unlike the herbalist's shop in Rua dos Curtidores.

On the table in front of Alice was a two-foot-long ivory model of a naked woman reclining on a rosewood stand shaped like a couch, her pale yellow body delicately engraved with Chinese characters outlined in black, the various medical regions of her torso and limbs delineated with thin scorings so she took on the weird appearance of a tattooed fairground freak. Next to her, on her hard couch, was an ivory needle mounted into a rosewood handle.

Alice had expected the doctor to be old and sage-like but he was a man only a few years older than herself. She thought for a moment that she recognised him. He was wearing a man's long gown from the hem of which protruded the toecap of modern shoes. He wore a gauche American university graduation ring on one of his fingers, the large purple-ish stone in the centre surrounded by embossed lettering. It was too large for his thin fingers and kept slipping sideways. His wristwatch ticked audibly in the quiet of his consulting room.

'Good morning, Miss Soon,' he greeted her with an American Chinese accent as she entered. 'I don't think we've met since your husband introduced us at the theatre — oh, some months ago now.' He thought for a moment before adding, 'Maybe over a year since. Before the war.'

For most Chinese, addressing a woman as 'Miss' and then referring to her husband would have been an act of calculated rudeness but for Dr Mak it was a mere statement of fact.

'We have not met since then.' She blushed, recalling him now. 'How are you, doctor?'

He was seated behind the desk and smiled at her over the reclining figure.

'Isn't that the question I should be asking you? But never mind. I'm fine. But you're not, otherwise you wouldn't be here. And I can see you didn't expect me.' He spoke quietly, his voice humorous, at once putting her at ease. 'Perhaps you expected my father. He's retired and I've taken over the practice. It seems most strange, after medical school in America, to be examining my first professional patients in such a surgery and under such dire circumstances, too. But I believe the present situation can teach me — us, perhaps — a little of value. The old quacks had something and we can use it . . . along with our newly-acquired knowledge.'

He undid the top buttons of his gown, exposing an open-necked shirt, a stethoscope around his neck.

'I'll check your pulse while you tell me the problem.'

He pressed the stethoscope against her arm and squeezed upon her biceps. He felt her wrist, his index finger and thumb moving to locate the artery.

'I'm late,' Alice said simply.

Mak hummed and studied the second hand on his watch.

'Have you been late before? Have you a history of irregularity?'

'Not recently. I used to be quite irregular when . . .'

She stopped abruptly and wondered if he could feel her pulse rate fluctuate.

'I don't think I need to resort to Blanche here, do I?' the doctor asked, letting Alice's wrist go.

'I'm sorry? I don't understand.'

Perching himself on the edge of the desk, Dr Mak said, 'Miss Soon, when I was a medical student in Los Angeles, I had a girlfriend. Her name was Blanche Schulte and she came from Nebraska, right in the middle of America. Her parents were first generation Americans from Bavaria, in Germany. She had a very white skin, like the snows of a prairie winter — I visited her once in winter: it was forty degrees below zero — and bobbed blonde hair. Her name means white, too. In French. Of course, I never told my parents of this for they've had a young lady in Canton lined up for me from way back. So I'm taking you into my confidence.'

He looked at her pointedly and Alice nodded.

'Now, in the days of my father and his father — who were both Chinese doctors, as opposed to a Yankie one like me — it was forbidden for the doctor to touch his lady patients. Sometimes he conversed with her only through an intermediary, usually a female servant. So he could know where the pain or problem was, he brought out one of these' — he lifted the reclining ivory figure — 'and the patient pointed to the relevant parts with the needle there.'

'It's a very beautiful carving,' Alice commented.

The doctor passed it to her, the ivory like firm, cool flesh. Every feature of the female body was exquisitely carved from the strands of hair tied in a bun to the slit of the vagina and the lines on the soles of the feet.

'I call her Blanche. To myself. She sits there to free the older patients from any worries. After all, to them I'm a young man *and* a Western doctor. And she is off-white.'

Alice laughed sedately. She did not know how to accept the doctor's very un-Chinese approach to patient psychology.

'Right,' said Dr Mak, 'I've let you into my secret and you must . . . Well, I know but I want you to confirm it to me. I'll be as quiet as one of the priests in the confessionals. Isn't Macau churchy? There are hundreds of them. Did you have very irregular periods when you were working as a courtesan?'

The suddenness with which he sprung the question left Alice speechless.

'Don't be embarrassed. Or shy. And don't withhold the facts. I need to know. I'm sorry Blanche can't answer for you.'

Gathering her composure and her courage, Alice admitted, 'I was irregular from time to time. It depended on the month and how much work . . . how many . . .'

'Have you ever been pregnant?'

'No, never. We had the men take precautions when we could and they often did so anyway to avoid catching anything.'

It seemed so utterly despicable now, from the perspective of several years away from The Line, to be speaking of those days in such coldly clinical terms: but it had been a coldly clinical job most of the while.

'That was my next question. Have you ever contracted anything?'

'Twice. Both times it was just the clap.'

As she made the admission, Alice realised she knew no other word for it.

'Gonorrhoea?'

'Yes — at least, I think that was it.'

They all lived in fear of veneral disease. It would so quickly ruin one's appearance, take away business, stop the flow of money and one would die mad, or of starvation, ugly and rejected.

'Certain? It wasn't syphilis?'

'No,' Alice replied.

'I think I'll take a blood sample all the same.'

She was relieved to be having a proper examination at last, but worried in case she would be probed by the contents of the cabinet under the crocodile. Her anxiety ceased when the doctor opened a cupboard at the rear of the room to show a polished steel steriliser from which a wisp of steam was blowing. He opened the lid, allowing a billow to rise to the ceiling. With a pair of large pincers, he removed a chrome and glass syringe from the boiling water.

'I keep the modern equipment out of sight. It puts some of my father's long-term patients off. We can't afford to let them go.' He held up the syringe and lowered it into an enamel kidney dish.

With some blood drawn off and shaken in a test-tube with an anti-coagulant, he ordered Alice to remove her blouse. When she had done so, he felt her breasts, listened to her heart, tapped her sternum and her back and, loosening the waist band of her skirt, pressed his fingers gently into her stomach.

The examination over, he sat once more on his desk as she fastened her blouse.

'How late are you?'

'Seven weeks. It's been this long on occasion but not since Hong Kong.'

'I shall check the blood in the next quarter of an hour. It takes a while to stain the slide and scan it. I have my own microscope. Essential in the tropics, my professor told me. I think he had shares in the company. So many Americans have stock in businesses. Can you come back in an hour?' He did not wait for her answer. 'Good. But this is only a precaution. Tell me, are you happy?'

It was then she knew.

For the next hour, Alice walked the length of Praia Grande and on round Rua Praia do Bom Parto and the Avenida de Republica as far as the old Barra fortress. She took slow steps on her way to the fortress, lingering under the trees and gazing at the muddy tide. Her mind was in turmoil, her main concern being what Mulrenan's reaction might be to the news. It had never occurred to either of them she might one day conceive: they had not wanted to have a child and yet, sometimes, they had not tried to prevent it.

Every child sitting on the wall of the embankment, dangling its bare feet over the sea or fishing with a hand-held line for something with which to supplement the family's fare, became an object of interest. She stayed for fully five minutes watching one five-year-old who was having considerably better fortune than his peers further along the praia. By his side was a battered rattan basket with several dozen small fish in it, those on top flapping, their gill-slits red with the burning oxygen of the air. She rememberd a boy had been fishing the day they had gone to the races and Mulrenan had given her the amethyst and diamond ring: and that was the day she had first met Irina. How good it would have been, she thought sadly, to have shared these tidings with her.

As his amah showed her into the surgery, Dr Mak said, 'I'll bet my shirt you were walking along dreaming. All mothers-to-be do. Please, sit down.'

This time he did not hold the chair for her but remained behind his desk. On a folding baize-covered card table by the window balanced the brass body of a microscope hanging from its curving arm. The mirror under the slide platform had been angled to catch the sun which had now shifted in the sky, the mirror projecting a perfect orb of light onto the ceiling.

'Am I?' she asked.

'Oh, quite certain of it. I knew before you left. What I wanted to check for was not your pregnancy but for — well, anything that might be lurking in your blood. Gladly, there are no signs of any venereal disease. There are a few malarial parasites but the count is low — there aren't too many of the little fellas.' She did not know whether to smile at his Americanism or frown at his news. 'You appear not to be badly infected. Not enough to be a risk, anyway. I can't give you any quinine — and don't you dare tell anybody

I've still got some: I'm saving it for an epidemic or a very wet typhoon season — as it might abort you. One bad thing is you do have a lowish red blood count. You're anaemic. You need a tonic. That's no problem. I'll get you something.'

Much to Alice's astonishment, he took a jar from the bowing shelf, removing some grey powder from it with a bone scoop. He folded it into a triangle of paper, tucking the ends in so none might spill.

'Divide this into fifths and take one of the doses every day until it's finished.'

'What is it?'

'Do you really want to know?' he teased her.

'Yes. It looks herbal.'

'It's not.' His lips curled up in a grin. 'It's been nowhere near a plant. It's cobra's blood.' He saw her stare of disbelief. 'Well, that's what the index says. Jar fourteen: cobra's blood.' He checked the number of the label. 'Don't trust it, though. Probably any snake's blood.'

'Won't it be poisonous?' she asked with alarm.

'The poison isn't in the blood. It's in tiny sacs in the snake's head.'

She still gave the paper a wary glance.

'Some of these potions are rubbish,' Dr Mak said. 'Crushed tortoise shell for gallstones, powdered tigers' bones in tea for aching joints. Burned elephant skin paste for cuts. Rhino horn for TB. Baloney! But blood for tiredness? Seems right. You need iron to build up red blood cells and blood's a good source of it. And I've no iron pills anyway. So back to the drawingboard of my ancestors.'

Mulrenan was outwardly pleased. Alice broke the news to him gently and gradually, over their meal, but he already knew.

'You're expecting a baby.'

'Yes,' she confirmed. 'In the spring. Late May. I saw Dr Mak today.'

'I know.'

'How could you know! He . . .'

'I know you saw him,' Mulrenan explained. 'Ts'o was with you today.'

'That's true, but I've others. Macau's not huge and I need to know what's going on'. He put his chopsticks down across his bowl, signifying he had finished his meal. 'Are you pleased?'

'I think so,' she said after a pause.

'You need to be sure.'

'How do you feel?'

Mulrenan paused, too. It was not a position in which he had expected to find himself although the possibility had always been there.

'Quietly pleased. Of course, it means another mouth to feed,' he said gravely, 'and you'll need looking after. Mak will deliver you of the baby. And, before you go off to his surgery again, I have already settled the bill with him. He owes me a favour . . . But, yes, I'm pleased.'

Alice was secretly jubilant. It was every woman's dream, her ultimate fulfilment, to bear a child: or so it appeared to her. She was unable to consider the impending birth except in these terms, as the culmination of her life so far. She recalled the happiness of her childhood and her less joyful time spent in The Line as one of Mrs Morrison's ladies of leisure — a quaint phrase, she had always thought, for there was little leisurely about being a whore. She remembered then her release from what was little more than thinly-disguised slavery into her love affair with Mulrenan: he had been considerate at first, but their relationship had soured gradually. Now she believed it was his incapacity to love that had brought about her growing disregard for him.

The child now curling in her womb could be a fresh start for her. Just as its birth was an awakening for a new person, so it could be a new beginning for her, the turn of a leaf in her own life. She could, she hoped, use it not only as a widening of her future life but also as an exorcism of the past.

She would require Mulrenan's support for she had no way of keeping herself, and yet she did not want him influencing her son.

It was not *their* son nestling in her belly: this was her private act somehow. And, like any Chinese, she wished fervently she might be bearing a boy and told Mulrenan of her longing.

'You see,' he said, 'the Chinese in you comes through at all the seams of your personality. Like light leaking from a ill-fitting door. A son. What every Chinese wants. Daughters are of little use. And what will you call him? If it's a him.'

'Sean,' she answered. 'I'll call him Sean.'

'And what if he's a she?'

'Obvious. We'll call her Sian,' she said.

Alice was soon asleep that night, her fingers relaxing from his side and, after an hour, she turned over. Her arm moved across him like a rope being sucked into the sea by a craft leaving the quay and, in a way, that was what was happening: she was casting herself off from him and setting out on her own journey.

Yet he did not sleep and at midnight, as the air grew colder with the first hint of summer's dying, he went to the chest for a blanket to drape over the sheet under which they were lying. In tucking the mosquito net under the mattress, he accidentally allowed it to flitter across her cheek. She stirred and made to brush it aside, her hand reaching her face seconds after the net touched it.

Through the netting, where it hung over the bamboo frame above his head, Mulrenan stared at the ceiling. Behind the plaster, boards and beams lay the beaten gold strips. A number of those could be sewn into a belt or the collar of a coat. A few could be inserted into the lining of a case or portemanteau.

The Japanese presence in China was not the problem: that was the embryo folded in Alice's womb, the cells dividing and multiplying, developing and shaping into a replica of himself mixed with a replica of her. A quarter Irish, quarter Chinese — and half-English. The child would require feeding and money. The gold over their heads would do for a while; but what if the war lasted for years? Some believed it would; it was becoming a conflict not of military strategy but of attrition. It could go on and on, leaving him stranded with a mistress and a half-caste English bastard — just as he was, as she was.

On the other hand, he thought, if he were to get away from Macau, his absence would mean one less mouth to feed there.

It was easier said than done. A white face in a sea of yellow ones, especially a sea in turmoil and continuously monitored by an alien occupying power, stood out like a rose in a bed of thistles. A passport from his small collection would be useless: no one asked for identification prior to opening fire.

Yet he had the contacts. The pirates and the partisans were a fraternity in which he was well known, not only for his dealings but for being straight with his friends and ruthless with his enemies. Such a man can be trusted in a society of similar men. Besides, the boy with the diamond ring, Philip — he searched his brain for the lad's surname . . . Harrison, — Havisham — he had left Macau, spirited out somehow.

By dawn, Mulrenan had reached a decision. He would go, lessening the strain on their resources. He could send money back by way of the British consul or the Portuguese: these would be his *raisons d'etre* to Alice. And, he reminded himself, she was British with a passport to prove it: the

251

British were looking after their own so if he did fail, she and the baby would not starve.

As for himself, his escaping from Macau would bring a liberty he had forgotten and he would avoid being present at the birth of his half-English offspring.

The advantages, as he pondered them through the night, became increasingly appealing and his determination firmer.

21

In the first week of November, Mulrenan was walking along Rua Fernao Mendes Pinto near to Rotunda Carlos Da Maia. It was a warm, autumnal afternoon and he was making his way slowly, keeping to the shade, for the morning had been cold and he was wearing heavier clothes than he would have chosen had he known the weather would turn. He had met with a Portuguese Chinese who purchased gold and platinum and whom he believed would be a useful contact.

As he paused to cross the street, Mulrenan noticed Freddy Tsang approaching. He could not avoid him.

'Mr Mulrenan, good afternoon,' Tsang greeted him civilly. 'It has certainly developed into a fine day.

Mulrenan agreed.

'Let us walk. I want to have a word with you.'

With a sense of foreboding, and not speaking, Mulrenan walked by Tsang's side.

'I want you to do me a favour,' Tsang said when they reached a quiet street. 'Quite a considerable favour. It concerns Fukui, the Japanese consul.'

'I thought it might,' Mulrenan answered, adding, 'I haven't set eyes on him lately.'

'Hardly surprising as he's been in Hong Kong. New orders through from Tokyo . . .'

An amah came towards them along the pavement and Tsang was silent until she had passed.

'. . . which, needless to say, I've read. An acquaintance of yours works for me now. A Mr Leung. Young man, very talented.'

'How is he?'

'Doing very well,' Tsang said ambiguously.

'What do you want of me?' Mulrenan asked.

'A favour. But more of that later. Do you know Alice Soon's brother is alive?'

Mulrenan said nothing.

'He's in Stanley gaol. Not ill but not too good. He sends her his love.'

'I'll let her know. Thank you. And the favour?'

'Fukui,' Tsang replied. 'We are going to eliminate him.' He beamed. 'Doesn't that sound melodramatic! Like a line from a film.'

'And me?'

'We want you to help us.'

'If I can . . .' Mulrenan began.

'You can, Mr Mulrenan. Of that I'm quite sure.'

22

The note was delivered by a man who accosted Ah Shun at the market. She was in a straggled, disorderly queue waiting for a rice stall to open when he stood alongside her, thrust a sealed envelope into her hand and told her she was to give it secretly to her mistress and to no one else. To drive home his instructions, he painfully twisted her wrist.

Alice opened it in the privacy of the lavatory.

'Not long,' she read. 'All going according to plan. Be prepared. Next month most probably. Further instructions will be in the usual place at the usual time.'

It was signed *FT*.

She destroyed the note. Freddy Tsang was old friend, a good friend from her childhood and a one-time business associate of her father. He would not let her down.

23

In order she might take exercise, Alice and Mulrenan fell into the habit of evening walks to the façade of the ruined Sao Paolo cathedral. It was not far but just enough to tire her. The church had burned down in 1835 but its granite front had survived and they sat on the top of the steps before the facade and watched the sun go down. Behind them stone angels and saints, mingling with stone dragons and chimeræ carved Portuguese carracks, ornate fountains and shrubbery, peered over their heads from niches in the wall.

As they sat side by side on the stone, warm from the afternoon sun, Alice said quite suddenly, 'I've been thinking ever since you told me about Alec . . . And you must forgive me. But wouldn't it be good if we could get him out?'

She expressed the idea as if it had only just occurred to her.

'Why?' Mulrenan said, his voice dull with anger.

'Just to free him. I know you'd not let him live with us . . .'

'We could never bring him here. Besides, there're Japanese spies everywhere.'

As they walked slowly home Mulrenan, who had been silent, mentioned the matter again.

'You're right — I'd not want him here. He'd jeopardise all our lives. But he could be got out through China, perhaps. Just perhaps. There are ways, I've heard. Some people did escape — one of them was called Epstein — and they came here but had to go on. It wasn't safe. An organisation called the British Army Aid Group — they've representatives here, if you can unearth them.'

Mulrenan had known of the Epstein escapade: they had been civilian internees from Stanley. There were obviously possible ways out if one could find them.

'I've been thinking . . .'

Mulrenan went on to explain his thoughts on their financial situation, his ability to sell their gemstones at a better price out of Macau, his plans for getting the money back to support her and his impending child.

Alice's hand tightened on his arm and he decided to risk saying it, made it sound as if he had decided only after much reluctance.

'I'm going to get out of Macau, make my way through China to Chungking and from there to India. I'm certain to get a top price for the gems there. I'll send money back through the Portuguese. Perhaps, the war will be over sooner than we think. And I could . . .'

He made his words as optimistic as possible: yet as he spoke, wondering if she might reject his plan, his mind played with another possibility that would not fail to please her. He could suggest springing Alec Cowley out of his PoW camp, by which he might get to associate with the Aid Group, gaining for himself a safer and organised passage.

'Will you come back?' Alice asked softly.

The question was mere formula. She had considered the implications of her pregnancy and her action in collaborating with Freddy Tsang, and had accepted the probable consequences. A concubine without a lover and master was as worthless as a leaf on the wind: it was a proverb she had heard at some stage of her life in The Line. With a child as well, such a woman was less than nothing. The proof of her concubinage was forever around her, demanding her attention and affection. If Mulrenan did not send money at least at first, to tide her over from one life to the next, she would be in dire straits.

Yet, at that very moment of doubt, one memory surfaced in her: that of his savage blow across her face, and her one thought was that she must not allow him to take everything with him.

'Yes, I'll return. You know that,' he assured her.

She could not care less: he would be out of her life, leaving her at the mercy of fate, the Eurasian ex-whore who had lived with the Irish pianist who preyed on the unfortunate and bore his brat. Some people would not forget, but the passage of time would help to soften attitudes.

He would be taking with him his moods and his foul temper, would not be present to teach his brand of hatred to the child. She also knew that the child, being part English, would therefore be part despised by him.

She was certain she would be all right, would survive. What he did not carry out with him would be there for her. If he returned, it would not be before the end of the war, whenever that might be. By then, she would have established herself with the child, protected it from his hating.

Suddenly, her arm through his own, she realised that what she had loved of him was his English half, the considerate, unvengeful half, and that his kindness and generosity of spirit was living on in her womb — and she loved it the more.

Mulrenan thought further about matters as they walked the length of Rua Santo Antonio. If Tsang's plan to murder Fukui closely involved him, then once it was done he would be a marked man. He pondered on the chances of refusing to help the urbane Chinese, with his Oxford degree and his suave turn of phrase: but that, too, would mark him down for a knife in the back, if from a different quarter. The time was drawing nigh when he would not only like to leave Macau but would have to.

By St Anthony's church he removed her hand from his arm and, standing in front of her, said, 'If I'm to get out, the best way is to go with a properly planned escape route. I could pick Alec up on the way. And I think I know someone who'll help . . .'

Once spoken, he knew he had to do it. He had to get her loathsome half-brother out of Stanley gaol.

24

For three weeks, Mulrenan received no word from Tsang and his apprehension grew. He found he was not sleeping well, anticipating what Freddy might demand of him in the assassination of the Japanese consul.

During that time, he met the British Consul, Mr Reeves, a pleasant man who instantly distrusted Mulrenan and recognised him as a crook and a confidence trickster.

That he was Irish was an added mark against him in the consul's book. Admittedly there were Irishmen living in Macau and more in Hong Kong who were not interned and who avidly guarded their neutrality yet who nevertheless were striving behind the scenes in the Allied war effort. One, a former Hong Kong stockbroker, started and operated a chicken farm in Kowloon: the British, as a cover, accused him of collaboration, knowing that in fact he was acting against the Japanese and using his influence for the benefit of prisoners. The Irish priests in Wah Yan College took food to prisoners also, and had been accused of spying. But Mulrenan, Reeves knew, was not regarded in the same light. A self-centred criminal, with few positive qualities, he was neither to be admired nor trusted.

Despite several attempts to ingratiate himself with Reeves and draw the man out, Mulrenan got no further than a passing acknowledgement that there was an underground network but that the consul was not in touch with it.

Mulrenan was no fool. The consul had to be fully aware of it and of its modus operandi. He was just not prepared to pass on his knowledge to a Third National whom he clearly considered a security risk.

Finally, Mulrenan was sent a message from Tsang. It was to the point: he would be seeing Fukui, and then should arrange a further meeting. How he would come to meet the Japanese he was not informed but, the following day, as he was sitting in a tea-house, the meeting occurred.

Mulrenan was sitting at a table watching the surrounding clientele and considering how well some egg and rice flour biscuits would go with the weak tea, when a vehicle halted outside and the door opened to admit two Kempetai men. Both wore civilian clothes in imitation of a European cut. They wore their ties with a Windsor knot, but their trousers were too tight for the pre-war fashion. Their double-breasted jackets were buttoned. Behind them stood an officer in the uniform of the Imperial Japanese Army, his sword with its shark-skin hilt glittering in the sunlight. When all three had given the tea-house a cursory inspection, the officer beckoned outside and Fukui entered accompanied by a diminutive Japanese, not five feet high and podgily fat. From the street could be heard the slap of military tabi-clad feet on the cobbles. Sentries had been posted.

Fukui came directly across to Mulrenan's table and the officer pulled a chair out for him. The short, fat man was the interpreter.

'This Mister Fukui,' he introduced his senior and Mulrenan stood up and bowed. He knew the form. Fukui also bowed and sat, indicating Mulrenan should be seated. The interpreter removed a chair from an adjacent table and sat between them.

The interpreter spoke good Portuguese to the Chinese waiter, refusing to order tea, but his English was poor.

'Mister Fukui know you good dealer. Famous man in Macau for buy sell jewel stones. He want you sell him some jade.'

'I'm afraid I do not have any jade,' Mulrenan replied, speaking slowly for the interpreter's benefit. 'I do not deal in it. There is too much about and I am interested only in gemstones.'

'You can get jade? Mister Fukui want to buy some jade from Chinese dead.'

'Grave jade I have seen,' Mulrenan informed him politely, 'and I have had some but I sold it quite quickly. There are Portuguese people who collect this sort of carving.'

'Mister Fukui want to know name of Portuguese man.'

'There are a number. I don't remember who they are for I've not done much business with them. I'm sure Mister Fukui could find out these people more easily than from me.'

Throughout the converstion Fukui had been silent, his eyes not shifting from Mulrenan's face. It unnerved him but he forced himself not to show it, glancing occasionally at Fukui and smiling as if to include him in the discussion even though he was apparently ignorant of what was being said.

'Where you get stones?' asked the interpreter.

It was evident either that he was talking off his own initiative or that the whole meeting had been carefully orchestrated.

'I buy from people who need to raise money to live.'

'Where you get money to buy?'

'By selling things,' he explained. 'It is trade. Business.'

'Where you get money to start?'

'I brought it with me from Hong Kong. Some months before your victory over the British.'

'Before that? You piano player in the big hotel. That a good job?'

Mulrenan laughed briefly.

'No. The British pay badly. But I gamble and I dealt in gemstones.'

'You steal.'

It was a statement, not a query.

'Yes,' Mulrenan admitted, still smiling, 'but only from the British.'

This one sentence was the first to be translated for the benefit of Fukui who nodded gravely and spoke to the interpreter in rapid Japanese. His voice was quiet and soft yet insistent and, for a reason he could not explain, chilled Mulrenan to the marrow.

'Mister Fukui say,' the interpreter continued, 'can you buy jade?'

'I don't know. There might be some available.'

'He want you buy for him. Much jade.'

'I cannot promise. I do not know what is available.'

'OK.'

Mulrenan thought the interview was over. Fukui shifted in his seat as if to get up, but did not.

'Next. You do not like British. We know this. You like Japanese?'

Mulrenan grinned as charmingly as he could.

'How can I say no?'

The interpreter grinned back wolfishly.

'Understand,' he said. 'But why you trying to contact British spy people?'

His words were suddenly frozen, blank and stark.

'British spies?' Mulrenan said. 'Here? You must be joking with me. How could a British spy survive here? He would stick out like a sore thumb?'

The smile was lost on the interpreter who scowled.

'People would know him,' Mulrenan explained. 'Europeans do not look like Chinese or Japanese. He would be seen. He would stick up in the air like a broken finger.' He jabbed his thumb upwards as if seeking a hitch-hiker's lift out of what was becoming a very tricky situation.

'Ah, yes,' replied the interpreter and he spent several minutes going over the conversation with Fukui who fleetingly smiled when the metaphor was explained.

'Mister Fukui say you get him jade,' the interpreter said flatly. 'Also, if you meet British spies, you report to Japanese army officer.'

'Tell him I'll do my very best for Mister Fukui.'

'One week. You get jade. Mister Fukui meet you here same time.'

'If I get some earlier?' Mulrenan enquired, bearing in mind Tsang's message.

'You telephone,' said the interpreter.

'He's ready,' Alice wrote in her next communication. 'We have discussed his leaving Macau and I am sure he is resolute. He mentioned using an escape route and taking my brother, Alec Cowley, with him. If this could be arranged, I would be exceptionally grateful. I am sure that this would eradicate any obligation existing between us: indeed, I would guarantee this.

She hid the letter under the fourth pot of geraniums down on the right hand side of the steps leading to the top terrace of the cemetery. The reply was rapid.

'Excellent!' it went. 'Indeed, he had already seen me about the matter, no doubt as you were writing to me. We are arranging the details now and you can rest assured our utmost endeavours will be made to obtain the release of your brother using him. Our own plan, involving him, will necessitate his leaving immediately after completion. There will, of course, be some risk to you in this: be aware the J. may seek reprisal. However, you should be safe if you follow my advice as given.'

Alice turned the page over. The writing on the reverse was smudged from the damp base of the flower pot.

'Consider,' the letter concluded, '*The Ruba'iyat of Omar Khayyam*:

'Tis all a Chequer-board of Night and Days
Where Destiny with Men for Pieces plays:
Hither and thither moves, and mates, and slays,
And one by one back in the Closet lays . . .'

There are rooms better suited to living in at night and others more appropriate to the rough and tumble of the day. The formal, traditional room in Freddy Tsang's borrowed accommodation was of the former category for, by daylight, it appeared like a stage set arranged for a play, or a still life painting of furniture somehow brought to three-dimensional reality.

The heavy, square chairs seemed uncomfortable and the carpet had been brushed carefully so the tassles on the end spread out at perfect right angles to the weave. The cushions were undented and the egrets on the wall scrolls lifeless, mere cartoons of the natural creatures upon which they were modelled. Even the blossom on the artist's twigs was too pink or too white.

Drawn aside, the curtains revealed an uncharacteristic french window giving on to a tiny patio in the centre of which was a pond no bigger than a foot-bath. From the centre of the water protruded one slender stem of a water plant and just under the surface swam two small red and white blotched koi carp.

Across the patio rose a steep and high wall on top of which were the battlements of the Old Monte fortress. Plant pots stood in ranks against the cut stone of the wall where the sun might fall on them in the afternoon.

'Do you like fish?' Tsang asked Mulrenan as he came into the room, the door being closed behind him by a servant.

'Not especially. I see no point in keeping them.'

'That is very European,' Tsang observed. 'For me, a pool is like a universe and I like to be able to gaze out in the mornings and see an entire world at my window which I can order. At about eleven o'clock, the sun reaches down into that tiny garden and sparkles upon the water. The fish rise to the glitter and it is then they are fed. Ants' eggs. Or tiny pieces of doughy rice flour.

'The attraction is not merely aesthetic for I also like the concept that I own the world of the pool. From time to time, I move the position of the plant. For an hour or so, this confuses the fish but they soon grow to learn the new map. I like to think I can alter an entire world for, in our own lives, no matter how we try, we cannot manage such grandiose schemes.'

He sat on one of the uncomfortable chairs, arranging the cushions to ease his spine on the hard wood.

'That is why men fight wars. To control. Like mountaineers who risk everything climbing, merely in order to conquer.'

'And that's the only reason?' Mulrenan said.

'Of course not! Man is a complex animal. There are other reasons to fight — pride, anger, dignity, revenge . . . All of these you, in particular, fully understand, I'm sure. You do not fight to control . . .'

'I don't have much time,' Mulrenan interrupted. 'Can we get down to it?'

'So. "Ever the impatience of the white man." A negro student from Nigeria told me that when I was up at Oxford. "The difference between the white and the black," he said, "is that the white man wants to shape his day and the black lets the hours mould him." A generalisation, naturally.'

'Fukui came to me . . .'

'I know. In the tea-house. I said he would.'

Mulrenan did not question how the information — not to mention the prophecy — had come to Tsang. He assumed Tsang had somehow engineered the meeting.

'He wants jade and . . .'

'That I know, too. I am more than cognisant with what passed between you. The important thing is what we do from here.'

Mulrenan paced across the room and back, his hands clasped behind him.

'This is not like you,' Tsang remonstrated. 'When meeting with your pirates you are reported to be cool and collected. There is no need to worry now. Nothing will go wrong. Do sit down.'

There was a mild exasperation in Tsang's voice and Mulrenan chose a seat opposite.

'You need to say nothing. Everything will be arranged. You will meet Fukui and he will meet the ghost of his emperor's father. I believe that's who dead Japanese go to see? I'm not too certain.'

'Am I expected to bring about the reunion?'

'Not at all.'

Mulrenan was relieved. 'And afterwards?'

'Afterwards? Yes.'

He paused as if to suggest he had given the aftermath no thought: yet he had. Every conceivable possibility had been considered.

'When it is done, you will immediately go into hiding. As soon as the coast is clear — both literally and metaphorically — you will leave Macau for Chungking. There you will be received by the British — I'm sorry there is no Irish diplomatic presence in the current Nationalist capital, but there it is! — and be repatriated.'

Mulrenan leaned forward, his arms resting on the wide sides of the chair. He explained he wanted to escape by way of Hong Kong, to take Alec Cowley with him. Tsang gave the impression he was surprised at such a far-fetched request and he begged time to think it over.

That evening, a note was delivered to the house in Rua do Patane. Mulrenan tore it open. It was from Freddy Tsang and confirmed that arrangements were in hand to comply with his wishes.

Alice was, to Mulrenan's hidden annoyance, quietly jubilant.

The required jade was provided by Freddy Tsang. One piece was of muttonfat jade shaped like a rabbit: the second was an erotic carving. They were delivered by a man whom Mulrenan thought was a mute. He made no reply to questions. Instructions for Mulrenan were contained on a scrap of handmade paper in the fabric of which were knots of bark. The orders were simple: a time and a place. He telephoned Fukui.

At the appointed hour, Mulrenan arrived at the rendezvous in a tea-house he had not previously visited, to be met by the mute. Tsang was there. Mulrenan sat at a table, his hand in his pocket gripping his pistol, the mute sitting behind him at another. Fukui arrived punctually with his interpreter and two army officers. Several soldiers stood in the street.

It was all over in ten seconds. The apparent mute stood up, shouted something in a totally incomprehensible language, levelled an automatic pistol at Fukui and emptied the magazine into his chest. The interpreter was hit by splintered crockery and the officers and other customers in the tea-house threw themselves to the floor as Tsang's own revolver spattered shots about their heads. By the time they rose and the sentries had burst in through the door, Mulrenan, Tsang and the gunman had vanished behind a grey mist of gunsmoke. Spreadeagled on the floor was the corpse of Fukui, a hole in his chest the size of a rice bowl.

Mulrenan was ready to leave.

Tsang provided him with a small, British Army message pouch made of webbing with blackened brass buckles and a shoulder strap. In this he packed some basic rations, spare clothing, a small block of lard, a Gillette razor with two blades and a comb, and a child's compass.

The gemstones posed a problem. In them lay his greatest asset. If he was to be robbed, he would not mind sacrificing the gold strips inserted in his wide leather belt next to his skin, so long as he kept the jewels.

To preserve them, he took two precautions. One was to sew into his trouser legs, high against his groin, two narrow pockets each three inches long. They were made to take two gold casings. Mulrenan had had them fashioned by a goldsmith he felt he could trust: in any case, the man had never received such a commission before and could not imagine what the objects were.

Each casing was shaped like an cigar tube, both ends rounded, dividing half way along the barrel into two screw-threaded hollow sections, their sides milled to a thickness of two millimetres. Into them Mulrenan slipped the stones then slid the casings into the trouser legs. His second precaution was in having them made of gold for, if he suspected he might be risking the security of the gemstones, he could remove the casings, smear them with the lard and force them up his anus. Being made of gold did away with the risks of poisoning arising from a non-royal metal.

There was a triple knock on the door and Tsang's henchman opened it to allow entry to Alice and a boy in his early teens who immediately bowed to Tsang and spoke in quiet insistent tones to him in Cantonese.

'The Korean has been caught,' Tsang reported. 'They took him on his way to Canton so it is just as well you are going through via Hong Kong. Obviously, they expect you to take the same route as the Korean. He was questioned about your whereabouts but, naturally, he knows nothing.'

Alice stood by Tsang and watched Mulrenan buckling his message pouch.

She told Tsang, 'They've visited our house again — with the Portuguese police — but they did nothing. More questions. They believe I'm ignorant and merely a courtesan. And, of course, my British citizenship means they are wary of touching me. The Portuguese were very protective.'

The boy left and Tsang said, 'It is nearly time. You must be on your way within the hour.'

He left the room, signalling to his man to follow.

There was an awkwardness growing between Alice and Mulrenan, the uncomfortable limbo of those who know parting is inevitable and imminent.

'I shall be all right, Alice. You've no need to worry. Freddy Tsang has alerted Reeves and has bribed a Portuguese official. The Japanese'll do nothing more than question me and now the Korean has been captured . . .'

It occurred to Mulrenan, at that moment, perhaps the Korean had been sacrificed so that he himself could get away. He would not have put such a move beyond Tsang.

From below came an urgent, insistent knocking.

'I'll be back as soon as I'm able,' he assured her. 'As soon as the war's over.'

'Yes,' she said. 'Come back.'

There was no emotion in her words, no tears in her eyes.

'And I'll get money through to you. The Portuguese can manage it. Or the British. I'll write to you care of Reeves. That seems the best plan.'

'Yes.'

A door opened and closed in the building. The bolts were rammed home.

'I'll write. As often as I can.'

'Don't worry, I'll be all right.'

The door to the room opened and Tsang said, 'The sampan's ready. You must go.'

Mulrenan kissed her once, holding her close.

'Good luck,' she said. 'Take good care.'

She wanted to ask him to get Alec out safely but did not. He voiced her thoughts for her.

'I will,' he said. 'And I'll get that damn brother of yours free, too.'

He shouldered the pouch and left, going down the stairs, not looking up at her standing at the head of the flight. His footsteps rang hollowly on the wood.

He was gone. There was still no tears in her eyes. The realisation he might never return came to her but she did not worry over it. Then the baby nestling in her kicked.

29

The cover of the well had been removed. Someone had turned over the soil in the pots, spilling some. The afternoon sunlight shone on the mottled walls of the Old Monte Fortress and radiated into the courtyard.

Alice knocked upon the door. The manservant with the shaven head opened it, stepping aside.

The scrolls ruffled on the wall as the door closed, the watercolour egrets flexing their wings as if preparing to come to life and escape from the parchment.

'Has it all gone exactly to plan?' Alice asked.

'Perfectly,' Tsang said.

He was wearing a blue satin gown, a long ebony cigarette holder in his hand. For a moment, Alice thought, he resembled an Oriental Noel Coward for he wore European-style leather carpet slippers.

'The light is so beautiful at this hour of the day as it shines on the fortress walls.'

He sat on the double rosewood seat, facing the glass door.

'It is best he has gone.'

'For both of us,' Alice agreed, sitting next to him.

'He is unreliable. Too selfish. Too narrow. He is widely

travelled but has none of the attitudes of the internationalist.'

'No, he hasn't.'

'Mulrenan is a loser, my dear. He's a man without compassion and compassion is essential if one is to be ruthless and survive. The yin and the yang. To be evil one must be an expert in goodness. He is too — one-sided: an incompetent gambler and I know for I have watched him play; an adequate businessman but not one destined for great riches. I suspect he was a poor lover . ... However, enough talk of him. He's gone. I may or may not hear of him. You will, I am sure. But you need not fear him any longer.'

'I know that,' she replied.

In the pool, one of koi carp broke the surface of the water sending ripples out to the rim. The stalk of the waterplant agitated.

'When will he arrive in Hong Kong?'

'He should be there by now,' Tsang said. 'Tell me: do you know the saying "A man who has no master can have no home?" That's Mulrenan's problem. He has no master.'

'I think he has,' Alice contradicted him. 'It's his hatred.'

'Then he will destroy everything around him and, finally, himself.'

'Yes,' she repeated. 'He will.'

She watched the fish circling in the pool and stood up.

'I'm very grateful to you . . .' Alice began.

'It is nothing, my dear Alice. I was obligated to your father and welcomed the chance to repay him.' He reached forward and closed the door to the patio. 'What will you do now?'

Alice looked out at the warm sunlight on the stone walls.

'Live,' she said.

A Man, Running

1

Leung grinned expansively.

'Long time no see you. How you been keeping? Life good for you and you lady in Macau? I hear some story about you. Doing well with gold and diamonds.'

'And you?'

'I doing OK. I buy sell here in Hong Kong. Big black market for anyt'ing. I got many contacts. Japanese storeman, soldiers. Got more contacts in prison camps. I now fighting in Communist army. Kill Japanese soldiers in New Tewito'ies. Travel up to China. Tsang order me fix for you.'

In the half-light of the room, Mulrenan saw Leung was wearing a grubby singlet, a shabby and tattered pair of ex-army shorts and a pair of army boots much in need of polish. Around his head was wound a strip of cloth.

'Are you working as a coolie?' Mulrenan asked.

He had expected Leung to be better off if he was dealing in the black market. In war, a man in trade need not wear rags.

'Today I am a coolie. Tomo'wow another job. This for cover up.' He tugged at the singlet. 'You ve'y tired, must sleep. I come back later.'

'Where am I?' Mulrenan enquired as Leung stepped towards the door. His head ached from exhaustion.

'You in safe house. Kowloon-side. No wuwwy.'

He closed the door quietly and Mulrenan heard him talking in low tones. Later, as he half-dozed, Mulrenan listened to a train rumbling nearby. The noise of the engine suddenly cut off as it faded: he reckoned he was in Kowloon

Tong, not far from the entrance to the Lion Rock tunnel under the mountains.

For three days and nights, Mulrenan was kept in the house, formerly the home of a well-to-do merchant but now occupied by four families whose menfolk were incarcerated. One was Anglo-Chinese, the husband a Scotsman from Stirling who had worked for the Hong Kong and Whampoa Dock Company, and the other three were Portuguese Chinese. Their husbands had been members of the civilian volunteer force fighting alongside the regular troops.

The house was big with a flat roof and walled garden. In this the non-paying tenants had dug up the sparse lawn, the flower beds and the tennis court and planted them with vegetables irrigated partly from the taps, when these were running, and partly by stirrup pump from buckets scooped from the nullah in Waterloo Road. This water came from the hills behind Kowloon Tong but included sewage which manured the ground, so the vegetables had to be thoroughly washed and boiled before being eaten. Cholera ravaged the civilian population every summer.

For the sake of prudence, Mulrenan remained in the house during the daylight hours although he walked in the garden in the cool of the night. The Portuguese Chinese women questioned him incessantly about life in Macau and he was asked if he knew of friends or relatives.

'The population of Macau is huge now, swelled by refugees,' he explained patiently.

'We know but we also hope. Just one word will do. That you have come across just a mention of someone. . . Do you know a Mr Da Costa? Tall, thin and with a goatee beard? He has a scar on his right wrist, from a broken window when he was a boy at the Diocesan Boys' School and he wears a ring with a round carnelian in it. A red stone. Have you . . .?'

At times Mulrenan was tempted to say he had met their loved one, had conversed with him at length about life in Hong Kong, about stamp collecting, about his only visit to Lisbon: such a reply would cheer his companions and stop them pestering him with their futile inquiries. He was not tempted to tell them a more truthful story, that he might well have come across Da Costa and bought the ring for a paltry five patacas: carnelian was common and had no resale value.

No one gave a thought to how Mulrenan had got to Hong Kong or why he had left the safe haven of Macau. No one questioned him about his reasons for hiding in their midst — it was deemed best to remain ignorant — and no one asked him for a contribution towards his keep. He was fed the same meagre diet and drank the same tepid boiled water. Indeed, he was treated more as an honoured guest than a man on the run and a dangerous liability. He had a room all to himself, in which there were two beds: under the spare one was a large carboard box into which the regular occupants had stuffed their belongings. The room had been vacated especially for Mulrenan. When an apple arrived on the communal dining table one evening, Mulrenan was offered an entire quarter of it.

He passed the days loosening his muscles with press-ups and bunny hops, or reading. The rightful owners of the house must have been bibliophiles for there were three large bookcases in the shared living room, containing a wide range of literature from Charles Dickens to Thomas Hardy, Shakespeare to George Bernard Shaw. Many of the books were first editions — the copy of Graham Greene's *Brighton Rock* was signed in a spidery hand, 'for Billy; best regards Graham' — but were mildewed and damp. Some had been attacked by insects. Even *Brighton Rock*, only a few years old, had its hard covers warped by the humidity and heat.

Mulrenan found, at the end of one row, a two volume edition of James Joyce's *Ulysses*. It was bound in grey paper by The Odyssey Press. He had never read it: picking up the second volume, he opened it at random and read:
. . . the carnal bridal ring of the holy Roman catholic apostolic church, conserved in Calcata, were deserving of simple hyperduly or of the fourth degree of latria according to the abscission of such divine excrescences as hair and toenails.

He understood little of it. It did mention a ring. Yet as he scanned the words, he could hear the soft lilt of the magical Irish tongue running over them, and through them, and under them and they brought a lump to his throat.

On the fourth night, soon after dark, Leung arrived. He was no longer wearing coolie rags but a pair of grey trousers and a blue jacket once part of a naval uniform. Where the epaulettes and rings of rank had been the cloth was darker.

'How you feeling? You got some exercise?'.

'I've been in the garden at night. Not out of it. And up on the roof, lying in the sun. Always out of sight. I've done some press-ups.'

'Good.' He indicated Mulrenan follow him outside. 'Important you get you body ready for long walk,' he continued as they strolled in the garden, their voices muted. 'I got you t'ip fix up. All awwanged. I tell you about it after we leave here. Tomo'wow morning. I come ve'y early. You be ready four o'clock time. We go Hong Kong side.'

'How?' Mulrenan asked.

He was not only anxious, but also genuinely curious to know how they would cross the harbour.

'Star Ferry,' replied Leung enigmatically.

Mulrenan was appalled: the audacity of travelling across the harbour on the ferry struck him as foolhardy and dangerous.

Leung saw his surprise, interpreted his thoughts, and elaborated.

'Not c'azy,' he said. 'Few minute, we go inside, I show you. Fust, you listen to plan say you like or no like.'

At the end of the garden was a mimosa tree under which the owners had placed a wooden bench more like a seat from a London park than the furniture of a Chinese arbour. It was bulky and ugly, the paint peeled to reveal blotches of sun-bleached timber. The light of a waning moon gave the appearance of a rare and terrible sylvan disease attacking the slats. Leung brushed the seat with a neatly laundered silk handkerchief before sitting. Less fussily, Mulrenan just sat down and leaned on the arm of the bench.

'Better you clean fust,' Leung advised him. 'Cloths not easy to get now and you need to keep you cloths for you journey to China. Maybe some bird shit on seat.'

Mulrenan chuckled and Leung feared he was losing face.

'What you laugh at?' he bristled.

'You,' said Mulrenan, pausing before he expanded upon his apparent insult. 'Your English has improved a great deal. When we last worked together, you spoke only a poor peasant's language but now you speak so much better. Have you been taking lessons?'

Leung, realising he was not being insulted, replied proudly, 'No lessons. I learn from talking to many pwisoners. P'wrisoners,' he repeated to get the pronunciation correct. 'I see many working in Kowloon. Some digging in new airport at Kai Tak. Some working near docks at Tsim Sha Tsui railway station. I work as coolie sometime. Carry earth, fetch stones. Shovel. I listen, I talk. If p'wrisoner,' he deliberated over the word, 'want some t'ings, I get. If can do. If no can do, I not get.'

'What sort of things?'

'Medicine. Food — small chop. Maybe a fish. Salt. One day I get four ounce sugar. Tha' a lucky time.'

'What do they give you?'

Mulrenan was too shrewd to assume Leung did all this for the love of humanity. Business was business.

'I get gold ring, silver ring. Maybe brass tap. Copper wire. Watch. Fountung pen — good if point make of gold. If someone die, maybe get teeth. Not often. Only one, two time.'

It took Mulrenan a moment to realise the teeth would be the capped or filled ones.

'I get anyt'ing I can sell. Not difficult. In Hong Kong, can buy an' sell many t'ing because of war.'

A fast-moving cloud obscured the moon. A cicada, screeching in the branches of another mimosa across the tennis court cabbage patch, fell silent. Leung became instantly alert. When the moon was visible again, the cicada recommenced its noise and Leung relaxed.

'Only moon,' he explained. 'But better be sure.'

He shifted along the bench to be close enough to Mulrenan to speak into his ear, lowering his voice to a barely audible level.

'Moon die soon,' Leung whispered. 'Then we go. All fix up. You listen now careful.'

He looked about the shadows suspiciously and Mulrenan inwardly prayed he wasn't going to be this obvious when confronted by a Japanese guard checking identity papers at the ferry pier.

'We go Hong Kong side in morning. You travel wif me on bottom deck of Star Ferry. We get you cloths so you like Chinese man. Coolie maybe. All you luggage in basket I b'ing you. You got much?' he asked as an afterthought.

'No, not a lot.'

'When we get Hong Kong side go to friend in Shau Kei Wan. Stay in his house two days, maybe three. Then we work.'

'How do we get him out?' He hated to give Alice's brother his name.

'Mista Cowley al'eady told of plan. He know. What we do not too difficult. We go to Stanley walking, go in sampan to pwison. P'oper time, he come. We go in sampan. No p'oblem.'

'No problem!' Mulrenan exclaimed ruefully, his voice going just a little too loud.

Leung hushed him by waving his hand up and down in the air as if fanning the sound away like smoke.

'O, no. No p'oblem,' Leung quietly repeated. 'Sampan 'eady. Man to steer sampan 'eady. P'isoner 'eady. You me 'eady. Everybody 'eady.' He paused. 'Japanese not 'eady.'

The Chinese subtle but obvious sense of humour rushed a giddy hope into Mulrenan. They could, he thought, actually make it.

'So tomorrow morning I become Ah Pong, Coolie.'

'Yes.' Leung considered the pseudonym Mulrenan adopted then laughed. 'Ah Pong funny name for you. Make me think. You no wash again. You smell clean, got soap smell like *gweilo*. Coolies no wash wif soap. No good to go as coolie if you smell like taipan.'

Leung shook Mulrenan's hand as he left. A current of apprehension must have passed from the Irishman to the Chinese opportunist-cum-freedom fighter.

'You no wowwy,' Leung said. 'We be number one OK.'

2

Mulrenan slept fitfully, his dream crammed with ranks of Japanese soldiers, flashes of gunfire issuing from their eyes. He saw himself in a pool of blood, his hands sticky and his mouth tight shut with the glue of it. His ears were awash with blood slopping like warm syrup against the drums. When he turned over, he saw Alice standing by a grave, a small child holding her hand and staring upon a polished Chinese coffin with a complete lack of interest or even comprehension. Rain started to patter on the lid, run off the sleek surface of the varnish.

During the night, a basket was delivered and, by four am, Mulrenan was dressed in a baggy pair of trousers, a matching black, smock-like coat, leather sandals and, tied on with string, a short-brimmed conical rickshaw coolie's split cane hat. His feet were soft and clean, the toe-nails trimmed: to camouflage them, he rubbed dirt into them and smoothed mud under the short nails. His brown hair was hidden under the hat which was fixed so firmly on to his skull as to defy any cross-habour wind. He removed his watch and the ring he wore on the little finger of his right hand, inserting these into his money and gold belt which, in turn, he threaded through the fold-over top of the trousers. Traditional Chinese pants did not have buttons: they were simply folded around the stomach like a bath towel.

As he dressed, preparing himself like an actor, he worried over points of detail he might have overlooked. He was tanned sufficiently to pass as a Chinese. His hair was hidden and he shaved to do away with any beard: Chinese men seldom sprout thick, coarse stubble as Europeans do. His ears were partially hidden by the hat brim and so were his eyes. These gave him cause for concern but he knew a good many southern Chinese did not have the narrow eyes attributed to them by Western caricaturists: and the colour of his eyes would pass muster under the hat. What he had to consciously strive to imitate was the smaller step, the slightly bowed shoulders and the bent head.

Just before the appointed time for him to leave, Mulrenan's greatest fear surfaced in him. It was the possible loss of his treasure.

Unwrapping the contents of the basket, he removed the two gold cylinders and smeared them with the block of fat. Squatting down, he pushed first one and then the other into his anus. As they slipped through into him, the pain was intense, the muscles stretching and nearly tearing. He sucked his breath to dispell the agony. Once in, however, he did not feel them except as an ill-defined pressure inside his bowels. When he gingerly straightened, they shifted and settled inside his rectum.

He tried walking. It wasn't painful but it was awkward and he realised, with a wry inward smile, the gemstones in their gold repositories would force him to walk like a coolie.

At the Star Ferry pier, Leung went through the turnstile first. Mulrenan followed five passengers later. Two Japanese soldiers, their long rifles resting on their forearms with bayonets fitted, were posted by the entrance but neither gave him so much as a cursory glance. They were intent on watching for the approach of an officer to whom they would have to offer a very rapid and smart salute.

Mulrenan had never felt so alone, so vulnerable. As he paid his coin to the collector, he sensed how European his hand was despite the fact it was unwashed and smelled of his own faeces. He had not washed his fingers since inserting the gold tubes into himself.

The sun had been up for over an hour by the time the ferry crew cast off for the fifteen-minute journey across the harbour.

Around him, other coolies sat on the benches or stood by their loads. He lowered his basket to the deck and almost sighed with the relief. He wanted to rub his hands together to ease the numbness, to look at the redness of his palms, but he dared not. Coolies did not get blisters.

An amah left her seat by his side. Several of those standing made a rush for it but Mulrenan beat them to it. That was in keeping with coolie behaviour.

How many times, he considered, had he travelled on the Star Ferry, on the deck over his head, carrying his poker winnings or a few gemstones to the Hongkong and Shanghai Bank. How many of the gemstones now rammed up his arse, he wondered, had already made this journey in a soft chamois leather pouch in his pocket.

The ferry docked. He picked up the basket once more. Leung led the way. Mulrenan followed. Shau Kei Wan was a good five miles away, much further than the distance from Kowloon Tong to the Star Ferry pier in Tsim Sha Tsui. He was doubtful if he could manage to walk the whole distance. Leung knew this. He took Mulrenan to the tram stop to the right of the bank building, slipped him some change and they boarded an eastbound tram.

3

For three days, Mulrenan hid in the house of a carpenter in Shau Kei Wan, a rickety shack erected by the beach where the hulls of junks stood upon ramps in various stages of manufacture, shored up by a web of joists, struts and props. No intensive work was taking place upon them but the carpenter kept himself gainfully employed whittling pegs to join planks: little metal was used in the craft except good quality brass which, in wartime, was as scarce as gold.

Mulrenan, still disguised, strolled along the beach on his first evening, weaving between the unfinished vessels. The shadow from the mountain behind the bay was cast long over Lei Yue Mun, the narrow approach to Hong Kong harbour. Through the strait, making slow progress against the tide, was a Japanese patrol boat, the crew observing the shore through binoculars. They came in close to the beach but were not interested in the shipyard area, studying instead the steep hillsides.

'You no wuwwy,' the carpenter advised Mulrenan from under the stern of a junk. 'He no come in.'

'Are you sure?' Mulrenan replied in a hoarse whisper.

'He no come. You no wuwwy. Plenty peepul no like Japanese. Know you good man. All Chinese peepul in Shau Kei Wan you frien'.'

Mulrenan, glancing at the chugging gunboat across the lap of waves, noticed there were a number of Chinese boat-builders squatting beneath the junk. They were grinning, their white teeth glittering in the half-light. Around them the sand was soft with sawdust and shavings in which tiny translucent crabs foraged.

The second night, after a scanty meal of rice and fish with a few strands of cabbage, Leung returned and gave him the final details of their plan.

'We do this,' he said. 'We go to Stanley village. Two beach there, one one side of land, other other side. We go Tai Tam Bay side. Eleven o'clock night time. We get sampan, go round p'ison camp. No make noise. I show you map later. No p'oblem . . .'

Mulrenan, despite his apprehension, could not help being amused at the repetition of Leung's catch-phrase, his panacea for all anxieties.

'Go round p'ison to Tung Tau Wan. Not to beach. Too dangerous. We go to below p'ison hospital. One o'clock morning time, we go to wock. You go on shore, climb up. You find garden. In garden, you find Mista Cowley. You go back. We all go.'

'Go where?' Mulrenan asked.

'Go in sampan across Tai Tam Bay, go round mountain to Tai Tam harbour. Then walk here. Hide one day. Then go China.'

It appeared so feasible. There was no mention of patrols, guards, barbed wire or electric fencing, dogs, bullets, mines or traitors. No reference was made to the weather, the reliability of the sampan, the health of their cargo or the rigours of the long, forced marches.

'When do we go?'

He believed he already knew the answer: indeed, he did. Yet like a schoolboy who asks, after the first day of the holidays, about the exact hour of the departure of his train back to school while perfectly aware of it, he hoped that by merely asking again the fateful moment might be postponed, even cancelled.

'Tomo'wow,' Leung answered. 'We go tomo'wow.' He paused, like a man embarrassed. 'You got money?'

'Yes,' Mulrenan affirmed. 'Enough.'

He went to the folding bed on which he had slept the night before and took from beneath it his message pouch, removing three gold blocks each the size of a matchbox.

4

It was just before midnight when they arrived at a small group of fishermen's houses shut tight against the night and the war. A dog barked ferociously as they approached the beach but it fell silent once their footsteps were muffled by the sand.

There was no moon, yet the sky was clear and the starlight brilliant, the sea running with a light swell under an offshore breeze which would assist Mulrenan's going but hamper his return with Alice's half-brother.

Thirty yards from the beach, riding at anchor, were half-a-dozen sampans and a small coastal junk. They appeared as untidy black ghosts rather than solid silhouettes. A faint glimmer of light showed at the stern of the larger vessel. As Mulrenan watched the light was extinguished, though whether by design or by the gradual swinging of the junk he could not tell. A shadow detached itself from the larger darkness and began to approach the beach.

The oarsman was in his mid-twenties, a stocky, muscular

man with close-cropped hair and narrow eyes. No words were exchanged. Stepping over the gunwale, Mulrenan steeled himself on a thwart and Leung and the oarsman shoved the sampan off, jumping noiselessly aboard as it began to drift with the breeze.

It took twenty minutes to cross the inlet and round the headland upon which the prison camp was situated, a motley collection of three-storey staff quarters, residences, stores huts and bungalows occupied in the pre-war years by a school and the prison staff of the civil gaol, the walls of which loomed over the slight bay of Tung Tau Wan. On the crossing, the single oar began to creak loudly but was cured by the application of talcum powder: the scent of it reminded Mulrenan fleetingly of Alice. He wondered how the oarsman had come by it: by looting, probably.

The anchor, a heavy stone tied round with rope, was not thrown overboard but quietly lowered into the water. Leung put his chin on Mulrenan's shoulder.

'We little ea'ly,' he said, his lips close to Mulrenan's ear. 'We wait small time. Maybe half hour. Then you go.'

The wait was agonising. Although they lay down in the sampan with only their heads above the edge, Mulrenan still felt like a target on a shooting range. The Japanese were not likely, Leung claimed, to bother with a sampan, even if they spotted it. Fishermen still netted the bay. Besides, he said confidently, the sampan was tiny and not easily seen against the swell, the wavelets and the shifting reflections of the starlight.

The suspense got to Mulrenan's stomach. He wanted to belch, to urinate over the side. The two Chinese merely lay on their backs and faced the stars. He envied their composure and tried to imitate them: soon, he was relaxed and drowsy with the motion of the boat and the circling of the stars.

Leung nudged him alert, jerking his thumb shorewards. The oarsman raised the anchor stone, balanced it on the stern planks and flicked his oar from side to side in short, abrupt movements until there was a bump as the sampan jarred on a rock, scraping on the barnacles. The racket sounded like a building collapsing in an earthquake.

'Go!' muttered Leung.

Mulrenan, heedless of what lay ahead, jumped from the boat onto a rock. As soon as his feet touched the stone, the sampan backed swiftly away and he realised he had left his message pouch on board.

Turning, he saw the sampan bobbing about forty feet off the rocks, its bow pointing towards the distant islands on the horizon and the vastness of the South China Sea.

He cursed himself for his incredible stupidity and remained kneeling on the boulder. Fifteen yards away, on the tide, bobbed his entire fortune. Next to it was a ruthless Chinese guerrilla and a squint-eyed sampan boy whom Mulrenan would no more trust than kiss.

Leung was crouching in the stern, waving with his hand, signalling Mulrenan off the rock and onward to his rendezvous.

Mulrenan scrambled over the rocks, coming in a few yards upon scrub bushes and a pipe projecting from the ground. The stink issuing from it confirmed it was the sewage outlet from a hospital building to his right, behind some trees. To his left was the dark shadow of the jail wall towards which he was headed. Climbing higher up the shore, he discovered he was behind a former gun emplacement, or the foundations of a building. Even a low concrete shed of some sort. This worried him as it was not a landmark on Leung's map.

Ignoring it he moved on, praying he was going in the right direction, his every footfall as loud as a kettledrum, every twig cracking as a roll on a snare.

From the prison wall there was an audible click like a safety catch. It was the switching on of a small searchlight, its beam spinning over the trees behind him, quickly traversing the prisoner-of-war camp. The guard controlling it was not intent on checking the outside of the walls, however. He swivelled the light inside the prison and shone it up and down the compound.

Against the prison wall was a sloping patch of ground: at the end nearest the sea was a clump of saplings while at the other was a group of mature trees. The soil had been tilled and rows of low, sparse, nondescript plants were visible in the starlight.

If Alec Cowley was not there, Mulrenan had decided, he would not wait but would return to Leung and invent an excuse. Without the burden of the wretched man, he could make his own way through China, would stand a better chance.

The saplings parted and two men ran doubled-over towards him. They stepped nimbly among the vegetables and dropped beside Mulrenan.

Neither new arrival spoke. Mulrenan could not make out their faces until they were very close.

'Cowley?' he asked, *sotto voce*.

'Mulrenan?'

'We must go immediately. Are you ready?'

'Yes.'

Three more figures materialised from the saplings. They were darker than the night, walked upright and carried rifles in their hands.

'Holy Mother of God!' Mulrenan hissed as he spun round but the man by Alec Cowley's side whipped his arm out and seized Mulrenan's bicep.

'It's all right. Ours.' he murmued.

They were Europeans, two women and one elderly man. The former wore army trousers and battledress blouses, the man was clad only in a pair of shorts far too big for him and held to his waist by a suitcase strap. His muscles were like bundled string. They were carrying not rifles but twig brooms of the sort their garden servants would have used before the war.

'Cover the tracks,' explained Cowley's companion as he released Mulrenan's arm.

There was a hurried and muted leavetaking.

'Have you the letters safe?' one of the women whispered to Cowley.

'Yes.'

'And the lists?'

'Yes.'

'Give my love to Piccadilly.'

'I will.'

'Give mine to Lyons Corner House. And a cup of coffee.'

As they spoke, Mulrenan looked from one woman to the other. There was something vaguely familiar about the shorter of the two: her hair was untidy and her legs scratched by thorns or scarred with blisters, yet there was defiance in her eyes. Perhaps, Mulrenan thought, she had once danced to his music.

The old man shook Cowley's hand.

'Goodbye, Alec. Goodbye, George.'

'Goodbye, sir.'

'Give my regards to Ride and de Wiart when you get to Chungking. Tell them . . . Well, you know what to tell them. Off you go.' He might have been sending them home on a bus. 'Take care of yourselves.' He turned to Mulrenan. 'It's a very brave thing you lads are doing. Keep up the good work!'

The shorter woman stepped forward and, on tiptoes, pressed a kiss to Mulrenan's cheek. Her lips were dry and chapped

'Look after them. Please,' she said.

Despite himself, he put his arm round her and eased his fingers into the small of her back. She pressed against him and, in the starlight, he could see her eyes flash.

'Let's go!' Mulrenan ordered. 'We've a long trip ahead.'

Cowley and his partner followed Mulrenan through the bushes, past the sewage pipe and down to the rocks. The sampan, much to Mulrenan's relief, was rocking gently only a few yards off the littoral rocks.

Leung kept the sampan clear with his feet as Mulrenan and Cowley clumsily boarded. When the other man tried to step into the boat, both Leung and Mulrenan exchanged glances in the starlight. They had thought the man George was part of the farewell party.

'Who this?'

'Flight Sergeant George Doyle.'

Cowley's voice was barely discernable over the slap and suck of the waves on the rocky shore.

'What the hell's he doing here?' Mulrenan demanded in a fierce whisper.

'He's coming too.'

'The hell he is! We've only notification of one. You!' he retorted officiously. Notification was hardly the correct word for the message originally smuggled to the outside on a scrap of paper the size of a tram ticket. 'No one told us it was a mass escape.'

'Two's hardly a mass. He's coming.'

'Go, go!' Leung whispered, at the same time tugging Doyle by the arm into the sampan.

From the direction of the hospital came a strident voice.

The oarsman started to twist his wooden bladed oar with renewed vigour. The sampan, despite the breeze, weaved and rolled quickly away from the shore, heading north-east.

As soon as he was comfortably in his seat, Mulrenan felt for the pouch. He slipped one of the straps out of its buckle and moved his hand about inside. Everything was there, untampered with.

5

They arrived back at the carpenter's house just as dawn was breaking. His wife had bowls of warm fish soup prepared but before Mulrenan would allow them to eat, he took Cowley outside and into the shadows of the half-built junk.

'That was bloody stupid!' he growled, the enforced silence of their walk over the hills telling in his exasperation.

'What was?' Cowley bristled.

'Doyle! Another mouth to feed, another to watch out for. We'd no idea you were bringing him. Leung'll have fixed up for you and me, not half the bloody British army. He'll be a load of trouble from start to finish. If we finish . . .'

'Air Force,' Cowley corrected him. 'And he'll be no

trouble. Be downright useful, in fact. He's stronger than most and he knows the way. The route we'll take has to be through Waichow and George's been there. Before the war.'

There were soft hushing steps on the sand behind them as Leung and Doyle appeared in the starlight.

Mulrenan was unconvinced.

'We're hardly likely to get lost,' he said contemptuously. 'Leung knows the way. He devised it. He's guiding us. He's got the contacts and they're expecting two escapees, not three. They might smell a rat. One too many . . .'

'I'll be no nuisance,' Doyle defended himself. 'I flew over the route not long before Pearl Harbour. Photo recce flight. I reckon I could find the way if we get lost.'

'No p'oblem,' Leung interjected. 'I t'ink maybe can do. I send word ahead. One more Johnny.'

The two ex-prisoners ate the soup with the air of men accustomed to not knowing when their next meal might materialise.

'It was so easy,' said Doyle finally, as they talked quietly over a bowl of weak tea. 'I expected — I'm not sure what I expected.'

'Guns and shouting,' said Cowley. 'A whistle or an alarm of some sort. But nothing. A few loudish voices . . . probably Pat covering for the girls. It's as if the Nips wanted us to get away.'

Mulrenan had also been thinking, as they had walked over the mountain, Leung certainly knew his stuff.

Cowley put his bowl of tea down and leaned across the table, their quarrel forgotten now their bellies were full.

'Sean,' he said, 'you've no idea how grateful I am — we are. If there's something I can do . . .'

'Alice asked me to, Alec,' Mulrenan replied. 'I'm doing this for her.'

It was a lie and, though he was a past master at the arts of untruth, his cheeks warmed. He was doing this for himself: it was an act of survival and he was a survivor.

'Be that as it may, Sean, I'm still more grateful than I can say. I'm in you debt when we get to Chungking.'

That, Mulrenan reasoned, was something about which to be mildly pleased. He wondered if his name tasted as badly in Cowley's mouth as Alec did in his own.

'*If* we get to Chungking. It's a long way yet. You can buy me a beer in the officers' mess.'

It would be fun to drink with the bastard and his bastard chums: it might, he thought, lead to a good card game and then he'd get even . . .

Mulrenan was exhausted and fell asleep upon the folding bed — but not before surreptitiously checking the pouch.

6

Due north of Shau Kei Wan, across the Lei Yue Mun channel, was the fishing hamlet of Cha Kwo Ling, the starting point of their long journey: but first they had to reach it. The channel was heavily patrolled and overlooked from prominent guard posts, the tide raced through it, its shores were rock-strewn and the mountains funnelled the wind in. Aware of these hazards, Mulrenan slept uneasily, quizzing Leung next morning about this short but crucial first stage.

'We go to Cha Kwo Ling tonight,' Leung answered. 'I talk to boat man. He say best to go night-time in sampan with sail.'

'That's ridiculous,' Mulrenan said.

'Maybe,' Leung replied, not to be deterred. 'Maybe not. If you do what Japanese not t'ink you do, you can do it. Last place Japanese look is Lei Yue Mun. Boat there for sure fishing or going to islands. So. Cha Kwo Ling north from here. We wait. Evening time we go.'

He paused.

'I t'ink tonight best for sure,' he explained 'Wind coming f 'om sea, blow in harbour. Nine o'clock, tide running in to harbour, take us too. No moon until late then moon like eye-hair.'

Mulrenan accepted the winds and tides but was puzzled by the moon.

'Eye-hair. Hair over eye,' Leung reiterated. He ran his finger along his eye-brows.

Mulrenan smiled and nodded his understanding.

'So we go. No p'oblem.'

The fugitives spent the day in the carpenter's home, lying beneath the living quarters in a space where the man stored his tools, a few scrawny chickens restricted to a coop fashioned from a crate marked 'Marine Spares: manfctrd S. Diego, Calif. USA', and his dried fish. Under the floor sloshed flotsam and sewage-laden waves: through the boards came slaters and, by the lower end of the room which sloped towards the sea as if wishing to become flotsam itself, there occasionally appeared a mitten crab, its hairy pincers encrusted with green slime.

A Japanese platoon entered the village in the early afternoon. It was concerned not with house searches but purchasing fish. From the conversation filtering through the walls, conducted in a comic opera pidgin English, Mulrenan assessed it was an unofficial scavenging patrol, for the Chinese at first refused to supply fish. This produced a bullying and foot-stamping session, followed a resounding face-slapping. The local fishermen, to Mulrenan's relief, then parted with their catch and the patrol left. Had they not received their tithe, the Japanese might have gone through the buildings, to find more than Chinese children playing with wooden dolls and old ladies sewing rents in nets.

As night fell Cowley, who had spent most of the day either dozing or silent, moved across to Mulrenan's end of their hideaway.

'Do you think the Nips'll know we're gone by now?'

'Probably.' His reply was curt. 'But the other prisoners'll cover for you, though not for more than one or two parades, I'd guess.'

'When they know, what'll they do?'

'Tighten patrols. Watch the ferries. Keep an eye on the railway station. Snap-search junks and sampans and perk up their ears as to who says what in the New Territories villages. And give the prisoners a hard time, I should imagine. You would know.'

Cowley was quiet for some minutes before asking, 'Do you think we'll make it? What are the odds?'

Mulrenan squinted into the darker corner of the crawl space. A moth was edging through a hole in the planking, escaping from its dark diurnal roost. Its wings scraped against the splinters. Clear of the hole, it walked a few inches along the wood, its wing markings blending with the grain. With a shiver, it awakened its muscles and flicked upwards, flying to a hint of twilight above the chickens. Another moth appeared to follow the same flight path.

'Fair. We might make it. We might not. There's a lot of imponderables.'

'Others have escaped.'

'Apparently.'

'What happened?'

'Some were caught, tortured and executed. Some were shot outright or beheaded. Some roughed-about a bit and returned to their camp. Some made it.'

He watched a third moth make it.

Doyle, who had also been silent through the day and lost in his own thoughts, said. 'We'll make it. Of course we will. The odds're on our side. If we've got lady luck, we'll get through.'

There was a scuffling overhead. The chickens, settled for the night, shifted uneasily, ruffling their feathers. The leading hen clicked her beak and uttered a low, threatening cluck.

The floorboards over their heads were slid aside and Leung peered down.

'Mista Mul'enan,' he said, 'you come up.'

Standing on the top of the chicken coop, Mulrenan hauled himself upward and followed Leung into the night. They walked silently along the beach strewn with off-cuts of timber. In the darkness of a half-constructed, skeletal hull stood a figure.

'Ng-sap-saay.'

Leung introduced the indistinct shadow to Mulrenan by the number fifty-four. He offered his hand and it was accepted.

From the prow of the junk glowed a cigarette end. It was a tiny spark against a background of jet, oily sea.

'Baht. Look-out,' Leung explained noticing Mulrenan glance in the direction of the vessel.

Mulrenan turned his attention from Number 8 the look-out back to Number 54.

'This two men got no name,' Leung said, his voice only a fragment louder than a whisper. '54 take you to Cha Kwo Ling and on to next stage. But he say one big p'oblem.'

Suddenly the cigarette was extinguished. A cat mewed. Leung and 54 ducked, their hands on each of Mulrenan's shoulders, firmly drawing him down.

A woman walked out of the blackness of the buildings, squatting to relieve herself on the sand where a seeping trickle of fresh water met the tide mark. The stink of urine wafted over to them. When she was done, she shuffled her trousers into position, heading back to her hut. The three men did not stand but stayed on their hunkers.

'What problem?' Mulrenan asked anxiously.

'Sampan not ve'ry big.' Leung pointed with his chin in the direction of another dark shape on the sand twenty yards away. '54 say woom for t'ree persons. One for work sampan, two for passenger.'

'Can't we get a bigger one?'

'Not possible.'

'What about two trips?'

'Also not possible. One man stay here for one day. Later he come. Better to t'avel in small group. T'ree more lucky than four for you.'

'I'll sort it out,' Mulrenan offered, though the decision was easily made. He would be one of the two passengers. Who else came with him mattered not, but he was determined he would be going.

'How soon?'

'Wind blow more strong one hour. Maybe one, one half hour. Then go.'

Crouching low, Mulrenan returned to the carpenter's home and slipped down into the hiding place.

'What's wrong?'

Both of the escapees were tense. Although Mulrenan could see only a blur where their faces hung in the blackness, he could sense the electricity of fear sparking invisibly about them.

'Nothing too drastic. But the sampan can't take the three of us. Only two. One of us has got to stay. They weren't prepared for extra cargo,' he added pointedly.

The blurs changed shape as the men looked at each other.

'What's to be done, then?'

Doyle had been the first to question Mulrenan: now it was Cowley's chance.

'We could draw lots for it,' he suggested.

Mulrenan quashed that suggestion, saying, 'We can't. It's imperative I get through' — he did not offer a reason — 'so one of you must stay. I suggest, as the leader, in a manner of speaking, I decide.'

This recommendation met with no response.

'Very well,' Doyle said, after a moment of embarrassed silence. 'I suggest I stay for later. When will that be?'

'Tomorrow. That's a certainty.'

Mulrenan spoke with authority, as if he was the mastermind behind the whole operation. 'The sampan'll return. You might even catch us up as you'll be taking the same route. And as you know the way better than we do . . . perhaps you'll be safer — just you and a guide.'

This statement contained little truth or logic, but it was sufficient in the circumstances to meet with approval.

'Of course,' Doyle added, 'I'm a bit like the best man — the spare prick at the wedding. You weren't expecting another joy-rider along on the honeymoon, so it's only fair I hang on.'

Mulrenan accepted this decision and made grateful noises about it, patting Doyle on the arm encouragingly.

'Thank you, George,' said Cowley. 'I'm sorry you won't be with us, but . . . Well, when we meet in Chungking, the first round's on me.'

'Done!' Doyle manfully exclaimed.

An hour later, Leung shepherded Mulrenan and his mistress's half-brother across the beach and helped them into 54's sampan.

As they parted, Leung said, out of Cowley's hearing, 'Maybe see you again one time. After war finish. War no good for doing bizniz.'

'I hope so. Even after the war, though, business will be different,' Mulrenan prophesied.

'Business better maybe. We do good business. Big business. No more small-time.'

'Maybe.'

54 whispered urgently.

'Now you go. Safe journey. See you again.'

'Thank you. And I hope so.'

'For sure. Will do. No p'oblem.'

Swiftly Leung ran up the beach, his footsteps kicking up spurts of sand, then he was gone: possibly, Mulrenan thought, for good.

He had the message pouch hanging firmly over his shoulder and neck, the strap crossing his chest like a bandolier. It bulged with the addition of the contents of his clothing bundle. As the craft wallowed under a loose sail, he mentally inventoried his list of possessions — the now smaller block of lard, the change of clothes rolled tightly, the blunting razor blades, the belt, the Rolex watch which he wore face in to hide the luminous dial and, last but not least, the gold cylinders. One had worked its way into an awkward angle in his trousers and he shifted it with his hand.

'It is uncomfortable,' Cowley said, wriggling his bottom on the beam seat. 'Makes you decide to dress the other side.'

'No spik,' came a voice from above them.

The sail stiffened as the craft left the shelter of Shau Kei Wan bay, the journey taking less than thirty minutes. No patrol boat sailed round the headlands and no lights flashed from the hillsides. As soon as they beached, the three men leapt clear and hauled the vessel on the sand, lowering and stowing the sail and steering oar. 54 asked them to wait in the thick undergrowth by the beach. A narrow blade of moon rose and by its small light they could see 54 brushing out all their footsteps except his own with a leafy branch: he had removed his boots, since few boat people owned footware.

'Now we go,' he said. 'Long walk. No talk.'

Pushing through a screen of creepers, they came upon a path which avoided a hamlet before bending towards the hills sloping steeply from the shore. Had it been raining, the path would have been a torrent. The exposed rocks made climbing difficult. However, once at the top of the first ridge they met a well-defined pathway and struck out along the contours of the land.

7

At the apex of the valley, a stream rattled out of the trees through fallen boulders. Here they headed into the woods, following paths little used by mankind but much used, as was clear from the spore, by wild boar and deer.

The trees provided protection from both the sun and the eyes of patrols but, after two hours hard going, they reached the edge of the forest and were obliged to stop. Before them opened a wide valley, the slopes on either side wooded, the floor cut into terraced paddyfields which levelled lower down. Clumps of trees or bamboo dotted the field, birds dipping and flitting between them.

'What are the local people . . .?' Cowley muttered. Mulrenan shrugged.

54 instructed them to hide in a dense clump of bushes some twenty yards from the path, by a wide, tumbling stream, while he went on ahead to scout out the area. They were to answer no call unless it was his; when he returned he would call twice. He would say *to jai*, which meant little

rabbit: then he would say *Fei Ngo Shan*, the name of the mountain towering behind them through the trees.

'I come back night-time,' he told them.

After making sure that his charges were well hidden, 54 left. They watched him through the undergrowth, stepping away down the path towards paddyfields below.

At first, they were afraid to talk even in whispers. Below them their guide had drawn the attention of a number of men and women repairing a terrace wall. The peasants ceased their dyking and gathered round him, occasionally pointing or looking up at the trees. Eventually they let him go and he disappeared in the direction of the village.

After another half-hour, Mulrenan decided it was safe to speak and they relaxed, lying back on the leaf litter, peering up at the green blanket of the forest canopy. Not one ray of the sun, now near it zenith, succeeded in penetrating to their faces.

'How is Alice?' Cowley asked out of a long silence.

'Well now,' Mulrenan answered, not bothering to open his eyes. 'She's fine, living quite safely in Macau. We've a house there and she's provided for in my absence. Once I'm out I can send money back to her through the Portuguese.'

'Will you try to get her out?'

'No.'

Mulrenan hoped a blunt reply would force an end to the conversation, but it did not.

'Doesn't she want to come? I could look after her in Chungking. Or in India.'

'You've not taken much interest in her in the past — except to keep your relationship with her as secret as possible.'

'That's true, but I've had time to reflect upon things. In Stanley. There's nothing like imprisonment to concentrate your mind.'

'I doubt she'd want your help,' Mulrenan said cruelly. 'She's not given to thinking about you.'

'I thought you said it was she who'd asked you to get me out.'

Mulrenan realised he was much more tired than he had believed. He would not, under normal circumstances, have told a lie so easily queried. He opened his eyes and rubbed his knuckles into them, seeming drowsy and unworried.

'In part, she did. But I mentioned it first. I needed to get out of Macau and you provided an added excuse in her mind for my leaving.'

'Why did you have to go?'

Cowley's voice was not only curious but also suspicious and Mulrenan picked up the undertone.

'I'm not popular with the Japanese: they virtually run Macau and there's a lot of intrigue about. And their consul was recently murdered . . .'

He left the statement hanging in the air letting Cowley believe he had been the assassin.

'I see.' Cowley frowned. 'I thought you were neutral.'

'I am,' Mulrenan retorted.

He pressed his hand against his right breast pocket. The Irish passport was safely buttoned in and he smoothed the shirt so Cowley could see the outline of the document through the weave of the cloth.

Cowley persisted. 'I still think Alice should be offered the chance to leave Macau. I'm sure we could safely get her out through Canton. Obviously you've fixed her up with a suitable passport.'

Mulrenan looked at his enemy, this young Englishman he so detested. He was no longer the smoothly belligerent bank official of two years before: now he was thin-faced, his eyes were sunken and his flesh tinted with grey. His skin was blotchy and he frequently scratched at his legs where the red brands of ringworm showed lividly under their scabs and flaking cuticle. His hair was cut very short as a protection against lice and his fingernails were chipped or bitten to the quick. His teeth were the colour of the ivory keys of a piano left open to the sun. One of his ears wept a clear liquid which congealed on the lobe.

'She's pregnant,' Mulrenan said.

Cowley made no reply. He just stared at Mulrenan.

'Have you married her?' he asked at length.

298

Mulrenan shook his head.

'No time to,' he said, looking sorrowful. 'It's only recent. It was the deciding factor in my need to leave. To get money back to her. There's no money to be made in Macau now.'

Although unconvinced, Cowley lapsed into silence. He kept watch through the branches while Mulrenan dozed. The heat of the day had driven the farm labourers back to their village, leaving only a tethered buffalo in the fields. For a while it grazed then lay down to chew the cud. Even though it was three hundred yards away, Cowley could see its ears flick against pestering gnats.

So, he considered, Mulrenan was to father a child through Alice. That would make them related. He would be the uncle to the Irishman's baby. It was not a situation he relished but there was nothing he could do about it. He would have to make the best of it.

For more than an hour, he considered his opinion of Mulrenan. The man was a parasite, a person of little talent save at a keyboard — and even then it was not a concert grand but just a bar-room upright. Music was hardly a profession, anyway, hardly a job for a real man. All jobs in the arts were ephemeral. Real life, with which real men should be associated, involved making money, industry, commerce, production for the common good; it did not include the self-indulgence of artistic endeavour, the flippancy of mere entertainment. Furthermore, Mulrenan was a dubious character, living by gambling in the world of the card sharp, dealing in what, in his most charitable mind, Cowley classed 'doubtful commodities', the bar-room honky-tonk and red-painted ladies.

On the other hand, the war might have altered him. That Mulrenan had aided his escape might be a positive sign that the Irishman was no longer his former self. He had run a considerable risk in bringing the sampan in to the bay, a greater risk actually landing on the shore and climbing the rocks to the vegetable garden by the hospital. Perhaps he was no longer as selfish, as downright nasty as he had been.

There was, Cowley suddenly realised, yet another favourable aspect to Mulrenan: he had not left Alice.

Having picked her up, lifted her out of The Line, out of the clutches of Ethel Morrison, he had neither abandoned her nor treated her as a mere concubine. He had remained with her and, in his own way, had made at least a half-honest woman of her.

The more Cowley considered the Irishman asleep in the bush behind him, the more he felt sympathy for him. It was not an overwhelming, sudden revelation of friendship, but it was the start of something he felt he might encourage, allow to grow and prosper. Perhaps, after the war, with the common interest of a child between them, they might get to at least respect each other.

Cowley was prepared to accept the possibility that Mulrenan was reforming. Over the weeks ahead, as they made their way through occupied China, he hoped a bond of some sort would grow between them. If George caught up with them, which he admitted was hardly likely, he might be the catalyst to fire a reaction between them. Otherwise, they would have to do it on their own, two men, flung together in adversity.

He had seen it happen in Stanley. Corbin, of the Hong-kong Bank and McArthur of Butterfield and Swire had hated each other in civilian, pre-war life, an enmity founded upon their having accused each other of cheating in a yacht race. Yet, in the camp, thrust together in the same room with three other men and the ten-year-old son of one of them, they had soon patched up their quarrel and become not only dear friends but also partners-in-crime, raiding the Japanese quartermaster's store for iodine ointment and rice flour, tins of unissued British Army jam and nails.

When the evening shadow of Fei Ngo Shan had crept across the valley as far as the tethered buffalo, Mulrenan woke and took over the sentry watch. The paddyfields were bare of human activity and remained that way except for a child who ran out to lead the buffalo away towards a group of unseen buildings, the presence of which was betrayed by a haze of woodsmoke rising behind a copse of bamboo.

As darkness fell, Cowley seemed increasingly nervous.

'Do you think your man's left us?'

'I doubt it,' Mulrenan replied.

'Do you think something might've happened to him? Might he've been stopped, caught? The Japanese patrols . . .'

'It's not likely,' Mulrenan said. 'Unless he's been betrayed. But he's too wary to let himself fall in to a trap. He'll be back.'

Just as the last vestiges of daylight were fading, Mulrenan heard a quiet voice near at hand. Another spoke in response. Neither used the passwords. A torch flickered on, its unsteady beam shifting over the leaves. Mulrenan and Cowley crouched, hunching themselves to resemble rocks.

The whispering voices grew closer. They were not Japanese but neither did they use clear Cantonese. Mulrenan could only understand the occasional phrase.

A third then a fourth voice became apparent. Another torch was switched on. It had a more powerful beam and cut through the foliage, shining backwards and forwards at ground level. The brightness caused Mulrenan's eyes to smart and he closed them, not daring to move his head. One of the voices uttered a command and the bush around him was thrashed with a heavy stick; leaves, twigs and insects showered down. Leaf-dwelling ants fell upon Mulrenan's shoulders and began inspecting his collar and neck. He gritted his teeth against the itching of their tiny feet.

The searchers moved off. They beat at another area of heavy undergrowth and then gathered to walk back down the path to the farmland.

'Jesus Christ!' whispered Cowley. He moved his hand to swat a bug exploring his weeping ear.

Mulrenan lashed out just in time and stopped Cowley before his palm slapped on his skin.

They remained still for long minutes. There was further rustling in the trees and three more men advanced towards them. These did not speak, nor did they have bright torches, but one of them carried a dim battery-powered cycle lamp, the glass masked with paper. They came on quietly, secretly, their feet clicking twigs and their clothes brushing leaves but no more loudly than would an animal. They stopped every few yards to listen. Eventually, they reached the path and descended the hillside. When they gained the edge of the fields they began to talk freely as they strolled away towards the hidden village.

'Who were they?' Cowley asked, his voice barely audible.

'Japanese? Chinese working for them? Nationalist? How the hell should I know?'

'I think it's best we move off. They know we're in the vicinity.'

'And do what? Find our way across a hundred miles of China? Don't be so damn stupid. If we move, 54'll have no way of finding us. We stay. And we don't talk.'

'Do you think they have 54? If they have, we've nothing to lose by going on.'

The need to believe he was still free prompted Mulrenan to say, 'They haven't.'

'How can you be so sure?'

'Because if they had, he'd have been broken. They'd have known the passwords . . .'

'I don't like it,' Cowley said stating the obvious.

Mulrenan remained silent.

Around midnight, 54 returned, gave the passwords and they joined him on the path.

He quickly explained what had happened. Somehow, word had leaked out that fugitives were in the area. He had been greeted openly in the village below them, where he knew the locals were on the Allied side, but a tinker in the village, selling needles and twine, had been from away and had regarded him with suspicion. Before long, a posse from another village had arrived and combed several sections of forest, looking for escaped European prisoners.

'Night-time come now, we moof,' 54 said. 'More safe. We get some food.'

The agent had brought with him a Japanese army water bottle filled with diluted fresh milk. Cowley swallowed his share in gulps, pausing between them only to gain his breath. While he was busy drinking Mulrenan, who refused a share, made his way to a spring among the trees, roughly rubbing his face and hands alert with the cold water. 54 joined him.

'Maybe some t'ouble coming,' he confided. 'I tell you, not uvver man. You better you know. In case t'ouble, I got you this one.'

From the folds of his clothing he took a Smith & Wesson .38 revolver.

'Better you have this one gun,' he continued. 'Our f'ien' — ' he nodded his head in the direction of Kowloon to signifiy he was talking of Leung ' — tell me you no bad shoot. I t'ink uvver man no good shoot. So you take this one gun. Also,' he tugged at his pocket, 'got you small box bullet.'

Mulrenan accepted both with pleasure and gratitude. He had been in two minds about bringing his own pistol but had decided against risking being found with it: men will kill not only with a gun but for one, too. He shook the box gently: it did not rattle.

'Full box,' said 54.

The pathway down the valley was not as steep as it had appeared from the hiding place and they were soon in the fields, making their way carefully around the village disturbing not so much as a dog. After an hour's walking, making detours to avoid settlements, they reached a road running along the shore. To avoid patrols, they chose a parallel inland path.

'Hebe Haven,' Cowley told Mulrenan. 'I used to sail round here before the war. Sheltered here once from a tropical storm. Myself and some of the mess . . .' He broke off, obviously thinking of the men from the mess, all of them presumably now dead.

'Pak Sha Wan', the agent said, confirming their location, giving its Cantonese name.

The path was not much frequented and all but invisible in the leaf-filtered starlight. As it wound along it visited a number of graves cut into the hillside. The memorials were horseshoe-shaped and built like little quarries with higher backs and low sloping side walls surrounding a paved central area. In the rear walls were small stone doors tightly

303

sealed with mortar and carved with a series of characters outlined in red paint — the name of the family which owned the tomb and the names of those interred within. In one of the paved entrances, they paused to rest.

It was clearly a tiring march for Cowley. He was not strong and was unused to such physical demands. He quickly grew breathless, wheezing at every slight ascent of the track. He needed to drink often, stopping at any stream that 54 could vouch had not run through villages higher up the mountain. The last thing Mulrenan wanted was an outbreak of the trots, a scourging with dysentery.

'One-one-half mile we go to Sai Kung. Sai Kung friendly to Communist. Maybe good not good but we got some friend. They got boat but not here. Boat in Chek Keng. Long walk over mountain. Take two day but more safe. Can walk in daytime for number two day.'

'Where do we sleep?' Cowley asked. 'Rest in the day-time?'

'You see.'

They walked on and reached the outskirts of a substantial fishing village. As much fishing was done during the night by lantern, the village was not asleep. The fish market was lit by oil lamps, stall holders setting up their tables in readiness for the dawn return of the sampan fleet. The sharp odour of drying fish hovered in the still, warm air.

Keeping to the periphery of the village, they eventually reached a house in the yard of which hung racks of what appeared at first, in the faint light, to be a laundry wash consisting entirely of strips of rag. As Mulrenan brushed these aside, he found them to be stiff, rigid fillets of fish and the rubbery tentacles of recently landed squid.

54 knocked twice on the door which was hurriedly opened. There was no discernable light burning to give them away but, as soon as the door was closed behind them and the bolts slid, a hand raised the wick of an oil lamp.

Gazing around, Mulrenan saw the house was used by a fisherman. Cork floats were piled by the door and a half-repaired net lay crumpled by a chair on the seat of which was a ball of cord and a heavy steel needle. Against one wall

304

leaned an incompletely carved oar surrounded by shavings. In a far corner, a stone stove was crackling as the flames ate into driftwood. The salt in the fuel burned with yellow flares and spat chips of hot charcoal onto the flags of the floor.

The owner of the house seemed to be absent. The elderly man and woman who bowed to them were certainly well past raising nets and poling craft. The man had a wizened face and hands, his beard was long and greyed, his eyes were weak with age: the woman's grey-streaked hair was scraped into a severe bun, her hands were calloused with years of net-mending and fish-cleaning.

Mulrenan returned the bows courteously and Cowley copied him.

'M'koi,' Mulrenan said, not quite certain what words might be appropriate to the occasion. It was not every day he was welcomed into a Chinese home which his mere presence might destroy within the hour.

'You are welcome,' the old man said in flawless English. 'Please do sit down. We shall give you some food shortly.'

Mulrenan was taken aback by his command of the language. The old woman busied herself at the stove. Mulrenan quickly realised this ancient couple were used to escapees passing through their home.

'I see you are surprised. I should explain though I will not introduce myself, if you don't mind. It is a precaution we all take. I live here with my third son and his daughter. They are fishing tonight. This old lady is my daughter-in-law's mother. I am not a fisherman; before the Japanese came I worked for Taikoo Docks.'

'What did you do?' Mulrenan enquired.

'In the accounts. It was my job to assess costs.'

The old woman left the stove, laying on the table bowls and chopsticks, porcelain spoons and a dish for sauce.

'Do you often have prisoners come through?' Cowley asked tactlessly.

'Yes.'

It was a blunt and non-commital answer.

'Isn't this a risk? If the Japanese were to find out.'

'Yes, it is a great risk. Of course. But we must all take risks. Life is made of risk. My son may drown tonight. I am old: I may die tonight. A typhoon may destroy this village. A fishbone may catch in my neck and choke me.'

'But what of your neighbours? They might inform on you. You may — .'

'They will not,' the old man interrupted. 'They know me and will not — just as I will not inform on them for being Communists or Nationalists.'

'Are you a Communist?'

The old man beckoned to 54 and the two of them murmured together by the rear door, their backs to the room.

Mulrenan caught Cowley's eye and glowered at him.

'You're not in the bank now,' he hissed. 'Nor in Stanley. Surely you know better than to ask such blatant questions? Haven't you learnt anything about the Chinese in all your years out here?'

Cowley bridled. 'Of course I have.'

'Then keep your bloody mouth shut.'

Mulrenan ground the words out, furious at the man's gaucheness, his insensitivity, his lack of manners, his ignorance of etiquette — his utter Englishness.

'I don't think that's called for,' Cowley defended himself.

'I do. And I'm the driver on this mystery trip. You're the passenger. So do as you're told. If you want to speak, use some intelligence before opening your mouth.'

Even in the dim light of the oil lamp, Mulrenan could see Cowley redden with embarrassment and anger. 54 silently went out through the door, the old man going to the stove. Now he crossed the room towards them carrying a bowl from which thick steam was rising.

'You are both very tired,' he said. 'It is not easy doing what you are doing. Rest now. Your guide has gone to arrange the next stage in your journey.' He put the bowl on the table. 'Now we shall eat.'

The fish soup was followed by crabs. Such luxuries had not been known to Mulrenan for some months: for Cowley, he had not eaten so well since before the surrender.

When 54 returned, he was worried. He came in silently, suddenly appearing among them as a ghost might. But if Mulrenan and Cowley were startled by his quiet arrival, the old man was not: such unobtrusive comings and goings were a part of his life.

'We got small t'ouble,' the agent reported ominously. 'Chek Keng boat good, parf to Tai Mong Tsai busy. Many Japanese soljar at Tit Chi Shan.'

'Where's that?' Mulrenan enquired. 'Can't we go past there?'

He would rather have spoken in Cantonese, but thought it wiser to keep Cowley in the picture: perhaps he would then appreciate the odds against them.

'No can do. We go walk long way. Much hurry, no time. We no late for Chek Keng boat. If no come he sail.' Using a phrase Mulrenan had heard often enough from the walla-walla boat pilots in Hong Kong harbour, he added, 'No show, no go.'

'So what's to be done?'

'We go sampan. One more time. Go by Tai Mong Tsai to Wong Yi Chau. Can walk then, make good time if sampan go quick. We see. But not good. Japanese maybe see us.'

It was a risk they had to accept. Otherwise they would have to remain until another route could be planned, arranged and coordinated. It could take days, even weeks and the longer they were at large the more chance they ran of being captured. If that happened to Mulrenan it would be the end of everything. Gemstones would buy little, if anything — most probably, he'd be tortured then shot.

'When do we go?' he asked, resigning himself.

'Dawn.'

'Dawn?' he echoed incredulously. 'We go by day?'

'Must do. No can go night-time. Channel very small for sailing. Tide too fast for oar. Tide also bad time.'

The old man interrupted, saying, 'If you put on a jacket and perhaps wear a Chinese hat you may not be recognised, even from close. From the shore, it will be hard. If you help the sailor and your guide, the Japanese will think you are all of the same family.'

'I've already dressed as a coolie once,' Mulrenan replied. He looked at Cowley. 'Must get the walk right. That's the secret.'

For a few hours, they tried to sleep. The old couple took themselves behind a screen. 54 lay down on a blanket on the floor, hunched himself into a foetal curl, and slept easily without sound or movement. Cowley sat at the table and dropped his head onto his folded arms, half-sleeping restlessly, like a child forced to sit for long hours at a cramped desk in an examination hall.

Mulrenan crouched in a folding chair by the cooking stove. Although it was not a cold night, he was chilled and wondered anxiously if he was coming down with influenza. The fire in the stove had not gone out and he pushed a few more twigs of kindling into it. The little blackened cauldron on the top was filled with warm water which he occasionally sipped.

When he was certain the others were asleep, Mulrenan checked the Smith & Wesson. The weapon was in good condition, had recently been cleaned and oiled. He eased the cylinder round. It clicked decisively. When he opened the cardboard box, the flat eyes of the cartridge bases peered up at him from their rows. He pinched his fingernails around one of the rims and removed the bullet. The head was dull grey above the brass casing. Carefully, making no noise, he loaded the revolver, replaced it in his pocket and reassured himself about the contents of his trouser-leg pouches.

Just as dawn was breaking, there was a gentle tapping on the wall by the stove. The old man was instantly awake and quickly opened the door to admit a man in his thirties. His chest was bare, despite the pre-dawn chill in the air, his ribs protruded through taut, jaundiced skin. His face was skullish, his arms and hands thin as sticks. He coughed before he spoke, and Mulrenan realised he was in the terminal stages of tuberculosis. If he had worn a cloak instead of pantaloon trousers and rope sandals he could have been the ferryman across the Styx. For a moment, Mulrenan wondered if he would accept a diamond instead of a coin for the final crossing.

'Dis man take us,' 54 announced. He handed them peasant hats and tattered jackets.

There were a few people stirring in the village streets. Most were by the wooden pier where the night's fishing fleet was beginning to dock. From between the houses came the sounds of calling and shouting, insistent bargaining over the first catches and exclamations of annoyance or surprise at the prices offered.

The sampan was an old boat. Greasy water, in which floated fragments of long-dead fish, slopped in the bottom. A smear of scales adhered to the gunwale and a tangle of line had been shoved under the planking. The mast was worn smooth from the passage of years and ropes and the sail had been patched with squares and oblongs of any available material. Mulrenan identified the blue cotton of common peasant clothing, a length of serge suiting, two sections of sacking that had once held sugar (the lettering TAI — tear — OO — tear — GAR gave the information), a few fragments of tarpaulin and a large piece of khaki uniform upon which could be discerned the outline of a corporal's stripes.

Had the boatman been able to use such rags of wood on the hull as he had of cloth on the sail, no doubt he would have done so: the vessel was in urgent need of re-caulking. Water seeped between the planks, leaving the joints damp where timbers met.

A few hundred yards off-shore was an island. The boatman sailed to the north of it, the breeze stiff but not quite persistent enough to be a wind. Beyond the island was a group of rocks, waves just breaking over them. To avoid them, the Europeans lent a hand, Mulrenan taking the steering oar while the boatman and Cowley slackened the sail which flapped where the stitching was giving way to new rents. 54 was strenuously bailing out the water that poured in every time the sampan heeled.

Cowley had little idea of what to do. He tugged on a rope he should have let go and loosened one he should have tied, was clumsy in his movements and found keeping his balance difficult. His awkwardness would demolish his disguise if they came under scrutiny.

The breeze was warm and the spray more sweet than salt. Mulrenan narrowed his eyes to prevent it stinging but on his skin it was a purifying balm. He soon acquired the knack of steering the sampan — this was achieved not by moving the oar from side to side like a conventional rudder, but rather by twisting the blade on its axis, or even moving it in its entirety from port to starboard, as one might a punt pole. He began to enjoy himself and his thoughts took off into their own world.

Once, this might have been his life — a little boat on open sea with the fish veering by underneath, just waiting for the net to drop. If his two uncles had not drowned, while he was still a lad he might have joined them, fishing the Irish Sea . . . if his father had not taken himself off to the Isle of Man, had not been such an ambitious bastard and married his mother — his pink-cheeked, middle-class English mother . . .

The sampan drifted slightly off-course but Mulrenan deftly steered her back, keeping the prow facing between a headland to port and a low island to starboard.

54 now knelt in the bow. He seemed to be unscrambling the knots of line and net but Mulrenan guessed he was keeping watch ahead. They were nearing the peninsula at Tai Mong Tsai and he would be anxious to study where the Japanese patrol was stationed and what it was doing.

After a while, leaving his knots, he sat under the mast and beckoned to Mulrenan, who had returned control of the sampan to the tubercular boatman.

'Japanese gone,' he reported bluntly.

Mulrenan had not needed to be told; he, too, had been keeping an eye on the shore, watching either for the flash of a gun or perhaps the hazy drift of campfire smoke. And the proverb that said a tiger was not dangerous if its prey could watch it had drawn upon itself a distinct and unpleasant relevance.

'What do you think? Have they returned to Sai Kung? Or Kowloon?'

'I t'ink no. If he gone back Sai Kung or Kowloonside, we

hear. I t'ink he go where we go. Must be ve'y careful. Maybe we walk night-time. You can do? Must walk very quickly.'

Mulrenan believed he could but he had little confidence in Cowley's ability. The Englishman was hunched towards the stern, his knees to his chin and his arms encircling his shins. He had his eyes closed, possibly against the spray, but he was also plainly dog-tired.

54 followed Mulrenan's gaze.

'We ca'y him?' the agent suggested.

'No.' Mulrenan shrugged. 'We can't carry him over a mountain. He'll have to make it on his own or fail.'

It was harsh but Mulrenan was not reluctant to say it. He had agreed to get brother Alec out of prison. That was his promise made to Alice less than three weeks before: he had promised to get him free. Stanley free did not necessarily mean free of Allied China: he could hardly be held responsible for Cowley's condition, his general lack of stamina and poor physique.

'If he can't manage it,' he asked 54, quietly, 'is there somewhere we can safely leave him?'

54 thought for a moment. Mulrenan almost willed him to come up with a solution. If Cowley was in such bad shape now, what he would be like by the time they arrived in Weichow did not bear thinking about: before then, a hundred miles into a vague and hazardous future, they would somehow have to make their way through occupied China, a country crawling with Japanese, Communists and Nationalists, all fighting each other.

'Maybe. We go Chek Keng I talk wif one man. He can go back, get him to safe place. Not house. Hole in mountain. But warm and no people go there.'

Mulrenan nodded gravely but was inwardly elated. He might get rid of the millstone around his neck represented by the detestable Cowley. He begged the fates to force Cowley to collapse as soon as possible: it had to be before they reached Chek Keng. After that, across Mirs Bay and into China, there would be little chance of dumping him on the hospitality of locals.

The sail flapped as the sampan heeled to one side. 54 and Mulrenan hauled it down and the boatman began to oar the craft towards a cove. They travelled up an inlet, helped by a flowing tide, and were soon aground on a golden, sandy beach beside a hamlet of six or seven houses. 54 stepped out of the sampan ahead of the others and entered one of the houses.

Following him slowly, Mulrenan and Cowley scattered pecking hens with their feet. They left the boatman without a backward glance. A cat carrying half a fish in its mouth slouched by to squeeze behind a stack of driftwood. Mulrenan could hear a litter of kittens mewing.

54 came out of the house and pointed to a bench set against the wall upon which were piled folded fishing nets, out of sight of the hill and the few fields beyond the village.

'We no go inside,' 54 explained. 'Man live here sick with skin-drop-off. No good go inside, touch something, fall sick also.'

From those words, Mulrenan understood the building to be the home of a leper but, as it was in a village, he must have been suffering from the less contagious dry leprosy: the 'wet' variety made its sufferer a social outcast, a pariah to be avoided as precipitably as any devil or evil mountain spirit.

'What does he say?'

'Japanese solyer not come here. No see him dis side. This man say solyer gone norf to Kei Ling Ha Hoi.'

If this was true, it would place the patrol several miles and two mountains away to their west.

Cowley, who had hardly opened his mouth since being reprimanded by Mulrenan during the night, now spoke apprehensively.

'Are we to move in daylight?'

'Yes. There's a time factor in it now.' Mulrenan narrowed his eyes. 'We've got to arrive in Chek Keng by tomorrow morning,' he told him brutally.

He knew Cowley would have welcomed the chance to rest. He clearly had doubts he could cover the distance so quickly. They had only two and a half miles to walk but it was over mountain paths which rose to a height of over six hundred feet. With any luck Cowley would arrive in Chek Keng a wreck.

'What about cover? These hills are grassed. There's hardly a tree in sight. It will only take one aircraft to find three people and we'll be strafed off the face of the earth.'

He was playing for time and Mulrenan knew it.

'If they fly over we'll lie flat. The grass is not as short as it looks from here.' He cast an eye along the valley up which they would be going. 'We'll be able to hear them coming and we've got darkish clothes. The grass shadows will confuse our outlines.'

It was with satisfaction that he saw how little his words were doing to allay Cowley's worries. Mulrenan enjoyed seeing the man tighten with anxiety and self-doubt.

'Can we go slowly?'

54 said, 'No can go slowly. Must get over hills quick. Less time in open better for us.'

'Why not wait?' Cowley was grasping at straws. 'If the night's clear we can surely see the way.'

'Lis parf not easy. Not use much. Peoples stay Chek Keng. Not may peoples live dare. No come out. Use boats.'

'But you've been this way before.'

'No. First time. Before I go Ma On Shan.'

The reply sealed Cowley's fate. He had to go, had to make the effort, and had to keep up.

They drank some hot water provided by the leper whom they did not meet: a small boy delivered it in a cheap enamel basin handed out of the door. What they did not drink they used to sluice their faces. As they washed the child gazed at them with uninhibited curiosity: he had seldom seen a European, let alone two and dressed as coolies.

'Make sure you've got everything,' Mulrenan said.

Cowley had little to check: clothes and a ball of rice he had saved from the old man's table in Sai Kung. Mulrenan checked the contents of his bag. Everything was safe. He felt inside his shirt and tightened the buckle on the belt one more notch. He was losing weight but the belt, mercifully, was not: its contents remained secure. In his waistband, where he had transferred it and where it was pressing into his spine, was the .38.

54 refilled his Japanese water-bottle at a stream as they left the hamlet to start their long trek. The sun, which had been shining earlier, was obliterated by high clouds which Mulrenan knew would not be good for them. The humidity might rise, yet the chance of them getting sunstroke was not reduced. The impression of protection given by clouds was entirely false.

The path followed the shore of a narrow inlet into the head of which fed a rivulet, its source in the hills, dividing half a mile inland into two streams. It was along the right hand fork their way lay.

'Do you know,' Cowley said as they crossed a plank laid over a wide ditch of green stagnant water and grey floating scum, 'when I was a lad I used to hike all through these hills.'

Mulrenan made no comment, shifting his message pouch further round on his shoulder for comfort.

'They're beautiful in summer,' Cowley continued. 'Higher up the slopes breezes start to cool you from the heat of the climb.'

He fell silent and Mulrenan, casting a glance over his back to check their rear, noticed a faraway look in Cowley's eyes. He was returned to his boyhood.

As they walked in single file, Mulrenan scratched his chin, was reminded that he had not shaved for several days, and vowed he would as soon as they landed in China proper. The thick stubble was a weakness in his disguise.

In the sky, a bird hovered and chirped like a lark. When they crossed the rivulet by a ricketty bridge the water beneath their feet, shallow and clear as glass, was alive with darting fish flashing silver against the grey coarse sand.

They reached a junction. The more worn of the two paths bore left up a long valley. 54 went right, to the stream, and balanced across on stepping stones. Cowley followed him, stumbling but not falling into the water. Mulrenan crossed last, hopping very quickly from stone to stone.

Quite why he moved so fast, he could not be sure. For a moment, as he was in mid-stream, his spine had involuntarily contracted. He halted briefly, looked over his shoulder, but could see no-one. He tried to listen over the noise of the water. Nothing. No aircraft, no shouting, no distant gunfire. All he could hear apart from the others' footsteps was the song of the bird high overhead. He attempted to locate it against the high clouds and indistinct sun, but could not.

A small patch of level ground nearby had been turned into fields irrigated by the stream, beyond which was an area of woodland, the trees stunted by the wind and leaning. The path started to zigzag through the fields, following the intersections of the dykes built to retain water for the growing of rice. A new crop had recently been planted into the loose and watery mud, thin pencils of green projecting in rows above the surface.

As they crossed the open space, Cowley pointed ahead and said, 'There's the mountain. Once we're up there, it should be downhill all the way.'

He laughed ruefully at his pun.

The bird ceased its singing.

Instinctively 54, who was ten paces ahead, rolled into the paddyfield. Mulrenan dropped on one knee, hearing as he did so the squelch of 54's boots in the slushy mud. He flattened himself on the ground.

Cowley continued to walk.

A quick succession of shots rang out, the echoes rebounding on the valley sides long after Cowley lay still on the edge of the path, the dust kicked up by the misses drifting above him.

A scrabbling sound indicated 54 was dragging Cowley down into the paddy. Mulrenan thrust with his arms and pitched himself down off the path. He felt for the message pouch. The flap was securely buckled.

Cowley was lying on his back in the muddy shallow water of the paddyfield. He had been hit in the chest and his cheek was grazed where a riccochet had spat stone into his face. He was neither groaning nor moving. Already, a red wash was developing in the water by his left side. His mouth was twitching but his eyes were alert and fastened on Mulrenan as soon as he came into view.

'Gay do?' Mulrenan asked 54 in a recklessly loud whisper.

The words meant 'how much?' rather than 'how many?' but the agent understood. He raised his head very slightly over the defence offered by the path, keeping behind a tuft of grass. Mulrenan did the same.

Eight Japanese soldiers were advancing in a ragged line over some fallow fields beyond the stream. They carried their rifles, bayonets fixed, at the hip.

'You got gun?'

Mulrenan eased his arm round and pulled the Smith and Wesson free of his trousers. 54 saw it.

'You do lef' soljers. I do ovver soljers. Wait for him get to water,' he hissed.

Cowley gave a loud groan. It could not have been better timed by an actor. The Japanese, thirty yards away, heard it and halted. Several raised their rifles to their shoulders. When the paddy remained quiet and unthreatening, an NCO in their line issued a guttural order and they continued their advance. Their rifles were lowered again to the hip.

At that moment, Mulrenan realised he and 54 had a great advantage. The Japanese would not only be assuming that they had hit more than one of them but would also be expecting them to be Chinese peasants and therefore unarmed.

At the stream, the line halted, the NCO surveying the path. Mulrenan grunted as if having difficulty finding his breath. Cowley groaned once more, less loudly but still effectively.

When the NCO was satisfied he was dealing with wounded or dead Chinese, he issued another terse order and the line advanced into the stream. Its bed was rocky, the stones rounded and smooth, some of them coated with algae. The soldiers had to look to their feet as well as ahead.

Mulrenan and 54, in one action, leaned their forearms

upon the path and opened fire. The enemy was so close the shooting resembled target practice. The soldiers were trapped. Several tried to bring their rifles to bear. The NCO had a pistol but he was unbalanced by the slick rocks. Eleven shots dropped all eight of the foot patrol.

Not all were killed outright. Mulrenan covered 54 as he sprinted doubled up along the paddy dykes to see how many had survived.

He called to Mulrenan, who ran across to the agent and stood beside him on the bank of the stream. Four of the Japanese were alive but too badly wounded to offer any resistance. Two dead men were in the central current, their blood staining the water. One more was on the bank, his head face down, neatly fitting the depression made by a water buffalo's hoofprint. The last was half out of the water, his lifeless muscles flexing.

The four who were alive struggled in the shallow water to keep their heads above the surface. One found his gun and began to lift it. 54 kicked the man's arm and it submerged again.

'We had better shoot them,' Mulrenan said. He opened his pistol, discovering he had but one shell left in the chamber.

'No.' 54 lifted his hand as if to deflect the bullet. 'Amm-oo-ni-shun too little. I kill.'

One by one, he drowned the wounded. Mulrenan watched from the bank. The Japanese waiting their turn to die did not cry out, or beg for mercy, or pray to their gods, or try to get away. They lay quite still in the water, the current tugging at their uniforms, continued to keep their heads above the surface until their turn came to be thrust under. The NCO ineffectively flailed his arms at 54 but was soon made motionless by a kick to his temple.

When the killing was done, with Mulrenan's aid, 54 dragged the bodies from the water and laid them on the bank.

Five minutes before, Mulrenan thought, these weights of flesh had been moving, breathing people. Now, at his doing, they had become lifeless hulks, heavy with water and inactivity. As he dropped the last corpse on to the ground, he gazed at it. There was a hole in its back, the material of the uniform shredded around it. No blood oozed for there was nothing to pump it out and the stream had washed the jagged wound clean. Staring down at the dead Japanese, he felt no remorse, no guilt, no emotion whatsoever. His mind was a blank until the agent interrupted him.

'You look see Cow-lee,' he said, dropping the last Japanese onto the spongy soil. It was the first time he has used the Englishman's name.

Mulrenan returned across the paddy to where they had left Cowley lying in the mud. He had shifted himself since the firing and had succeeded in half-propping himself against the dyke wall. One of his arms hung limply at his side, the hand curled in like a monkey's. With his good arm, he was pushing the ball of his thumb into a wound in his side.

'Let me see it,' Mulrenan said, kneeling by him in the mud.

Cowley allowed Mulrenan to prise his hand away. His coolie jacket was tacky with blood. Mulrenan unbuttoned it. Through the shirt projected a smooth white stick with a pink pith. It was just like a bone in a butcher's shop, except that it moved when Cowley inhaled. Mulrenan covered it with the jacket and replaced Cowley's hand.

'How he?' 54 enquired, shouting from the stream.

Mulrenan looked up. 54 was engaged in collecting the weapons and ammunition pouches from the dead soldiers, tucking the rifles under the bank where the water had cut away the earth. The pouches he was stringing together for ease of carrying.

'M'ho,' he called shaking his head.

When 54's task was done, he inspected Cowley's wounds: he had been hit in the thigh as well as the chest.

'Not good,' he said, stepping out of Cowley's earshot. 'No can walk. We hide him in trees. Man from Chek Keng come for guns, he see Cowley, fix him up.'

Both he and Mulrenan knew that 'fixing up' Cowley would be work for skilled surgeons in an equipped theatre, not a family of peasants in a southern Chinese village, no matter how well-meaning they might be.

'We go see ahead,' 54 told Cowley. 'You wait five minute. We come back.'

Cowley nodded slightly.

'What we do?' 54 asked when they were thirty yards along the path. 'He not very fit now.'

'You walk on. I'll catch you up.'

54 gathered up the ammunition pouches and started walking. When he disappeared where the path entered a copse, Mulrenan retraced his steps to Cowley's side.

'I've got to leave you here, Alec.'

'I know,' Cowley croaked. 'Will you send someone back for me?'

'When we get to Chek Keng. You'll miss the boat, though.'

'I think I've missed the boat already,' he said and his head lolled onto his shoulder.

Mulrenan watched as tears began to well up and fall from Cowley's cheek onto the cloth of his jacket where they stained as the blood was staining lower down. Others fell into the paddy water like single drops of rain.

'Guard Alice well,' Cowley mumbled, his words distorted by his mouth pressing to his shoulder, 'and I'll hope to see you in Chungking. Or Delhi.'

Mulrenan turned away, saw that 54 had already gained the upper edge of the tree line and was pushing on up the hillside.

If the shots had been heard by another Japanese patrol, he thought, they might reach Cowley long before the man from Chek Keng could: after all, they had only to force march along the shore. The Chinese from Chek Keng had first to be found, informed and then sent back over the mountain that rose above the trees. He reckoned it would take several hours at the very least.

If Cowley were captured, the Japanese would hardly resort to their usual application of torture to interrogate him. He would be too weak to resist their questioning. One rifle butt in his side would be all that was necessary.

As soon as he had talked, the Japanese would be on Mulrenan's trail. They would be able to move fast, cover the ground quickly, arrange a gunboat interception of the junk, radio ahead to China to tighten patrols along the coast.

In his mind, Mulrenan rapidly assessed Cowley's wounds. The graze on his face was minimal — at worst, it would give him a jawache and it was not likely to bleed. Already a scab had formed on it. The thigh wound would make walking awkward, but not necessarily impossible. No bone had been shattered and the bullet had passed through the flesh and was not lodged in the tissue. The wound had clotted but it might bleed further if stressed: if Cowley could hobble along with Mulrenan's support, he might just make it. A tourniquet at the groin could help and a branch could be cut from the trees to act as a crude crutch.

The worst part would be climbing the mountain. After the crest, admittedly, it would be — as Cowley had put it — downhill all the way, but reaching the summit would be difficult. Once distanced from the scene of the shooting, Cowley could be hidden and perhaps treated. Possibly, Mulrenan reasoned, he could be taken along the coast by junk and put ashore where Japanese military activity was slight. The chest wound, however, posed a problem.

Mulrenan felt about his person for a length of cloth which might be used to bind Cowley's ribs. The pain would be excruciating. If Cowley passed out, Mulrenan realised, then he and 54 would have to carry him. Without a stretcher, that was not possible. Cowley would soon die of internal bleeding. Perhaps he might anyway.

54 was higher up the moutainside and had halted.

He was waving briefly but urgently to Mulrenan.

Mulrenan opened the revolver: the remaining live round was still one place away from the beach. The safety catch was in the 'off' position. His finger rested along the trigger guard. He felt it twitch as if suffering from pins and needles.

He snapped back the hammer of the Smith & Wesson, quickly aimed and jerked the trigger. His mind went blank except for an awesome whistling that might have been his rushing blood.

Cowley juddered under the impact and toppled into the water, his good arm folding under him. His legs spasmed briefly, the muddy water splashing under them. Heavy ripples struck the paddy dyke. He fell face down in the ooze.

As he walked after 54, following the agent's wet boot-prints on the path, Mulrenan's thoughts were in turmoil. This was not what he had intended. And he had done it so quickly, so dispassionately, so automatically. He was horrified with himself. It was as if some uncontrollable and irrational instinct had governed his actions. He remembered then how he had felt in those moments just before he had struck Alice on discovering she had secretly met her half-brother: he had wondered, afterwards, what it was that had operated his arm, what had possessed him . . . and had it perhaps possessed him only a few minutes ago. Then, too, there had been that whistling noise in his ears.

He told himself, searching for excuses, he had done all he could. If he had allowed Cowley to die slowly and alone, it would have been inhumanly cruel, for no man should have to face the encroaching darkness of death on his own. Had Cowley survived, he was sure to eventually be recaptured by the Japanese who would torture him and doubtless behead him, a far more gruesome an ending than to die from a bullet, quickly, in a paddyfield.

'His wounds were unrepairable.'

He spoke out loud, and his words seemed to refer not to a man but to a rundown, clockwork toy.

He realised with surprise he felt a compassion for Alec Cowley, that he had shot him in order to save him as well as himself. It was not an act of hatred or surrender, not a means towards the end of his own safety. It was a spontaneous act of basic — almost bestial — generosity. He had killed Cowley much as he would have put down a faithful dog.

'Love,' he exclaimed to the copse of stunted trees through which he was climbing. 'Could I possibly — even for split second — have loved the damned man?'

A light gust soughed no answer: Mulrenan heard, as if through aeons of time, Cowley saying, 'Higher up the breezes start and cool you . . . '

Once above the trees, Mulrenan paused to look back: 54 was a long way ahead up the moutainside, trudging against the incline under the weight of the Japanese soldiers' pouches.

All was quiet. Mulrenan could see Cowley's corpse crumpled in the paddyfield and the line of dead Japanese soldiers on the stream bank. The bird had recommenced its piping in the sky.

A Good and Gentle Woman

1

Alice gave no thought to Mulrenan after his departure. She felt no guilt at having connived with Freddy Tsang, her only fear being that Mulrenan might have, at the last minute, decided to stay and bluff it out.

She was aware he had been tiring either of her, or of Macau, or of both. She also knew he would have to leave if she and the baby were to survive and be happy. His going was a financial gamble she had to take: she had to hope it would pay off with him sending money. That he would succeed in reaching Chungking she was in no doubt — he was a survivor — and that he would take her half-brother with him was also strangely certain.

Her pregnancy continued normally. Once, she stumbled in the street and was helped up by T'so who remained with her after Mulrenan's departure. He no longer saw his role simply as bodyguard but more as manservant. He chopped firewood when he could get it, and repaired the building. The herbalist downstairs died and Alice relet the shop at an increased rent to the cobbler from the hovel in Rua do Patane, the scent of herbs subborned by the tang of tanned leather, the confidences of patients becoming the tap of the hammer on the last.

When she went into labour, Alice suffered little. Dr Mak attended the birth because he was worried Alice's years in The Line might have affected her uterus but they had not. Her labour began in the late evening and she feared a night-long ordeal, but three hours later the baby was born, leaving her feeling surprisingly strong.

As the child was sucked from her into the air, Dr Mak looked across her sagging belly and smiled broadly in the lamp light.

'You are very lucky, Alice Soon. You have a firstborn son. Many Chinese women pray for a son. Have you so prayed?'

'No,' she said and she laughed. Her whole body filled with happiness and she laughed until it hurt.

'What are you going to call him?' the doctor asked, handing the child to Ah Shun who lay him on a thick mattress of flannel towels in a cot, swabbing his body clean with lukewarm water.

'Alec,' Alice replied without hesitation. 'Alec Sean Soon.'

Later that night, Alice woke from a strange dream: she had been walking on a shore where the sand was mingled with pine needles that pricked her bare feet. Some way off, through the trees, she could see incense smoke rising: quite suddenly she was transported to the temple, but there were no images within — no red and gold statues, no bowls of fruit or sweetmeats on offer to the gods, no candles burning or banners hanging from the ceiling. As she started about, a tiny white moth emerged from the murk in the rafters and alighted on the ground before her. On its back were markings in the shapes of the characters *yat* and *tsai* — 'one' and 'son'.

'Ah Shun!' she called weakly and the amah, fearful for her mistress, came rushing up the stairs, her tiny feet tapping like a bird's upon the wooden steps. 'I've seen the white moth.'

As she spoke, Alice raised herself from her pillow, her belly hurting. The amah took her in her arms and embraced her.

'There is no need to worry,' she said, speaking as a mother might to a child scared of the dark. 'It is only good.'

Alice sank back on to the bed.

'I know,' she replied. 'I know.'

In the weeks following the birth, Alice began to take stock of her possessions, her life and her future. When she had been carrying her son, she had found all her time taken up with the essential needs of pregnancy and the banalities of everyday existence. Now the child was in the world, alive and seemingly well, she considered it time to make plans.

With the same care at concealment she had exercised during Mulrenan's stay — the time he lived with her was already concertina-ing in her memory from years into months — she opened his hiding place behind the altar.

The best jewels had gone but there remained a large number of fine stones. She weighed them, placed them in envelopes with their colour, classification and caratage written on the flap, and catalogued them in a notebook. She also went through the rest of the house gathering all the other odds and sods that were salted away, placing these in the same god-protected niche. She had some superb pieces of fifteenth century grave jade, over two dozen bars of fine gold, three dozen of silver and one small, single ingot of platinum. There were also two ivory carvings wrapped in cotton waste and tied with twine. She constructed for herself several small, new hiding places in the walls or under the floorboards, in addition to those she had had when Mulrenan lived with her and, as a reserve against a fire in the house, she hollowed a space beneath the outside door step and hid in it a few gemstones.

Then, during her period of classifying the gemstones, one in particular caught her attention. She was sure she had seen it before, but neither in the hiding place nor shown to her by Mulrenan.

The stone was a sapphire and it struck her at first because it was the only one she had seen cut in a Dutch rose. It was just over three carats in weight and contained few inclusions, thus having a deeper and richer colour. Then she became certain she knew the stone and after she had sealed it in its envelope, she could not get it out of her mind. A fortnight later she discovered its source.

It was a sultry afternoon and Alice, while feeding the baby, was suddenly overcome with nostalgia. Sitting on the balcony with the breast flap of her *cheong sam* unbuttoned, the child suckling at her, she let her mind pass over the years. Initially, she could remember only vague details of her time in The Line. There were very few clients, she thought, who stood out in her mind: she laughed aloud at this choice of crudely appropriate metaphor.

The infant let go of her nipple for a moment, startled by its mother's noise, but it quickly fastened itself to her flesh again, kneading her with its miniature hands.

Her first months with Mulrenan gathered into focus and she reeled through her memories: the occasion of his first taking her out to dinner, her first meeting with other Europeans in his company, his first gift and their first real lovemaking. She remembered the parties on The Peak to which he had taken her, the beach picnics or dances, the races.

People passed before her eyes. The Deldertons, Audrey Christabel Burroughs who would rather be called Chrissie, Mr & Mrs Antrobus, Irina. She always thought of Irina as Irina-Of-Several-Husbands. Irina who had died so horridly in a street less than a mile from where Alice now sat nursing her tiny son.

When she grew dry and the baby's sucking pained her, Alice lifted him over her shoulder and rubbed his back. After several belchings, she gave him into the charge of Ah Shun and went into the bedroom.

From the camphorwood chest she removed a fat brown envelope with a scarlet stain on the flap where a seal had been pressed in wax. Sitting cross-legged on the pillow and tipping the contents out, Alice began to shuffle through the photographs. Some were sharply black and white but others had faded to tones of grey. Not a few had turned sepia as the chemicals had deteriorated. Some had curled or creased.

Each rekindled a lost memory. She picked them up and, having drawn a fragment of time out of each, slid them back into the envelope.

Halfway through the collection, Alice unearthed three pictures held together by a paper clip. The steel had rusted, staining the left hand corner of the uppermost photograph with a red U to which clung flakes of rust. She removed the clip and rubbed the rust free with her thumbnail.

The top photograph was of a group of Europeans. Alice was standing to the right of the group, nervously smiling. Next to her was a tall man with a pith helmet under his arm. The middle picture was almost exactly the same, except that the man with the helmet was missing and, in his place, was Irina. The continuing presence of the man was evident, however — his shadow intruded at the bottom of the photo: he had put his helmet on to leave his hands free for the camera. The third snap was of Alice and Irina, standing next to each other. Irina was holding a fluted glass, and in the background was a crowd of other, blurred drinkers. Alice turned the photograph over and read 'Kwan Tei Races 1939. Me and Irina', to which Mulrenan had appended 'with characteristic bubbley.'

She remembered how she had chided him for his spelling.

'You Irish!' she had exclaimed: he liked being addressed so. 'You have to have whisk-e-y and now you have bubbl-e-y. There's no 'e' in bubbly.'

'It's the Americans who have whisk-*e*-y,' he argued.

'Probably the influence of immigrant Irishmen,' she had teased.

Looking at the photograph brought on a wave of sorrow. She studied Irina's features as if to be sure of recognising her when next they met in the street. Or at the races.

Irina's hand holding the glass could be clearly seen and upon it was a ring containing, Alice was sure, the sapphire. She fetched the magnifying glass Mulrenan had used to assess gems. On inspection it was, without doubt, the same stone.

'I never take it off,' she heard Irina say from somewhere in the recesses of her memory. 'Once belonged to — well, let's say a very special man. When I was just a slip of a girl . . . '

That evening, after Ah Shun and T'so had bade her goodnight and retreated downstairs, Alice sat in the doorway to the balcony wrapped in her thoughts. Across Rua do Patane, an evening wind shifted the trees in the cemetery.

Irina had never removed that ring: Alice was certain. She would have had it on her when she was killed. Alice recalled with an involuntary shiver seeing her sprawled in the street, her blunted, lacerated arms lying like clubs of meat on the cobbles, the ragged stubs where her fingers had been. Poor Irina, whose multitude of passports had served no purpose.

The rings must have been bought by Mulrenan. The father of her child had purchased them. All the stones must have come from such tragedies. The serious face of Philip Haversham, old before its time and yearning for love but wary of asking for it in case it — like all good things — was to prove too brief, rose in front of her.

How Mulrenan had obtained the jewels Alice could only surmise. She knew he was connected with the underworld of thieves and pickpockets, the coshers and stabbers. She assumed he had been fencing for them.

It occurred to her then he might not have been so much of a middleman as the actual instigator of the crimes: he had perhaps ordered Irina's death for the sake of her rings.

It was absurd, yet the more she dwelt upon it the more feasible it became. Could he have been a mastermind, his jewel trading not merely financing his gun and medicine dealing and the comfortable way in which they had lived, but actually organised by him in the first instance? If this was true, she had been living on blood money, income derived from the deaths of others, even of her friends.

She undressed and lay down on her bed but was unable to sleep. Her mind feverishly examined Mulrenan's activities. Eventually, she accepted that although he was probably only one of the spokes in a criminal wheel, he had created a demand and others had met that demand, so that he undeniably shared responsibility for the misfortunes of many different and unknown people.

Viewing the whole matter philosophically, however, she came to believe that Mulrenan had, after all, done *some* good. The boy could not have realised his mother's jewellery alone, and she was also certain that many other of Mulrenan's dealings, no matter how selfishly motivated, had saved people from penury, and even starvation.

Yet the doubt remained. He might have been a party to the murder of Irina Boyd.

2

Over the first months of Mulrenan's absence, the last traces of her love for him faded. They did not fester into hatred. They merely diminished until he was like any other of her many clients from The Line. He became just another masculine experience: true, he was one of the better ones, but he was nonetheless what the American girls had termed 'a john'.

As her love lessened, her fear increased. She was afraid he would return one day, reclaim her and the gemstones and, worst of all, his son. She was frightened in case her love for the baby might lessen similarly, because of his father, and the more she was afraid of that, the stronger their bond grew. She gave the boy less into the charge of Ah Shun and spent many nights with him sleeping and burbling by her side in her own bed.

With calculated deliberation, Alice devised a plan for the future. It was simple and, being uncomplex, she considered it certain of success.

Her plan was that she herself would live on as little as possible, but make no sacrifices where Alec Sean was concerned. If Mulrenan failed her she would work at anything other than whoring. The gems would be used only in the most dire circumstances. She would salt most of them away in the new hiding places and, should he return, she would concoct a story to explain their absence.

So unsure was Alice of Mulrenan, that she began to set her plan in motion at once, by searching for a job. On account of her command of English and her lively intelligence, she was appointed to a part-time position in one of the convent schools as a teacher. The work was pleasant, the timetable agreeable and the children eager to learn.

Alice enjoyed her hours in the classroom, secure from the outside world in a haven of books and young people who, despite what the adults were doing, continued to be engrossed by small wonders. Her spirits were often lifted by her pupils: one morning she watched two Eurasian girls, one aged eight and the other six, stare with complete fascination for half an hour at a silk moth caterpillar as it wove and spun its buff-coloured cocoon upon a twig placed inside a cracked aquarium. She asked the children what they thought it was doing.

'It's making silk, Miss,' the older answered matter-of-factly.

This explanation was unacceptable to the younger child, who blurted out, 'She's wrong, Miss. It is hiding from the guns and things.'

The salary offered by the nuns was low but better than nothing, and they did not demand their teachers be Roman Catholics. In peacetime, a calling would have been of primary consideration but now the mother superior of the convent was forced to waive that rule.

'Do you believe in a god?' she had quizzed Alice at her interview.

'What do you mean?' Alice had replied. 'I am not a Christian, though I have been to a few Christian services.'

'Why did you go?'

'To accompany a friend who was afraid to walk the streets alone.'

'Do you believe in your own god, though, if not in Our Lord? Are you a Buddhist, perhaps?'

'I believe in my own god,' Alice assured her. 'I'm not sure who he is, but he exists.'

The mother superior had smiled benevolently.

'That is good. Maybe we shall even make a Catholic out of you. In the meantime, however, let us make a teacher of you instead.'

'What shall I teach?' Alice had asked, worried now she was appointed that she might not be up to the task.

'You speak Cantonese and you speak English. Teach them both.'

Alice's income was supplemented in other ways. The British consul, John Pownall Reeves, knowing her to be the daughter of an Englishwoman, arranged for her to receive a stipend from London. When the occasion arose, she worked for him as a clerk and became friendly with him and his small staff, particularly Joy Wilson of whom Philip Haversham had spoken.

As the winter months wore on and the cold winds swept in from the north, Alice forgot what Mulrenan looked like. She flicked through the photographs in the envelope, sustaining the image of him, but soon it was the photographs she remembered rather than the man. She never forgot his hitting her, but she also never forgot his gentle touch and his telling he loved the Chinese part of her.

Gradually, she became known as Mrs Alice Soon, the teacher at the convent whose husband had disappeared in the war. And, just as gradually the people, engrossed with their own day-to-day survival, forgot Mulrenan.

3

From time to time, Mulrenan sent messages back to Macau. Often they were skimpily worded sentences scrawled on postcards — on one occasion, his brief message was written in mauve, indelible pencil on the inside of a Players cigarette packet, the picture of the sailor on the reverse gazing at Alice as she opened the envelope: it was as if the matelot was conniving with Mulrenan in his dismissal of her. The brevity of so many of the letters upset and angered her, but gradually she grew to ignore them, sometimes leaving them unopened for hours — even days — unless they felt thick enough to contain folded currency.

The messages arrived with no regularity. Once she received two in a week: another time, she heard no word for seven months. Most reached her through the diplomatic bag and had taken months from the date of posting to get to her. If Mulrenan had failed to send the letters as soon as he had written them, then the scanty news they contained would be even more out of date.

By the time a message had reached her, she thought, he might have been months dead. The letters came, she considered, like light from the stars which had left them before the world began.

The first message came through from Chungking and was the only one from him not to come through official diplomatic channels. It was written on army memo pad, had been folded very small to fit into a seam in a jacket, was curt and meaningful:

Arrived Cg in one piece. All A1. S.

There was no reference to the trials and tribulations of the journey. She assumed the note implied that both he and Alec had made it. His next two letters still made no reference to the journey out of Hong Kong or to her half-brother. Perhaps, she thought, Mulrenan had been instructed not to name anyone else with whom he had travelled. And yet the remainder of the letter was quite detailed and bore very few censor's deletions.

No word reached her after that for some months except for a diplomatic communiqué but when it did, it was a fairly long letter from which seemingly random place names and proper nouns had been heavily inked out by a censor. However, reading the letter made it plain to her that Mulrenan had flown to India over The Hump, the eastern Himalayas.

Thereafter, his infrequent correspondence informed her that he was trying to make a living but that it was hard. He was doing some dealing, he wrote, although she had no idea in what commodity nor to what degree of success. Then he wrote he had lost a lot of his money. After more months of non-communication, a short note told her he was back playing the piano in a small hotel.

At no time, in any of his letters, did he make even a passing mention of her half-brother.

Some — but by no means all — of the letters contained money. He seldom sent large sums and the size of his contributions towards Alice's keep were quite obviously insufficient. She wondered how he could think she and the baby were surviving on these small sums and nothing else. She believed he was evidently giving little thought to her.

None of his letters carried an address. Mulrenan was never in one place long enough to receive a reply and his failure to give Alice a means of communicating back to him was, in any case, a relief to her for she was not of a mind to answer. She had nothing she wanted to tell him, found no desire to remonstrate with him over his small payments. She preferred to keep her troubles and her joys, her son and their life together utterly separate from him.

Similarly, none of his letters indicated any signs of real love existing in him for her. She was always 'Dear Alice' or 'Dear A.' He always signed off either with 'Love, Sean' or 'Love, S.' No fondness shone through the bleakness of his signature.

4

Towards the end of Alice's first term at the school, Helena, one of the cleverer students, did not attend her classes for five days. She mentioned the absence to the mother superior on the second day as was the rule. One day of missed classes was overlooked, two days prompted a note in the register, three days suggested action and four days, at the latest, saw it put into motion.

It was not that the nuns were out to catch truants. Truancy was rare for the children wanted to attend school not only to learn but also as a means of temporary escape from the rigours of life in a city all but beseiged. Even the youngest was aware anarchy ruled only a few kilometres away, through the border gate with China. Macau, for all its shortcomings, was a safer place than Canton or any of the villages in the surrounding province.

The aim of the attendance report was to ascertain an absence and then discover its cause, giving assistance where possible. A child away from school could have a number of causes: the parents might be sick, or one of them might have died, leaving the family starving or freezing.

It was the mother superior's practice, on the third or fourth day, to send to the missing child's home one of the sisters accompanied by a priest from the seminary. The nun would look into the absence and the priest cater for the spiritual needs of the family. On frequent occasions, he would arrive in time only to give a final absolution.

In Helena's case, matters were different. The mother superior and four of the nuns were themselves ill. The fish eaten the previous Friday had not been gutted soon enough after being landed. There was no one to spare for an investigation into the girl's non-attendance and so Alice volunteered to go with the priest.

'How old is the child?' asked the priest as they walked through the crowded streets.

'Fifteen. Or so we think.'

'You are not sure?' he exclaimed. 'She is your student.'

The priest was an Italian. He had arrived in Macau just before his country entered the war, sent out from the Vatican on an errand for a cardinal. His task was incompleted when the shooting started and so he had been marooned. Life in Macau was still a puzzle to him.

Alice shook her head.

'No: it is only a guess. We don't pry too deeply into the pupils' families. If they want to tell us, they will. Besides, with the Chinese, it's open to conjecture: a Chinese child is one year old on the day it is born.'

'She is Chinese?'

'She is actually half Chinese,' Alice replied. 'Like myself. Her mother is Chinese, her father Portuguese. The father, however, was drowned last year in the typhoon.'

'How?'

'He was walking along the Priai Grande when a wave

swept him against the embankment wall. It knocked him unconscious and then, on its next thrust, carried him through a storm drain.'

'How do you know of this? Were there witnesses?'

'Helena,' Alice answered and the priest fell silent.

They crossed Estrada do Repouso and began to walk past the prison in Rua do Almirante Costa Cabral. From over the high walls came a wailing human cry followed by a sharp bellow and a faint scream.

'You are not part Portuguese,' the priest observed.

'No. I am part English. My father was Chinese.'

'In Hong Kong?'

'He was. Now he is dead.'

'May he rest in peace with Christ,' the priest said. 'How far have we to go?'

'Not far,' Alice told him, 'unless they have moved. We can never know . . . '

She was interrupted by a beggar shuffling out of the shadows cast by a number of planks leaning against the wall of a carpenter's workshop. The aroma of camphor-wood and teak scented the air.

'Kum shaw?' the beggar enquired, holding out a filthy hand thinly bandaged in a length of cloth stiff with grime and congealed pus.

'Si!'

The priest lifted his soutane up like a skirt, felt inside his trouser pocket and removed a coin which he dropped onto the bandage.

'Why do they not come for treatment?' he asked Alice as they walked on. 'They must know we can wash their wounds and put permanganate or gentian violet on them. It is not much, but . . . '

'They are afraid,' Alice said simply.

'Of the medicine?'

'No.'

'Of priests?' he said shrewdly.

'No. They are afraid for their spirits. They fear you will steal them.'

The address to which they were going turned out to be a

semi-derelict building at the end of a noxious alley. At some time the building had caught fire, leaving the stones above the windows soot-blackened. There was no second storey but there was a roof of sorts, cobbled together with offcuts of timber, sheets of tin and an assortment of ill-fitting pantiles. This carcase of a house was divided into four rooms by means of curtains or oblongs of tarpaulin.

About to enter the building through a door hanging on one hinge, Alice was accosted by a Chinese woman, brusquely demanding to know what she wanted.

'Wan pin wai ne?'

'Helena. Sin shaang,' Alice said, pointing to herself and gazing about her at the squalor of the living space in the centre of which a tiny brazier was smouldering, the smoke filling the roof space. On the charcoal was simmering a tin can, the liquid spilling over to hiss in the embers.

The woman ignored her. She tried again.

'Helena yau mo lai?'

'Mo.'

The priest, though ignorant of Cantonese, guessed the gist of their exchange.

'Why do we not go in?'

'Nei hai m hai hui?' the woman demanded emphatically.

'Wait here,' Alice instructed. 'I'll go round the back. It is you she is worried about, not me.'

As Alice passed the woman, she screeched, 'Nei hui m hui!'

'Ngoh m hui,' Alice responded gently, her soft voice quietening the complaints.

In the third division of the house Alice discovered Helena. She was lying on her side in the centre of a damp mattress. She was naked from the waist down and her legs were smeared with dried blood.

'You have found her?' called the priest, concerned. 'Do you need my assistance?'

'Yes. I have found her. But do not come in. Get a rickshaw. Quickly.'

'Subito!' the priest confirmed and she heard his footsteps running down the alley.

338

Alice helped her sit up which she did with difficulty, sobbing as she moved.

'Miss Soon,' the girl said, haltingly. 'I am ve'y sorry but . . . We have no food . . . My mother is old . . . The coolie was a young man . . . We could not beg . . . '

Alice pressed her fingers to the girl's lips.

'I understand, Helena.'

'Will you tell . . . '

Of course, Alice would have to inform the mother superior: yet she knew the old nun, for all her harsh exterior and strict discipline, would also understand and forgive.

5

The senior girls were weary. The classroom was sweltering in the first hot day of the spring and Alice had set them a difficult dictation from a dog-eared copy of 'Jane Eyre' she had borrowed from Dr Mak. The girls were checking through their work when there was a knock on the door.

'Come in,' Alice said quietly so as not to disturb the girls. Failure in an exercise meant a strict talking-to from the mother superior.

One of the novices, a shy Chinese girl, entered and whispered, 'A message from Mrs Wilson at the consulate, Miss Soon. Please expect her to call at your home this evening.'

The evening was sunny and humid, the walls radiating the stored heat of the day. Alice was on the verandah, kneeling by Alec Sean who was crawling round a play pen constructed by T'so who had also fashioned a high chair for him.

The street below was a hubbub of noises: a rickshaw had broken its axle and shed its load of sacks of sawdust which had burst open. The feet of passer-by had scuffed the sawdust across the cobbles and into the shop downstairs.

The shoe-mender was slanging the rickshaw coolie at the top of his voice, coughing intermittently and pausing in his tirade only to spit. As Alice pressed her forehead to the railings to gaze down on the commotion, she saw Joy Wilson pushing her way through the gathering crowd.

'Nei ho ma?' enquired a friendly woman's voice a moment later on the stairs.

'Ho, nei ho ma,' replied Ah Shun.

'Ho, nei yau sam.'

The door opened and Joy Wilson came in, a much soiled leather briefcase under her arm.

Alice was pleased to see her, but clearly something was not right. She could not tell how she knew: perhaps the jollity of the greetings with Ah Shun had been just too jolly.

'I'm fine, too,' Alice welcomed her. 'It's good to have you call.' She caught Ah Shun's eye. 'Ning yat poon cha lai,' she requested.

'No,' Joy Wilson said quickly, 'M' yiu cha. I'll not have a cuppa. Must hurry. I've left a rickshaw waiting.'

'What's wrong?' Alice asked.

'Sit down, my dear.' She clicked the brass catch of the case and flipped the cover over. 'We've had a couple of messages through from Chungking today. Mr Reeves has just finished deciphering them and I'm in a rush to get to HE with the despatch.'

'HE' was their slang for His Excellency the Portuguese Governor: it was the same in Hong Kong — 'HE's at the races' or 'HE's coming to dinner.'

'But,' she went on, 'there was a bit for you. Not good, I'm afraid.'

From the case, she removed a single folded sheet of paper upon which the typewriting was faint. The consulate office used ribbons until they were all but devoid of ink.

'It's been a while coming,' she said. 'The trouble with the bag is it takes such a long time — this has gone from Chungking to Assam, on to Delhi, across to London — via The Cape, no doubt, not Suez — down to Lisbon and then back here. So very tedious . . . '

She gave it to Alice.

340

'Start. Chungking, —th. day of —— , 194–.' it ran, the dates blacked out. '*Arrived safely two persons ex. HK. One civilian, one RAF. Confirm to Macau civilian a leprechaun. Other civilian (HKVDF) lost. Inform sister said resident Macau. Stop.*'

It was signed incomprehensibly with a mauve indelible lead pencil, perhaps the same one Mulrenan had used on the cigarette packet.

'Your brother. I'm afraid he didn't make it. We've received confirmation.'

Alice made no reply. No words came to mind. She did not want to cry out nor did she want to weep. She just sat quite motionless, the paper in her hand.

'He was my half-brother,' she said at last.

Joy Wilson touched Alice's arm.

'I'm sorry,' she said. 'Really I am.'

'Yes,' Alice muttered. 'So am I.'

6

On the very same day, Alice received two envelopes.

Both were delivered personally by Mr Reeves: one had travelled in a Portuguese diplomatic bag and contained one hundred American dollars in denominations of fives and tens. With the money was a postcard of a quaint, Indian castle entitled 'The Red Fort, Agra.' It read, briefly, 'Reached Delhi. Here's the first lot. Hope you and baby are well. Love SM.'

The other had arrived at the Embassy by way of the ordinary postal service. It had been mailed in Lisbon some months before, the stamps having been franked several times and the envelope besmirched with grime and an inky thumb-print.

She opened the envelope and, as she extracted the letter, some grains of sand fell loosely into her palm. Unfolding the letter, she read;

'Dear Miss Soon-Mulrenan,

341

You do not know of me, my name is George Doyle, RAF, flight sergeant. I was in Stanley with your brother Alec Cowley. He and I escaped together with the help of your husband and a number of Chinese fifth columnists. I can say no more for security reasons, I am sure you will understand.

I am writing to let you know that, due to circumstances, we were separated during our escape and I followed on a day later. In the course of my escape, I came upon the body of your brother. He had been shot both in the body and in the head. It is my belief he was murdered, not shot whilst resisting arrest although I was told some dead Japanese had been found nearby. He was shot in the head by an un-Japanese caliber slug. I feel you should know this. I can draw no conclusion, but feel you may like to know this for after the war.

Your brother is buried secretly in a tomb of the Ling clan near the village of Wong Keng Tei: after the war you will be able to find him, I am sure. I said the Lord's Prayer over him, do tell any priest that, it may be important.

I have had the good fortune to reach Europe and will be back in England in a week or so, I am posting this in the hope it gets to you in Lisbon as Portugal is neutral and I am told you live in Macau which is also neutral, even though you are British.

As he had nothing on him to send, except his dog-tag which I felt it best he keep for identification after the war, I enclose a lock of Alec's hair.

Yours sincerely,
G.Doyle. Flt. Sgnt. RAF.'
The hair was not enclosed with the letter.

7

The pavement outside the hospital was crowded with
bodies. Some were emaciated and some bloated, a travesty
of the hunger wracking them. Many were covered with
sores, seeping blisters or pus-filled scabs, and all were
dressed in rags. The stench from them was worse than that
rising from the sewers. Passers-by, stepping off the pavement to avoid them, were assaulted with pleas for money,
for food or clothing, for mercy.

Every Tuesday and Friday, Sister Agnes and a novice
visited the pavement with a cauldron of weak fish soup.
Anything stronger would be vomitted as soon as it reached
the stomachs of the starving. She knew the soup was
nothing more than a sop to the spirits of the suffering. Their
flesh was doomed.

Sister Agnes was one of the few English nuns in Macau.
In her late fifties, she was a state registered nurse who had
received her training in her home town of Sheffield, a city of
which she spoke with what she called 'the love of hatred.'

One Friday, Alice accompanied the two women on their
mercy errand. She knelt with the starving and held bowls
for them as they noisily sucked the soup through loose
teeth, cracked lips and bleeding gums.

On that day, Alice was scared by two events, almost
insignificant at the time, simply a part of the overall
inhumanity of living through a war, yet each terrible and
horribly shocking in its own way. She watched several
orderlies from the hospital carry out a corpse and dump it
on the pavement where it lay against the wall, its head
lolling as if it was a passenger asleep on a ferry or omnibus:
it was then she realised the other sleepers by it were also
dead and awaiting the municipal cart.

Later, as she was holding a young woman's hand whilst
she drank, Alice noticed how terribly thin the dying

woman's wrist was. And how thin was her own.

8

It was drizzling, a sorry dampness hanging in the air like cold, dismal steam. Alice, returning home from school, hurried along the street for dusk was approaching and she was unaccompanied. T'so had requested the afternoon off and she had given him permission without a second thought. Whenever he took time for himself he usually returned with meat. Although often only a few taels'-worth it was always lean, without gristle or bone and he was eager to share it with his mistress, her baby and Ah Shun.

Once she had asked him where he went on his days off, but he became defensive and etiquette prevented her from prying more deeply. She assumed he had a lady friend somewhere or frequented the coolie brothels and tea-houses where young girls could be purchased cheaply.

In Rua dos Mercadores, Alice met one of the nuns hurrying in the opposite direction, a rattan basket in her hand. It was Sister Agnes.

'Alice! You are out late, my child.'

'I'm on my way home. I was detained by Sister Michael: we had to discuss Felicity . . .'

'That awful girl! Oh! There I go again! Three Hail Marys for uncharitable thoughts. Forty years next Easter I'll have worn a wimple and I still can't get it right. I hope Our Lord has a generous demeanour on the day I kiss His hand! But she is a frightful little thing. So spiteful. I'll bet you were talking about her fighting . . .'

'We were,' Alice interrupted, eager to be on her way. Sister Agnes was notorious for talking when her Order's quiet hours were over.

'And with that pretty little dark Chinese girl with the limp! Ha!' She laughed once, like a man. 'There I go. Ever seen a big, fair Chinese girl?' Her voice mellowed. 'Or an ugly one, come to that. The Chinese, I find — still, after eighteen years — extraordinarily beautiful people.'

'Where have you been?' Alice asked, responding warmly to the praise.

'Tending the sick. As ever. Satan's work is never healed. If it isn't dysentery, or a wound, or worse — gangrene — it's the canker of sin. Still! I leave that largely to the fathers. My job lies with the body more than the spirit. I really was *not* cut out to be a missionary. Yet here I am. And now I must be getting along. And so must you. I'm safe as a sock on a foot. No one in Macau attacks a nun. But you . . . Run along, my dear. I'll see you in the morning. At devotions . . .'

'Goodnight,' Alice said, but already the nun was five yards off and vanishing into the drizzle.

Ah Shun was standing at the door as Alice entered the courtyard at the rear of the house. She was cracking her fingers, a habit she had when anxious.

'I am sorry I'm late,' Alice said in Cantonese. 'There was some trouble in the school. How is Alec?'

'He is asleep,' Ah Shun said dismissively. 'But Ts'o has not returned. It is already seven o'clock.'

'There's no need to worry,' Alice assured her. 'He will come back soon. He can look after himself.'

As the evening wore on, T'so did not appear. They waited for him then finally ate a scanty meal of boiled rice, gritty with the sand the merchants added to bolster the weight, and the tough outer leaves of a cabbage. Two water chestnuts were diced into the rice. They were reluctant to let the food spoil by holding it back for him.

'He has decided to stay the night where he is,' Alice decided as she washed her face and hands before slipping into her bed next to her child who was breathing lustily with the blanket pulled to his chin.

Ah Shun lifted the basin from the table just as there was a loud thump in the courtyard.

'T'so,' she said with relief, putting the basin down and starting to descend the stairs.

345

'Wait!'

There was a knock on the door.

Alice searched in a drawer and found the gun Mulrenan had given her. She had never used it and fumbled to check it was loaded. With difficulty, for it was stiff with hardening grease, she thumbed the safety catch and went down the stairs, the amah following behind her.

'Pin koh . . . Yiu mat ye ne?' she called.

'Tso mat ye!' Ah Shun shouted, her voice shrill with fear. No sound came from outside.

Cautiously, Alice unlatched the door. In the courtyard was a lantern, its glimmer shining over the rain slick cobbles on which it stood. In its faint glare was a black, huddled heap in the centre of which grimaced Ts'o's face.

The courtyard gate was shut. Alice ran to it, driving in the bolts, returning to tend to her manservant.

Ts'o was cold, several hours dead. Rigor mortis was setting in to his joints, his flesh already unresilent. He had been garrotted.

9

'You have no cause for worry,' Freddy Tsang said, lowering his chopsticks onto the carved ivory rests by the side of his bowl. 'Ts'o's death was unconnected with you.'

'Are you certain?'

'Quite. My man has discovered Ts'o was in debt to a moneylender. Heavily in debt. A figure was mentioned . . .'

'How much?' Alice asked.

'Three hundred and twenty patacas. It seems he spent his spare time gambling in a doss-house in Rua da Erva. Dice. And cricket fighting. Apparently, he owned a very good cricket but it met its match and was killed a fortnight ago since when his fortunes have declined.'

'Rua da Erva is only just around the corner from my house.'

'Yes. But he was murdered on the hill near to the Guia lighthouse. In the trees . . . They needed a place where he could be killed without silence. They did much to him before the end.'

'I know.'

Alice twisted her empty tea bowl in her fingers. She had barely touched her food even though she was hungry.

'Three hundred patacas,' she mused. 'I could have paid that so easily — he must have known.'

'Yes,' Tsang replied, 'I'm sure he did. But he was a good servant and would not approach you. It was good for you to pay for his funeral.'

'I went to the temple yesterday,' Alice said. 'In the midday break from lessons. Ma Kok Mui, below Colina de Penha. I burnt some incense and asked the gods to look after his spirit. I hope he is more businesslike in his next life.'

'You must eat,' Tsang demanded. 'I did not buy a whole chicken for you merely to look at. With prices rising and the currency worth less by the week, a chicken is not easily acquired.'

As she ate, they discussed Alec Sean's progress. He was taking his first steps and had learnt to speak two words.

'What are they?' Tsang asked.

'One English, one Cantonese,' she told him, laughing for the first time in days. 'I suppose that's appropriate. He can say 'captain' and 'fei kei see' although I cannot imagine where he heard either.'

'A seaman and an aviator,' Tsang commented. 'Perhaps he will become a military man!'

When the meal was over, they sat in the twilight by the pool. Neither spoke. The fish opened their mouths and gobbed bubbles of air onto the surface.

'You are happy now?' Tsang asked.

'In a manner of speaking, I suppose I am. I have a job and the sisters treat me well. They know of my' — she paused, for the memory of those years still hurt her — 'past, but they choose to ignore it.'

'They are realists. I wonder how many of those nuns

347

have personal histories they keep well hidden? Sometimes, joining a convent is for a woman what signing on with the French Foreign Legion is for a man.'

'Yet they are good people,' Alice rejoined defensively, 'who see goodness. Their past does not matter.'

'Any more than yours does,' Tsang said, adding after a moment, 'Do you know what a jade pavilion is?'

Alice shook her head.

'It is a well-used metaphor found in Chinese literature over a thousand years old. A jade pavilion is a house of pleasure . . . Such as you were once in.'

'But from which I'm now free,' she exclaimed quietly.

'Quite so. But you must be sure never to return to such a place . . .'

'I do not need your advice on that.' Her words were curt. 'My lesson is well learnt.'

'Forgive me, Alice. I think you do need my advice. Of course, you will never return to being a concubine but there are other means of selling yourself. Think of Mulrenan, and be sure you avoid prostitution in the wider sense of the word.'

Tsang could see she was puzzled and hurt at his mentioning the topic.

'Consider your present predicament,' he continued. 'You are settled in your teaching, are among friends, have a fine son to raise. You are your own mistress. For you, the jade pavilion has flung wide its doors and let you go free. But for Mulrenan . . .'

One of the goldfish broke the surface of the pool, its fins wafting soft currents from side to side.

'I'm not sure what you mean.'

'T'so: he was living in the jade pavilion of his gambling habit. In Mulrenan's case, his soul is sold to something worse — to his hatred, to his bigotry, just as his body and mind are dedicated to greed. He lives in a jade pavilion: he always has. Now you yourself no longer have to sell your body for a stranger's erotic satisfaction, but there are other equally bad contracts to be struck. The moral is — never market yourself. As you know, the customer always abuses the shopkeeper . . .'

348

Alice stayed silent, pondering his words.

'Everyone has a personal jade pavilion,' Tsang ended. 'It is best to be aware of it and keep it securely locked.'

He was, she realised, correct. Mulrenan had surrendered himself, and lived entirely by selfish drives. She wondered if he was capable of real love, actual human emotion, anything other than the taking advantage of and the hating.

'Do you have anything to sell?' Tsang enquired, breaking into Alice's thoughts. He was not, she knew, referring to their previous conversation.

'Maybe,' she answered.

'What is it?'

'A statuette of imperial jade. Eleven inches high and, I think, sixteenth century. It's a carving of a goddess, perhaps Kwan Yin. I'm not sure.'

'No gemstones?'

Alice shook her head.

Tsang always asked her whenever they met in the street or visited each other if she had any jewels to sell but her answer was always negative: she would say Mulrenan took them, selling the residue before he left.

'I will buy the statue. Will you accept my price?'

It was the last piece of jade Alice possessed.

'As ever. And I'm very grateful to you for your help . . .'

'This will be the final time. I am leaving Macau very soon.'

Alice was taken aback at the news: she had not expected Tsang to take her into his confidence, and she was amazed he should consider going.

'Where to?'

'That I cannot tell you. The war is changing, though. The Japanese are going to lose it. Of that I am utterly convinced, although I can give you no reason. But it is so. Another year — eighteen months at the most. My mission in Macau is over. I am required elsewhere.'

'When are you going?'

'Not long. I wanted to tell you but you must let no one else know. If it were to become public knowledge, I would not reach the border gate.

'I am telling you because we are friends and because, after the war, I hope we might meet again, in China. I am not a young man and therefore memories are important to me. And dreams. I hope, one day, you might take a part in one of my dreams, making China a unified nation. She will need people like you.'

Before she left the house, Alice was handed a battered leather suitcase with the initials 'FT' embossed beneath the handle.

'I bought the case in Oxford when I was a student. It's served me well and now it will serve you. It is heavy and so a rickshaw has been called for you. I'm certain you will be able to put the contents to good use. And here . . . ' he placed in her hands seven hundred patacas '. . . is payment for the statue. Send it round. Tonight. Tomorrow may be too late.'

When she reached home, Alice opened the suitcase. It contained children's clothing wrapped around several hundred quinine tablets, some vials of morphine, jars of vaseline, calomine lotion, talcum powder, bottles of gentian violet, potassium permangate crystals and kaolin mixture and three packets of pristine scalpel blades.

10

'My dear Alice, this is crazy. You must let me pay you.'
She was adamant.
'In that case, I cannot accept.'
'Yes you can. You know you can because you must. You need these things. The scalpel blades alone are worth gold to you.'
'Then let me pay you!'
Dr Mak was frustrated with her.
'Sit down!' she ordered him. 'And listen. When I was pregnant, you helped me. I paid you nothing. When I went

into labour you delivered my child and accepted no payment. I pressed money upon you: only then did you take it. I owe you much. Now I have a chance to help not only you and your practice but also your patients.

'I know you treat most people for nothing. I also know they pay you in food — when they can. Now I am paying you in medicine. So do not argue with me. Besides, what can I do with all this? And I have kept the children's clothing for my son . . . '

'You could sell the contents of this suitcase for food. There are many who would exchange rice for quinine . . . '

She shrugged her shoulders and he capitulated.

'You don't know how grateful I am,' he said, taking hold of her hand. 'You will save many people with this . . . '

'No,' she replied, smiling at him and squeezing his fingers. 'I won't, you will.'

11

It was a warm, sunny day in mid-summer. Alice sat on the verandah, Alec Sean burbling and muttering as he played at her feet. Only weeks before he died Ts'o had made a counting frame for him from a length of wire nailed to a strip of wood and hung with twenty glass beads. The sun was so bright it shone through the beads, marking the verandah floor with tiny colours which delighted the child.

In the street, two children were playing with a hoop of iron, the track from a cart wheel. It rang and chimed upon the stone, was cursed at by pedestrians into whom it bumped and barked at by a dog driven to a frenzy by its noisy rolling.

From the shop came the rhythmical percussion of the cobbler's hammer and the solid thud of leather as he banged the pieces down to shape them. His shoes were more clogs, rough and ready objects made of leather and cut-down vehicle tyres mounted on wooden soles which he shaped himself in a vice. He whistled tunelessly as he worked, interrupted only by a customer or the comings and goings of his wife who spent her waking hours scouring the streets for the raw materials of her husband's trade.

In the cemetery, the breeze had stopped. The sky was hazy and still. Alice thought if time could stop it would be like this. Life would go on at a personal level but the universe would cease its spinning, the skies hold their breath.

She had been reading Sherlock Holmes. A long-disused cupboard in the seminary had been opened to reveal four wooden boxes of what the mother superior dismissively termed 'modern literature'. They had been given to Alice on the assumption one or two might be suitable for use in her classes.

She eagerly opened the boxes as soon as they reached her home, carried through the streets on a coolie's pole. The authors she found inside excited her: E.M. Forster, Thomas Hardy, Joseph Conrad, Mark Twain, H.G. Wells, Poe, Kipling, Conan Doyle . . . All the books were novels and none was more than fifty years old. She began to plan a reading programme for the senior girls and decided to read the Sherlock Holmes stories to the more junior, using them as an approach to studying England in the times of Queen Victoria. The Conan Doyle was conveniently illustrated.

She put her book down on the verandah floor: Holmes had solved the mystery of 'The Three Garridebs' and she was wondering how she would get permission from the mother superior to read a story to the girls which contained such lines as 'For God's sake, say that you are not hurt.' She would also have to omit mentions of Holmes' addiction, too. His shag tobacco was one thing, but . . .

Her thoughts were brought to a halt by Alec Sean. He had lifted himself onto his feet, was clinging onto the verandah railing and, tottering unsteadily, pointing to the sky.

'Fei kei see!' he chattered. 'Fei kei see!'

Alice smiled at him indulgently. Aircraft were not uncommon over Macau. Zeros cruised low overhead and Japanese seaplanes occasionally landed in the Porto Exterior. She traced the line of his stubby finger and listened.

These aircraft were higher than usual, the engines only just audible over the sounds of the cobbler and the children's hoop. She could see one through the heat haze, dark circled stars painted on its wings. There was a brief, shrill whistling which drowned the cobbler's tune, followed by a whoomfing sound. A wave of warm air swept along the verandah like a summer zephyr, flicking the pages of the book. Yet it smelled tart, like the smoke from New Year Festival firecrackers.

For a moment, Alice's thoughts were confused. Ah Shun, in the kitchen, shouted. The cobbler's hammer stopped. Alice grabbed her son and rushed down the stairs.

'In the store!' she screamed. 'Shelter in the store!'

She and Ah Shun flung open the door and burrowed under the piled boxes and tea-chests, chairs and tables and bundles.

'Why are the Japanese bombing us?' Ah Shun asked, terrified.

'Americans,' Alice replied. 'They are Americans.'

The knowledge filled her with both fear and an all-embracing joy. 'Freddy Tsang was perhaps right after all,' she thought.

12

Ah Shun had been gone since six-thirty in the morning. It being Sunday, Alice was not required in the convent, although the mother superior tried to persuade her to attend a service once in a while. She still had a lingering hope she might convert the one-time concubine.

In her opinion, Alice was well on the way to redemption. She had borne an illegimate son, it was true, and had lived in a state of sin for some years with the Irishman, but even that was nearer a state of grace than her previous position in the most notorious bordello in the Far East. With her lover departed, Alice had moved away from sin and nearer to the Lord by seeking her present employment. Since then, she had shown many acts of charity, of goodness, of love. She guided and guarded her pupils, assisted the nuns in their missions of mercy, and adored her son as a real mother should. As Mary had adored the child Jesus. Had Alice not lost her virginity, she would have been a most appropriate candidate for entry into the order.

Alice did not see the matter in such a light. In her eyes, she was merely being human. People suffered: she had the means to alleviate their suffering, and so she acted when she was able. It was simple human love she believed she felt: it had nothing to do with the gods.

She gave the most love to Alec Sean who, as time passed, she called Alec. The child was doted upon although not spoilt. Alice was not beyond giving him a spanking if he misbehaved or ignored her instructions. He tried, when he was just two-and-a-half, to be rude to Ah Shun — a throwback to the Irish in him, his mother decided — by imitating what he had seen urchins doing in the street. He had wiggled his right index finger in a circle made of his left index finger and thumb.

Being innocent, however, he had not done this behind her back, as the urchins did, but in front of her as she cooked his midday meal. Alice was told on her return in the evening and Alec missed one of the few meals of his life, taking to his small bed in choking tears of bemusement, fright and infantile rage.

Usually, he was fed well. His rice was scooped from the top of the pan to avoid the sand which sank during the cooking. His fish was filletted and he was never served the head which Alice or Ah Shun chewed for the juices. If only one egg was purchased, he ate it. If milk was available, he drank first. If Ah Shun, by some miracle of bartering or bullying, succeeded in getting five tsin of sugar, the child was allowed to dip his finger into it and suck the crystals.

Any fruit was his first, the bruised going to his mother and amah.

As the child flourished, so Alice grew thinner. She suffered from headaches, became tired easily, fell prey to any minor illness going the rounds in the convent. Yet she was careful to keep her strength above the threshold once over which there was no return. She would not die, for Alec's sake.

When, finally, Ah Shun returned just before dusk, she was exhausted, collapsing on her narrow bed by the stove, lowering a package carefully onto the floor. She rubbed her small feet.

'Where have you been?'

'Shopping,' she replied, enigmatically.

'At this hour?'

'I had to go a very long way.'

Alice filled a bowl of lukewarm water into which a pinch of salt and sugar had been dissolved.

'Drink,' she instructed.

'What is today?' asked the amah after she had drained the bowl.

Alice thought then replied, 'Sunday.'

'What else?'

'Nothing. It is a saint's day, but I don't know which one. It's not a festival.'

Ah Shun's smile beamed in the semi-darkness of the kitchen.

'It is your birthday!' she exclaimed, lifting the package from the floor. 'This is my gift.'

Alice was speechless. She accepted the package and kissed the amah on her cheek, her moist eyes smudging the old woman's skin.

'On your birthday, you should be happy and you have no parents and so it is my task . . .'

The wrapping was a copy of the *Hong Kong News*, the Japanese newspaper of occupation. Inside was a bolt of silver brocade embroidered with chrysanthemum flowers.

'Eight cheks long,' Ah Shun said proudly. 'Now you can make a dress for yourself. Like in the old days.'

In the main room, Alice unwound the cloth and draped it over the chairs, taking care to avoid any projecting nails.

'It's wonderful!' she said. 'Quite wonderful.' She paused, then added, hugging the old amah, 'And I do love you.'

There was a knock below.

'Take care,' she advised.

There was a sharp, long knife kept stuck into the inside of the door. Although the door was chained, it was still a necessary precaution. Ah Shun released the chain, however, without hesitation and steps sounded on the wooden stairs. Dr Mak entered the room.

'Happy birthday, Alice,' he greeted her and held out a small box.

'You, too!'

'Macau's a tiny place. There're no secrets here.'

Alice kissed him on his cheek and opened the box. It was made of cardboard and bore the name of a drugs company on the side. She first lifted out an ivory bangle, intricately carved with elephants holding each other's tails. Next came a bar of Cadbury's chocolate and, lastly, a reel of silver threat and four new needles in their original paper envelope with 'Made in Manchester, NH' printed on the reverse.

She slipped the bangle on and thrust her arm out to look at it.

'Thank you,' she stammered, lost for words.

'Small gifts, but in the circumstance . . . '

'No. Huge and fabulous gifts.' She turned to Ah Shun. 'From both of you.'

She broke the chocolate open, not bothering to remove the wrapper, and shared it out. Alec, playing with the fraying edge of the brocade, was picked up by Ah Shun who balanced him on her knee.

'His first taste of chocolate,' Alice observed and they all laughed.

'How on earth did you get the cloth?'

'There is a saying. "Ask not how the gods make the rice grow: tend it and harvest it and offer thanks," ' replied Ah Shun, cryptically. 'I was owed a favour. From before the war. From a friend . . . In China.'

'You've been over the border?'

The amah nodded.

'That's dangerous!'

'Not by junk,' answered Ah Shun. 'And I know the captain. From before the war . . . '

'And the chocolate?' Alice asked, turning to Dr Mak.

'Yes?'

'What about it?'

'It's smeared your lips.'

She wiped her mouth with her finger and licked it clean.

'You know what I mean!'

'It's not just letters and despatches that come in diplomatic bags.'

'And the thread? I've not seen good quality thread since Hong Kong. Or needles. And the silver thread matches the . . . You two have connived!'

'Yes,' Dr Mak admitted, grinning broadly.

13

The cobbler's hands were as horned as the soles of his feet, the skin calloused and the ball of his thumb tough as the leather and tyre rubber with which he worked. His hair was close cut and his face and back bronzed: in the summer months he worked on the pavement, balancing on his three-legged stool and passing the time of day with coolies and would-be customers as he cut and shaped and tacked. In the winter, he worked at the rear of his shop, sitting as near to his brazier as he could, his teeth chattering nevertheless. He had to take care in the winter for if his hands became too cold, they grew clumsy and to cut one of them would mean a hold-up in his work and no work meant no food.

In the winter of 1944, the accident he dreaded happened. His fingers, chilled for lack of charcoal to burn in his brazier, slipped whilst he was razoring through the woven canvas in a particularly tough tyre. The blade slipped and cut deeply across the third joint of three of his fingers. He screamed. Ah Shun heard him and rushed into the shop. Quickly, she bound his hand tightly in cloth, applying a tourniquet to his wrist while his wife who assisted him in his work hurtled into Rua Coelho do Amaral to hail a rickshaw.

Dr Mak treated him, stitched the gashes, pouring gentian violet over them, and then bandaged the hand. All through the treatment, the cobbler muttered he could not pay but the doctor allayed his fears.

'You need not pay me. Just get well. We can come to some arrangement to suit you, I am sure. If we must.'

'I cannot pay,' the cobbler reiterated in rapid Cantonese. 'How can I? I have no money to buy charcoal. The wood shavings in my shop burn too quickly. In Macau I cannot get charcoal now even if I was a rich man. Now I cannot work. I cannot earn money to feed my family. We shall starve. We shall have no home. I cannot pay my rent . . .'

That evening, Alice was approached by the cobbler, his hand swathed in cloth and held close to his chest by a triangular sling.

Uncharacteristically, he came straight to the point.

'Missy,' he said in pidgin English, 'I no can pay money.'

He held out his good hand in the palm of which lay three patacas.

'is las' money. For wung more week.'

Alice asked him to sit down which he did, evidently embarrassed.

'You do not need to pay me rent,' she said in Cantonese. 'You have been a good tenant, always paying on time. Now you may remain in the shop until you are fit to work. On the first day you are working properly again you will pay me one week's rent for the time of your illness. After that, you will continue to pay me as you have until now.'

She spoke brusquely for it was her place as landlord to do so. To have given the man his shop totally free would have been to insult him, to treat him as a beggar. He had, as she knew every man had — be they coolie or compradore — his pride. When she looked at him, he was crying.

'Toh tse!' was all he could say.

On the first day of his returning to full-time work, Alice hung a thin strand of firecrackers from the verandah and lit them to ward off evil spirits and bring the cobbler luck. Within a week, she was presented with a pair of soft leather shoes. Alec was given a stout pair of European style children's sandals and Ah Shun a pair of black cloth slippers. All three pairs fitted perfectly.

14

'Look, mama! Look at the airplane.'

Alice looked up, stopping in the street so suddenly a man walking behind collided with her. He, too, followed her gaze. Others, observing them looking upwards, did likewise.

The aircraft with the American star on its wings was circling, dropping lower all the while.

Up and down the street were knots of other skywatchers.

When it was down to three thousand feet, the rear of the aircraft seemed to shimmer for a moment.

'What is it, mama?'

'I don't know,' Alice said.

She was afraid. There had been no bombing for some months except in Hong Kong, the thunder of the raids rolling across the Pearl River estuary on an easterly summer wind.

'Chi!' shouted a man standing by her.

'Yes!' Alec shouted. 'It's paper, mama. Lots of paper.'

The leaflets took ten minutes to reach the ground. There was a scurry as people ran for them, those who could not read searching around for someone who could.

Ah Shun had the news long before her mistress returned.

'Over,' Alice said. 'The war is over. Japan has surrendered.'

The amah was silent. Somehow peace was terrifying.

15

Alice was recovering from a mild fever and Dr Mak, calling round to give her a check-up, mentioned that he was leaving Macau within a few days.

'How long will you be in Hong Kong?' Alice asked.

'I'm not going to Hong Kong,' he replied. 'At least, I'm not staying there. I'm going to Hawaii. My papers've come through from the Americans and I'm being allowed to settle there. It seems they're short of doctors since the war — expecially those who can and will treat what they term as non-Caucasian peoples. There's a big Chinese population in Hawaii.'

Alice took hold of his hand as his fingers gently explored the glands under her ears.

'I shall miss you. Very much. You've been very kind to me and my amah. And my son. It was you who delivered him.'

She lightly kissed his fingers on their very tips. They smelt of methylated spirits and carbolic soap.

'I'll bet that tasted none too pleasant,' he joked. 'I'm on my way back from the hospital.'

She grimaced as he disentangled his fingers from hers and returned to pressing beneath her jawbones.

'I, too, shall miss you, Alice Soon,' he said, his eyes avoiding hers and his head craning to concentrate on her neck. 'I don't think you know it but you've been a positive tower of strength to me. And to others.'

She blushed delicately.

'You're very polite and a poor liar, for a doctor. I always thought doctors were proficient liars.'

'They are. And I'm good at lying. But this is no lie. You see,' he signalled for her to slip her Chinese smock down her back and he unclasped the buttons behind her neck to help her, 'you have achieved with such grace what many of us either failed to manage or else did so only with much effort . . . '

She shrugged the material off her shoulders and he moved behind her, adjusting his stethoscope in his ears and tapping her back with his hand as he listened to her lungs.

'You've been dignified through all the adversity of war. So courageous. You've not been the only one — I'm not holding you up as a saint — but people like you have an inner light which has lit the road ahead for the rest of us. You've struggled as we all have, but . . . I don't know. It's just that when I've felt things were going from bad to hopeless, I've only had to think of you.'

She was embarrassed but secretly very pleased. She knew she had survived because of her stubborn determination. There was no virtue in it. It had just happened.

'You're being unfair,' she answered. 'To hide behind my back and then speak such rubbish is unfair.'

'Let me tell you something,' he said, lifting the smock so she could pull it back over her shoulders. 'In the summer of 1944, when we were worried about your son, I had a couple come to me with their child. He was a boy of seven or eight. Their family name was Lee. The boy was dying. He had been coughing blood and was so thin the bones of his wrist stretched against the skin. He was so pale, you could pick out the vessels running the blood just beneath the epidermis. He had TB, of course. Complicated with other things — a touch of malaria and starvation. He was badly dehydrated.'

He coughed, as if the mere recollection of the boy filled his throat with the same diseased spittle that had sapped the child's life.

'There was little I could do,' he continued. 'I gave him some of the few quinine doses I had left, but I knew there was no way the child could survive more than a week. I suggested they go the herbalist to get a painkiller — the child was in pain with every breath. The mother led the child away and I told the father his son had no chance.'

'He wasn't an old man — maybe thirty years of age — but he looked fifty. Watching his only son die by degrees had pulled the years over him like a blanket over a corpse. And just as I predicted, the boy died a week later.'

He removed the stethoscope from his ears and folded it into his much-battered case. Alice reached over her head and did up the buttons on her smock.

'Several days later, Mrs Lee arrived at my home. Would I come quickly? Her husband was dying. I rushed round in a rickshaw. The father was sitting in a chair, bolt upright. He didn't show a sign of life except he was breathing shallowly and, once in a while, his eyes blinked. I felt his pulse. It was hardly there, faltering. He was like a cheap clock running down. I pricked him in the finger with a pin to get a blood smear. He did not flinch. I sat before him and tried to reason with him, but he did or would not hear me.'

He closed his case, lifting it from the table on to the floor. Alice's eyes followed his face as he leaned over.

'Do you know, Alice,' he said as he straightened himself, 'I watched the man die. It took less than thirty minutes. The strange thing was when he died, he did not fall. He remained just as he was, but he was dead. His eyes glazed, his arms relaxed. His hands loosened. That was all.'

'What was wrong with him?'

'He had no will. He wanted to be with his son. You know how important sons are. He died — well, there's no medical term for it, I suppose — of a broken heart.'

Alice gazed into Dr Mak's eyes. There were tears gathering there and, as she watched, they rolled free and down his chin. It surprised her that a doctor, for whom death was a regular part of his working day, could cry.

'I'm sorry,' she muttered. There was nothing else she could think to say.

'That's why I want to leave Macau,' he added, rubbing his index finger along each cheekbone. 'I can cure much illness with my skills but I can't cure the human spirit when it is dying. I'll never forget that man: I remember him vividly whenever I pass by the end of the street in which he lived. I can't spend all of my life avoiding one street in a tiny city like this. So I'm going where I can help people. I could do nothing for him.'

Alice stood up and adjusted her smock, pulling the hem down to hang over the waist of her Chinese trousers.

'But you, Alice Soon: whenever I saw you, in the worst times with Alec Sean howling for food and you having nothing to give him but thin gruel made of fishbones, even then I saw hope. And in that instant you blotted out, for just a moment, the vision of Mr Lee sitting up dead in his chair.'

'When do you leave Macau?'

'Tomorrow. I shall be sailing on the ferry when it returns to Hong Kong in the afternoon.' He rubbed his hands together. 'If I rub hard enough, I bet I could get a flame off the stench of my hands. Meths! I hate it. And me a doctor.' He lifted his case. 'Now I must be off. Give my love to your son.'

'I will.'

'Under different circumstances, perhaps we might have . . .' He smiled at her. 'But the war and Macau. And I don't think you'd like doctoring.'

'I might,' she whispered, but the words were so faint he did not hear them.

'I'll keep in touch,' he said. 'I'd like to know how things go. I'll write care of the bank in Hong Kong. You've an account there?'

She nodded.

'Do write,' she said.

When he had gone, she did not cry but left the house. Early on the following day, Dr Mak found a small package had been delivered to his home. His servant gave it to him with his morning tea. When he opened it there fell out of the wrapping a small bag containing an exquisite star sapphire. With it was a note which read, simply:

'Love from Alice, and her son.'

Winners and Losers

1

It was in the spring of 1948 that the telegram was delivered by a young boy on a bicycle. Alice had seen him bumping along the cobbles, struggling to keep his balance on a machine far too big for him. He was not riding with his legs on either side of the crossbar, but with one leg through the space under it so the bicycle maintained an angle of forty-five degrees the whole time it was moving. To dismount, the boy merely slowed until the momentum was no longer sufficient to keep the angle constant. The bicycle crashed to the ground and the boy leapt clear of the scraping metal and spinning spokes.

She slit the message open but did not immediately read it. She put it on the table, unfolding it and smoothing the creases caused by its journey in the boy's pocket from the telegraph office in Avenida Almeida Ribeiro. As she ran her palm over it, she clearly remembered receiving the despatch from Chungking informing her of Mulrenan's successful flight and the loss of a civilian.

One corner of the sheet was folded inwards and she pressed it out with her nail: any action to delay the deciphering of the scribbled message was more than welcome. When, at last, she could put it off no longer, she read the words with a detachment befitting a prisoner presented with a sentence against which there was no appeal.

The message was bleak, short in order to save the tranmission cost:

'Returning fifteenth. Sean.'

It had been sent from Manila and the Filipino clerk

taking down the details had made a number of spelling errors: Alice's surname was written as 'Sun' and she had been given the honour of being 'Mrs' rather than 'Miss'. Yet for all its brevity, its functional imparting of information which she thought so appropriate after the infrequent letters and postcards of the past five years, it opened an anxious void in her. Today was the ninth. He would arrive in six day's time.

2

Her diary was open on the bed when the cobbler called the following day, for the last time to settle his rent. He was transferring his tenancy to his son in order to move to Hong Kong where he planned to establish a new business with, he hoped, a shoe shop as well as a repair concern. The son, also a shoemaker, would manufacture footwear for sale in the shop. They would grow rich, he believed, because there were opportunities to be found in the post-war developments occurring in the colony to the east.

He had been considering moving from Macau ever since the war ended but, like peasants the world over, he was cautious of rash decisions and had decided to wait, to test the financial current before plugging into it.

Alice herself had considered leaving for Canton soon after Dr Mak's departure, but she shared the caution of her tenant and, as the end of 1945 turned into the following spring, and then the summer and typhoon-haunted autumn, she was glad she had decided to stay.

China was in inevitable turmoil. With the Japanese defeated, the Chinese turned inward once more upon themselves and it was safe to assume the Communists would eventually win the civil struggle that had flared up after merely smouldering during the Japanese occupancy. The Nationalists under their generalissimo, Chiang Kai-shek, were planning a retreat to Formosa and the Marxist forces were increasingly successful and confident. By the winter of 1947, Alice had been convinced she, her son and amah would find a more secure living in Macau or Hong Kong than in the new China.

Immediately after the war, the mother superior sent some Chinese nuns to Foochow with instructions to establish a school and clinic there. By Christmas 1946 they were back, unwelcomed by the Communists and regarded with suspicion by the locals.

'Mark my words!' the mother superior told Alice one day after a staff meeting. 'The time is coming when China will be a far more dangerous place under her own rulers than under an alien oppressor. We'll be glad of our little haven here then all the more.'

A mild spring breeze idling from the sea had blown into the bedroom and riffled the diary's pages. Alice thumbed through them to the back. The last few sheets were a mass of numbers written in her smallest hand with a fine nib. Weighting the page flat with a hair brush, Alice ran her finger down the columns, mumbling the addition under her breath.

Her calculations completed she sat upright and said ironically, 'Two hundred and ninety-eight American dollars, one hundred and eight pounds sterling. Since 1943! So much for the stones and the belt of gold . . . '

It was all Mulrenan had sent her. Every time an envelope had arrived from him, she had entered any money it contained in the back pages of her diary beside her own earnings, thus keeping a faithful account of all her finances — with the exception of her sales of the treasures hidden behind the altar.

Mulrenan's not sending her sufficient money had rankled at first but, as the years passed, she learnt not to expect his help. Now looking at his contributions to her income and reading his telegram over, she was reminded of his letters. From the hiding place in which she kept her diary she removed the thin bundle that contained all his correspondence. The rubber band that held the sheets in place

369

was perished and was adhering to the top letter. As she pulled it free, it left a red, sticky blur across the writing.

At first, she had read his letters with some interest but, as time passed, she began to skip sections in later deliveries until finally she was merely scanning his neat, cursive writing and filing the letters in their rubber band unstudied, and for the most part, unwanted. She did not look forward to them except in that they might contain promised money.

Sometimes the money would indeed arrive. Often, the envelope showed signs of having been tampered with but the money was never stolen. The unknown eavesdropper was an official censor rather than a thieving postal clerk.

His first message to her had been the military memo sheet sent from Chungking and smuggled down the escape line. It had been terse, and anyway unnecessary, for the official decoded message had soon told Alice all she wanted to know. Mulrenan had made no reference to her half-brother.

His second letter had followed soon after and was a long narrative of his arrival in Chungking from Kweilin. There was still no mention of his and Alec's journey from Hong Kong.

She unfolded the sheets and looked at the first lines:

'Dearest Alice,

I can't write of my getting here: the censor and Capt. Probyn have warned me not to mention military things like that — but I can tell you of my arrival in Chungking. It was not a little exciting . . . '

Turning the flimsy sheet over, Alice began to read again halfway down the page. The paper was of poor, wartime quality, recycled and yellowing with age. It was brittle at the edges and creased, Mulrenan's writing blurred where veining in the paper had sucked the ink from his words.

' . . . Chungking has the strange atmosphere of a thousand-year-old Chinese city mixed with a modern one. It was for a time within Japanese bomber range and has suffered occasional strafing missions but not lately — it is the headquarters of the Allied and Kuomintang forces.

'It is a complex place: military missions exist alongside Christian ones, university undergraduates work as sing-song girls, the upper-class Chinese ladies wear *cheong sams* over Western bras and panties — which are a form of currency here, almost — and urchins collect by bus stops to gather bucketsful of the oil seeping from the sumps: the fuel and grit mixture is crudely purified and reused either in the buses or domestic lamps — the streets reek in the evening from the noxious smoke.'

Despite herself she read on, curious to rediscover what he had written. His earlier letters were interesting.

'I flew in on a . . . from . . . ' The censor's pencil had unsuccessfuly blotted out 'DC3' and 'Kweilin' in red. 'It was a bumpy trip through low clouds: a squadron of Zeros was said to be about and the pilot steered by compass. We overshot Chungking by ten minutes and dropped to get a bearing. He recognised a hill, a monastery perching on its slope and summit, banked the aircraft and broke radio silence.

'The pilot was an American flying for the Chinese civil airline — abbrievated to CNAC often lengthened to "C-NACkered" — and shouted, "We're goin' down. Chungking next stop. Hold on tight 'cos this one's a helluva strip."

'The din of the engines and the wind outside which leaked through the door frames and around the window seals was deafening. I had a fellow passenger, a civilian in a pinstripe suit and carrying an attaché case and an umbrella just like a bank manager.

'I grabbed a joist in the cabin airframe. Outside, strands of cloud whisked by: I saw a deepish river gorge, terraced fields, then Chungking hove in sight. The airstrip's on an island in the river. The pilot jiggled with the controls and the wings wobbled. Then with a sudden jolt, the nose of the aircraft lifted and the engines howled. The pilot hollered, "No good. Try again!"

'As we climbed, the cargo groaned and creaked, the webbing straps holding it in place expanding and tugging at the mountings. I was terrified it would break loose. A bit did — a cardboard carton slid across the floor, banging over the plating and clouting my shin.

' "Mind that one!" yelled the bank manager. "It's Dewar's."

'We made a second descent. The aircraft shook and wiggled, my ears hurt. As we touched down gravel spattered on the fuselage. The engines howled and the whole thing began to vibrate, shiver and slow down. As we taxied I saw a partly burned-out . . .' This time the censor's pencil had successfully erased the aircraft type. ' . . . lying on the water's edge.

'The co-pilot noticed me looking at it as we disembarked and said, "Last month. Flew in over The Hump. Misjudged the approach. Bang! Into the river. All killed. When they got the fire out found some dumb bastards had hung gold ingots from the aileron wires. In the wings! Zammo!" '

Alice skipped a page.

'My billet is a building divided into bedrooms leading off a balcony, facing a central courtyard. In the middle is a stone lion. The drawing-room's furnished with a three-piece suite, assorted Indian chairs and two upright Chinese rosewood seats. I seem to be the only visitor. In my bedroom was a box of essential toiletries and in a heavy oak wardrobe, once a missionary's — it has "CMS. Keys to Rev. Cooke, please" stencilled on the inside — I discovered some clothing smelling of mothballs.

'There's a boy here called Chan. The captain calls him Charlie. He speaks no Cantonese, which I found out as soon as I saw him. He came into my room, saying, "Bahfu 'eady. You loom an' you clowfs. Sop in box. You wan' somet'ing you arsk me. I fetch."

'That much I understood and not having shaved since . . . ' The censor had deleted another place name. 'I requested a razor. Chan looked blank. "Razor," I said. "So p'aau." Not a blink so I mimed shaving. Of course, Charlie then says, "Laser!" and I get one.'

She folded the letter, the paper cracking, and placed it at the bottom of the pile. Her fingers shuffled through to a pair of postcards. The topmost was the picture of The Red Fort at Agra and was that which had arrived in an envelope with one hundred dollars on the same day as the letter from Doyle. The other was later, a view of a mountain lake upon which were sailing dinghies of the sort she had watched, before the war, tacking around Kellett Island and the course buoys laid by the stewards of the Royal Hong Kong Yacht Club. Alec had sailed a bit, once, she thought.

The next letter she picked out was also sent from Chungking and was, in many ways, a continuation from the first. She had not stacked the letters in chronological order.

The first sheet was faded so badly that the writing was hard to read but, as she turned it over, it became more comprehensible. Perhaps, she thought, she had at some time left the letter lying in the sun and the paper had bleached.

'My debriefing with Probyn took place in the drawing room and was not as detailed as the gruelling three-hour session . . . '

Alice ignored the next two pages to find a passage more typical of Mulrenan.

' . . . the lance corporal driving it saluted me smartly and said, "Captain Probyn's compliments, sir. Are you ready, sir? The drive'll take half an hour at this time of day."

'The streets were narrow and packed with stalls and hawkers, kerb-traders and barrow owners vying for space at the expense of the pedestrians and the motor vehicles. The town's built on a hillside so the streets are ill-cambered, caved away in places, and tight cornered. The jeep stayed in first or second gear. I asked the driver how long he'd been in Chungking.

' " 'bout a year, sir," he said in a broad Cockney accent. "Came over from Calcu'a." I asked him what he thought of it and he told me. I can remember most of what he said. "No' be'er than India. No' so bloody 'ot" and "the food's spicy but it ain't like curry. And we don't get it in quar'ers like there. Don't live in barracks, neither." He slewed the jeep round the corners, gunned the pedal like fury, squawked the horn at the crowd.

' "This town's bloody incredible," he went on. "Jus' look

at it! I swear it's 'eld on to this mountain by shit, faith and telephone wires. If you'll excuse me language, sir."

'Every time he spoke, he called me "sir" but I told him he didn't have to: I wasn't an officer.

'Anyhow, it seems, as he put it, Chungking's a "good place to get a few old things." I asked him what old things? He said, "Carved stone things, jade bits and bobs, wood statues. All real old. I had a mate — flew back last month — bought some little ivory do-dahs. Dirty little things they were! 'bout as big as a walnut and carved all over. If you gave 'em an artful twist, you could open 'em up. Inside there's two Chinese shaggin' away. No lie! I seen a few myself since then. Got two, but they're just carvings, not inside these little nut cases. I reckon they'll go a bomb back home. If I can get 'em back."

'His very words! I had to laugh! But it set my mind to thinking.

' "What do you buy these things with?" I asked. I wasn't too keen to dip into my resources.

' "Whatever they want. Depends on the seller. They'll take any foreign money. Dollars, rupees, pounds. If it's a high-class bint" — it's slang for a woman — "selling the goods, she'll go for silk stockings or suspender belts, knickers — anything like that. And they all like gold. Hungry for it, they are. Not a lot about, but what there is they go for. You can get anything for gold. Even a girl slave, I've heard tell."

'I think I might see what's what . . . '

She shoved the letter beneath the rest and lay the pile on the bed. Before she put them away, she would need a new rubber band.

The main points of his other letters remained in her head. She did not need to read them to remember the synopsis of his life after Chungking. He had flown over The Hump to Assam, found his way to Delhi, made a few deals, lost the bulk of money and his resources, as he had put them . . .

The last letter she had received was the one she most enjoyed reading, the only one she had re-read from time to time. It showed Mulrenan returned to his former self, the

station in life from which he had risen and to which she felt
his conduct deserved he be reduced once more. It was not
with spite that she relished the letter. Nor was it with a
feeling of justified revenge or with emotions of pleasure. She
could not reason to herself why it was she found the letter so
satisfying. Much of his correspondence, after the first few
letters, had been sketchy. Even when sending money, he
wrote just a note. She flicked through several of them,
casting her eyes over them to remind herself of what she had
accepted as his growing indifference.

'Dear Alice,

Enclosed another instalment. Lost a deal with two Muslims. Bit hard up at present. More in a fortnight.

Love, Sean.'

The next missive bore a violet date seal three months on.

'Dear A.,

Find attached seven pounds ten shillings in Stg. Sold one
of the Ch'king ivories. Goodish price but market gen.
deflated. Hope all good. No word from Moradabad or
Lucknow yet.

Love, S.'

She had no idea what word he expected to receive and
she had to look in the atlas in Sister Bernadette's classroom
to find the towns in question.

The last letter was, like the earliest, a long one, more than
twenty pages, evidently written over a number of days: the
ink was varied and three different types of paper had been
used. It was as if he was atoning for all his past brevities,
trying to make up for lost words and withheld money by
seeking to ingratiate himself with an over-abundance of
news. It failed to touch her heart but it gave her the
pleasure of savouring his predicament.

The letter had been written in the hill station of Naini Tal
in the north of the United Provinces, in the angle of India
tucked against the western border of Nepal and close to the
rim of the Himalayas. The first few sheets were letter-
headed 'The Metropole Hotel, Naini Tal. UP.'

It began with the customary 'Dear Alice,' but was soon
deep into the narrative of Mulrenan's life on the day the

war finally ended. She unfolded the pages, tapping them to get them into shape before reading them once more.

'. . . I glanced over his shoulder – the maitre d'hotel was dodging between the tables frantically waving a square of buff paper. He caught his hip on the corner of one of the tables: the cutlery rattled and a wine glass toppled over, hit the silver-plated cruet and shattered. He ignored it, didn't seem to notice it. He's a finnicky, particular man who prides himself on running "a tight restaurant": he's fair to the Indian servants but not beyond handing out a lambasting.

'I put the tin of polish on the piano stool — I was giving it its weekly going-over. "What's up, Tec?" I asked.

'The MD's name's James Holmes, so we nickname him Tec after the detective Sherlock Holmes. He's a Canadian, served in Malaya but lost three fingers in an engine and was invalided out. In civvy life he was a head waiter. Mind you, he's not worked the best spots! His last employer was a cashiered naval officer who was the proprietor of a clip joint in the dockland of Vancouver, more like a cat-house. He puts it as "a french fries, fritters and fucking shop."'

From that one sentence, Alice knew Mulrenan had changed. Before the war and in Macau, he would never have used such language save in anger.

'Before that,' the letter continued, 'Tec had worked in Anchorage, Los Angeles and Chicago and as a waiter upon Canadian Pacific. He took to me as soon as I got to Naini. I suppose he saw me as a kindred spirit. And I needed work because of the damned Muslims so he talked the manager into taking me on as the resident piano player.'

Ah Shun called from below, asking if Alice wanted to buy some fresh sugar cane. She answered in a joyful affirmative and attempted to recall, at the same time, when she had last had the luxury of sucking the juice out of a length of cane and who the damned Muslims were.

'I've not told you about the Metropole. It's one of the better of the Naini Tal hotels, set just below St. John-in-the-Wilderness which looks for all the world like an English parish church. There are steep, tree-covered mountains —

except for Cheena Peak which is mostly bare rock — and houses all around and the bazaar is just down the hill, on the way to the lake. I'll enclose a postcard. It's popular with the ICS (civil service) as well as the military who pop in and out of Naini. The local businessmen patronise the place and it's quite a hive of industry some nights. I guess it'll see even better times now, too.

'Anyway, Tec reached the piano breathless — the hotel porch is 6513 feet above sea level and you can get short of wind very easily — and says, "Just you looky here!" He handed me a cablegram — copy of one, actually. "It's over," he stuttered. "The goddam war's over. The Yanks have dropped a big one on the Japs and they've surrendered. It's over."

'I couldn't believe it, grabbed the cablegram and read it.

'You can't imagine how I felt. The war was finally over. It's taken far longer than I hoped. My first thoughts were of you and the baby — return to Macau and find you both. When the war ended in Europe I thought to claim an expatriate passage but felt no inclination to go back to the British Isles. Or even Eire.'

Ah Shun entered the bedroom with two lengths of sugar cane each about a foot long and wrapped in rice paper. One was for Alice and the other for the boy. As she handed Alice the sappy stick, she frowned disapprovingly at the letter.

Alice bit into the cane, tearing at the woody pith, the fibres catching in the gaps between her teeth which had increased through the war years.

That Mulrenan gave his first thoughts to Alice and their son she doubted: more probably, he was thinking of the remaining gems and gold.

'I was terrified, all of a sudden. Now that peace was come — even though I think some of us expected it fairly soon — I started to look to the future. And I couldn't see much . . .'

That, Alice thought, was the truth glimmering through his writing. Unless he could regain his Macanese hoard, he might not be able to rise again above being just a cabaret pianist. He had made no progress whereas she had: she was now respected as a teacher and a mother ill-treated by the war.

'Tec said I should play the piano, said I should make a fair living, said I should go to the States. The next night there was a victory dance. That afternoon, I checked the sheet music in the piano stool. There was a good deal tucked under the seat and I sorted out waltzes and tangos, jazz numbers. Some of tricky stuff I'd not touched since The Pen. — rags and the like. Fast pieces. It hurt my fingers after the Palm Court stuff of the last months.'

The paper changed to a flimsy onion skin, Mulrenan's writing showing through from the other side and making reading awkward.

'I live in The Manor House,' the new page began, 'a sort of boarding house owned by a Mrs Chandler, an elderly lady with faded fair hair she wears in a bun down on the nape of her neck — she always pats it as she talks. She prefers it to be called "an 'otel". I rent a room in the annex. It's a strange building which looks more like a two-storeyed Swiss chalet than an Indian doss-house. Junior officers often stay here and box wallahs: the top brass stay at the Grand down on the lake. Or the Metropole.

'I've got a little sitting room with an old settee — comfortable, though — and a table much ringed by glasses. There's a fireplace — it snows here in the winter, quite deeply — and the wall over the mantel's blackened by smoke: the chimney's too narrow to draw properly. Behind the living room is a dark bedroom and, behind that, there's a bathroom. The chokidar says it's haunted and he won't come round at night. I'm on the ground floor — the pukka rooms upstairs cost more — with a verandah outside shared with the other lower rooms.

'One good thing is Mrs C. doesn't charge too much. She's not cheap by a long chalk so I don't get to save anything — but she is within my means (just) and places are scarce here. What with the bloody Muslims and all the rest, things haven't really turned out too well, have they?'

Again, Alice thought, the mysterious Muslims.

She accepted his letter more as an ingratiation than a communication. She felt Mulrenan was trying to bring himself back into her life and she was not sure if she resented or pitied him for it.

The sun was warm outside. Early September had seen the last of the typhoons of the year and, towards the end of the month, the weather had turned hot without being unbearably humid. Alice put the letter down and went onto her own verandah, holding the postcard around which Mulrenan had folded the letter.

It was a black and white photograph which had been hand-tinted and showed a panorama of Naini Tal taken, according to the scrawled title, from 'Snow View, on Alma Peak.' The buildings of the town clustered around the head of the lake and the houses fitted snugly into the horseshoe-shaped valley. The lake was smooth and tinted a brilliant azure which did not reflect the washed blue of the sky. Upon the water sailed two tiny smudges that were yachts. The artist touching up the photograph had tried to paint the sails red but the colour had run into the lake water where it hung like a faint blur of blood.

On the reverse of the card, Mulrenan had written, 'Manor Hse. is off to the right of the picture. The Metropole is just out of sight on the same. Attached is what I got from the major . . .'

A five pound note had accompanied the card. There was no mention in the letter of a major.

3

In retrospect, the five years since Mulrenan had departed, hurried along by Alice's scheming with Tsang, had passed peaceably. It was strange to regard them so, for they had been a time of war and fighting, of terror with the American bombing and the Japanese reprisals over the border in China, not to mention the inter-faction fighting amongst the Chinese. There had been months of living on the verges of starvation, of queueing and black market buying, of worry and sickness, of hot sun and the fears of cholera, of cold winters and the fears of influenza. She had had to face the illness of her son, T'so's murder and her own inward fears of what would happen when — if — Mulrenan returned. Yet the overall impression, helped by Dr Mak, was still one of quietness and tranquil growth.

She was glad Mulrenan had left her life. The hardships and changing attitudes of the society in the middle of a war had dulled curiosity as to her background and the identity of her child's father. She was like everyone else, poor, suffering at the hands of common circumstance. No one made allowances for her and no one cared who or what she had been: she was Alice Soon from Hong Kong, who worked as a teacher. She was kind and intelligent, pretty and had a little boy. That was all they knew or cared to know.

A few remembered Mulrenan as the Irishman who dealt in gemstones. If one needed to raise any money, he was the one to approach. He drove a hard bargain but he was fair, or so the passage of the years had made him. He avoided blackmailing his clients and he was not as usurous as the money-lenders. Unconnected directly with the triad societies and the criminal fraternity, he had lived as a free agent. One had something to sell: he bought it.

In the six days after the delivery of the telegram, Alice prepared for Mulrenan's homecoming. She felt little emotion for him: even her hatred was barely alive. Yet she believed she had to make the effort to welcome him back, even if she resented him. He too had suffered, she supposed. He deserved a modicum of civility from her. She could not forget that he had at least helped her out of The Line and she had, albeit without his knowledge, been living partly off his hoard of treasure. She owed him this much but not, she told herself over and over again, anything more. She purchased two catties of a good grade of rice, ordered a large fish from the father of one of her pupils and arranged with the mother superior to have three days' release from her teaching duties. Ah Shun cleaned the house thoroughly and extra charcoal was purchased for the brazier which had replaced the oil stove in the living quarters. During the war, the brazier had served to burn anything inflammable: oil had become so scarce as to be unobtainable even to those with money. Yet these were only Alice's material preparations: the others were far harder to accomplish.

The first of these was preparing her mind to accept him back. She had grown accustomed to thinking of him only as a distant figure, a sender of brief messages and, very occasionally, small sums of money. In her mind, he had assumed a character not dissimilar to that of her half-brother in the pre-war years: he, too, had sent only a rare postcard and showed no interest in her life. In Mulrenan's case, however, the feelings of being apart were intensified by her inability to reply.

She had forgotten what he looked like, in the same way she had forgotten her brother Alec or Irina. There were few photographs to strengthen her memory and fewer objects. Most of his wardrobe she had given away or sold: his remaining clothes brought back reminiscences but only of the events at which he had worn them.

As for his voice, his company, his lovemaking: these had been dispelled by time. Sometimes, when she felt the need for a man in her bed, she tried to remember what he was like and thought she might have recaptured his closeness, the scent of his body or the surface texture of his skin, but no sooner had she decided these were Mulrenan's than she had the doubt they were not his but those of another, previous man, one of her clients, her many tricks.

Facing the mirror, she tried to arrange herself so he, at least, could recognise her. She had had her hair cut in a style he would know. She studied the photograph of herself at the Kwanti races so she might imitate the make-up.

Whenever she held that photograph, she remembered the sapphire and her friend Irina dead in the torch-lit street. The memory prompted her recalling the letter from the man Doyle and those two fragments of paper — the one turning sepia and the other weak at the folds from so many openings and closings — brought back to her the pain she had had to endure alone, the anger she had had to assimilate then dissipate.

How she would react to Mulrenan was something she could not tell and it worried her. For once, the self-confidence she had developed in his absence seemed frail.

Her second preparation was the manner in which she made her son ready for his first meeting with his father. Now nearly five years old, Alec was attending his first classes with the nuns, learning to read English and speak Chinese. He was as proficient with chopsticks as any Chinese child but he could also use a knife and fork, if clumsily. He could write his alphabet passably well in a childish scrawl and his brushwork on characters was beginning to show some form. He could manage the calligraphy of the numbers from one to ten and write his surname: Soon.

Alice told him his father was coming, and that Sean, his second given name, was his father's. Mulrenan's reaction to his son having as his first name that of her detested half-brother was something she would just have to face.

4

She barely recognised him. As he crossed the gangplank and entered the customs and immigration building, Alice knew it was he because he was the only disembarking European. And he, emerging from the building with a battered leather suitcase in one hand and a mackintosh screwed up in the other, did not immediately recognise her in the jostling stevedores, eager and happy relatives and chivvying officials.

When he did spy her, it was not her appearance which drew his attention but her intense calm. She was standing in the milling throng, shoved and pressed on all sides, but she herself did not move. Like a tree in a storm she bent but did not shift her ground. It was the strength of her will which caught his attention and, as he watched her, so he understood this now was Alice.

The crowd of arriving Chinese started to turn and he had to struggle against the obstinacy of their tide. A pillar hid Alice from sight.

When he had last been with her, she had been lithe and graceful, her shoulders straight with a pride he could never quite fathom. She was no longer lithe now, but thin, the bones on her face were more prominent, more Chinese. Her hair, cut much as it had been in 1942, lacked lustre and was touched with grey and her skin, as sallow as ever, no longer shone as if there was an inexhaustable light burning within her. He decided it was not that it was extinguished, merely that it was struggling to stay alight.

As he elbowed his way towards her, he noticed she was wearing a *cheong sam* but not of silk brocade as she might have worn before the war. It was cut from blue cotton and the slit in the skirt was only inches long: it was not a dress to entice but just to cover the body. Through the material he could see her hip bones jutting, unbalancing a little bag suspended by a cord from her shoulder. Beneath the hem, her legs were thinner. She was wearing a padded jacket too small for her and flat slipper-like Chinese shoes. Her wrists were narrow below the too-short cuffs.

There was nothing he could say to her. On the steamer from Calcutta, on the cargo boat from Singapore via Manila and the ferry from Hong Kong, he had rehearsed how he would greet her but with each rehearsal he changed his script until finally, at the moment of meeting her, he was without words.

'Did you stay at The Pen in Hong Kong?' were her first words to him.

From a far distant, lost past, a memory came to him. He did not feel it was from his own life: more, it was a scene viewed in a film of someone else's. He could almost hear the buzz of a projector, a strange black-and-white face on a screen, only the room behind it familiar.

'No. Not quite. I stayed in the YMCA next door.'

She smiled, pointing a finger in the direction of a group of squatting coolies. One rose from his haunches and took Mulrenan's case.

'We have to walk,' she said, 'but it's not far. As you know.'

They made their way through the streets, the coolie ahead of them with the case hanging from his pole in a sling: to counterbalance it he had a pannier containing a few catties of cabbages collected from the same ferry. He could just as easily have carried the case by the handle, for it was light and he knew his services had been needed purely as a matter of status. To carry it from his pole, however, gave the impression of effort and it was for effort he was paid.

As they walked, they did not talk. Her small bag bounced against her side and she held it closer. It was not until they were in sight of the house that he spoke.

'You are still living here,' he commented, and she noticed a hint of relief in his voice.

'Yes. We could not have moved, in any case. Housing has been very short. Like everything, in the war years. Sometimes I had to rent a room out. To pay for fuel for heating. Then Ah Shun and I lived in the bedroom with . . .'

The moment had arrived. Mulrenan was, once more, stepping with her over the familiar cobbles. A dog barked at them from a doorway down Rua do Patane.

'Alec Sean,' she said 'Your son is called Alec Sean.'

Gradually, to her surprise, a smile came over his face. It was not the one she had known from the pre-war years, a grin of wicked humour born of a lightning mind; nor was it avaricious, that which she had watched cross his face when he was about to take an Englishman for everything he was worth. It was a tired smile, of resignation.

'Where is he?' Mulrenan asked, gazing up at the balcony as if hoping the child would appear to wave to him.

'At school.'

'Already? But he's only . . .'

The coolie lowered his burden to the cobbles and Mulrenan removed the suitcase from the sling.

'I have no Macanese coins,' he said apologetically.

'It won't matter. Anyone will take any money these days.' she replied.

'Actually, I've no money at all,' he admitted.

She had expected as much and he looked away with embarrassment as she paid the coolie who haggled for a higher rate. She softly remonstrated with him but he, with an unusual temerity, argued back. She cowed him with a curt retort, her cruel sarcasm still quiet. The coolie begrudgingly accepted the coins, slipping them into a pouch on his belt before going down on his hunkers to redistribute the weight of his cabbages between each end of his bamboo pole.

In the doorway to what Mulrenan remembered had been the herbalist's shop, he heard a voice ask about his identity.

'Kui hai pin koh?'

'M shik,' a second voice exclaimed. It was an old man's wavering voice.

'Ngoh m hai m shik! Kui hai M-wey-nan.'

Alice twisted her key in the padlock on the door.

'The same padlock,' he observed.

'It served us all well. There were times when I was glad of your sense of security.'

She made no attempt to elaborate and he wished she would. A break into such an explanation might open up the channels of communication between them. Yet she remained silent, going ahead of him up the steep stairs. Her feet level with his face, he noticed how narrow her ankles had become.

Most of the furniture was the same as when he had left the room. It was even in the same positions. He found himself involuntarily searching for the household altar hanging on the wall. The plaster looking worryingly new and so did the god.

'Ah Shun is out to the market,' Alice said to explain the emptiness of the house.

Mulrenan sat on an upright chair by the table: it seemed somehow impertinent to sit in one of the more comfortable seats. Although this room was what he considered his home, he felt he was a stranger in it; it no longer belonged to him but to Alice. His life had been absent for so long it now had no right to be there, whereas her life had gone on, shared with others of whom he was ignorant. She was the new owner by his default.

'When I was in India, I was invited on a tiger hunt,' he said. 'Would you like to hear of it?' She nodded and he continued, 'I was the guest of a maharajah and we went out to shoot tigers in the forest. We sat in howdahs on elephants — they are cane boxes with seats inside, strapped on the elephants' backs — and a line of beaters banging on drums and sheets of tin or hollow logs marched towards us through the trees. Right across the valley they came, through a shallow river. Other elephants stood on the flanks. The tigers were driven in our direction. One was shot, although not by me. I shot a leopard instead.'

She made no comment and he realised a day's promised excitement and danger, camaraderies and colour had been reduced by his words to a sham of the reality.

'You must tell Alec — Alec Sean — that story. He likes tigers,' Alice said.

Ah Shun entered, critically and silently looking Mulrenan up and down as he greeted her. She grinned wanly in reply.

Alice explained she had a job as a teacher but added she had a few days release from her duties. They spoke very little in the hour before it was time to fetch the boy from school. Alice pottered about the apartment, talking to Ah Shun, tidying or flicking already neat and dusted objects with a feather duster, or discussing their evening meal with her amah. Eventually, she told Mulrenan she had to leave to bring her son home.

'Can I come with you?' he requested. 'I'd like to see him leaving his first school with . . .'

'No!' she interrupted him quite emphatically, 'I shall get him on my own. You'll meet him soon enough. I'll be gone half an hour.'

When she had left, Ah Shun busied herself and did not converse with him. Any comment he made was met by a subservient silence which ill disguised the old woman's dislike for her mistress's former — and now, she assumed, reinstated — master.

As he sat alone, Mulrenan considered how Alice had altered. The firm manner in which she had forbade him to accompany her to the school was unlike the woman he had known. As on the dock she was calm and self-assured. In paying off the coolie, too, she had indicated a confidence he had never seen before. The war had given her strength and he realised she must have needed it. It could not have been easy living in a blockaded city. Life had been getting tougher when he left and he now wondered if he would have had the same inner determination to survive. Yet he had survived in India. Despite losing his security in a failed arms deal with anti-British Muslims he had gone on, regardless of the odds against him. He had fallen back on his resourcefulness, even if that *had* meant playing the piano for British officers.

Now he had returned to Macau and was face to face with Alice, he sensed a new shame growing. No matter how grim things had been for him in India, at least he was never reduced to near-starvation, as, he suspected, she clearly must have been. Her stick-like ankles had shocked him.

He promised himself her life would improve: he was quite determined to look after her, share in the upbringing of their son. They could move back to Hong Kong and he would set himself up in business. His Macanese assets would have held good and he thanked the gods that guarded him she had not moved from the building. A move would have presented insurmountable difficulties.

Calling Ah Shun from the kitchen, Mulrenan asked her to get him a sharp knife. Apprehensively, the amah brought him a knife sickled with so much sharpening. Even the cutlery, Mulrenan thought, had grown thin in the war.

Dismissing her, he removed the new altar from its nail in the wall and set it carefully on the table, ensuring the god within still faced in the same direction. Something told him pagan deities did not like to be forced to observe other views. Besides, he did not want even the household god to watch him.

The nail was new, too: he remembered the old one well. It had had a flat head whereas this one was tapered.

With mounting concern, he plunged the knife at the wall, pressing the blade in with the ball of his thumb. The knife did not penetrate the plaster as readily as he had anticipated. Sawing with the blade, he cut out a jagged circle two feet across. It fell inwards and he reached for it, pulling it out, fragments of plaster tumbling to the floor scattered with shavings. His shoes were a pinky-cream with the dust. With his hand, he probed the cavity. It was empty.

When Alice returned she found Mulrenan sitting bent over in the upright chair. His hands were to his face. As she entered the room, he removed his hands and she saw where streaks of plaster dust had adhered to his tears. Behind him the hole gaped. The household god resided in a temporary kingdom on the floor below it.

She stood before Mulrenan, holding the little boy by her left hand. Alec Sean studied his father for a long moment before craning his neck to look up at his mother.

'Hi koh shue tso mat ye?' he asked with the quiet curiosity of a child for a man's tears.

She shook her head, slowly.

'Mo yan chi,' she answered.

Yet she knew why the boy's father wept.

Leaving Mulrenan, she led Alec Sean away to wash him in a basin in the bedroom and change his clothes.

Remaining in the chair, Mulrenan drove his loss out of his mind with considerations of his son. He was a handsome child with dark brown hair and a sensitive expression. In it, he saw his own grandfather by the fire in his cottage, a fishing net draped across the old man's knees like an invalid's blanket. Yet in his son, in tiny ways he could not define, he also saw Alec Cowley and remembered the body crumpled in the paddy.

While she prepared the evening meal with Ah Shun, Alice's mind reconstructed the events of the day. Mulrenan had not reacted as she had expected to the naming of his son. He seemed to accept it. Indeed, he had not been himself. He was not the man she had known and loved and been hit by and had gradually grown not exactly to hate but more to disregard. He was less outward-looking, not so full of the essences of living. His finding the wall cavity empty had, she suspected, broken him.

What would he want now? She no longer loved him, no longer wanted him in her bed or even in her house: that the house was partly his was of no consequence. If he started to argue ownership she was certain someone would come to her aid with a skilful legal diatribe or a swift knife in an alleyway. Either solution to her problem would be acceptable. She realised her thoughts were extrapolating farther than they need. He might leave them now he had discovered the jewels were gone.

Her carefully contrived tale of what had apparently happened to the gemstones had gone through many revisions and her final version was concocted and published while she was preparing dinner, basting the fish as it crisply browned in the hot oil.

'The fish is very good,' he complimented her as they sat opposite each other across the table, breaking a long silence. 'In India, there's a huge river fish called a mahseer which I ate on a number of occasions. The meat's sweetish and they make little cakes out of it mixed with chickpea flour and spices. I learnt to cook it. I'll make it for you if you like. Carp might taste similar.'

Her chopsticks rattled on the waste bowl in front of her as she knocked free a bone.

'I doubt it,' she said. 'River fish live in white water and eat other fish. The carp lives in ponds and is a bottom feeder. It eats mud with its food and the mud flavours its flesh unless you keep it in a tank for a long time.'

'Then I'll do that.'

'We have no tank large enough.'

'Won't a big bucket do?'

'No, not really.'

He fell silent wondering if she was deliberately sabotaging his attempts to talk and establish a bond.

'Do you want to know about the wall?' she enquired, her eyes staring him straight in the face.

'I suppose so.'

Above her, the hole still gaped. Mulrenan spooned more rice into his bowl and placed a cube of fish upon it. The steam from the rice lifted before him in a temporary mist.

He asked 'You know why I cut the hole?'

'I can guess.' Alice rested her chopsticks across her bowl. 'You must have had money hidden there.'

'Not money. Stones. Some of very good quality — the very best I had obtained and did not take with me.'

She turned to survey the hole. It was dark inside yet she could see the lath and plasterwork of the wall at the rear of the cavity. Now was the time to put her story to the test.

'During the war,' she told him, 'the Americans bombed Macau. We were not hit but the shockwaves from the explosions cracked the plaster and, over a few weeks, the cracks widened. We were afraid the wall might collapse. This room was occupied by Mr Kwan, his wife and three young children. We were worried in case the wall fell on the children who slept against it, so Mr Kwan asked me if he could strip the plaster and repair it. He said he'd do it himself. He had worked for a building company before the war. I agreed for he offered to share the cost with me.'

Mulrenan was not eating. The rice had ceased to steam and the sauce on the fish was dulling as it congealed.

'I went off to school one day and, when I returned in the afternoon, the wall was down. There was nothing there. Over the next few days, Mr Kwan rebuilt the plaster as it is now.'

'Where did the Kwans go?'

'They left a few months later for Canton.'

'Did you not suspect that? After all, how could they go through occupied China?'

'By then, the Japanese were retreating. I had no cause to be suspicious. Why should I? You didn't tell me you'd anything hidden there.'

He put the piece of fish in his mouth. It was cold and the sauce gelatinous. He separated the flesh from the bones which he spat on to his hand. She noticed he had forgotten his etiquette. One should remove bones or gristle with chopsticks.

'If you'd told me the wall contained a secret, I should have made other arrangements.'

She did not speak as if to chastise him but she hoped that he felt the sting of criticism nonetheless.

'Could we trace the Kwan family?'

She made no reply.

'Everything else I've had to spend,' she said, pre-empting his next question. 'You didn't send us very much. Things became very expensive after you left. Food became scarce, disease increased. Cholera, leprosy — there were many lepers in the streets. We could buy rice most of the time but you had to sieve it because the merchants put sand and small stones in it to cheat on the weight. Meat was rare. We grew some vegetables in pots on the verandah — tomatoes.'

She left the table and, picking up the altar, hung it from the nail so that it covered most of the hole. Its emptiness nagged at her conscience.

'Life was very hard. Most refugees lived in centres run by the British consul or the Portuguese. The Jesuits started St Aloysuis' College for refugee boys: over three hundred passed through it. The nuns I teach for started a school for the girls.

'Medicine was scarce. Dr Mak took good care of us but he's left Macau now. He was a good friend to us. Murder was common. T'so was killed: people would kill you for anything. I lost my wristwatch one night to a man who cut it from my wrist with a razor. It was lucky he did not do worse.'

She turned her left arm over and Mulrenan could see a scar so straight it could have been a surgeon's careful incision.

'He missed the artery,' she went on, 'and Dr Mak had some catgut he had made by shredding a tennis racquet. There was much prostitution, too,' She paused to note his reaction. His eyes were blank. 'I did not revert to that.'

'I'm glad,' he said, putting down his chopsticks which

rolled off his bowl and clattered on the table.

Taking her left hand in both his, he twisted her wrist to see again the scar. It was like the burn she had received falling against the Valor stove.

'Did it hurt?'

'A bit. I was more scared than hurt. If you lost a lot of blood . . . and all our resistances to disease were low. I was terrified I'd get gangrene . . .'

'I'm sorry,' he said, letting go of her hand 'It's not . . .'

'Don't worry.' Her voice was suddenly tired. 'History will take care of all that.'

From the bedroom a small voice called, 'Mama!' twice.

'I'll go to him,' Mulrenan said.

'No. He doesn't know you yet. I'll go.'

5

Many of Mulrenan's former acquaintances had disappeared. He did the round of his old haunts but most people did not know him. His reputation remained but had been convoluted by legend and rumour. To some he was a renegade, an outsider to be avoided at all costs: to others, he was a just man who would not cheat you beyond the bounds of expectancy. No one, however, was prepared to deal with him, or to deal him in.

The gold business was almost entirely dominated by one man, Dr Pedro Lobo. He was the most powerful man in Macau, the owner of the gambling franchises and much more besides. The decision of the Portuguese government to exclude Macau from the international agreements on gold trading had given the colony an unique position in the Far East: gold could be openly traded there whereas in other countries bullion dealing was restricted to a few approved merchants and the biggest of the banks.

The enigmatic Dr Lobo was a small and trim Portuguese

Chinese. He was polite, withdrawn and wore gold-rimmed spectacles high upon the bridge of his broad nose. He was as ruthless as he was respectable, as efficient in his business as he was retiring and aloof. His home, Villa Verde, was unpretentious but rumoured to be sumptuous inside, with cabinets of Stuart cut glass lining the walls.

Lobo's business operations were simple: he purchased gold from bullion dealers in London, Amsterdam or Geneva, and flew or shipped it to Macau. Once there, he sold it at a profit to anyone who would pay what he set as his own personal gold standard. Once purchased, it was their responsibility to remove it from Macau, if they so wished. Export was legal: import into most other countries was not or it was highly controlled. Hong Kong, the nearest comparatively politically-stable territory, was usually the first halt for the smuggler. The Hong Kong customs officials kept an eagle eye open for the illicit exit traffic in bullion.

To break into the gold business in Macau was impossible. Mulrenan quickly realised he had lost his contacts by leaving Macau. Precious stones were no longer of interest, even if Mulrenan had owned any. Opium smuggling was a possibility but the rewards minimal for the considerable risks: fellow smugglers would kill for a quality cargo and the authorities were vigorously clamping down on narcotics — which Mulrenan anyway regarded as a dirty business. It was British opium which had corrupted China.

For several weeks, Mulrenan struggled to find an entrée into a world that had left him behind. He obtained a number of louis d'or from a gold dealer, using money Alice lent him for the venture and waited for the price to rise. It did. He sold. The commission on a small transaction was high and he made no significant profit.

The salary Alice continued to earn from the school kept them from going hungry but it was not a situation Mulrenan relished: as a kept man he was belittled, if only in his own eyes.

Alice did not begrudge him his keep. For as long as she was paying, she could control their joint lives. They did not sleep together. She delicately steered him away from the

393

subject of a sexual attachment, using the thin excuse that she had not had a man for many years and wanted to ease herself back into a state of physical familiarity. He, being held in her power, had to agree and spent his nights on a folding campbed in the main room. Over his feet, whenever he lay in bed, was the household god and the patch of fresh unwhitewashed plaster behind the wooden shrine.

Mulrenan spent his days in the house or wandering the streets. Like an old coolie, he was unemployed and unlikely to obtain work. He sat in the cafes drinking coffee slowly; he perched on the wall of the Praia Grande and watched the semi-pellucid waters of the Pearl River suck and wash at the stones; he watched the ferry to Hong Kong sail by, its black funnel with two white bands belching smoke which hung in the humid air. On the superstructure of the vessel, as if to taunt him, was painted a Union Jack.

One day in late May, he spotted a purse lying in the gutter in Travessa do Bom Jesus. It had evidently been lying there for a while; the leather was stained by rainwater and the cheap metal clasp pocked with rust. A fine fur of mould was flourishing on one corner. Walking past, he glanced upon it but not obviously so. The clasp was shut.

There were only a few people in sight yet he was reluctant to be noticed stooping to an object in the drain. Reaching the end of the street Mulrenan halted, peered about as if not sure of where he was and retraced his steps. Two amahs chattering in a doorway prevented him from retrieving the purse but on his third journey down the street, he found them gone. Hastily, as if committing a crime, Mulrenan bent and picked the purse up.

He walked down the hill towards the Praia Grande, his steps forced to hurry by the incline and his shame. He arrived in Rua do Chunambeiro at a half-trot. Crossing the road, he sat on one of the benches overlooking the bay and, laying the purse on the wooden slats of the seat, tugged at the clasp. It was rusted shut but he forced it, his fingers tearing the leather.

The sparse contents, though wrinkled with damp, were not stained. There was a photograph of a Chinese couple standing by a bronze statue of a lion, a badly smudged letter written with a brush and ink, two keys and a wad of notes wrapped around two small, worn gold coins, probably representing the owner's entire life savings. It amounted at best to not more than a few hundred Hong Kong dollars.

Thankful for his good fortune Mulrenan refolded the notes, slipping them into his own shabby leather wallet, pressing the coins into a pocket within it designed to hold postage stamps. The thinness of the coins allowed them to fit: they were worn as if, like Alice and her kitchen knife, they had suffered in the war.

To be found in possession of the purse was inadvisable. He could be accused of stealing it.

It was only two paces to the praia wall beyond which the sea was slapping idly against the embankment. Mulrenan scooped up a handful of sandy gravel from behind the sea wall and poured it into the purse covering the replaced letter and photograph. As the grey grains pattered on the photograph, his attention was caught by it: the lion by which the couple were posing was one of the lucky bronzes before the Hongkong and Shanghai Bank.

'So they do bring good fortune,' he said ironically.

The purse made but the slightest splash as it hit the surface: the leather bubbled for a moment, then winged its way like an ugly brown moth down into the murk. The tide was rising and Mulrenan prayed the currents would drag it out to sea before low tide came around to expose the mud against the stone wall. Not that it would matter: no one would associate him with a piece of flotsam.

It had been his rule to dress as smartly as he could when going out. Now, provided for by fortune, he considered the vista of possibilities opening before him. He could visit the casino, a good hotel bar or a restaurant. He could buy Alice a present but he had no sooner considered that course than he abandoned it. To purchase her a gift would entail explaining where the money came from and he was not prepared to tell her. Pride prevented him from admitting he had found it in the gutter.

He was only a few hundred yards from the Bela Vista Hotel and it was not long after midday. He decided to walk up to the hotel, enter the restaurant and order a beer for himself on the balcony.

The entrance to the hotel in Rua do Comendador Kou Ho Neng was not as he remembered it. The steps were unswept except in the very centre and the wooden doors were in need of varnishing. He passed through them to find the lobby more or less unaltered except that the paint was peeling against the ceiling and the potted palms were dusty. They had been over-watered: in the soil at the base of the one by the reception desk, an etiolated toadstool had sprouted, hanging its pale umbrella over the rim of the glazed porcelain container.

The balcony was the same. Here, time and war had had no effect. The wooden blades of the overhead fans still spun slowly and ineffectually. The stone balustrade still lined the view down to the now-deserted dance floor in the centre of which was parked a battered Austin. Oil spots elsewhere on the dance floor indicated where vehicles were usually left.

'Yiu mat ye?'

The waiter's uniform was as it had been before the war but the cuffs of his starched white jacket were frayed and there was a faded brown stain on the collar.

'Beer, please.'

If he closed his eyes, Mulrenan could almost hear the band playing on the terrace below.

'Boy!'

His daydream was dispelled by the scraping of chairs and British voices at the far end of the balcony.

'Boy!'

The waiter returned bearing Mulrenan's glass of beer on a tray.

The Englishman raised his voice. 'Leung gor gin an' ton-ick. Fide-fide-ah!'

The waiter brought Mulrenan's beer. The silver electro-plating on the tray had been worn through to the brass with polishing.

'M'koi,' Mulrenan thanked him and nodded his head in

the direction of the two men who were wearing light tropical suits and tan shoes, asking unsurely, for he had forgotten much of his Cantonese, 'Ni ti hai mat yan?'

The waiter understood him

'Dey B'tish offiss',' he replied in equally uncertain English.

When their drinks arrived, the two men raised their glasses and chimed them together. Their dark blue ties upon which were embroided small insignia were neatly knotted.

'Cheers!' said one.

'Yaam sing!' replied the other and they laughed.

'You know, I reckon this is a pretty cushy posting,' commented the first, a man in his mid-twenties with fair hair and a freckled face.

'How do you work that out?'

'Suppose we were stationed in Europe. All the problems of repatriation of aliens, monetary controls, hatred of the locals. I heard from Barnie last week. Stuck in Munich sorting out the poor bloody Jews: caught between pillar and post. The Jews don't like him because they want to get out as fast as they can and bugger the red tape. The local Germans, by and large, hate his guts. Half the bars in the town are off limits and the other half aren't worth it.' He drank noisily, the ice and lemon bobbing his lip. 'No, I still think we're the best off.'

'Maybe. No unfriendly locals to speak of. Most of our time's spent learning the lingo and the lie of the land.'

'And the ladies . . .'

'Too true, chum! Toddled down to Wanchai with those two RAOC blokes we came out with. Fenwick Street, just along from the China Fleet Club . . .' He whistled as he sucked his breath and lowered his voice.

Mulrenan sipped his beer and, as he did so, an idea dawned on him. Emptying his glass, he left his table and went in search of the manager.

A glass-panelled door suggested in Portuguese this might be where the manager was to be found: some of the painted letters on the glass had been scratched off. Mulrenan knocked and a voice replied incomprehensibly.

The office contained a large desk littered with papers and a black telephone off its receiver. The manager was not the man Mulrenan recalled from the early years of the war: there would be no favours due from him upon which to draw.

Evidently noting the man before him to be neither a fellow Portuguese nor Chinese, the manager assumed him to be British and greeted him politely.

'Good morning, sir. What can I do for you? I trust you had a restful night.'

'Good morning. And I'm not a guest,' Mulrenan admitted. 'I live in Macau and have a proposition for you, sir.'

The return of the compliment he hoped would have an effect. It did. The manager, who had stood up on his entering the room, sat down again.

'What is it? You can see I am very busy,' he announced impatiently, indicating the telephone receiver, the interrupted call.

'I understand you now have a largely European clientele with a quick turnover.'

It was an assumption, but Mulrenan guessed he was near the truth.

'That is correct. The British forces in Hong Kong use the hotel as a recreation place for officers and the Hong Kong Government have their civil servants stay here whilst they undergo a course in Cantonese and Mandarin.'

'What entertainment have they?' Mulrenan asked.

'What do you mean? They go to the casino, or they drink in the bar . . .'

'If you'll allow me?' Mulrenan sat on a chair in front of the desk. 'Before the war, I used to visit this hotel — as a guest — and I can clearly remember the charming summer evenings when there was a dance band outside. I even played here once or twice myself, just for the fun of it. Might I suggest you re-institute those evenings?'

The manager placed his elbows on the blotting pad and leaned over the clutter of papers.

'Also, before the war,' Mulrenan continued before the

manager could make a comment. 'I was the resident pianist at The Peninsula Hotel. And the Repulse Bay Hotel. Now I am seeking a new position . . .'

'Why should I hire you?' the manager rejoined with bluntness. 'I have no need to attact business. There are too few hotel rooms in Macau. We are not in competition with each other.'

'It may be true, sir,' Mulrenan said, 'that you are not in competition for rooms. But what about bar takings? If you held dances here, especially in such a romantic setting as the hotel offers, I am sure guests from other hotels would attend — and dances mean an extra person for each guest for they will bring a partner. Word will spread easily through the officers' messes.'

'Our dance floor is now for cars.'

'There is ample room in the street for parking. Or down on the praia. It's not far to walk.'

'How good is your piano playing, Mister . . .?'

'Mulrenan.'

He stretched forwards over the desk, offering his hand across the unpaid invoices and unanswered letters. The telephone receiver hummed. Mulrenan knew his plan would burgeon.

6

The lights in the wrought iron and glass lanterns above the dance floor had fallen into disuse during the war and rewiring was too expensive. In place of the electric bulbs fat candles were inserted. The piano was wheeled onto the terrace and a long table erected as a bar and buffet. The dance floor itself was scrubbed free of oil, though a few persistent stains remained, the wall below the balcony was distempered and the pot plants were pruned. Along the terrace were positioned folding chairs and circular wooden tables borrowed, at a price, from a restaurant: upon each was a vase of night-scenting flowers and a small candle, glinting cutlery and glasses. The tablecloths were fixed to the table tops with drawing pins the brass heads of which had been painstakingly coloured white.

Mulrenan arrived early in the evening, wearing a charcoal grey suit with a white shirt and a grey tie. His black shoes had been polished by Ah Shun, his shirt ironed by Alice. To avoid soiling his clothes by a hot walk through the streets, he had taken a rickshaw paid for in advance by Alice.

'You are ready?' the manager asked, nervously welcoming him at the hotel entrance.

'Certainly. Ready as you are.'

Mulrenan sat at the piano, adjusted the stool and wiggled his fingers. He had been practising a few of the latest tunes there in the morning, after most of the guests had left. He had grown rusty and needed to loosen his joints and sharpen his ears for the correct chord progressions.

'Do you have your repertoire arranged?' questioned the manager. He was plainly anxious his gamble should pay off, not only to cover the expense but also to save his face with the other hoteliers.

'Don't worry.' Mulrenan put on his best Irish accent. 'We'll be all right, for sure. It'll be a piece of cake.'

The opening tune of the evening was *Clair de Lune* and playing the first bars put into Mulrenan's mind the two charioteers he had not seen for years. Perhaps they no longer rode their wall at The Pen but had been removed to make way for the kimono-clad geishas preferred by the Japanese occupiers.

By nine o'clock, there were well over three hundred and fifty guests. More tables and chairs had been found, more sandwiches cut. The manager, previously worried that he might lose his investment, was now terrified of running out of ice, tonic water, gin or scotch.

Mulrenan played almost continuously from seven-thirty until after one in the morning. He broke off only to relieve himself and to snatch a tough roast-beef sandwich which had been made without any butter and a superfluity of mustard.

All through the evening, dancers whirled before him, requests were handed to him by the waiters or the officers who attended in their best mess uniforms, their brass buttons or gold braid shining above the silver cutlery and glassware. Miniature medals clinked above left breast pockets and sword scabbards rattled on the frames of the metal folding chairs.

The women who accompanied the officers were of two sorts — wives and whores. The former danced cheek-to-cheek, their right hands held by their husbands, their waists encircled by their spouses, so that an onlooker could have slid a pocket bible into the spaces between them. The latter danced closer, pressing in with every back step, both their arms on their partners' shoulders: the men kept their hands spread across the tops of their ladies' buttocks.

At midnight, Mulrenan quietened the music and played soft, cocktail hour melodies in slow tempo. The wives and husbands departed in their rickshaws or cars and the bachelor officers, or those whose wives were in Britain, remained on the dance floor with their escorts or slunk off two by two to their hotel rooms.

When, at one-thirty, Mulrenan ceased playing, there were only five couples left. The men, he assumed, were those who either had nowhere to take their women or were afraid to go with them.

Increasingly throughout the evening, Mulrenan had despised himself for playing for them, the officers and gentlemen of the British Empire, the liberators of the East who were the oppressors and opportunists of the world. He had hoped to pick up on a poker game that night and use his fingers to greater advantage than smoothing out waltzes or thumping out tangos. Yet the new order of Englishmen was not apparently interested in card games. They were, he saw, more interested in straight fornication. Back in India, he thought, it had been degrading enough playing for the summer visitors and all-season residents of Naini Tal but at least that had afforded him the opportunities to reap some

401

gainful revenge over a card table or in the occasional bed of some grass widow or lascivious daughter. Here in Macau, however, with his own position precarious both socially and domestically, he could not afford to run such risks. His circumstances reduced him to expressing his hatred by other, more subtle means.

Over the next fortnight the Bela Vista held five dances, and the reputation of these events soon reached Hong Kong. Each dance exceeded the last in numbers of guests and consequent profits: the manager was able to redecorate the hotel, purchase new linen and have the main structural faults of the building repaired. Mulrenan became known again as a pianist, as he had been before the war.

And it was through his music that he had his sweet revenge against the British. The one thing, Mulrenan knew, which the British could not abide was to look foolish. They were ever prepared to laugh at themselves, but to be laughed at by others brought them feelings of insecurity, the loss of all-important face.

The dances, as they became more crowded, became more riotous. Champagne — the manager had been obliged to send for a huge stock of assorted drink from Hong Kong — was poured down the front of ladies' dresses. Games were played. One night a banana tied to a string was passed through everyone's clothing and then the line was pulled tight. On another occasion someone from a Royal Naval ship at anchor in Hong Kong harbour brought a yard-of-ale glass from the able seamen's mess, and it provided a fine source of frolicsome gaiety.

The Portuguese who attended these dances joined in with the bemused air of Methodists at Mass: the Chinese guests, who came only at the invitation of Europeans, viewed the proceedings with disdainful incredulity. Only the Chinese ladies accompanying the single offficers actually took part in the games: for them, it was another trick to be learnt for future use in a Wanchai bar.

Into this mêlée Mulrenan introduced a new dance. He called it *The Macanese Tango*. He had found, while staying at Manor House, a freemason's handbook belonging to a member of the lodge in Naini Tal, a brother in the Craft having accidentally left it on one of the verandah tables. Much of the book was printed in semi-code but one aspect of the ritual was decipherable — the positions of the feet at various junctures in the ceremonies. And, with this knowledge, Mulrenan devised a series of steps.

At the third of the dances, he stopped the proceedings and chose a partner, the pretty blonde wife of a sub-lieutenant. He led her to the centre of the dance floor and, with everyone's attention on him, commenced to explain the footwork, how to tuck the heels in to the insteps, how to swivel on one toe and hold their hands in certain gestures. He informed the gathering that the finger signs were borrowed from ancient Chinese dances.

Returning to the piano, he struck up the chords and played the first few bars for the sub-lieutenant and his wife. They cavorted and stumbled, laughed and shouted and waved others onto the floor. Soon, Mulrenan had fifty couples falling over themselves, those who were worse for drink persevering all the harder to get the steps correct. Everyone enjoyed themselves, but Mulrenan's satisfaction came when he overheard two of the waiters quietly talking by the piano about the undignified, pathetic *gweilos*. They might not know how ridiculous they were, but he did.

The sixth dance was to be the last for a while. Other hotels in Macau, not to be outdone, had started their own dances, and the manager of the Bela Vista, having made a handsome profit and re-established the name of the hotel, was prepared to retire from the fray. He was satisfied to have started the trend.

At the sixth and final dance, advertised widely as a gala affair to which fancy dress could be worn, Mulrenan played three sets. The first began at seven-thirty and ended at nine: he then had fifteen minutes off.

As usual, within a quarter of an hour or so of starting, someone bought him a drink. Generally, he was not asked what he would like. The glass or bottle was just placed on the piano by one of the waiters who would then bend close to his ear and let him know who the benefactor was:

Mulrenan, in a few minutes, would turn and smile his supposed thanks.

This evening, however, just before his first set ended, a second drink was put on the piano and the waiter indicated a note pushed under it.

'Dw'ink come man by kumquat,' the waiter informed him.

As he completed the last tune, Mulrenan looked in the direction of the large kumquat bush growing in a pot on the edge of the terrace. The small table beside it was empty but bore a reserved sign. He finished playing *In the Mood* and sipped the drink. It was neat tonic without the gin. He unfolded the square of paper which bore a simple message.

'Sit at the table and wait.'

Curious, Mulrenan carried his tonic water to the table and did as the note ordered.

After a few minutes, a Chinese man approached the table and sat down. He was, Mulrenan guessed, about thirty years old, smartly dressed in a dark beige suit. His light blue shirt was without a crease and his wide, dark brown tie was knotted in the American square style. His hair was trimmed in a western cut and from his breast pocket there protruded a dark brown handkerchief. On the little finger of his left hand he wore a diamond set in yellow gold. Mulrenan, though out of practice, assessed it as at least a six carat gem.

'Mr Mul-renan, good even-ing,' the Chinese said, his almond eyes sharply noting the direction of Mulrenan's gaze. He broke some of his words into their syllables as if taking care to get his pronunciation correct. 'I can tell you are guessing the weight. For your in-form-ation, it is seven point two-five carats. The stone is South African, of course and you will appreci-ate its value.'

There was a slightly nasal twang to the man's voice which gave his words a strange accent.

'Now you are wondering who I am and where I come from. Cali-fornia, perhaps, from China Town in San Fran-cisco?'

'You do have the advantage of me,' Mulrenan admitted. 'And you seem to know a good deal about me.'

'You do not re-ember me, Mista Mu'enan?' He mocked himself with his pidgin English. 'Long time you do bisnis wif me. We do goot. Lo p'oblum.'

'Leung!' Mulrenan exclaimed. He struggled with his memory for the given names. 'Leung Tse-tung! There is no way I could recognise you.'

'Now I am Francis Leung. I have given myself an English name since we last met. It saves me being confused with Mao Tse-tung.'

He smiled mechanically at his own sense of humour.

'I owe you a deal of thanks,' Mulrenan said. 'I would not be here if it was not for you.'

'You are right, I did you some good favours. Made possible your escape to Chung-king — at the beginning, anyway. And gave you the chance to rid your-self of your mistress's half-brother.'

There was no calculation in the man's eyes, no intention of using the information to advantage. This was not an attempt at blackmail.

'So,' Leung continued, 'you are back playing the piano. And this is the last night for you.'

'Not for long. My reputation is growing again. I hope to get a spot in Hong Kong before too long. Or even Manila. There are American bases being set up in Subic Bay, I'm told. Where there's troops there's bars and where there's bars, there's music.'

Leung snapped his fingers and a waiter, who had been attentively watching the table, came smartly over.

'Whisky and soda,' Leung ordered in English, 'and another tonic water for Mr Mulrenan. Put fresh lemon in it.' The waiter left as promptly as he had arrived. 'You are wonder-ing why I am so rude as to not buy you a gin and tonic, so I will ask you some-thing. Can you do without it?'

'Of course.' Mulrenan bridled. 'I'm not a bloody colonial soak . . .'

Leung cut him short.

'That is good. But I have to be sure. I do not want a

partner who, over the war, has found his happiness with a Scottish dist-ilery.'

Partner: the word rang as true as the best bell metal. Here in a former assistant, a procurer of pirate contacts, a professional go-between and a Communist partisan, lay the opportunity for which Mulrenan had been hunting. He was cautious however — no one simply emerged from the past and made an offer without there being some considerable snags.

'What do you mean?'

'And I trust you are not in love with the dragon? Even an occasional pipe blunts the reflexes. I need a man who can keep his head, a man who is a sur-viv-or. Like I think you are and as re-ports coming to me suggest you are.'

'What do you mean?' Mulrenan repeated. 'A partner?'

'Enough of that for now. Tell me: how was India? Do you still hate the British?' It was a rhetorical question. 'But of course you do. I have watched you playing for them.'

The waiter returned with the drinks and set them on the table. Leung paid with a high denomination bill without checking the amount on the chit.

'Are you not staying?' Mulrenan asked. Usually guests settled their bills at the end of the evening.

'No. I did not come here to dance. Besides, I have no lady with me. I came to see and talk with you.'

Mulrenan raised up his glass. The sides were cold with condensation, the lemon a chrome yellow disc in the candle light, floating under the layer of crushed ice like a reflected sun.

'You mean,' he said, 'you came to see me for yourself as you can only trust reports so far.'

Leung chuckled briefly. Again, when he laughed, his eyes remaining unmoved by emotion.

'That is true and proves to me you are as alert as you were in our earlier . . . trading days. Since then, as you can tell,' he cast a quick glance downwards over his suit, 'I have changed.'

'You have certainly improved your English. When we last met . . .'

'English was "lo ploblum". . . . but by the end of the war, I had gathered some money and so I travelled to San Francisco. Then to Los Angeles. There I was able to learn English whilst working for some of my — friends.'

Mulrenan could readily guess who the friends were: Los Angeles and San Francisco had small but elite Chinese criminal fraternities into which a young and impressionable but experienced member of the same trade guild would quickly fit.

'I have learnt many things in America but I also learnt many things from you. It was you who started my education and you were a good junior grade teacher. When I was introduced to you by Mr Fong that day in the restaurant I was only a messenger boy — not even that — for a man I had never met.'

'Kao Lee-sung?'

'Precisely! But do not mention him now. He is not . . . I'm sure you under-stand.'

Mulrenan did: it was the nature of warlords and barons, leaders of secret societies and gangs, to rise in power and be quickly removed from office, usually with a narrow shiv between the shoulder-blades, or a bullet in a dark street, or a length of piano wire around the throat. A few were afforded honourable deaths by the short sword. One day, it would be Leung's turn.

'It was Mr Fong who set me on the road but it was you who drove me forward, taught me much of how to deal with people. All you did not teach me was your language.' He lifted his glass but held it in mid-air, not putting it to his lips. 'You mentioned you owed me thanks. You do and I accept them with much grate-ful-ness. But I also owed you, so I helped you to pass safely through Hong Kong. Now we are equal and I come to you as an equal with a proposition. But later. I do not want to speak of that here.'

As he looked around to emphasise his point, Mulrenan realised more than a quarter of an hour must have passed. Leung noticed him glance at his empty wrist.

'Soon, you will be able to have another good watch. Another Rolex, perhaps? You will not need to win this from a British soldier, either. I expect you had to sell it in India?'

'Yes, I did.'

The memory rankled for he had been obliged to part with it, for a paltry fifteen pounds, to a Squadron Leader in Lucknow.

'It was secondhand,' Leung said, dismissively, 'and you surely deserve better. But, of course, there was the joy of obtaining it.'

'What time is it?' Mulrenan asked. 'Not having the Rolex . . .'

'Do not worry. You will not be in trouble for failing to return to the piano. We have finished our talk, I think. I will be in touch. You will hear from me.'

He left the table and walked around the side of the hotel, leaving by way of the tradesman's gate.

For the remainder of the evening and well in to the early hours, although Mulrenan played through his repertoire he gave the music little thought. He was noticing with what new deference, even reverence, the waiters treated him. Where as they had previously joked and talked with him, practising their English, now they served him as an honoured guest. The change of attitude had been immediate.

7

At eleven the next morning, Mulrenan returned to the hotel to collect his night's earnings. The manager ushered him into the office where he announced he was giving Mulrenan a bonus for not only making the music but also for initiating the dances. The bonus, Mulrenan discovered on looking into the envelope, was the equivalent of double his agreed nightly wage.

'I really don't know what to say,' he said, suspecting Francis Leung might be the instigator of this exhibition of generosity.

'Say nothing,' the manager told him. 'You had a very good idea and we have all benefitted. Now, will you join me in a cocktail?'

They sat together on the balcony. From a window upstairs came the chanting of a European civil servant language student revising his tables of final sounds.

'. . .ik, im — no, dammit! — *ee*m, in, ing, ip, it. iu, o, oh, oi, ok, om — no, ohm as in *home* . . .'

'The canticle of the future,' Mulrenan said.

'I'm sorry?'

'The sound of the future: now they are all learning Cantonese. It is the new desire to conquer. The Japanese are beaten. That was easy. In a war, things are black and white. The man in the other uniform, shouting orders you do not understand and with a gun, is the enemy. He is obvious and you kill him. These invaders are very different. They wear no uniform — or if they do they'll get you wearing it, too — and they speak the local language. They are far harder to get rid of.'

The manager understood now.

'We Portuguese . . .' he began.

'Yes, you too, to some extent. You tried to corrupt China with religion but that scheme was born of sixteenth century ignorance or bigotry, not greed. You wanted trade of course, and you got it — but not at the cost of ruining a civilisation. The Spanish, on the other hand, the conquistadores of South America — they were like the British. They eradicated a culture by the sword, by disease and with their god.'

'You are a strange man, Mr Mulrenan. If you so dislike the British, why do you stay here?'

'I am trapped,' Mulrenan replied. 'I cannot get out because the East is my home now. When I first came out, nearly ten years ago, it was on a short contract to The Peninsula Hotel. A one-year guarantee with a promise to renew for a further year if both parties were agreeable. I played well and they were pleased. I accepted the second year. But I began to put down roots. I met a young lady — whom I think you know about? — and set up in my own

409

business. By the time my piano playing contract expired. I was tied. Then the war came . . .'

'Did you not leave Macau and escape to India?'

Mulrenan nodded.

'Then why did you return? From India you could easily have gone back to your homeland.'

'I did not have enough money. My business affairs in India were not a success,' he admitted.

'Perhaps,' the manager suggested, 'you did not want to be with your own people again.'

Mulrenan made no answer. He gazed across the brown, silt-laden sea towards the islands of Taipa and Coloane. The Hong Kong ferry was vanishing over the horizon trailing a smut of smoke. A junk with its three sails full of wind moved rapidly by.

'It is not so bad living in the East,' the manager continued. 'My family have lived here for nearly two hundred years. I myself have never been to Lisbon: indeed, the farthest west I have been is our colony of Goa. In India,' he added, as if searching for a bond with Mulrenan. 'We have a good existence here, are accepted by the Chinese and have accepted or even adopted their way of life. It does not matter where in the world one lives if one is happy.'

The smudge of smoke was dissolved by the sky and the junk altered course to round Barra Point.

'Have you ever had your fortune told?' Mulrenan enquired.

'Often. It is one of the Chinese habits I personally have held to.'

'How?'

'How?' For a moment the other man was perplexed. 'There are several methods. Palmistry is usually very accurate. Reading the lines of the face. Sometimes the shaken sticks are very good, too. And the tortoise shell and the three coins. Have you seen that done?'

Mulrenan ignored the question. 'Have you ever used the birds?'

'Yes, if you mean the white finch.'

'I do. But consider that bird: it lives in a cage barely big enough for it to flap its wings. Once in a while, the cage door opens and the bird hops out, removes one card from a fan of the things and, after receiving a grain to eat, hops back into its cage. That is its life. It never ignores the cards and flies off. It just obeys its master. Its destiny is set. Until it dies, it will chose cards, eat grain and live in a cage.'

The junk was out of sight. In its place thumped a small coal-fired coaster, its decks laden with piles of bound bamboo cane. The din of its antiquated engine vibrated across the sea.

'I feel like that bird, caged by its master. Like a god, he controls its future. He could kill it if he wanted to.'

'But he would not,' observed the manager, 'for to do that would be to lose his earnings. Besides all living things are inter' — he sought for the word but could not find it — 'need each other.'

'In whose hand is the bird's fate?'

'That of the master of the fortune teller.'

'I believe,' Mulrenan told him, 'that the bird's fate is in its own control. When the cage door next opens, it should ignore the cards and fly off.'

'Then, if you are like the bird,' asked the manager, 'why do you not fly off when the cage opens?'

'My cage never opens.'

'Surely your cage opened in the war.'

Mulrenan again made no answer: the coaster sounded its horn to clear a sampan from its course.

'You have money,' the manager reminded him. 'In your pocket is enough for you to leave Macau. On the ferry, by the new seaplane service — on one of those small ships.' He pointed to the coaster: from the belched gouts of sooty steam it might have been a railway locomotive rather than a vessel. 'There is nothing to stop you.'

'I'm not trapped just in Macau,' Mulrenan said. 'Perhaps I'm held in more than one cage. Like those stone boxes within other boxes people buy as curios. It is difficult to give up what is familiar, what is one's self.'

The manager was thoughful for a moment before commenting, 'We are all like those Chinese finches. We all have cages.'

8

'You'll have to be most careful,' Alice told Mulrenan on hearing of his meeting with Leung. 'He is a powerful man now, not a runner for you. His dealings are not with small-time pirates from Swatow.'

Mulrenan listened to her with growing impatience.

'But Leung knows he owes me a favour for old time's sake,' he said, adjusting the truth. 'He actually told me so. And he had a partnership in mind.'

'By powerful,' Alice continued, stopping sewing a tear in one of Alec Sean's shirts, 'I also mean dangerous. He is an important man . . .'

'I know!' Mulrenan's exasperation was increasing.

' . . .and not in circles you will want to move in. He is said to be a leading member of the Wo clan of the Black Societies, the Hak Sha Ui. They made much money in the war by operating brothels for Japanese officers in Hong Kong. Leung Tse-tung, now called Francis, is a 415 officer, White Paper Fan. This position gives him financial control of his society. Only Second and First Route Marshalls are higher than he is. Soon he will be a Mountain Lord for he is ambitious.'

Mulrenan was taken aback by Alice's knowledge of the structure of the criminal secret societies.

'Of course, I am not sure of my facts. I can only say what I have heard,' she continued.

'From whom?'

'From people,' she answered non-commitally. 'But it suggests you must be careful. He will use you. You will not be a real partner. The societies are for Chinese only. No foreigner may join.'

'You can leave my affairs to me.' Mulrenan lost his temper. 'You didn't involve yourself with them before and you need not now. If I get any gemstones,' he added sarcastically, 'I'll be sure to ask your advice as to their quality and marketability.'

'You will not be able to sell them in Macau. In Hong Kong, maybe. There are people who will buy gems in Kennedy Town. And, of course, in Kowloon City.'

She returned her attention to her sewing. His anger no longer scared or worried her. She had known, as soon as she received his cable, that there would come a moment when she would press him to the limits of his patience, and that moment would be yet another test for her. She was not certain she could stand up to him.

There was a scrabbling on the door and a small voice begged to be let in.

'Mkoi nei hoi moon pei ngoh yap lai.'

Alice put down her sewing, balancing the garment on the arm of her chair and going to open the door. Alec came in holding a very battered, off-gold-coloured teddy bear. Its nose was squashed flat with its face and the black boot-button eyes wandered as if the toy suffered from acute astigmatism. One of its ears was loose and the joints of the limbs were without stiffening so the arms swung insanely.

'Ho yee lat ke,' the boy exclaimed, pinching the derelict ear with his fingers.

Alice smiled at him and said, 'Yau kui hai nu shue. And now we talk in English for your father. His Cantonese is not as good as yours.'

'Yes, mama,' he replied haltingly. He spoke her nickname as if he had learnt it from a mechanical doll: both syllables sounded alike and pitched flat.

Mulrenan held out his hand.

'Come to me.'

The child began to edge towards its father but looked to its mother for support or approval. She waved him on with the back of her hand and resumed her needlework: yet she did not once take her attention from her son.

'In a few weeks, do you know what is coming to Macau?' Mulrenan asked.

After a pause, the boy shook his head.

'A circus.'

The word meant nothing to the child but he did not ask the meaning. Instead, he twisted his head over his shoulder.

'Your father will tell you,' Alice said.

'It is a huge tent — like a godown made of canvas — and in it are animals and funny men called clowns and people who ride on the air on ropes.'

'What ani-muls?' the boy enquired.

'Elephants and horses and seals and lions . . .'

'Tigers?' the boy interrupted hopefully.

'Sometimes.'

'We go?'

'Are we going?' Alice corrected him.

'Yes. We are,' Mulrenan said. 'All three of us. It is called the Kamala Circus and the ringmaster is a man called Mr Moskevitch. He is coming to Macau next week to find a place to pitch the big tent.'

'What is ring-master?'

'The ringmaster is the manager of the circus. He stands with all the animals and people and commands them. He wears a red coat and black trousers and a tall hat. Would you like to go?'

'I would like to go,' the boy answered, transposing the words as he would in exercises from a textbook.

9

Mulrenan woke late. Alec Sean had left for school and it was arranged he should visit the home of one of his friends when the afternoon session ended. Alice was back at her teaching job and likely to return late because the children were sitting examinations. Ah Shun was doing her shopping and the round of her cronies as all amahs did in the mornings, gathering in groups at the markets or in the streets, their sleeked hair pulled into tightly woven buns, the wide sleeves of their white smock-like tops flapping as they gesticulated or tried to drive the incessantly pestering flies away from their heads. Mulrenan had additionally given her the afternoon off as she had expressed a desire to visit one of her friends just over the border with China: she too would not return before the evening.

It was the opportunity for which he had waited ever since returning to the house and which, until now, he had not been able to engineer. He had never been sure how long he would be left alone in the house and therefore he had been unable to conduct a thorough search. Just as Alice had, years before, he systematically began to scour their home.

The hiding places they had shared were either permanently sealed or empty. He gently tapped the walls with a metal spoon, listening for the echo the bowl of the spoon would amplify, but he located only one excavated cavity, behind a skirting board: it had been soundproofed with cloth but the material had crumbled. He lifted selected flooring planks but uncovered only the hatched cases of cockroach eggs or elastic, dirt-laden spiders' webs. He also shifted ceiling timbers but this produced nothing except dried bird droppings and stone dust.

His efforts created a lot of grit and grime and he spent an hour removing all signs of his search. He was scrupulous, lifting carpets to avoid leaving a rim of dust, moving and wiping beneath everything so no ring or stain remained. He even shook the bedding out of the window which caused consternation with the neighbours: European men who employed an amah did not engage themselves with domestic chores.

With the whole of their apartment cleaned and the kitchen cursorily gone over, Mulrenan fixed his attention upon the storeroom door. It was bolted but not padlocked. He pulled the bolt aside. It was rusted and in need of oiling: evidently, it had not been opened for a long while. Inside, as he had half expected, the belongings they had brought from Hong Kong years before were still piled high. He stood before the undisturbed heap and decided nothing could be hidden there. Even the webs hanging from the ceiling were old and abandoned. A crack in the tiny window high up in the wall had allowed rain water to seep in, discolouring the pale plaster with a streak of blue-green mould reminding him of veined cheese.

In the main room upstairs, he sat and brooded. Alice must surely have some assets remaining from their better days. He could not believe she had sold everything. Yet when he seriously considered the situation, he realised she must have: she was still thin, and the war had been over for two and a half years. She and the boy might not live frugally now, but they did not live well by any means. He was constantly reminded he was an additional burden on their small resources: food was not plentiful and Alice darned and repaired their clothing over and over again. She did not smoke. Ah Shun accepted as wages what amounted to no more than pocket money. Soft European soap was used only to wash their bodies, and but once weekly: laundry was done with a coarse soap made locally and sold by a hawker. It was bought in cakes the size of a book and as hard: cutting it into manageable blocks could take up to an hour of sawing with a sharp knife. Crockery and cooking utensils were cleaned with a mixture of sand, charcoal ash and sea water.

If Alice was keeping a bank deposit box or operating a savings account, Mulrenan thought, there would have to be, somewhere in the house, either a key, a pass document or a statement. He therefore set about hunting for it. It was in this process of routing about he found what he had not expected.

One of the two drawers beneath the wardrobe was looser than the other, the runners slick and smooth and the sides worn: the lower edges were dented and chipped. Obviously it was opened and shut more often, but Mulrenan could not work out why for it contained mostly winter clothes. He pulled the drawer free of the cupboard and when the weight of it dropped it into the floor he noticed there were marks in the floorboards corresponding with the regular point of impact.

Beneath the drawer space was a hollow section between

the lower runners and the floor. In this, Mulrenan saw Alice's carved wooden jewel case.

Carefully noting exactly how it was positioned, he removed it and lifted the brass hasp. He had hoped to find her jewellery inside: instead there were her Hong Kong passport, her birth certificate and similar family documents. A bank statement was not amongst them, nor was a key. There was, in the bottom of the box, the pistol he had bought after the murder of Irina Boyd: it was loaded but the brass shell casings were marked with verdigris. The barrel was pitted and the trigger stiff to pull. There was a little money secreted in the box, mostly pre-war sterling notes.

As he replaced the box he caught a glimpse of something white against the interior panelling of the cupboard. Tucked behind the strips along which the drawer ran was a flat cardboard box of the sort in which bespoke tailors packed shirts. It was tied round with a faded red ribbon shot with threads of gold. With infinite care, he slid the ribbon off the box so as to avoid ruffling or weakening the knot.

Inside was a sheaf of the communications he had sent her — the letters, cheap, ill-painted postcards and brief notes. They looked so petty and insignificant held together by a single metal clip. He fleetingly read a few of them: they were trite and shallow. Next to them was an equally small pile of postcards and letters from Alec Cowley, most of them bearing postage stamps from the Malay States. Those, like his own, only bore words for the sake of filling the space: they said nothing and meant less.

Under the two piles of pathetic letters and cards were a number of other papers including letters from London concerning her refugee stipend, from Reeves the consul about her nationality and status, and from the mother superior of the school dealing with her employment. There was a brown envelope with a faded red stain on the reverse: it was full of photographs which Mulrenan ignored.

Also in the box was a hardback notebook. It had a marbled board cover and the cream-coloured pages were richly textured. He opened the book at the first page. It bore an entry for December 23rd, 1941. He read it and flicked through the pages ahead. The book was a diary, some of it written in code and some Chinese calligraphy.

As he thumbed through the pages, he dared not read them: the words at the foot of the first page were sufficient — '*Sean hit me.*'

From the book, as he closed it, fell a single letter. It was contained in a buff envelope of the type used by officials in governments or lawyers in expensive chambers. It had been sealed and bore her name, given as 'Alice Soon — possibly a.k.a Alice Mulrenan', on the front followed by 'care of The British Ambassador, The British Embassy, Macao, China'. Above, on the same line in the paper as the cancellation mark over a Portuguese stamp, was written 'Highly Confidential.' From the spelling Mulrenan wondered if it had been written by a Portuguese. He opened the flap and unfolded the single sheet. It had not: it was signed *G. Doyle. Flt. Sgt. RAF.*

He began to read, instantly absorbed. Unnoticed, a slip of paper that had lain in the notebook, under the letters, floated to the floor and drifted beneath the bed. It was a betting slip, on which were scrawled the words *Miss Macao*, and the odds, *15-1.*

10

His discovery of the diary and Doyle's letter unnerved and unsettled Mulrenan. He was no longer sure, as he had been in their years together, of what thoughts were circulating in Alice's mind. Whenever she was reading a book, or sewing, or listening to programmes beamed from Hong Kong on the old valve radio they had succeeded in buying from the widow of a Chinese merchant, he was unable to tell if she was paying attention or lost in a reverie of her own.

The radio was her favourite morning luxury before she left to teach her classes. She would switch the set on to hear, through the static, the words, 'This is The World Service of the BBC. The time is midnight, Greenwich Mean Time and here is the world news read by . . .' The newscasters varied from day to day, but she knew them all, accepting their slow, well-pronounced diction as an anchoring point for her day. Some of her senior pupils tuned in to the same broadcast and she was able to discuss with them, in English, points raised by the news items.

Any attempts Mulrenan made at conversation when Alice was lost in her thoughts met with failure. She would merely nod at him or mutter, 'Can you wait a moment? I've got to get this button on' or 'Shush! I want to hear the news.' She was never rude but he knew she was deliberately ignoring him.

What galled him most was her apparent lack of interest in his pending deal with Francis Leung. After her initial warning, she had made no further comment and, whenever he sought her opinion or tried to excite her with the possibitilites of the situation, she was quick to steer the talk another way.

Matters came to a head on the morning of the Tuesday he was to meet with Leung. Frustrated by her continuing indifference, Mulrenan confronted Alice.

'Can I have a word with you before you go?' he requested.

She had switched the radio off and was patting sheets of school exercises into neat bundles. The night before, she had been marking pupils's work and had used this as an excuse not to speak with him.

'Of course you can,' she answered lightly. Her smile was as false as if it was shaped in wax. She did not stop what she was doing.

'I want to ask you what is wrong.'

'Nothing,' she said. 'Nothing's wrong. It's as I told you, I have to get used to your company around the house after so long without a man. And I think it would not be right if we . . . Well, I don't want to upset Alec — Sean. It will take him a little time to adjust.'

The involuntary and tiny pause between the two names

419

fuelled his mounting anger. Mulrenan knew she thought of the boy as Alec.

'I have been back a couple of months now,' he replied defensively, 'but it wasn't that I was thinking of. What else is wrong between us?'

'Nothing.'

She had patted all the sheafs of papers into three piles and was counting pencils in a box.

'Can't you pay attention to me for just a few moments?' he asked, his words short and hard.

'I must go. I'll be late and I have to get these papers to Sister Joseph. The news ended at least five minutes ago.'

'Just sit down and talk to me for a moment.' He was struggling to keep control of himself.

'Can't we talk tonight? Or at lunch. I'll be home about one. It'll be an early night, too, as we've no meeting. The exam results are all worked out.'

'No, we can't talk tonight. Because when tonight comes, you'll have another excuse. You'll sew or listen to the music and then go to bed. We never talk.'

'Well, I can't now.' She sounded contrite. 'I'll be late.'

'Sod the school!' He stood up from the table, knocking it violently and slopping the coffee in his cup.

She gave him a withering look and called down the stairs.

'Ah Shun? Master spilt coffee.'

There was a rattling below as the amah rummaged amongst the pans for a dish cloth.

'Never mind Ah Shun!' he said bitterly. 'What about me?'

No sooner had he spoken than he realised how selfish his words must sound: he was losing the battle before she had fired a single shot.

'What about you?'

She carried on checking her pencils, her bundle of crayons, her tobacco tin full of erasers and her box of powdery, brittle sticks of chalk.

'You pay me not the slightest heed,' he accused her. 'I'm less to you than a lodger. I'd wager you had a better relationship with the Kwans who lived here and ran off with our future.'

'I did,' she readily admitted. 'And now I'm going to teach.'

She had a wicker basket in which to carry her school paraphenalia and commenced packing the papers into it.

'What's more important?' Mulrenan's teeth ground and the words came out through rigid lips. 'Us or those bloody children?'

'Us?' She stopped filling the basket. 'Us? You mean yourself, don't you?'

'No.'

'Yes. You aren't going in with Francis Leung for *our* good. You're doing it for yourself. To get back into business, as you term it, to get more money for yourself, to raise your own prestige. Whatever I get out of this will be incidental. We aren't a team, a man and a woman, lovers. We are just two people temporarily united by circumstances. Personal history, if you like.'

She did not raise her voice as he did: she spoke calmly and rationally. But at least she was talking and for that he was thankful.

'Now I must be off,' she said. 'I'll have to get a rickshaw as it is.'

'You'll stay,' he ordered. 'Now we've started talking, you're going to continue.'

'I've nothing to say.'

This annoyed him more than anything else.

'The hell you haven't!' he exploded. 'You've got more bottled up in you than . . .'

No metaphor seemed suitable, and he had not time to find one.

'Yes, I have,' she quickly agreed, 'and it's staying there.'

'Sit down,' he commanded her.

She did not. Instead, she picked up the basket.

'I'm going now.'

He grabbed the basket from her hand and flung it across the room. It hit the wall and the contents tipped out. The pencils and chalk clattered and the carefully ordered exercises slid or fluttered across the floor.

She turned from the disarray of her work.

'You bastard,' she said quietly.

Not once, in all their years together, not even on the occasion of his hitting her, had she uttered such words. They were not only abuse but also a condemnation of all he was and ever had been. Her anger, stored like a treasure for so many years, was about to break out.

'If you want to talk, we will. Just wait a moment.'

She called down the stairs once more to tell Ah Shun not to bother with the spilled coffee but to go to the school and offer her apologies: she would be late. That done, she glowered at Mulrenan and spoke to him as she had always hoped she would one day dare.

'Right,' she began. 'You want to talk. We'll talk. What about?'

'Us,' Mulrenan repeated. 'We're . . .'

'Good. Then we'll talk about us. Or, more correctly, we'll talk about me and you.' She sat down at the table, righting the coffee cup and placing a sheet of foolscap paper over the spillage. 'First, we'll talk about me. I waited here for you, Sean: through the war, through the disease and shortages of food, through the bodies thrown over the hospital wall into the street a hundred yards from here. I raised my son by you. I waited for money to come from you and it didn't. A bit here and there reached me, but — '

'I had nothing to send,' he defended himself. 'I lost my money . . . A deal with the Muslim League fell through . . .'

' . . . Whoever they were. You've not told me.'

'They are a political body seeking their own country. Free of the Hindus, Pakistan, they call it. They needed arms . . .'

'One of the commodities you are an expert in, according to local rumour.'

'Not so expert, I'm afraid. I had to lay out virtually all my money up front. They reneged on me.'

'Reneged?'

'That's right. They cheated me. I should have insisted on guarantees.'

'No doubt these Mulsims were anti-British as well as anti-Hindu,' she said.

422

'Yes, they were.'

'I guessed as much.' She looked him squarely in the face. 'You're selfish and arrrogant, riddled with a hatred even you can't justify. How ironic it was the British who kept me going through the war.' She saw he was confused by this and added, 'Where do you think the money for me to live on came from? Reeves and London. As a British national I was eligible for expatriate assistance. Refugee money. That's where my comfort and support came from — not from an Irishman but an Englishman. All those stupid passports: they did me as much good as Irina's did her. All I needed was the Hong Kong one, the British Commonwealth one.'

'And how do you think I felt? I had your son, I lived with you, I was your concubine, but it was they who kept us alive.

'And let me tell you something else. After you left people started to call on me: remember how very few visitors we had when you were here . . . They asked me to tutor their children, they talked to me. I was invited to their houses. All this wasn't because of some past favour they believed they owed you. None of your big tips and grand gestures paid off. They gave me their help because of the common bond between us of living in bad times. Not just Chinese but Europeans, too. They helped me out of love . . .

'But then, all you live for is hate. Hate for those better than you are, luckier than you are, more handsome and rich and powerful and happier than you are. You are nothing but a volcano of hatred. And what you hate most is yourself — not just the English half — all of you. Anthing you touch is tainted with hate.'

She stopped to draw breath. The sheet of foolscap was saturated with spilled coffee so she peeled it off the table and dropped it into the waste basket where it flopped over the screwed up sheets of her work from the night before. In its place she laid a second oblong of paper.

During her tirade, he made no attempt to interrupt but sat glaring at her, his face white with suppressed rage.

As soon as the new sheet was soaking up the coffee, she **started again.**

'You didn't even tell me Alec was dead. Why not?'

'The authorities would have told you at the time. I didn't want to upset you,' he replied sullenly.

She sensed the undertone of defensiveness, and was pleased. The minute had come, the minute for which she had waited five years.

She dropped her voice and demanded quietly, 'How did Alec die?'

Mulrenan told her of a Japanese ambush, of an exchange of gunfire, how he and the agent had fought back successfully but how Alec Cowley had been shot.

'By a British weapon?'

'No. By a Japanese rifle. He was hit in the chest and the thigh.'

'And the head,' she said in a detached way. 'He was shot in the head by a British bullet. That was yours.'

He opened his mouth to reply to the charge but she did not let him.

'I'll tell you what happened. He was badly wounded and you shot him like a dog, to put him out of his misery. You couldn't be bothered to take him on with you, get him to safety. So you shot him.'

'He was practically dead,' Mulrenan protested. 'I couldn't move him. Neither of us could. If I'd left him he'd have died slowly in the paddyfield . . . And he asked me to look after you. Those were his last words.'

'You haven't done too well then, have you? Hitting me. Killing Alec. Leaving — us — Alec and me — alone . . .'

Her words trailed off and he took a moment to realise the second Alec was their son.

'You can't love,' she went on, quieter now. 'You want and own and think that is love. But that is not you . . . You no more loved me than you did' — she cast her mind back for an appropriate image and found it — 'that Rolex watch. You even got hold of one of Irina's ring stones . . .'

Silence fell between them. There was, he knew, no point in an apology. She would not believe he had purchased the stone weeks after her friend's murder, that he had played no part in her death. If he had not bought that sapphire cut in a distinctive Dutch rose, someone else would have done: yet she would not want to understand now. In the heat of their argument it did not occur to him to consider how she knew of his possession of the gem.

It was quite plain to him their relationship was at an end. An apology would have been to accept the truth of her accusations and he was damned if he would do that: he simply stared at her. Then he decided to hit back.

'Aren't you grateful for everything I've done for you?' he demanded. 'I saved you from whoring, I bought you respectability . . .'

'How dare you!'

She shouted at him and he recoiled from her outburst: Chinese whores were notorious for their temper tantrums but he had never heard her actually scream with fury before.

'You bought me respectability? Never! I've *earned* it, you despicable bastard! I've worked for it week after week, year after year, as a teacher and a mother. You got me out of The Line all right. But why? Philanthropy? You did it because you wanted to possess me just as you wanted money and gold watches.

'Oh! I'm grateful: you can be sure of that. But what a price I've paid for your help!' She calmed and said coolly, 'You can stay here for another month. Until you can get fixed up somewhere, preferably out of Macau. I'll pay for you to get to Hong Kong. I can borrow your fare against my salary.'

'I'll make it on my own,' he said furiously. 'I don't need your help. Once I get this deal fixed with Francis Leung, I'll be all right. I'll be off then.'

'Good!'

She started to reassemble all the jumbled papers, replace the pencils and erasers and chalk. The rubber band holding the crayons had snapped and she wrapped them in a sheet of paper.

Just as she was about to leave, she said to him, 'I'm sorry. Truly, I am. But we have nothing now.'

'No. We haven't. That's for sure.' He put a tinge of the

Irish accent in his words, taunting her with their past happiness. 'I'll not be here when you get back.'

'Very well.'

She went down the steps and out into the bright morning sunlight. She did not feel sad or happy, just empty. He was gone and she would not have to set eyes on him again. As she turned the corner and hailed a rickshaw she realised, not once in their whole argument, had he mentioned their son.

11

The bare bulbs hanging in the shops cast harsh beams and deep shadows across the twilit streets as Mulrenan walked purposefully through the crowds towards the shop and No. 39, Estrada de Coelho do Amaral. During the afternoon, he had packed his bags and moved into a cheap Chinese boarding house at the northern end of Avenida do Conselheiro Ferreira de Almeida.

It was a gloomy, nineteenth century building occupied by the upper echelons of the lowest ranks of Chinese society: company clerks, refugees from the troubles in China living on their last money before having to swallow their pride and accept employment well below their expectations, girls making a part-time living in the match factories by day and offering themselves by night to coolies. There were no rooms as such: the patrons lived in plywood cubicles six feet square and open at the top like those in a public lavatory. Mulrenan was the only European in the place, causing much curiosity and many covert glances.

He was not bothered at having to live like the poor in the Kennedy Town and Western District areas of Hong Kong before the war. It was only a temporary measure, he told himself, and it would do his soul good to be reminded of how the less privileged existed under colonial rule. He could have moved to a Macanese hotel — even the Bela Vista — but decided not to: it was better, he considered, to drop from sight. Once he and Francis Leung had set themselves up, Mulrenan planned to move to Hong Kong, rent a property in the Mid-Levels and live as he had in the days when he had money.

Although in fact he was desperate to succeed as he had once, he would not admit this to himself: in his own mind, he was merely taking life as it came, jumping at opportunities and ducking punches much as he had always done. Undeniably, however, he had lost face. And for a European to be so demeaned in an Oriental setting was unpardonable. Standards had to be maintained.

The shop at Number 39, Estrada de Coelho do Amaral was doing a brisk trade in bolts of cheap cotton. The aroma of newly printed cloth hung in the air, an unpleasant chemical smell which gripped the nostrils. The electric light bulbs swinging in a slight breeze over the stacked rolls of material shifted the shadows at the back of the shelves, inching them forwards and nudging them back.

From across the street, the building appeared to be the last house in Macau suitable as a secret rendezvous. It was on a junction of two main thoroughfares and cyclists, a few motor vehicles, rickshaws and pedestrians passed before it in a blur of activity illuminated by the shops and the single light hanging on wires over the centre of the crossroads. All around, other shops were thronged with evening customers and from overhead came the calls of children, the rattle of mahjong tiles and the hubbub of Chinese family life.

Above the shop was the characteristic balcony of eighteenth century Macanese buildings, a stone balustrade running along its short length and it was protected from above by a wide projecting roof. Two windows and a door gave onto the balcony and from within shone a light diffused by a large clump of thin bamboo growing in a pot. From the roof hung a wicker cage containing two laughing-thrushes trilling in the close evening air.

Drawing the inquisitive attention of two women haggling over a length of cloth, Mulrenan passed through the shop, mounting the stairs to the first floor. He was about to knock on the door facing him when a pretty young Chinese woman opened it, ushering him in. She wore her hair in a loose ponytail tied with a ribbon of the same material as the women were arguing over in the shop below: the sound of bargaining drifted up the stair well.

The room looking out onto the balcony was plainly furnished with scrubbed deal chairs and a table, a bed in one corner and a cupboard in the other by a chest of drawers. There were glasses on the table and several bottles of local beer. Seated on the bed was a Chinese woman of about forty with a thin, angular face. Around the table were five Chinese men: one of them was Francis Leung. As Mulrenan entered, they all ceased speaking.

'Sean,' Leung welcomed him, 'come in, please. Take a seat.

The young woman produced a chair from another room and placed it behind Mulrenan.

'Kwai sing ming a?' asked one of the Chinese, a man with delicate hands but strong arms, wearing a short-sleeved European-style shirt.

Mulrenan gave his name, adding, 'Sin shaang ne?'

Leung interrupted.

'Let me introduce them all to you. You need to know them for you will be working together soon enough.' He turned his gaze upon each man as he spoke. 'This man, who has just asked your name, is Chiu Tok. He is their leader. Next to him is Chiu Cheong. By me here is Wong Yu-man and next to you' — Mulrenan turned to acknowledge him — 'is Chiu Chou. As you may have guessed from their names, with the exception of Mr Wong, they are all of the same clan. Their village in China is called Nam Mun. The lady sitting on the bed is Chiu Min Vo, who is a sister and the young lady behind you is Chiu Ik Chan. This is her home.' Chiu Tok nodded and Mulrenan realised he understood English. 'Now you know all the people, we can go on.'

'Nei hai pin shue chue a?' the leader asked.

'Rua dos Curtidores,' replied Wong Yu-man, giving him Mulrenan's earlier address.

Mulrenan corrected him. 'Avenida do Conselheiro Ferreira de Almeida.'

'Pin kaan uk ne?'

'I know you speak English,' Mulrenan said, 'so can we use that? My Cantonese is not as good as it used to be.'

Chiu Tok laughed and answered with an American accent.

'OK. We talk in En'lish. Why you livin' in Chinese doss-house?'

'I am no longer living with my concubine.'

Putting it so bluntly was an act of catharsis. At the time, he had regretted the break and was momentarily a little afraid of what the future might hold. But now he felt he was free of her, and the future was up to him.

'Good. It is good you are now un-attached,' Leung said. 'Our enter-prise demands a firm sense of direction and no regretful thoughts. You must put yourself to the purpose. If you accept it.'

Chiu Tok opened a bottle of beer by slapping the metal top down on the edge of the table. The contents hissed as the top loosened. Mulrenan was given the bottle first and he poured himself a small amount into a glass before passing it on. It was best to keep a clear head.

Leung recognised the move. 'It is good to see you drink very little. I'm sorry there is no tonic water.'

'What are we doing?'

Chiu Tok turned to the women who were both sitting on the bed and said, 'Nei hui m hui. . .'

They rose together and the pretty one followed the elder out and down the stairs.

'Shaan moon!' Chiu Tok shouted and the younger returned and quietly closed the door.

'Let me give you the background to this meeting,' Leung said formally, speaking as if he was addressing a board of directors.

Mulrenan leaned on the table and pressed his elbows onto the wood, wriggling them to find a smooth area of grain.

'The Chiu clan members — with another who has left

recently, to be replaced by Wong Yu-man — have come up with a very good idea. A quite novel idea, in fact. They came to me to ask if I would carry it out but I told them it was their plan and they should conduct it themselves. However, it required capital so I invested in the scheme to the sum of three thousand Hong Kong. In truth, I bought some rice fields from them for this sum. As co-lateral. I shall take a share of the overall profits from their idea — as you will: you are part of my investment, Sean.'

'The plan is my idea,' Chiu Tok interjected, anxious that credit be given where it was due.

'Quite true,' Leung continued. 'Entirely his. It is based upon the fact Chiu Tok can fly aeroplanes. He learnt this during the war, in Manila. The Americans taught him.'

Mulrenan was no nearer to guessing what their plan might involve. There was no airstrip in Macau and the only aircraft to visit the enclave was the Catalina flying boat which had not long before started a service between Macau and Hong Kong where, being amphibious, it landed on the airfield at Kai Tak.

'At this moment,' Leung said, staring Mulrenan hard in the face, 'I must ask you if you are in with these gentleman — and myself — or not.'

'What is there at the end?' Mulrenan enquired.

Leung grinned and said, 'A million Hong Kong dollars. Perhaps even more. One cannot tell the limit. These men will each earn fifty thousand. That is two hundred thousand to them. The remainder is for me and for you.'

'There must be risks.'

'Yes, there are. Of course. But they are not as great as those you faced escaping from Hong Kong.'

For a minute, there was silence in the room. The Chinese men looked at Mulrenan who, like a true gambler, played the hand dealt him with care. Running his bluff to the limit, he sipped his beer and put the glass down, watching the bubbles meandering through the straw-coloured liquid. He set it exactly in the ring of condensation from which he had lifted it.

'Very well,' he said. 'I shall join you, even though I don't know what I have to do.'

'You have the easiest part.'

Leung rubbed his hand across his brow and Mulrenan noticed the room was so hot because the windows facing the balcony where closed.

'What does it involve?'

'Bringing the gold to me.'

Leung spoke so matter-of-factly it sounded simple, as rowing a sampan under the noses of the Japanese had turned out to be.

'What gold? Where does this gold come from?'

For a moment, Mulrenan was afraid Leung was planning to attack Lobo to steal his bullion. Such a plan would be a suicide mission.

'We are going to be pirates,' Leung said.

'Which ship?'

'The *Miss Macao*,' Leung answered.

Mulrenan wondered if a vessel of that name was likely to be carrying so much bullion. With a local name, it would have to be a small coaster rather than a deep sea cargo ship. But certainly, to hit at Dr Lobo's bullion while it was in transit would be the most sensible way to try such a heist. He asked about the size of the cargo boat.

'It is the wrong question,' Leung informed him. 'The *Miss Macao* is the Catalina flying boat of the Macao Air Transport Company.'

Chiu Tok watched Mulrenan's reaction. The other Chinese, although their English was not good, had followed the gist of the conversation and they too studied his response.

Mulrenan turned from one to the other of the men. He could not disguise his astonishment.

'It's audacious,' he said finally. 'But so much gold? . . .'

'We ca'ch Cat-a-leena on way Heung Kong . . .' began Chiu Cheong.

'I will explain,' Leung interposed. 'This aircraft transports gold. It also takes very rich people who carry gold, too: and they can be held to ransom. It is our plan to capture the aircraft in mid-flight between Macau and Hong

Kong, to have Chiu Tok fly it to a secret place and then to rob the passengers and remove any gold cargo.'

'If you steal gold,' Mulrenan advised, 'there will be only the usual piracy patrols out to catch you. But if you kidnap wealthy people, everyone will be alerted. Aircraft will fly over to find the Catalina. Land forces will search for you without stopping. Rich people have powerful friends. I suggest the passengers be set free.'

'You are correct. If there is too little gold,' Leung decided, 'then we can hold and ransom the passengers. Otherwise, we shall let them go in the mountains on Seong Chau. They will soon be found.'

'And my part in all of this?'

Mulrenan was worried. Robbery was one thing: kidnap and possible murder was another. He was in no way reluctant to steal from Lobo, whose bullion trading he suspected — as did everyone in Macau — was assisted by the British authorities and the banks in Hong Kong through which he handled his transactions. The wealthy Chinese on the aircraft would be similarly connected. To strike at them would be to deal a blow at the same paymasters and power-brokers: the British colonials. There might even be rich British on the aircraft which would give the whole design an even sweeter aspect. Yet a kidnapping — for which, if he was caught, the penalty could be death — was not something to which he was willing to be a party to.

Risking all, he expressed his doubts.

'Is OK,' said Chiu Tok. 'Wong also no like. He no doin' it. He our nawigator.'

'What you do,' Leung instructed Mulrenan, 'is not difficult but most important. We want you to fly as an ordinary passenger to Hong Kong and back in the aircraft. Watch what the pilot and the other members of the crew do. Chiu Tok will tell you what information he wants. Then, on the day of the plan, you travel as a passenger again. You do nothing during the capture of the aircraft. Just pretend you are a passenger with the others. Allow yourself to be treated like them. When the aircraft has landed, you will be taken with the passengers while the others remove the gold.'

For the first time, Leung turned his head to Chiu Tok for agreement and received it.

'When they have the gold, you will be taken away from the passengers to be a hostage messenger. That is what we will tell them. You will bring the gold with Wong Yu-man to me at Tai O on Lan Tau Island. He will receive payment of two hundred thousand dollars and return with it to the others. You and I will go to Hong Kong in a junk and you will be paid for your services. I will purchase for you a sea ticket out of Hong Kong to Honolulu. You will not have your own name, of course. By all of this, you will not be compromised. What do you think?'

Mulrenan instantly agreed and it was arranged he should meet Francis Leung the following day to obtain his expenses for the reconnaissance.

12

Alice readjusted her veil, pushing a hairpin through the lace to secure it. Ah Shun had starched the material and it hung in crisp folds which rubbed her neck. She was reminded, as she stepped over the lintel into the quiet gloom of the church, of the tough-minded English priest and his belief that a clerical collar was a form of holy retribution.

The recollection of the priest caused her to think of the old crone she had visited and the fortune teller with his slivers of wood carved with characters and his white finch with its pink legs and red beak. From the dimness of the past, she remembered quite clearly the woman's advice over encounters with moon moths: 'For some it is a sign of wealth but for you a warning . . . be warned of things that fly and beware of those that glide.'

The sun shone down starkly and the shadow within the doorway was intense and deep and cool.

'They can make you rich,' the old woman had said. 'Even give you sons.'

Indeed, that much had almost come true, she reasoned, just as the fortune teller's prophesy had: she could see him now, dressed in his padded coat against the winds blowing down from central China, his rolled up sleeves and his army boots. He had said she would be a queen — she took that to mean a lady — and there had been much trouble in her life. And she had suffered and had borne a son. She had lost what she had wanted, in Mulrenan, but had gained much in his stead. Within the hour, she believed she would be richer still. And had not the old man warned her of flying creatures, too?

She was no longer afraid of the memory of the priest, or the predictions of the crone and the coolie's prophet: she was convinced the priest had not been flesh but a premonition sent to set her on the road towards this very moment.

In the front pew Sister Joseph from the school was kneeling, her fingers interlocked at her brow. By her side was Sister Maria. Their wimples caught the glow of sunlight from the open door and stood out sharply in the half-light.

The altar was lit by candles. Above it, upon his cross, hung a plaster Christ. His skin was pale and the agony of a man disappointed and betrayed shone in his glass eyes. From the wounds dripped blood as bright as scarlet wax. The crown of thorns upon his head drew beads of redness from his scalp and his beard was matted.

Alice went down on one knee at the centre of the altar and bowed her head, her right hand moving in the outline of the cross. Unused to the action, she gestured broadly, making the sign across her entire body.

The confessional stood in a side aisle off the main nave and she walked around the rear of the pews to reach it. The priest was within his half of the panelled wooden box. She knew he was there for the small rectangle of white card to be placed by the door when he was present was resting in its slot.

She entered the confessional, thinking how like it was to a cage — and yet how it was not built to contain her but her sins. She knelt on the step before the grid of latticed wood to

434

the outer side of which was pinned a thickness of butter muslin.

'Bless me, Father, for I have sinned.'

She could hear the priest breathing loudly and knew it was old Father Ignatius who had given Alice six months' instruction, guiding her towards conversion, and who suffered from asthma when the summer heat grew intense. He muttered something to her in Latin she could not understand.

'This is my first confession,' she said. 'I accuse myself of many sins . . .'

It was so good to be rid of them. The years of whoring for Ethel Morrison, of lying on her back with her legs spread for a taipan or initiating his son in the mysteries of a woman's flesh; the guilt of living from Mulrenan's criminal earnings for which she hoped her subsequent life had partially atoned; her harbouring of hatred for her lover; her bearing a bastard son . . . they were shed and she was glad of it. It was like washing her soul clean of years of grimy life.

She did not have to go into detail. She knew God was aware of her misdemeanours.

As she completed her confession the priest wheezingly coughed, and pressed his mouth nearer to the grid.

'For your penance you must say the first three decades of The Sorrowful Mysteries of The Rosary.'

'Yes, father,' she said, continuing, 'Oh, my God, I am heartily sorry and beg pardon for all my sins. I detest them above all things . . .'

Over her voice, as if she was made of two persons, not one, she could hear Father Ignatius intoning.

'Ego te absolve . . .'

As she spoke she cried, yet she knew not why for she was neither happy nor sad. She was simply somehow new, somehow a very different person.

'. . . in nomine patrii, et fillii, et spiritui sancti . . ,' the priest went on.

Outside the church, in the shade of a tree leaning over a wall and cracking the topmost stones, the two nuns were waiting. As Alice came into the sunshine they ran excitedly to her side like children in the playground of their school.

13

'Why do you need me on the plane?'

Mulrenan had been served a soda without the scotch. The waiter had considerately added a slice of lime to the glass. It collected the gas and released it in batches to the surface.

'To guard my investment,' Leung answered. 'I cannot really trust these men you met yesterday. They are not known to me and are not — I'm sure you know what I mean — brothers of mine. They may be foolish enough to attempt to cheat me. If they did, they would be found and punished, of course. But that would not settle matters and I should have made a loss regardless. You are one of the few people in whom I can put my faith in such an adventure.'

Flattered, Mulrenan replied, 'I'll do my best. I should, however, like some sort of insurance.'

'Naturally,' Leung exclaimed. 'That is taken care of in the briefcase.'

At the side of Mulrenan's chair was a smart leather briefcase with solid brass catches. The key to the locks was on a short chain in his pocket. Attached to one end of the chain was the Chinese character 'sow' — it denoted long life — cast in heavy silver.

'You are booked on this Saturday's five o'clock flight to Kai Tak. The ticket is in your name. That night, you have a room reserved, also in your real name, at The Grand Hotel in Carnarvon Road in Tsim Sha Tsui. You return the next day on the one o'clock flight and you meet with Chiu Tok at eight in the house in which we met last evening.'

'Understood,' Mulrenan said.

'You are not afraid of the dangers?'

'Yes, I'm very afraid of them,' he admitted, 'but they're the price to pay.'

436

'That is indeed so.' Leung parted his hands in agreement. 'All worthwhile gains are expensive.'

Mulrenan nodded. 'I was a gambling man once, as you know only too well. And, like all gamblers, I can assess the odds, those which are too short and those which are worth risking. I think this little game is one I can take a chance upon . . . Besides, once I'm away from Hong Kong I'll be all right. The world is a big place. And I'll grow a beard.'

He'd added this touch of melodrama as a joke but Francis Leung accepted it with gravity, saying, 'I think that is most wise of you. And to speed your escape, I have a seat held on a flight out of Hong Kong three days after our business is done. The ship to Honolulu will take too long and can be recalled to its harbour.'

'So there is a date set?'

'There is. But you are not to be told it yet. All in good time.'

Leung did not drink more than a third of his glass of beer. Mulrenan drank all his soda: the excitement of being back in business made his mouth dry.

'One last thing you should know before I go.' Leung put down his glass. 'Wong is not to be trusted. He is being kept in because it is safer. His landing site for the aircraft is not to be used: Chiu Chou is to guide you somewhere else. From there, you will still bring the gold to me with Wong. But the junk will be mine and, on the way, I want Wong killed. You will have to do that.'

Mulrenan said nothing. He knew he had to accept.

The briefcase contained the insurance he had asked for: six hundred dollars, a return ticket to Hong Kong, a letter of confirmation from the hotel reservations manager — and a .22 revolver with twenty rounds. The serial numbers had been filed from the weapon.

Dressed smartly in his best tropical suit with a white shirt
and a dark tie, all of them recently laundered by a washer
woman living in an alley near his doss-house, Mulrenan
stepped into the airline company's launch at exactly a
quarter to five on Saturday. He stood in the passenger well,
looking forward, out across the harbour.

The Catalina was moored to a buoy in the Porto Exterior,
rocking gently in the slight swell from a five hundred ton
coaster steaming past her stern. On the rear of the aircraft,
just under the tail wing and in front of the rudder, was
painted a Union Jack and this firmed Mulrenan's resolve to
take the plane and its passengers for all that they were
worth. On the side of the fuselage, where it rose from the
water behind the passenger entrance, were painted the
code letters VR-HDT, and below the cockpit was emblazoned a shield, divided into three sectors — the bottom
sector contained four painted waves and was only just
above the actual waterline. Over the device were the letters
MATCO — Macao Air Transport Company.

There were four passengers in addition to Mulrenan: two
were Chinese — a husband and wife — and the others
European men. No one spoke to him. The Chinese couple
were standing apart with a coolie watching over their
luggage: the two Europeans were deep in conversation.

As the passenger launch veered around the nose of the
aircraft and down its seaward side, making towards the
port blister — a bulging window which opened to allow
passenger entry — another, larger launch cast off from the
aircraft. It was grey-hulled and on the deck were three
armed men, their rifles not casually slung over their shoulders but positioned at the hip. The craft had just delivered a
gold shipment for transportation.

A Chinese air hostess welcomed the passengers aboard,

helping them into the aircraft from the bobbing launch. She checked their tickets as she showed them to their places.

Mulrenan took stock of his surroundings.

There were twenty-three single seats in the aircraft, twelve down the starboard side and eleven on the port. Below the entrance blister was a folding seat, and behind both blisters were two further seats. In the centre of the aircraft, above the aisle and below the point where the wings joined the fuselage was a seat for a flight engineer. Beneath the wings, where the wheels folded up when the aircraft was on water, there was a gap in the seating. At the front of the long cabin the cockpit had two seats in it, for pilot and co-pilot. All the passenger seats were placed singly: this, Mulrenan thought, would make Leung's plan much easier. In bigger seaplanes, he remembered, the seating was arranged in pairs so that to leave a window seat meant clambering over a fellow passenger.

Mulrenan looked about, observing the storage lockers and shelves. A small wooden crate bearing wax seals was tied to the rear bulkhead.

'Good afternoon, ladies and gentlemen.' The hostess addressed them in perfect English just tainted by an Australian accent. 'Welcome aboard our flight to Hong Kong. For those who have not flown with us before, our journey will take approximately twenty minutes. We shall be flying to the north of Lan Tau Island, change course over Tsing Yi island and land at Kai Tak in Kowloon. We shall take off in just a few minutes.'

As if at her command, the engines coughed, turned over, fired and howled into life, the aircraft beginning to move very slowly forwards in the water.

The tone of the two engines changed to a deep-bellied roar and the aircraft surged forward, spray blurring the window by Mulrenan's head. He could feel the aircraft heavy with its contact on the sea: then the wings wobbled and the aircraft lifted onto the step of its boat-shaped hull. In a moment, they were airborne: the spume died and the water on the window by Mulrenan's head drifted away in ripples. Below, he could make out houses and the fortress on Colina de Mong Ha.

The aircraft tilted to starboard and the hill and buildings vanished under the aircraft as Ilha Verde drew closer. The pilot climbed to three thousand feet and Mulrenan had a clear view, in the late afternoon sunlight, right up the western coastline of the Pearl River estuary. A blunt peninsula jutted out towards a group of three islands, the largest of which he recalled sailing past at night on a number of occasions, on journeys not altogether unlike his present one: they had been business, too.

The sea was ochreous with mud-laden river water as they steered a direct course on an east-north-easterly bearing. Within a matter of minutes, Mulrenan caught his first sight of Castle Peak and, peering across the cabin and through the opposite window over seat number two — he had memorised the numbering pattern — he could plainly see the mountains of Lan Tau with streaks of shadow cast by the dipping sun on the ridges. He could not help thinking how, in a few weeks at the very most, he would be down among those wooded hills with a million dollars' worth of gold. Or more.

The first officer lowered the landing gear while the Catalina was flying over Tsing Yi island, south of Tai Mo Shan, the highest of Hong Kong's mountains. The aircraft began its descent, flying over Lai Chi Kok and Kowloon Tong. Mulrenan tried to spot the house in which he, as an enforced guest of the Portuguese Chinese families to whom he had been tempted to lie about their loved ones, had hidden during the war, but he could not: new roads had been built which upset his sense of direction.

He caught a taxi from Kai Tak and spent the night in the Grand Hotel, seated at the writing desk in his room and listening to the incessant banter rising from the rickshaw stand in the street below his window. He did not venture into the streets, deeming it best not to be seen by anyone who might recognise him. The following morning, he returned in a taxi to the airport and flew back to Macau along the same route. In his briefcase were his detailed notes of everything he had studied in the aircraft.

15

After Chiu Tok had gone over the notes, he requested of Mulrenan some definite points of information: how were the seats allocated? Where did the stewardess sit? What speed did the pilot maintain for cruising? Where did he make course corrections, if any? He wrote out a long list and Mulrenan once again booked a flight for Hong Kong on the morning of the following Saturday.

He spent the week either in his cubicle at the boarding house or in a tea-house or hotel bar. On several occasions, he visited the Bela Vista at midday, chatted with the manager and was asked to play the piano in the hotel dining room for tiffin on the Thursday. He obliged because he was grateful for his earlier employment, because he wanted Alice to hear that he was still in Macau and enjoying himself, and because it was best to keep in with those whom one might need again — although he sincerely hoped he would never again set foot in Macau, Hong Kong or any other part of the benighted East.

At no time did he feel he wanted to see Alice or his son. Even when he noticed preparations being made on an area of waste land near Colina da Guia for the arrival of the circus he did not regret his actions. They were moves in the past just as Alice and her son were now people of the past. The future loomed ahead, glistening with opportunity.

As he sat in the tea-house or lay on his narrow bed, reading the Hong Kong newspapers, he wondered what he might do with the money. Only a minimum cut of the proceeds would be a quarter of a million Hong Kong dollars. With that kind of money . . . He worked out that such a basic sum would be the equivalent of twenty thousand pounds sterling. If he went to America, he could set up his own night club in Los Angeles or New York. With his knowledge of gemstones, he could start a dealing business or a jewellery concern. He could even return to Ireland and buy a small farm, a bar in Dublin or a modest country house where he could live on his investments.

The dream of going to Ireland set his thoughts in another direction. With so much money, he could not only live comfortably but could also afford to be generous. If he was to make even more than the quarter of a million, greater possibilities opened before him.

Sitting in the bar of the Central Hotel, a small beer on the glass-topped table before him and a folded copy of the *South China Morning Post* on his lap, he decided he would give ten per cent of whatever he arrived in Eire with to the Republican cause. His Irish father would have approved, his English mother would not: his grandfather would have rejoiced.

As he pledged the donation in his mind, Mulrenan was prompted to consider what he had done so far for his country. The answer, he concluded, was precious little. He had harrassed expatriate Britishers, cheated them, belittled them, and profited from them but all this was to his own ends rather than to those of mother Ireland. Now, he decided, it was time he acted for her as well as himself.

He unfolded the newspaper. It would not be long, he considered, scanning the headlines, before his actions with the Chiu clansmen and Wong Yu-man would be printed in hard black headlines across this paper's front page. The mid-air piracy of an aircrraft loaded with gold and immensely wealthy passengers — that would make the bloody British authorities sit up and take notice. It was in fact a shame that he must feature merely as a missing passenger, rather than one of the perpetrators.

Specifically paying attention to Chiu Tok's newly-posed questions, Mulrenan flew in to Kai Tak on the mid-morning flight from Macau on July 10: he had his return ticket booked for the 4.00pm flight.

The hostess recognised him as being a recent passenger and gave him an added welcome as he climbed from the launch into the perspex blister.

'Good morning, sir,' she greeted him. 'I'm glad to see you on *Miss Macao* again.'

'Thank you. After my last trip, I vowed this was the way to go. Most exciting! I'd not flown before. It really is very exhilarating.'

'Then I hope today's flight will be as enjoyable.'

She attended to another passenger, an elderly Chinese woman who bore on her right hand a diamond ring Mulrenan guessed was at least three carats in weight. He hoped she would be booked again on the final trip he planned to make on this aircraft — which journey was certain to be *most* exciting.

The aircraft took off on time at ten o'clock and by a quarter to eleven, Mulrenan was seated in a taxi driving down Nathan Road, past the Alhambra Cinema, the Nathan Road Barracks and St Andrew's Church towards the Star Ferry. He had five hours to fill and had decided on the flight just what he would do.

His last ferry crossing of Hong Kong harbour had been on the lower deck with his hand stinking of his own excrement and with a fortune in gold and gemstones slid up his anus. This time, as he went on board, he wondered if this was the very same vessel. Now he was on the upper deck, just as he had been in the old days, carrying a briefcase. Ironically, he was immeasurably poorer than he had been as a Chinese peasant — but, he told himself, not for long.

The lions in front of the Hongkong Bank headquarters building had been removed during the war and transported to Japan in order to be melted down into bullets. Such a use for the bronze would, in Mulrenan's opinion, have been not only a fitting irony but a just dessert. However, they had in fact escaped the furnace and been reinstated, but were not now in such good condition as they had entered the war: the shrapnel scars of captivity had scored deeply into the metal and riccocheting bullets had marked them.

Mulrenan stood by the bank's entrance as he had in the pre-war years. It was not long before a young coolie, dressed in tattered shorts and wearing a shallow-brimmed conical rattan hat, upon which were painted Chinese characters in red, paused before the left-hand lion and stroked its front paw, running his fingers over the spread toes and down the sheathed claws. When the coolie had departed, Mulrenan strolled over to the lion and discreetly repeated the poor man's movements. For the coolie, it merely expressed general hope; for Mulrenan it was an act precisely directed towards his coming enterprise.

The Peninsula Hotel was encased in a complex latticework of bamboo scaffolding upon which swarmed an antlike battalion of workers engaged in removing the last of the camouflage paint applied to the building during the war and cleaning the stonework: quite why anyone had bothered to attempt to conceal it was beyond imagining. It was the largest building in Kowloon, prominently situated near to the Star Ferry pier, the general post office, the railway station and the end of Nathan Road: any bomber pilot required to hit it or use it as a beacon to mark other targets would have had no problem. His bomb aimer or observer could have picked it out by its shadow alone.

With easy strides, Mulrenan walked round the pavement on the sweeping curve of the short drive to the main entrance. As he ascended the six steps and passed between the two lamp standards with their spherical white shades, for all the world looking like inverted pawnbroker's signs, a calmness borne of great satisfaction came upon him. The first time he had entered those doors he had been a servant of the mangement. Now, on the last occasion, he could play the respected guest. One of the bellboys, in a white uniform and pork-pie hat, opened the golden door for him, thereby completing Mulrenan's delight.

The lobby was little changed. The chandeliers still hung from the ceiling and a multitude of bulbs glittered in the crystal: the fans hummed and spun. The floor had been recently carpeted and the walls redecorated.

Mulrenan strode purposefully towards the main staircase and climbed floor by floor through the hotel: his progress was almost majestic. He could have used the lift but it would have been too rapid for him, too impersonal.

He wanted to rise through the building slowly, feel it around him.

Arriving on the sixth floor on which The Rose Room was situated, he found his sense of triumph deflated.

It had been his intention to take tiffin in the room where formerly he had been a mere piano hack, watching the British wine and dine, connive and rule. His plan was to have sat near the dais and listened to some Filipino or Chinese attempting to play the latest tunes, smiling obsequiously over his shoulder as he received a drink or acknowledged a request.

He was hugely disappointed. The Rose Room was no more. The blue ceiling remained in need of a coat of paint, but the polished floor was badly scuffed and the windows were hidden by a series of fibreboard partitions off a central alleyway dividing the former restaurant and dancefloor into makeshift bedrooms. Overhead, at the far end of the alleyway, rode the stucco charioteers, their muscles and steeds outlined with dust: from somewhere in this warren Mulrenan could clearly hear someone snoring stertorously.

The door of one of the temporary rooms opened and a man came out. He was wearing a white uniform with epaulettes and a peaked cap upon which was a gold braid badge. In one hand was a clipboard filled with stiff sheets of paper which rustled against his shirt as he tucked them under his arm: in the other was a small suitcase more appropriate to a woman.

'Can I help you?' he enquired as he drew level with Mulrenan.

'This used to be The Rose Room.'

'Yes, I believe it did.'

'What's happened to it?'

'Shortage of accommodation, I suppose. This floor's quarters for BOAC flight crews and station staff.'

Disheartened, Mulrenan descended in the lift. He would go to the Moorish Bar and have a drink: but that, too, had gone. It was now a passenger assembly desk for those flying to Europe — over where the bar had been was a discreet sign with the words 'British Overseas Airways Corporation' and a blue symbol representing a bird. On the desk was a framed photograph of the flying boat used on the UK-Far East service. From a rack, Mulrenan took a timetable card and slipped it into his briefcase.

Having to make do with the lobby, Mulrenan settled himself in a chair and ordered a gin and tonic. For once, he reasoned, he was out of range of Leung's spies and he could hardly order a tonic on its own in The Pen.

The hotel was doing good business. Cars arrived with impressive regularity at the entrance, tourists and passengers in transit checked in or settled their bills and departed. Two liners lying alongside Kowloon Docks were providing the hotel with a lucrative passing trade.

He sat watching the wealthy come and go, remembering when he had not only played for them but had mixed with them as an equal and on his own terms. Those times, he was certain, would come again.

A commotion started at one end of the lobby. A tourist was complaining in a penetrating voice about the sandwiches served with his beer. The lobby manager was called but the tourist was not to be so easily consoled: he wanted to have words with *the* manager. Soon after his demand had been made the general manager arrived in person, escorted by two deputies, one European and one Chinese. The tourist was placated and Mulrenan, watching the skilful handling of the trouble, realised that the general manager was none other than Leo Gaddi, whom he had known as a Swiss chef in The Hongkong Hotel. He looked taller in a pinstripe suit and his hair was receding, but he still had the bearing of a military man and wore a thin moustache. During the war years he had been a Third National as had Mulrenan: but whereas the Irishman had used the war for his own benefit, Gaddi had worked as a volunteer cook in the Red Cross centre. As the general manager walked briskly away from the tourist, he pointed to a vase of flowers: immediately, one of his lieutenants summoned a waiter who lifted the offending ornament and wiped the ring of water from the base.

Mulrenan was in two minds whether or not to introduce

himself but caution dictated he stay silent: in a few weeks at the most, he might have to check in with the BOAC clerk and then he'd be using an assumed name.

As he left the hotel to hail a taxi for Kai Tak, Mulrenan paused by the reservations desk, making sure before he did so that Joseph Collins was not in sight. Probably, he thought, the reception clerk was long dead, a casualty of the Japanese occupation. He asked for and was given a room tariff folder. It was a cheap but adequate souvenir.

While he was waiting to embark once more upon the *Miss Macao*, Mulrenan was treated to the display of one of the huge intercontinental flying boats landing in Kowloon Bay. It flew in through Lei Yue Mun and gradually dropped to the sea until it seemed as if it was hovering: then, suddenly, a huge cloud of spray erupted from both sides of the aircraft and the engines screamed within their aluminium cowlings. The aircraft slowed and moved round, making headway towards its mooring. Through the square windows set in the silver body of the aircraft, Mulrenan could see tiny pink faces eagerly surveying the shore. Upon the tail fin was the Union Jack.

16

The classroom was crowded with pupils and parents. On the desks, on the rickety tables that lined the walls and strewn across Alice's desk on its low dais, were exercise books, textbooks, novels and poetry books, sheets of music and folders of work. Upon the notice board and tacked to the panelling were paintings, drawings, maps and a frieze made of scraps of cloth and paper glued to squares of cardboard, depicting the history of Macau.

'If anyone turns over a section of the frieze,' Alice said quietly to Sister Catherine, her words barely audible over the hubbub, 'they'll be in for a shock.'

'What have you been up to this time?' the nun asked, a hint of mischief in her voice.

'That bit by the door,' she confided, 'with the routing of the Dutch in 1622 . . .'

'The gruesome bit with the African slaves cutting off the heads of the retreating men?'

'Yes,' Alice confirmed. 'That was drawn by Maria Marques.'

'Which explains a lot!' exclaimed Sister Catherine. 'But what about the backing?'

'Johnny Walker,' Alice answered.

Sister Catherine gave Alice a look of incomprehension.

'It's from a cardboard box full of whisky bottles,' Alice explained.

'I see. Well, if anyone asks, say you found it in the refectory . . . Or you were given it by one of— yes!' She was delighted at the thought. 'Instead, say you were given it by one of the Jesuit fathers.'

'You're as bad as I am,' Alice mocked her.

The nun winked. 'Perhaps.' She paused, grew serious. 'Yet I wish in meditation sometimes that I was as good as you, too.'

'Miss Soon?'

A parent had approached the two teachers, sparing Alice the need to answer Sister Catherine. He was a gaunt Chinese with high cheekbones wearing a European suit which was very much the worse for wear and evidently causing him discomfort. He would plainly have been more at ease in a traditional jacket and baggy trousers.

'Good evening,' Alice greeted him in English, opening her register. 'Welcome to our classroom. May I have your child's name, please?'

'I am Mr Ling.' He gave a slight bow, his hands together by the buckle of the belt that was holding in tucks of superfluous waistband. 'My daughter is May Ling.'

Alice ticked off the pupil's name with her red crayon.

'I am pleased to say that May is progressing very well,' Alice began. 'Her English is improving and her mathematics have reached a very high standard indeed, Already, she is on Book 4 . . .'

'Excuse me, Miss Soon,' the parent interrupted her. 'I know of my daughter's studies. She is working hard.'

He seemed on edge and Alice, assuming he might have a complaint, politely asked him for it.

'No. I have no bad things to say. Only that my wife and I are very grateful to you' — he paused, unsure how to continue — 'for your unnecessary kindness.'

'I don't understand, Mr Ling,' Alice said perplexed.

'We have no sons and so must look in our old age to our daughters. One of them is not so good, but May is not like her . . . We are grateful to you for spending so much time on a daughter.'

A mere daughter, Alice thought. She sighed. Society would have to change. The reliance on sons would have to end. Already the binding of feet, the system of *muitsai* girl slavery, the murder of unwanted girl children, the keeping of concubines — all these were ended or on the decline. Times would be different, she hoped, for all their sakes. And for her own, too.

'It is my job to teach your daughter,' she explained. 'I do nothing for her I do not do for all my students. No one is special.'

Mr Ling made no reply. Instead, he bowed again and made his way through the throng of people by the frieze who were gazing at the vividly beheaded Dutch sailors. Alice watched him go and, as she did so, saw one of the parents start to turn the cardboard section over.

As the last parents were leaving, the mother superior summoned Alice to her cramped office near the main entrance to the school.

'Do sit down, Alice,' she said, indicating a chair by the side of her desk rather than the one in front of it. 'How has your first full parents' evening gone?'

'Well, I think.' Alice sat, neatly, balancing her register on her knees.

'I have had a few parents come to me about your classroom.' The mother superior's voice was somewhat stern. 'I think a number of them were at a loss as to what to make of your music and art lessons.'

'I'm afraid I'm not sure what you mean,' Alice replied defensively.

'Mr da Silva Mendes,' the mother superior said, 'commented upon the fact that your music sheets included a lesson on the rhythms of' — she glanced at a note before her on a leather-rimmed blotter, squinting at her own writing — 'ragtime. Could you explain this?'

'I believe,' Alice began, 'that our pupils should be acquainted with all forms of artistic expression. I agree that ragtime is perhaps —'

'Yes, yes!' the elderly nun interjected. 'We must press forward the bounds of learning.' To lend emphasis to her agreement her hands, resting on the blotter, pushed the paper into a ruck. 'What I want to know is — what is ragtime? I've never heard of it.'

'Jazz,' Alice informed her. 'This is a form often played on a piano. Or with a small band.' She wondered if her employer would understand the meaning of *band* in that context and added, 'Of musicians.'

'Can you play it?'

'A little.'

'I should like you to do so at some time,' the mother superior said. 'Now, on to the subject of your class project — the frieze. Many parents commented to me on the imaginative way in which you have taught your girls the history of Macau. I don't think that has been tried before. However,' she again peered at the paper before her, 'I should like to know where you obtained so much excellent cardboard. It is, to say the least, in short supply. We could gladly use some more. What is not taken as fuel . . .'

'I can explain,' Alice said. 'Some I obtained from the shopkeeper beneath my home and some' — she hesitated — 'some was given to me by the Jesuit fathers.'

'What does your shopkeeper sell?'

'Shoes. He is a shoemaker.'

'I see,' answered the mother superior. From her tone of voice Alice could tell she was puzzling over the matter. Alice rose discreetly to go.

As she turned the door handle, the mother superior

asked, 'Did you talk to Mr Ling?'

'Yes. I did.'

'He gave us twenty-three patacas as a donation.' It was a comparatively small sum, but the Ling family were poor and such a gift was a sign of very deep gratitude indeed. 'You know, Alice,' the mother superior continued, 'you are a credit to us here.'

'I do my best.'

'Continue to do so, my child.' The mother superior smiled and, as she did so, the tight sides to her wimple creased. 'And tell me, before you go home, which of the fathers was it who gave you the boxes.'

'I don't remember,' Alice said, grinning sheepishly.

'In that case, Father Dominic has a bit of investigating to do.' She screwed up the sheet of paper and tossed it accurately into the centre of the rattan waste basket by a wooden filing cabinet next to the window. 'We would be a lot of boring old women if we didn't have you, Alice Soon, to check a bit of life into us. Now — goodnight.'

'Goodnight, mother superior,' Alice replied.

17

'Ni koh lai paai,' said Chiu Tok when the conspirators met in the morning of 15th July at the house in Estrada de Coelho do Amaral.

That something was about to happen was plain: they had not previously met in the day but always in the late evening.

'Kei shi? Mat ye shi kaan?'

'Lai paai ng. Ng tim chung.'

Mulrenan was dubious they would be ready on time: Friday at five pm. It was the next day. When he complained to Chiu Tok about such short notice, he met with a hard stare.

'We are goin' tomowwow. F''iday got some good passenger.'

The plan was outlined once more and Mulrenan was handed an envelope from Francis Leung. He did not want to open it in front of them, but was ordered to do so. Obviously the Chiu clan were suspicious that Mulrenan might be one of Leung's entourage, even if only a peripheral member without initiation. They seemed unaware of the impossibility of a *gweilo* ever becoming a member of a tong.

The envelope contained a BOAC flight ticket on the following Tuesday departure for Ceylon via Malaya. It was in the name of Langley and was pinned to a British passport for the same name, the space for a photograph left blank but the embossed stamp which should have covered a corner of the picture was complete and just missed the empty square — it was intended to represent the work of a careless clerk in a passport office, issuing many documents in a hurry. Alongside the ticket and passport were seven American ten dollar bills to cover Mulrenan's immediate expenses. The Chiu clan inspected ticket, passport, and money, and were grudgingly satisfied.

When Mulrenan reached his cubicle in the boarding house, however, he discovered waiting for him a further note from Francis Leung. The message was terse.

'Not Tai O. Siu A Chau. Sunday six o'clock. Boat has new instruction.'

That evening, Mulrenan called in to a photographer's studio in Rua das Estalagens and had three passport photographs taken of himself, waiting while they were processed in a back room and demanding the negatives. With these in his pocket, he visited a stationery shop and hunted through a shelf of maps until he found one of Hong Kong.

The island of Siu A Chau, to which he was being redirected, was the northernmost of the dozen or so islands constituting the Soko group south of Lan Tau. They were just within Hong Kong territorial waters and appeared from the map to be largely uninhabited: between all of them there were only three hamlets, one on Siu A Chau and two on the southerly Tai A Chau where there was also light-house. Mulrenan examined Siu A Chau closely. Leung could follow one of two courses from the island, depending on how things were shaping after the taking of the Catalina. If they were being pursued, he could collect his gold and make a run for the open sea and the chain of larger islands that squatted low on the horizon: if all was clear, he could make a leisurely and quiet journey in to Hong Kong by way of the dumb-bell-shaped island of Cheung Chau. Mulrenan was prepared to go wherever Leung dictated: from the Lema Island chain thirty miles to the south he could make his way to Formosa or the Philippines. Whichever was to be the case, he would be safe.

He spent the evening eating alone in a small restaurant, and the rest of the night lying on his back in his bed, a sheet draped over his naked body. It was hot. The air did not stir in the boarding house and, in the early hours, he left the building, walking through the near deserted streets, round the tree-covered slopes of Colina da Guia and on to the monument to Ferreira do Amaral — passing, just as the dawn broke, the jetty from which, later in the day, he would leave Macau for ever.

At half past nine in the morning he met with his fellow adventurers, as he liked to think of them, at the house of Chiu Ik Chan. She welcomed them with a meal of plain rice and dumplings, a freshly-landed grouper with sweet and sour sauce, beef and bamboo shoots and green tea. After the meal, Chiu Tok pulled a small black bag with a metal zipper from under his chair and placed it in the central drawer of the chest of drawers.

Ik Chan enquired innocently after the contents: she had not seen the bag before. Tok fiercely instructed her and Min Vo they were not to touch the bag under any circumstances. They both dipped their heads with acquiescence but Mulrenan was experienced enough in the guile of Chinese womanhood to know that as soon as they all left, the bag would be investigated. He knew also, from previous briefings, that the bag contained a .45 and two .38s with loaded chambers or magazines, depending upon the manufacturer: if the guns had been supplied by Francis Leung they, like his own, would have had the maker's serial numbers erased.

453

The four Chinese were jumpy. They ate with unnecessary haste and Wong was unable to swallow without the aid of a drink. Only Mulrenan was at ease. His experience of pirates and their peculiar trade was greater than those of the four village hobble-de-hoys turned bandit.

'Now we are goin' out to have some coffee,' Tok declared. 'It will smoove our nerves and help us pass time.' He addressed Mulrenan directly. 'You not come to d'ink coffee but we meet you at the Cat-a-lina. You sure you know all of plan?'

'Yes,' Mulrenan confirmed.

'You no know us.'

'No. I don't know you,' he agreed.

He followed the Chinese distantly. On Avenida Almeida Ribeiro they entered a tailor's shop. Later, as he sat in a restaurant with a bottle of Portuguese rosé wine and some cheese, they came in wearing new cheap European suits to 'd'ink coffee', and he obligingly left.

Although Mulrenan arrived slightly early for the flight, some of the passengers had already congregated ahead of him. It was a mixed group of British, Americans, Australians and Chinese: one was an imposing man with an Eastern European accent who was talking to two teenagers, one a girl of about sixteen and her younger brother. Mulrenan, his eye ready to spot any factor which might affect their plan, noted the girl was holding a much-thumbed and battered Bible with a scratched cross in gold leaf upon the cover. He fervently hoped it would be but a first sample of the metal he would be in close proximity with for the rest of his life.

'Are you staying in Hong Kong for very long?' asked the man with the Balkan accent.

'I don't know, sir,' replied the teenage boy in a voice bred in the mid-West of America. He turned to a tall, austere man wearing a clerical collar. 'How long are we staying in Hawng Kawng, father?'

'Two-three days, son,' was the answer.

'In that case,' boomed the man, reaching into his pocket, 'please accept these with the compliments of Mr Genady

Moskevitch, ringmaster of The Kamala Circus.' He gave them passes to the big top. 'Please feel free to use them when you like. There are four — for all of you. I hope you will allow me to present these to your charming children, pastor?'

'Daniel Nelson, sir,' the minister introduced himself. 'United World Action in China.'

He smiled pleasantly as the homely-looking woman beside him, presumably his wife, accepted the passes gratefully and Mr Moskevitch snapped his heels together and bowed.

How like the church, Mulrenan thought, to grab at any free pickings that might come their way. He tried to recall which English king had asked to be rid of a meddlesome priest: a rare outburst of sense from the British monarchy.

'Major Hodgeman! How good to see you again. How are you?'

A couple had arrived, their large suitcase carried between them by a coolie. They walked either side of the man as if guarding not only their baggage but the porter as well.

'Mr & Mrs Stewart, isn't it?' asked a solidly-built man with a booming, army officer's voice. 'I'm in fine fettle, thank you. Don't think you know my wife.' The three shook hands. 'How's the oil business?'

'Coming along, you know, coming along. I owe you a deal of thanks, too. You brought me in a tidy sum at Happy Valley not once but twice. April 17th and May Day. That's one hell of a horse you have there!'

His exclamation drew an askance glance from Nelson: hell was clearly not a place one mentioned in front of the children of an American minister.

'Rebel?' the major rejoined. 'Yes. A fine beast. Won on him in January, too.'

A taxi arrived and from it emerged Mulrenan's four fellow adventurers. They had lost their nervousness, as if dressing in new European clothes gave them an impregnable disguise. Chiu Tok was carrying his black bag, the sides limp with emptiness. It would not be long before it was bulging with jewellery and hard cash.

They paid attention neither to Mulrenan nor to the other passengers. They stayed together, a tight group apart, and ignored even the other Chinese: it was not their place to join in conversation with them. The others were of the wealthy classes.

Mulrenan recognised that several of these were millionaires in American rather than Hong Kong dollars. Wong Chung-pang, who was speaking with a Chinese woman travelling alone, was the co-proprietor of the Hang Shun bullion company in Macau: he was reputed never to travel without half a million dollars in gold in his possession. Wu Sau-man was the Shanghai agent for Coca Cola: five of his children were being educated in a convent school in Hong Kong while his eldest daughter was studying at university in New York: he, Tok had assessed, would be worth a tidy ransom — as would all the foreigners.

Mulrenan unobtrusively observed Wong Chung-pang's waist. If he was carrying gold or high denomination notes they would be in a standard money belt, next to his stomach. He was no smuggler but a legitimate gold merchant.

The Catalina landed by the Macau breakwater and moored to the reserved buoy. The launch brought a number of incoming passengers ashore and tied up alongside. Mulrenan was pleased to notice another craft, grey-hulled, approaching the seaplane from the direction of the Praia Grande. It remained by the aircraft just long enough to unload a small wooden box which it took two men to lift aboard by its rope handles. During the transfer a man stood lookout on the fuselage of the Catalina: two others, armed with rifles, patrolled the decks of the vessel. Out of the corner of his eye, Mulrenan glimpsed Tok registering the stowing of this cargo.

The sun was warm as it came out from behind high clouds drifting over the sea. The wavelets sparkled against the stern of the launch and the blue sky to the east was bright with the expectation of promises about to be fulfilled.

The launch gradually filled with the passengers and their scanty luggage. A deckhand cast off and the motor burbled as the propellor churned the water. The stone wall of the quay fell away astern and Mulrenan took a last look at the shoreline of Macau.

Somewhere in the late afternoon heat haze distorting the outline of the buildings and the low hills of the Portuguese colony was his former concubine turned schoolmistress, his bastard son who bore her half-brother's hated name, and the house in Rua dos Curtidores where he had lived and from which he had escaped not once, but twice. Now, as the launch drew sluggishly away towards the Catalina, he vowed he would never return.

The flight hostess aided the passengers from the launch, through the glasshouse-like blister and into the cabin. Inside the aircraft it was hot and there was the smell of aviation fuel and warm metal. In the cockpit, the captain was conducting his pre-flight check. Atop the companion-way in the centre of the aircraft was a man out of uniform but occupying the flight engineer's seat.

Tok sat himself in seat 5 and Cheong in seat 1, opposite each other and directly behind the cockpit. Choi sat in 9, halfway down the starboard side and Wong, who boarded last, sat himself next to the entrance blister. Mulrenan discovered he was without a place to sit.

'Full up today,' Major Hodgeman remarked jovially. 'Standing room on top only!'

The hostess, who had planned to sit on the hinged seat in the entrance, gave it to Mulrenan who therefore found himself sitting by Wong. He politely greeted him in English but Wong only smiled sheepishly and stared at his feet.

Check list completed, the captain called out, 'Cast off, Ken!'

The first officer at the bow slipped the rope from the buoy, stowed it, and returned to his seat on the right hand side of the cockpit, bringing with him the metal flag post which, while the Catalina had been at her mooring, had flown the airline's courtesy flag. The engines sputtered then rumbled into life and a wall of spray built up to flow over the windows and trickle down the perspex as the aircraft turned and began its take-off.

The captain opened the two throttle levers over his head to full and held them to resist any jarring from the waves through which the Catalina began to plough. As the speed increased, he rocked the wings and the aircraft lifted on to her planing step. Half a minute later he eased back on the control column and the aircraft rose free of the Porto Exterior and began her climb over Macau. The aircraft rolled gently to starboard, onto her bearing for the course north of Lan Tau Island and, as she levelled out from her banking, the first officer swung his legs round to climb to the engineer's seat and switch the control to retract the floats. The man not in uniform prepared to move himself out of the first officer's way.

This was the moment the pirates had been waiting for: with one man out of the cockpit there was room for Tok to seat himself and take over.

Together, Tok and Cheong stood up quickly and pulled their revolvers from the waistbands of their trousers.

'You out. I flying this plane,' Tok yelled at the captain.

Cheong aimed his .38 through the cockpit doorway at the pilot's head.

The pilot made no move other than to glance back over his shoulder at what was happening behind his seat.

One of the European women screamed but no one else made a sound or a movement.

Choi leapt from his seat and stepped smartly to the foot of the engineer's companionway. He briskly ordered all the passengers across to the starboard side of the cabin so that he could more easily cover them with his gun. The aircraft tipped slightly, bumping in a pocket of turbulence and Choi moved his feet to keep his balance. Major Hodgeman, spotting his chance, made a grab for Choi's gun. Choi shouted an obscenity and struck at the major with his gun barrel. Cheong, distracted, turned his attention to the brief struggle. Tok watched them, undecided and panic-stricken.

The first officer, half-standing in the cockpit entrance, snatched the flag post from beside his co-pilot's seat and struck at Cheong with it, beating his arm down to his side.

Cheong lurched away from the flailing metal rod, bellowing with pain. He stumbled against Tok.

The last swing of the rod glanced off Cheong's arm and hit Tok in the ribs. He lost his balance and, as if controlled by a hand far greater than his own, fired his revolver. The bullet hit the pilot in the base of his skull.

Sliding sideways, the pilot's body hit the airframe and folded forwards, his chest and shoulder snagging on the control column. It stayed poised on the fulcrum of the column then slowly toppled towards the instrument panel, an inch at a time.

Terrified, the three pirates mindlessly opened fire, emptying their guns, their bullets thumping into the airframe around the cockpit, penetrating the skin of the fuselage and punching into the lifeless body of the captain.

All the passengers were screaming now, grabbing for hand holds and trying to hide behind each other. The minister and his wife were shielding their children from the spit of sharp splinters of aluminium.

Mulrenan was struck on the shoulder by a clenched fist, then thrust to the floor by Wong who was struggling to release the blister door. The *Miss Macao* turned sharply left, veered hard right and pitched her nose down.

Through Mulrenan's mind flashed lights, the shatter of sunlight through diamonds. He saw Alice and the boy, the lake at Naini Tal and his room in the annex of Manor House, the Black Watch officer wearing his Rolex once again and Alec Cowley lying in the paddy with his legs flexing.

An immediate thought then possessed him, angrily obliterating the past: these bloody Chink amateurs were blowing the best opportunity he — or they — would ever have. He had to do something to right this mess.

The tossing of the aircraft threw Mulrenan from side to side, rolling him about. Baggage broke loose and a case struck him in the small of his back. He attempted to get up but could only grasp at someone's ankle.

The aircraft's juddering worsened. Mulrenan twisted his head to see the small, wooden box with its rope handles glissading across the floor plates, aiming straight at his face. He put up an arm to ward it off. Someone stood on his thigh and a burning ache shot through his ribs.

He began to slide, let go of the ankle and linked both hands behind his head, cradled it within his elbows. He shouted at the top of his voice but heard nothing over the screech of the engines and the banshee whistling of the wind. Through the din, a voice kept calling incessantly to him, saying, 'Higher up the breezes start . . . Higher up the breezes start . . .'

He thrust his hands to his ears but the voice persisted, swelling until it blessedly ceased as Wong kicked at him. He opened his eyes to see nothing but the side of the box of bullion, the rope handles swinging wildly.

Then, with all switches on and the engines at full cruising throttle, the Catalina plunged into the sea.

18

In the water floated a man's body. Fung Man-yau hove to his motorised fishing junk and gave orders for it to be hooked aboard. One of his crew leaned over with a large iron gaff on a bamboo pole and was about to spear the body when it moved of its own human volition. The man was clutching a seat cushion and near him on the surface floated a briefcase.

The Chinese survivor was lifted on to the deck. He was in deep shock, heavily bruised and shivering, his leg dangling limply, badly broken.

'Kwai sing ming a?' asked Fung Man-yau.

'Siu sing Wong . . . Wong Yu-man.'

The junk master had the briefcase brought to him and, when he docked in Macau, surrendered it to the Portuguese authorities.

When opened it was found to contain a sodden British

passport with the printing ink so badly run the name of the bearer was indecipherable, a British Overseas Airways Corporation ticket and timetable card similarly ruined by sea water, a Peninsular Hotel room tariff brochure, a small brass key on a silver chain attached to the silver character 'sow', and a jeweller's eyeglass.

19

The briefcase posed no great puzzle to the authorities. It was assumed to have belonged to one of the missing British citizens on board the crashed Catalina, and although a check with the BOAC reservations desk in the Peninsula Hotel revealed that no one on the *Miss Macao* passenger manifest was also booked on an outward-bound BOAC flight, no conclusions were drawn. The passenger might have been carrying the ticket for a third party, or it could well have belonged to one of the flight crew: speculations were in any case soon crowded out by Wong Yu-man's inconclusive story and eventual confession.

Alice, on the other hand, was certain she knew to whom the briefcase had belonged and attempted to claim it, but without success. She had learned of the contents by bribing a police official and was curious to obtain the key even though she was ignorant of the whereabouts of the lock it fitted. She then attempted to purchase the entire briefcase from the official but he was loath to oblige her: there was too much attention being paid to the evidence for him to risk it. He would not even chance taking a wax impression of the key.

For several weeks after Wong Yu-man admitted his part in the affair, Alice followed the revelations in the Hong Kong newspapers as to what had happened to the aircraft and the whereabouts of the gold — it was generally known, although never officially confirmed, that there was a shipment of Lobo's bullion on board.

Twice in the days after the wreckage had been located, Alice chartered a small fishing junk and sailed to the site of the crash, the owner steering his craft in a figure-of-eight pattern over the area whilst she scanned the sea for further flotsam.

She was not sure what she wanted to find: a scrap of clothing she could recognise, a shoe, a suitcase. Ideally, she would have liked to have discovered Mulrenan's body.

The chartered junk pitching through the choppy currents towards Macau on its last return journey, Alice sat hunched in the creaking, cramped cabin with the junk-owner's family, the smell of fish and seaweed stinging her nostrils, and tried to identify her emotions.

There were no morbid motivations in her mind. She was not anxious to give Mulrenan a burial: of that she was certain. He had never been a religious man, certainly not a godly one. His only deity — apart from his consuming hatred — was money and he had died for that: although he had kept her in the dark as to his plans, she was shrewd enough to understand that the big deal he had been involved in had somehow led to the crash of the *Miss Macao* after the attempted theft of the bullion cargo.

Quite often, as the junk yawed and rolled in the swell, she fidgetted with her rosary, slipping the beads through her fingers, considering how her faith would protect her. And yet the fortune teller and the old crone had been so exact in their predictions: both had warned of flying creatures. The moth, she mused wryly, had transformed itself into the Catalina and brought her freedom.

As the junk spun its bow around Barra Point and slowed for the quayside in the Porto Interior, Alice finally realised, through the jumble of her feelings, just why she was so adamant to find Mulrenan's corpse. She wanted to be certain he was dead. Completely gone. If he was to reappear, she wanted to be sure it was only as a ghost, as a spirit or a devil such as those hanging in the twilight of the temple in Hollywood Road: yet she knew also that the worst devils were not those inhabiting the outside world but those residing in the human soul. By seeing him dead, she would succeed in laying them.

On more than one occasion, she was tempted to trace Leung and ask him for details, but every time the thought occurred she dismissed it. It was advisable not to become associated with such a man: she had spent enough of her life with one crook to be wise enough to keep clear of a second.

A month had passed by when she received an anonymous note which she believed must have come from Leung or one of his henchmen. It was typewritten on a sheet of stationery from a seedy hotel in the Wanchai district of Hong Kong, an establishment which she had frequented on a few occasions before Ethel Morrison had taken her under her wing on a full-time basis.

The note was terse: it gave just a surname and a map reference followed by the initials 'SM'. Studying a pre-war marine chart Mulrenan had used. Alice discovered the reference lay on the western extremity of Lan Tau Island, in a bay beside the fishing hamlet of Fan Lau.

So it was that, in bright sunlight a week later, Alice stepped ashore from a sampan on to the Lan Tau beach, to be met by a thin young fisherman, bare to the waist with his trouser top rolled over tightly and his hands red with fishes' blood. On his own craft, dragged up the sand from the high tide mark, were several dozen gutted groupers, four gulls nearby fighting noisily over the discarded entrails.

The fisherman, on hearing the surname Alice read from the note, reached out and took the slip of paper from her hand: he wanted to assure himself that this pretty woman really did want the person she mentioned. The fact confirmed, he returned the note, a bloody thumbprint obliterating the initials and the last number of the map reference.

'He liff ofer d'ere,' he said, speaking in broken English, assuming from her appearance that she spoke no Cantonese. He pointed with a bloodstained finger to the headland across the paddyfields.

'Toh tse,' she thanked him.

He replied, still in English, 'You no wan' go. Man no good. For lady, he no good.'

He shook his head vigorously.

463

'Thank you. But I have to see him.'

She spoke slowly so that the fisherman could understand. He was undeterred.

'No good man for lady,' he repeated, wagging his finger at her. 'No good . . .'

Yet Alice would not be put off and, turning, she set off across the beach: the fisherman watched her go and then started to rinse his hands clean in the sea.

As she approached the place through the brush and trees, the path thin and all but invisible in places, Alice felt a terrible foreboding creep over her. If Mulrenan had survived and was being nurtured by a hermit — but the thought, romantic and preposterous as it was, quickly left her. He could not, must not be alive. She felt in her handbag where her fingers touching the pistol reassured her.

There was no one in the ruins. Set in a copse of wind-stunted trees and once a tiny fort, they had been partially reconstructed as a makeshift dwelling. A singlet was spread out on a bush, drying in the sunny breeze and a fire of driftwood was crackling in a hearth of coarse stones: from branches and upon some of the flat stones of the ruins were hung or spread fish skeletons, dessicated seaweed, cuttle-fish bones and warped, dried sea horses. In a lean-to without a door was a narrow bed of salt-bleached boards and a stool surrounded by the barest of essentials.

Alice called out and there was no reply, yet she believed she was being observed from nearby. She glanced at the shadows under the bushes but could see no living creature — only more dead fish crawling with ants.

Whoever the absentee inhabitant of this macabre dwelling was, Alice felt a sympathy for him. Clearly the living gave him no succour or friendship and his only relationships were with the dead creatures of the sea. It was his place to exist with death, drawing into himself the pain of lost souls unable to achieve entry into the spirit world. As with the sin-eaters and purchasers of warts and leprosy, he was one of this sad category of mankind — she assumed the occupant to be male — condemned to living with evil, disfigurement and death.

Reluctant to leave without discovering at least a part of the purpose behind the note, she once more looked about the ruins and it was then she found a second lean-to beside the first, partially hidden from sight by a tangle of bushes and a collapsed heap of creeper-strewn masonry.

Again there was no door and, tossing aside a screen of cut branches, she peered in to see, almost completely filling the space, a heap under a ragged tarpaulin. She bent to lift the edge.

'You no opung!'

The sudden voice startled her and she dropped the tarpaulin, spinning round to see the young fisherman standing behind her with another, older man wearing a black cotton jacket.

'No good opung!' the older man repeated. 'Man liff here many year fin' it more two week gone. He c'azy man. Like to liff wiff what come f'om sea.' He tapped the side of his head with his finger. 'He wife dead fish. He child'un dead fish,' he went on by way of added explanation. 'He gone look-see water. Get more —'

'I want to see him. I want to speak to him,' Alice said adamantly.

'No can do. He gone longway. No come back long time,' the older man told her.

The young fisherman took Alice by the elbow and guided her over to the fire. The smoke drifted by her, scented sweetly and hazy in the sunlight. Small flames crackled, and spat with the salt soaked into the driftwood fuel.

Exchanging a look with his partner, the fisherman asked, 'You got lettah?'

Alice was surprised that these men had somehow been expecting her. She gave the note to him: in turn he passed it to the man in the jacket.

'Good! You Missy Soon, come Macau-side,' he said, confirming her identity in his mind. 'You wan' know noos of Mistah Mu'wennung.'

She nodded.

'He dead. Man liff here fin' him. He in . . .' He jerked his hand in the direction of the tarpaulin.

465

She looked at the dark heap.

'No can go look-see. No good!'

'How do you know that is Mister Mulrenan?' she asked, keeping obstinately to English though Cantonese would have been better.

'I no know. One man Hong Kong-side tell me. Tell you.'

'I want to see it.'

She moved towards the lean-to but as she reached it the young fisherman, with a strength that belied his appearance, grabbed her around the chest, pinioning her arms with his own.

'I show you small-small . . .'

The man lifted just one corner of the tarpaulin and, in the deep shadow of the lean-to, there glowed what appeared to be an unearthly white log upon which was draped a newly-landed fish, its teeth sunk into it. A line of ants was meandering towards a crack beneath the stones, each worker carrying a tiny morsel. As the corner of the tarpaulin fell, a strong odour of seaweed, shellfish and death puffed out.

The fisherman lowered his arms and Alice turned away slowly. The men, exchanging glances, were caught off their guard. Alice snapped open her handbag, whipped round, ran back a few short steps towards the tarpaulin and fired four shots in to it. The reports thundered in the confines of the ruins.

Standing with the muzzle of the pistol smoking she said, quietly but with firm conviction. 'Now there will be a future.'